HOT FOR IT

Books by Melissa MacNeal

ALL NIGHT LONG

HOT FOR IT

THE HAREM
(with Celia May Hart, Emma Leigh, and Noelle Mack)

NAUGHTY, NAUGHTY
(with P.J. Mellor and Valerie Martinez)

Published by Kensington Publishing Corporation

HOT FOR IT

MELISSA MacNEAL

APHRODISIA

KENSINGTON PUBLISHING CORP.

http://www.kensingtonbooks.com

APHRODISIA BOOKS are published by

Kensington Publishing Corp.
850 Third Avenue
New York, NY 10022

All Kensington Titles, Imprints, and Distributed Lines are available at special quantity discounts for bulk purchases for sales promotions, premiums, fund-raising, and educational or institutional use.

Special book excerpts or customized printings can also be created to fit specific needs. For details, write or phone the office of the Kensington special sales manager: Kensington Publishing Corp., 850 Third Avenue, New York, NY 10022, attn: Special Sales Department, Phone: 1-800-221-2647.

Aphrodisia and the A logo Reg. U.S. Pat & TM Off

ISBN-13: 978-0-7582-1412-6
ISBN-10: 0-7582-1412-X

First Trade Paperback Printing: October 2007

10 9 8 7 6 5 4 3 2 1

Printed in the United States of America

For Leslie and Julie, cousins who love a good pirate yarn—or just a good pirate! Thanks for your love and laughter, girls!

1

Cat Gamble rested her aching head in her hands, squinting at the manuscript page on her laptop screen. Her lips moved as she read silently.

Clarissa's heart thundered when he tossed her onto his bed. The pirate's lips, so brutally chiseled into his sea-beaten but handsome face, parted in a hard smile as he ripped open her bodice.

"Ah, such lush beauties, these," he breathed, wedging his knee between her thighs. "Peaks like berries, just awaitin' my tongue . . . lappin' at your creamy skin, sweet lady, as I feast upon your fleshly delights."

Gasping at the sandpaper texture of his face, Clarissa curled in upon herself. Quite against her will, she writhed beneath his hot, solid weight. That was no ordinary sword pressing into her abdomen . . . surely long and thick enough to ravage her down there, the way this swashbuckler had already taken her imagination captive. Again against her will, of course.

"Please, sir," she rasped. *"I'm betrothed to Lord Lust-ingworth, pledged to him as a virgin bride—"*

"Lustingworth, eh?" The buccaneer raised up, shaking with his laughter. *"You haven't heard about all his little bastards? By all the wenches a-workin' in his castle? He won't notice your bein' broke in. Ripe and ready for—"*

"YO, HO, HO!"

"—and a bottle of rum!"

"—it's a poi-rate's loife fer me!"

"No! No! That's the wrong frickin' movie, Trev!" came a strident cry. "You can't play Captain Jack if you're gonna mess up the script and—"

A startled intake of breath made Cat look up from her story. From her nook in the loft, she peered over the railing to see the tallest of the three costumed swashbucklers pressing the point of his glimmering sword to his challenger's bare chest . . . right between the swells of that low-cut hot pink evening gown.

"It's my house," came Trevor Teague's terse reply. "If you don't like the way I play pirate, take your balls and bat and go elsewhere, Bruce."

"Gentlemen, gentlemen!" Grant Carey crooned. The sleeves of his flowing laced-front shirt billowed as he stepped up to deflect Trevor's sword with his finger. "I see no need for bickering over petty—"

"I am *not* being petty!" Bruce insisted with a swish of his long blond wig. "As Elizabeth—the *smart* one, who gets things accomplished!—I'm only pointing out—"

"If you want to make points, stud your bra," Trevor muttered. "Cat should play the part of Elizabeth. She would at least bring some originality—and real breasts—to the role. Something besides flicking that fake hair in my face every time—"

"Don't even think about it, guys. I'm *trying* to work." Cat immediately regretted the frustration in her voice, but it was getting late and she hadn't reached her page quota for today. Her story felt way too clichéd, and Lord Lustingworth's name had flown too far over the top. She'd lost sight of the solid grounding this whole book needed but didn't have a clue what to do about it.

She had no room for whining or feeling ungrateful, however: as Trevor's house guest, living rent-free, thanks to the architect's compassion, she was damn glad for this loft . . . even if, as the choir loft of a Catholic church he'd renovated, it overlooked the open great room where voices carried with crystal clarity up into the vaulted, frescoed ceilings he'd restored.

"Oh, dear, we've interrupted you again," he said with an apologetic smile. "I'm terribly sorry, sweetheart. Rough day?"

Her shoulders sagged. Cat shook her head, more at herself than at the three gay blades who loved to cavort in costume. This huge unique house was the perfect place to pretend they were pirates instead of an architect, an attorney, and a landscape designer, and she envied them their sense of play. She'd never known grown men who gave themselves over to role playing with such childlike glee and dedication to detail.

"Just a little distracted. Conflicted. Whatever," she muttered. "The beginnings of books are always the hardest part."

"You've had enough on your plate since Laird died to distract even the most disciplined writer," Grant remarked. He placed a placating hand on his companions' shoulders. "Come on, guys, let's give her some peace and quiet while she—"

"No, it's all right. Tomorrow *is* another day," she drawled, trying to match their sense of movie drama. "Didn't mean to spoil your fun with my funk."

The three smiled up at her, raising two swords and a beaded fan in salute. They exited the great room through the door behind the tall carved pulpit that Trevor had ingeniously transformed into a freestanding waterfall.

The room—still a sanctuary in a very real sense—sighed

with silence and the sound of the trickling water then. Tall stained-glass windows depicting the miracles of Christ glowed with the direct rays of the sunset, casting the cavernous room in brilliant hues of ruby, cobalt, and amber. These colors had inspired Trevor's decor when he removed the pews and chose the groupings of furniture that made his unique home such a showplace. Cat sighed again, awed by the beauty of this sanctum . . . at how fortunate she was to be here after her husband's suicide had revealed his extensive gambling debts and an excessive lifestyle she'd had no idea about.

Things would be so much easier if she'd suspected Laird's secrets—if his creditors hadn't swooped down on the accounts and repo'd her car and her home the day after his funeral. She'd felt damn lucky to come away from the ordeal with her clothes and computer. Gazing alongside this choir loft at the stained-glass Shepherd holding His sheep, Cat wished *He'd* work a miracle for her about now.

But all this wishful thinking wasn't getting her new book written, was it? She couldn't keep calling herself a writer if she didn't land another contract soon. Couldn't land another contract if she didn't get a handle on these gawdawful characters who eluded her efforts to motivate them.

Cat looked at the half page of crap she'd struggled over all day and clicked the file closed. Maybe writing a pirate romance wasn't such a hot idea—no matter *how* those *Pirates of the Caribbean* movies had recaptured the romance of swashbuckling and bad-boy heroes. She gathered up the notes she'd scribbled, wishing she'd been a better sport with Trevor and his friends. Where would she be if Trev hadn't invited her to live here? Or if Grant Carey hadn't taken her as a pro-bono client, to fight the tangle of red tape those creditors had tied her up with?

As she focused on the top slip of paper, Cat blinked. It was a Powerball ticket, compliments of Bruce Bigelow—who, thank goodness, designed industrial parks and city greenways with more élan than he played the part of Elizabeth Swann. When the jackpot had swelled to $258 million last night, he'd bought tickets for all of them. Liquor had spurred his generosity, but the numbers still counted, didn't they?

"And I hope you win it, honey! The whole frickin' jackpot!" he'd slurred as he closed her hands around the ticket. "Nobody deserves a new life more than you, sweetheart."

Cat's gut fluttered. A whole new life . . . maybe even like the ones she'd been researching for her book, complete with a private island villa and a high-dollar yacht . . . white sand beaches with palm trees. The images in her mind were so vivid she could feel the ocean breeze caressing her cheek—

And that's the whole damn problem with you and your imagination, her mind muttered. *Always wishing—spinning something from nothing. Then you get upset because it isn't real.*

She stepped outside to the small balcony Trevor had built between the bell tower and the main building. Maybe some cold evening air would clear her head. It was a brisk winter night just made for cuddling naked under the covers with a lover.

"Oh, stop it!" Cat hugged herself, blinking at tears—tears that came way too easily these days. When would she get past this mess Laird had left her in? When would she feel like herself again, competent and capable and—

When you wish upon a star . . .

She held her breath, listening. Had the guys tuned in to an old Disney flick? It was the voice she remembered from her childhood crooning that sentimental tune—Jiminy Cricket in *Pinocchio*—wasn't it? The music swelled, taking her weary heart with it, and she sighed up at the evening sky with tears dribbling down her cheeks. Wouldn't it be wonderful to be a child again, to *believe* she could wish upon a star and her dreams would come true?

"I wish I could find a man who truly loved me," she whispered.

The solitary star above her shimmered. And then it *winked.*

Cat's mouth dropped open. She had *not* imagined that! That star had flickered—at her! And as she watched, it winked again—and then it shot across the sky with a glorious burst of star fire!

Got your attention yet, Cat?

She glanced quickly around. Had one of the guys come upstairs? Had anyone else heard that voice—or seen that shooting star?

Nope. It's just you and me, babe.

Cat swallowed hard. She gripped the railing, aware that her pulse was pounding and goose bumps were running up and down her spine. Was this how it felt when you lost your mind? First you thought stars were signaling, and then you heard disembodied voices, and then—

I'm not gonna show myself, so you better listen up. Check your Powerball numbers, got it?

"Who *are* you?" Cat was shaking now, looking anxiously around the little balcony. Inside, the loft she'd just left was shadowy enough that she was half afraid some weirdo was hiding behind the pipe organ to pounce on her if she—

Angels don't pounce, Cat. Get a grip.

"Angels," she rasped. "Right. An angel's telling me to check my Powerball ticket. Like I'm supposed to believe that."

Believing in things you can't see is the first lesson in Wish Fulfillment 101. I'm Spike, by the way. Your guardian angel, reporting for active duty.

Her pirate story was over the top, but *this*! Now she was hearing voices—some tough guy named Spike, claiming he was her guardian angel—

You've always wanted to believe in me, so here I am. It was a street-savvy baritone that spouted attitude all over the place and smelled like a sports bar on play-off night.

Cat wrinkled her nose. She *did* smell cigarettes! And beer!

Okay, fine, I'll take my Luckies and my Bud and butt outta your life, Cat. But I'm tellin' ya, you're already a winner. If you don't believe me, it's your loss, doll.

"Doll?" Cat snickered at the hint of gangster in his tone, still wondering why she was even holding this conversation. Yet she could see him perfectly in her mind's eye . . . realized her body was thrumming on a whole new wave length now. She felt the caress of an unseen hand as surely as she'd imagined the Caribbean breeze earlier.

And then he was gone. Only the subtle apple-wood smoke from Trevor's fireplace wafted around her now.

She glanced inside again, wondering what to believe. Should she check those numbers? Should she—

On instinct, Cat looked up. The dusk had deepened, and another star above her shone more brightly than the others coming out around it. When it winked at her, she went inside: who was she to disregard a third sign? Messing with stuff like that meant trouble . . . especially since there were no witnesses to this little incident. Except for Spike, of course.

She opened her laptop again, willing it to hurry as the familiar beeps and whirring sounds brought pictures to her screen. Wistfully she picked up the lottery ticket, wishing she could believe the brief conversation with an angel that already felt, well—unreal.

Cat typed in the URL listed on the ticket . . . Powerball. com. By now, the day's numbers would be displayed and they'd have upped the jackpot amount because no one's numbers matched—

WINNER! WINNER! WINNER! flashed across the screen.

Cat scrolled down to where the numbers were listed—on a ticket purchased in Crystal City, just south of here, the sidebar said! Hadn't Bruce bought their tickets in a trendy little watering hole near the interstate?

She held her breath, glancing from the cash-register receipt to the screen. 34—and 34.18—and 18.48—and 48—

Voices rose below her as the three pretend pirates cussed the television in the parlor.

"Damn! Isn't Crystal City where you bought these—"

"So much for retiring early."

"Hey, I bought you the damn chances, guys!" Bruce's tenor whine rang out. "It's not like *my* numbers were any better than—"

"Holy shit," Cat whispered. Her hand shook so badly the receipt fluttered to the floor. Surely she'd misread; she turned on the desk lamp to compare those numbers again.

A few moments later Trevor's voice ascended the narrow wooden stairway ahead of their footsteps. "Let's see if Cat's checked her numbers yet. We need to help her lighten up tonight, guys. Maybe order in some pizzas and—"

She stared at the three men approaching from the other side of the pipe organ console. Trevor Teague in his mascara and beaded scarf; Grant Carey in his flowing shirt with a sword swinging from his magenta sash; Bruce Bigelow who'd ditched the blond wig but still wore a fitted gown of hot-pink brocade with matching kid slippers.

"Are you all right, Cat? You—"

"—look like you saw a ghost or—"

"I won," she squeaked. "I think, anyway. Here—*you* check the numbers!"

Trevor snatched the receipt from her hand and then murmured the digits in turn as he checked her screen. "Holy mother of God, would you look at—she won it!" he crowed. "Our very own Cat Woman won the fuckin' *Powerball*!"

"On my ticket!" Bruce chimed in. "Do I know how to pick numbers or *what*?!"

"And—and by all rights that money is yours. Fair and square, Bruce."

Cat swallowed hard and held out the receipt. Damn that

angel for showing up and telling her she'd won, when it wasn't rightfully her money anyway!

Bruce Bigelow's eyes glowed an enhanced emerald green as he gripped the other end of the lottery ticket. He had the sun-bleached hair and perfectly bronzed pecs of an all-American surf bum, and Cat had no trouble imagining him as some rich bitch's cabana boy, hot and tanned and alluring in his Speedo. Without the dress, of course.

Bruce folded her fingers around the receipt and then kissed her fist. "This calls for champagne. A toast to your new life, Catalina Gamble."

"Hear, hear!" Trevor cried. "I'll go fetch a bottle from the cellar!"

"If—if the lottery board verifies these numbers for two hundred fifty-eight *million* dollars," Grant intoned in his low courtroom voice, "you'll have some important decisions to make very quickly, my dear. If your husband's creditors get wind of this, they'll try to—"

"Screw them."

Cat looked into hypnotic eyes that glistened like indigo crystals. Just like that bad-ass angel had said, she suddenly had answers to all her problems! And thanks to her hours of online research, she knew exactly what she would do and where she wanted to go. At last, she could escape the annoying phone calls and threatening letters from Laird's loan sharks!

"You're my attorney, Grant," she said earnestly, "and you're going to get those bastards off my back. I did *not* accumulate those gambling debts, nor did I put the house in hock, and—and I'm not going to answer another one of their calls or accusations!"

Grant arched an eyebrow. "You're not suggesting I blow them off? I'm not sure we can—"

"Whatever it takes. Keep it legal without caving in to them," she breathed. "This windfall has just bought you all the time you need, and it's my ticket out of a nightmare."

"You *go*, girl!" Bruce hooted.

Still in shock from this lucky turn of events, Cat placed her hand on Bigelow's smooth bronzed shoulder. "Even if I split this jackpot with you, Bruce, I'll have more than enough to—"

"I want you to dream *big*, Cat," the landscaper replied with a happy sigh. "Hey—I never figured on winning, so I won't miss it. Easy come, easy go."

"Don't you tell those guys a *thing* before I get back up there!" Trevor called from downstairs. "I'm coming as fast as I can!"

"That is *so* Trevor," Bruce breathed with a roll of his eyes.

Cat smiled. Idiosyncrasies aside, these guys were better friends than she'd had for a long, long time. The perfect buffers and pick-me-ups during the bleak six months since Laird took that overdose. Had Grant Carey not read of her predicament in the papers, she wouldn't be sitting in this remodeled cathedral with a silver fox of an attorney dressed in a flowing poet's shirt . . . and tights that hugged a whole lot of manhood. Nor would Grant's friend Trevor have invited her to be his house guest, with perfectly honorable intentions! Too bad these three fascinating men were after each other rather than her.

But thanks to them, she had a new dream to plan—a whole new life to plot out! It sounded like a helluva lot more fun than bemoaning the crappy pirate drivel she'd written today and wondering if she'd ever sell another book. The thunder of boots in the stairway prompted her to click into Yahoo so she could access her bookmarks.

"Here's the scoop, guys," she began, breathless with feeling so alive again. "I took this online class about how to disappear—*legally*," she added with a pointed look toward Grant. "So now I can get a J2 phone—load up on calling cards—and—and buy myself an *island*! I'll—"

"What's a J2 phone?" Trevor peeled the foil from the neck of his champagne bottle and then shot the cork over the railing with a satisfying *pop*. "You're sharp, Cat, but you don't impress me as the cloak-and-dagger type. Too damn beautiful to remain hidden or anonymous for long, no matter where you go. Technology being what it is, and all."

She grinned brightly. Teague had never told her she was beautiful—and by God, she was starting to feel that way now! "J2 phone calls can't be traced, which means Laird's loan sharks can't harass me. And here—I've got URLs for opening offshore accounts! What do you know about setting those up, Grant?"

The attorney leaned closer to her laptop screen, absently accepting a flute of fizzing champagne from Trevor. "I have colleagues who do it all the time for corporate clients diverting assets away from taxes. Cat, honey, you're moving awfully fast here—"

"Not when you consider I've been looking into this stuff for months, as research for a book someday. Look!"

She clicked to another site . . . pointed at a listing of articles about how to find jobs and buy homes on the cheap, in places like Nicaragua and Guam and the Pacific Islands. "Here's info on how to have my mail forwarded to a mail drop. Real estate listings for entire islands that cost less than this house, Trev!"

Her host handed her a glass with fizzy bubbles dancing around its rim. "Escape Artist dot com?" he demanded. "Cat, this sounds like something your husband should've looked into before—well, before he did such a number on *you*!"

"Makes it sound like there's a whole frickin' *world* of people from the States relocating to these places!"

"You're right on the money, Bruce. Expatriates living abroad . . . for whatever reason," she said, clicking through to her favorite bookmarked site. "And get a load of this place! I've been imagining it as my setting for a book—four bedrooms;

rosewood staircase, cabinets, and floors. Wraparound balconies with a Jacuzzi facing the sunsets and a full view of the ocean, where you can watch the dolphins play. Lush tropical trees and flowering—"

"Cat, this place runs a million eight."

"And your point would be?" Giddy triumph surged through her as she raised her glass to the three astounded men hovering around her laptop. "Why would I *not* want it? Even after the taxes on my jackpot, I'll have plenty to spend on such a home. And with four bedrooms—"

"We could be *your* house guests!" Trevor crowed. He tapped his flute to hers, and the ringing of crystal lingered in the loft. "Here's to Cat's new life and new home!"

"Long may she wave!" Bruce called out. He downed half his champagne before Cat got her glass to her lips.

Ah, it was sweet, this victory. Far more exhilarating than the rush of cold fizz down her throat. Grant, ever the practical one, had taken her mouse to click on the pictures of this idyllic property, his indigo eyes narrowing.

"You'll have to arrange for a viewing of this property, dear heart," he mused aloud. "Pictures don't always tell the whole story—"

"Of course I will! And I might find something just as nice for less!"

"—and you'll need a passport to leave the US—"

"Got one."

"—and before any of this can come to pass," he continued, gazing at her over his champagne, "we'll need to confirm your winnings with the lottery board and see if other winners share your pot. We'll have papers to sign. Payments to arrange."

Cat drained her glass, gazing at him over its rim. This alluring attorney was probably ten years her senior but *hot* to the point of making her wet. So powerful was Grant Carey in legal

circles she'd been totally intimidated by his custom-cut suits—
his awesome *presence*—and those dark shining eyes that seemed
to see through to her deepest secrets. Until now.

She winked at him, holding her flute toward Trevor for more
champagne. "So what're you doing tomorrow, Grant?"

2

Cat stomped her feet in the frigid air that whipped along the curbside check-in area at the St. Louis airport. Just a week ago she'd been languishing in the loft at Trevor Teague's, worrying where her next check was coming from, and here she was shipping off to an island paradise beyond her wildest dreams. To *buy* the damned island!

Maybe.

She reminded herself that, yes, the photographs on the Web site had looked too good to be true. And yeah, the arrangements for her offshore accounts and for the flight to view this island property had fallen into place as though her guardian angel—this time in the form of Grant Carey—had waved a magic wand. As he hefted her suitcases from the trunk of his Lexus into the check-in line, the breeze caught his steely hair and gave his cheeks a ruddy glow. A glow of sincere joy for her.

"I'll be in touch, sweetheart," he murmured, bussing her cheek. "Keep me apprised of your findings, and I'll be sure all your new accounts and connections remain confidential."

"If there's anything we can do—" Bruce chimed in. Then he

grabbed her in a huge hug. "This is so exciting, Cat! Have a fabulous time!"

"You'll be the first one I call if I need a groundskeeper," she insisted, returning his grin. "I owe you big-time, Mr. Bigelow."

"And don't forget to e-mail us soon as you get there." Trevor slipped the strap of her computer case over her shoulder, letting his hand linger for a squeeze. "With that theft-detection software I installed, your laptop—not to mention your new book!—will be traced immediately if a thug snags your Mac. Can't be too careful in countries where technology's scarce."

Cat bit back a remark about how protective they were all being. After all, they just wanted her to be safe and have the time of her life, now that she *had* a life. "And what does that do, again?"

"Every time you send an e-mail, a separate message goes to the account address I've set up, and it tells us the location of your laptop," he explained patiently. "So if someone swipes it, you call the software company and they'll know where your Mac is as soon as the thieves go online with it."

Cat nodded as though she understood. "Like having an OnStar chip in a car?"

"Pretty much." The architect stuffed his hands in his overcoat pockets, his grin tentative. "But we'll think positive thoughts, Cat. You're going on the adventure of a lifetime here, and we're all wishing we could, too!"

She threw her arms around his neck, basking in his warmth and the subtle scent of his cologne . . . the way his close-cropped beard teased her cheek when he kissed it. "Soon as I'm settled, you might as well come see me," she insisted to the three of them. "Why spend the rest of your winter in St. Louis when you could be sunbathing on my white sand beach watching the dolphins frolic?"

"Oh, stop! Just get on the plane, you tease!"

After a final round of hugs as she checked her luggage, Cat

strode resolutely toward the terminal doors. When they opened automatically, as if recognizing her as the queen of her own ocean domain, she turned for a final wave. Three gorgeous guys raised their arms as though saluting her with their pirate swords, and she laughed.

It was a big improvement over bursting into tears, wasn't it?

The trouble with flying alone, first to San Juan and then to St. Lucia, was having so much time to think. Oh, she'd brought along the stack of information she'd received about Porto Di Angelo, the island she was viewing, but she couldn't focus on it. Cat alternated between little-girl giddiness over this adventure—was she really flying down to buy her own slice of paradise?!—and the gnawing fear that Laird King's creditors would somehow shatter her new plans, despite the safeguards Grant had put into place.

And now that the first rush of hitting the jackpot had settled, she felt overwhelmed by loneliness. Surrounded by strangers and preoccupied flight attendants, Cat had to face emotions she hadn't expected. She stared out the window a lot so the kid in the aisle seat wouldn't think she was a nutcase when she went from tears to gleeful grins.

It felt odd to be setting out by herself, after nearly fifteen years of marriage to Laird. While she'd been shocked and pissed at the mess he'd left her, she couldn't just erase the good life he'd provided her—at least on the surface. Then came the condolence calls and those damn threats from bloodsuckers trying to wrench money from her after they snatched her house and her car. Scary, to think how she could've ended up in a homeless shelter, had Trevor Teague not invited her into the house he shared with Grant and Bruce.

While she'd always loved to travel—she and Laird had gone abroad or cruised every year—as a writer, she'd spent most of her time alone. In imaginary worlds of her own creation. But this trip was taking her to a whole new reality, where she didn't know a soul. She'd really jumped off the edge—mostly because that shooting star and the swaggering voice who called himself Spike had pushed her.

What if her parachute didn't open?

What if this leap of faith landed her among sharks and crocs who smelled her fear and swallowed her whole? Would that theft-detection software protect *her*, half a world away from everything and everyone she knew?

When she got off the plane in San Juan, she still had no answers. Thank God her travels had taught her how to navigate airports: this one was colossal, and she was alone in a sea of people moving toward their gates with their own concerns. Their own companions.

Hey, you got me, doll!

Cat fought the urge to gaze crazily around her. She was approaching the security checkpoint and didn't need those uniformed agents thinking she was wacko. The smell of cigarettes was suddenly so strong, she could've been in one of the glassed-in lounges where they confined smokers these days.

"Where were you when I was feeling so lonely on the plane, huh?" she muttered. She stepped out of the stream of people funneling toward the X-ray machines, in case anyone was watching her talk to herself.

Like you would've talked to me on that plane, Spike replied. *I was in the center seat the whole time. Watching the movie.*

"Right. You could've told me you were there—"

You needed that time alone, babe. I've learned to never come between a woman and her mood swings. He cleared his throat ceremoniously. *Better get your sweet self into that security line, missy. It's a loooong way to your gate, and if you miss this plane for St. Lucia—*

"Are you telling me what to do?" Cat stepped out of the restroom doorway, smiling apologetically at the dark-skinned lady who came out and stared at her funny.

Okay, fine, doll. I got work to do, anyway. If you're gonna get all pissy—

"I'm not getting—"

And by the way, I can hear you just fine if you think *your part of the conversation. See ya around, sugah—if you make your plane, that is.*

Half an hour later, Cat scurried aboard the little express jet.

"Thank you for waiting," she gasped at the glaring blond flight attendant. She beelined to her seat, avoiding the eyes of the passengers who'd been there several minutes ago. The door *whumped* shut behind her, and as they taxied away from the terminal the spiel about plane safety came over the speaker system.

What a relief that, again, no one occupied the aisle seat beside her. She could catch her breath and regroup without—

Without so much as a thanks or a kiss-my-ass! The pilot had to take a sudden leak, or we'd be long gone, girlfriend. See if I ever hold a plane for you again!

"I am not your—" Cat caught herself and let out a long sigh. *I am not your girlfriend, Spike—or whoever the hell you are! How come I smell your beer and cigarettes now when I didn't before?*

Spike chortled. *That's how I share my charming self when I wanna get your attention. Had plenty of time for a smoke and a couple cold ones, waiting for you to get down the concourse.*

With a disgusted sigh, she stuffed her laptop under the seat in front of her. All these years she'd wanted to believe she had a guardian angel, and now he turned out to be a rude, crude—

Don't forget lewd! Love the way those knit slacks hug your ass when you bend over, baby.

The heat rose to her cheeks as she sat bolt upright and glared at the empty seat between her and the aisle.

"Something to drink, miss? Coffee, or perhaps some wine or a cocktail?"

Cat looked up, her face aflame. The uniformed steward had leaned over his rolling refreshment cart to speak to her in an exotic accent that crossed Bob Marley with Ricardo Montalban. His sexy, sun-kissed face belonged on the cover of *GQ* magazine, and his twinkly blue eyes suggested something much more addictive than liquor.

"Not here on the plane. Everyone will want to watch," she quipped.

Then she felt stupid and crude: he was simply doing his job, and she'd come on like a shameless hussy—or like Spike had put such words in her mouth.

The corners of those eyes crinkled. "Too bad I have to work the return run," he replied with a quiet laugh. "I could show you all the hot spots and private island playgrounds. I grew up on St. Lucia."

Cat grabbed her tote bag. Maybe there was something to this angelic intervention thing! "Do you know about this island that's for sale? It's a gorgeous estate—amenities out the wazoo," she gushed, "but I've never found out *why* it's on the market. Who would want to move away from *here*?"

When she showed him the photo and online fact sheet she'd printed out, his face softened in recognition.

"You are looking at Porto Di Angelo? You will find it a lovely, gracious hideaway—just as these photos suggest," he murmured. The steward glanced around and then sat down in the empty seat so the other passengers couldn't hear. "It's for sale because the Contessa—Valenzia Borgia—disappeared. It remains one of the unsolved mysteries of the Caribbean."

"The Contessa? Valenzia Borgia?" A shiver of intrigue went

down her spine. "That would explain the grandeur of the estate. But why didn't the Web listing mention this?"

The steward placed his lips near the rim of her ear. "Pirates," he whispered. "We suspect they kidnapped her—held her for ransom. She's not been seen for perhaps two years now."

Cat listened with wide eyes, wanting to giggle—yet sensing this man was deadly serious. It was more than the warm tickle of his breath against her neck that had her squirming in her seat. Weren't the Borgias known for poisoning people? "And no one put up the money to—"

"She had no family. Only her devoted staff, who—the way I heard it—put the island up for sale out of desperation," he replied softly. He reached into his shirt pocket. "With no authority to access her accounts, they had no way to offer the ransom, you see. No way to maintain the Contessa's home, much less pay a detective to look for her. It's all very sad. And very strange.

"Be careful, Ms. Gamble," he added, gazing pointedly into her eyes. "A beautiful woman like yourself . . . unaccompanied . . . might give those pirates reason to strike again."

Pirates! Why did the image of Johnny Depp in beads and eyeliner ambush all rational thought when the sexy steward said that word? He sounded totally sincere—

And as Cat read the card he left beneath the mimosa he didn't charge her for, she didn't know whether to laugh—or go straight home. ARIEL GAETANO, PRIVATE INVESTIGATIONS, it said above his phone number.

At first she was flattered. Then reality set in.

Now, how can an airline employee be doing investigations, huh? Your mind's running away with that Contessa story—already planning to pump the staff as research for a book! she warned herself. *Never mind that he might be associated with those pirates.*

Hey, doll, you shouldn't believe anything a good-lookin' guy tells you—except me, of course. They're only after one thing, ya know.

She could imagine Grant or Trevor ranting at her that way, too. And they'd be right. Life in the single lane was different from holing up with her computer, and she'd better shift into a higher gear pronto.

She glanced at the steward, who was now at the front of the cabin. He was pouring juice, chatting up another passenger in a language she didn't recognize—but then his gaze flickered back to meet hers.

Cat held his eyes for a moment and then focused on the stack of printouts in her lap. Not even on the island, and already she was embroiled in something suspicious the Escape Artist site hadn't mentioned. Like she should trust anything from a site with *that* name!

What have I done here? Why didn't I listen to Grant's practicality and Trevor's protective questions? She gazed out the window at a sea of sparkling turquoise. Not a speck of land in sight. *And why didn't you warn me about this situation, Spike?*

You didn't ask. You were wishing for true love, remember?

The air from the overhead blower suddenly smelled cool and fresh. Her guardian angel had vanished, just when he could've given her information that might prove important. Useful, even.

But it was too late for second-guessing: the popping of her ears signaled the little jet's descent, and fifteen minutes later they landed at the airport near Castries, St. Lucia's capital city. Cat smiled flirtatiously at the steward and then trotted across the tarmac toward a relic of a terminal, too excited and nervous to wonder if everything here was so far behind the times. She was to look for a uniformed driver with a sign—the man who'd be taking her to her future home, if all went well!

She followed the other passengers to the creaking baggage carousel and nearly peed her pants.

There was no missing the sign that proclaimed MS. GAMBLE

in bold black letters—and it was held be a *very* tall, *very* black man who sported a diabolical goatee and had a braided pigtail hanging from the back of his head. He had the longest fingers she'd ever seen.

Is it my imagination, or are his thumbnails filed to a point?

She tried to smile. It wasn't like three other blondes named Cat Gamble were going to rush over and claim a ride with this man. And it wasn't like this stuffy, antiquated airport had a phone bank where she could summon another driver—even if she could tell him where to take her.

The man's predatory smile told her he knew exactly who she was and what she was thinking. He was watching her sweat, and enjoying it.

She saw her cranberry suitcase chugging by on the conveyor belt and lunged for it, just as Mr. Sinister did.

"Allow *me*, madam."

Who was she to argue? That voice belonged to Barry White and the moves were Shaquille O'Neal—and had Cat tried swinging the huge suitcase by its handle that way, she'd have shot-putted herself across the terminal. Or at least pulled her arm out of its socket.

"Thanks, but—I'm not a madam—I mean—I'm not married—anymore, anyway—and I—"

Her mouth froze, open, when he stooped slightly and suavely extended his hand. He was wearing a pinstripe suit with a crisp white shirt and a colorful paisley tie—better dressed than most American men she'd met lately. Cat shook his hand, afraid not to.

"Cat Gamble," she rasped as his large, dark fingers swallowed her tiny white ones.

"And I am Ramon," he crooned, rolling that R in a chocolate-sauce voice spiked with island spices. "Leilani and I are so very happy to have you, pretty princess. You'll make a fine new mistress for our home on Porto Di Angelo. She needs a classy lady like you to bring her back to life."

So much for first impressions. Cat relaxed, smiling for real this time. With Ramon's courtly voice still lingering in her ears, it was easy to discount that steward's talk of abductions and ransom.

Or was she a fool to fall for this man's grand manners? He didn't wear an eye patch or a hoop earring, but plenty of corporate pirates had plundered unsuspecting buyers on dry land . . . something she'd learned the hard way when her husband's habits came to light after he died.

But what choice did she have? She hadn't traveled all this way to get spooked by a black man who escorted her to a black sedan with black-tinted windows, and then held open the door to its black leather interior.

Am I walking into a black hole I might never come out of? She was summoning Spike as much as asking herself this question, but her guardian angel apparently had better things to do when she needed him most.

"I—wasn't expecting such a—a fine car," she stammered, gesturing at the tropical wilderness within view of the airport and the obvious poverty of passersby who jabbered in the local language. They carried chickens in crates, and on their heads.

He moved with a graceful gallantry, stepping between her and that glimpse of harsh reality to close her door. Then he slipped into the driver's seat beside her. The car, a big vintage Cadillac that would make collectors in the States drool, purred to a start. Cool air blew from the vents, circulating the scent of fine leather warmed by the afternoon sun.

"The Contessa insisted upon nothing but the best," her chauffeur said in that cultivated voice. "You've probably not heard of Valenzia Borgia, but she was Italian nobility who lived with a sense of adventure and—"

"Lived? As in, past tense?"

Ramon smiled wryly. "She disappeared nearly two years ago, while on her evening walk along the beach. We have only my wife, Leilani's, divination to go on, but Valenzia's spirit guides instructed her to put the estate up for sale. The Contessa has no further use for it."

Who did she believe? That hot airline steward or her driver?

"Do you think she drowned?" Cat hoped her questions didn't sound nosy, Especially since Ramon's talk of divination and spirit guides introduced a whole new set of issues.

"Miss Borgia was an excellent swimmer. Careful about herself," he replied pensively. He swung the Caddie around a hairpin turn in the narrow road, which ended at the bottom of the hill. "Knowing how Valenzia had a highly developed sense of adventure, we suspect she either arranged for a . . . rendezvous that lasted longer than she anticipated—"

"Two years?" Cat murmured.

"—or she was abducted and has made the most of it."

He flashed a white smile as he stopped the car at the very edge of the road, where nothing but the Caribbean Sea stretched before them. True, it was the most gorgeous shade of shimmering blue-turquoise she'd ever seen, but what the hell were they going to do *now*?

"And . . . and you never went after her? Never tried to find her?"

"Not all who wander are lost, Miss Gamble."

What was *that* supposed to mean? And what was she supposed to believe? This man had just fed her a whopper about an Italian adventuress—without the least sign of anxiety about the Contessa's life—and now they were sitting at land's end like a couple of lovers out parking. The waves lapped at the rocky shore, accentuating the silence and the fact that there wasn't another sign of civilization in sight. The fan circulated the scent of Ramon's musky cologne with its cool air.

"We're early," Ramon remarked as he glanced at his watch. "The only way to take the car from here to Porto Di Angelo is by ferry. I hope Rodrigo remembers to come for us. When he dropped me here earlier, he and his pretty lady were taking a bottle of wine from a picnic hamper."

When her face fell, the man beside her chuckled . . . a rich, seductive sound that, under different circumstances, might've made her, well—horny.

"You'll learn quickly, Miss Gamble, that we islanders believe God gave us these little spots of paradise in the sea so we could enjoy every beautiful moment we spend on them. It's a philosophy you'll want to consider, if you plan to prosper here."

Paradise . . . philosophy . . . prosper. Coming from the tall, dark—and, yes, devilishly handsome—Ramon in the pinstriped suit, those words made perfect sense in the same sentence. And yet . . . Cat toyed with the idea that he was mentally feeling her up. Partly out of allegiance to the Contessa, because he couldn't sell his mistress's estate to just anyone—

Oooh, and was she his mistress? Spike whispered.

—while sensing he was also sizing her up as a woman he might be living with . . . in whatever sense of that word applied. The hush of the engine, playing a duet with the waves licking the shoreline, cast a spell over her travel-tired mind.

Or did Ramon possess mysterious otherworldly powers, as his wife apparently did? It wasn't much of a stretch to see this man with the close-cut, pointed goatee—and thumbnails—in the role of shaman or witch doctor. His eyes assessed her with leisurely curiosity. He exuded a comfortable sense of total control.

"And why do you want to buy Porto Di Angelo, Miss Gamble?" he asked in a deceptively dapper tone. "Many who can afford the Contessa's playground aren't prepared for the—culture shock, shall we call it?—of living such an isolated life. They're not ready to depend upon a generator for electrical power, or to rely on a ferry operator like Rodrigo to get them to the mainland for groceries and supplies. Or when a hurricane's blowing in."

Cat caught herself following his lush lips, thinking how he'd make a wonderful late-night radio show host. Or hypnotist.

She blinked—maybe because Spike nudged her? While she couldn't smell him, Cat had a tingly little sense of her angel's presence. So . . . what was it Ramon had asked her?

"I—like Miss Borgia—am a bit of an adventuress," she fudged, frantically fishing for a coherent reply. "I'm a romance novelist, Ramon, and my online research led me to the advertisement for your property, and—"

She swallowed, not yet ready to mention the Powerball jackpot or Laird's death to this stranger. Which left damn little truth to draw upon.

"And you imagined yourself living in the exquisite luxury those photographs depict," he continued for her, "without any real sense of the . . . potential threats we Caribbeans live with every day."

"Are you one of them, Ramon?"

Cat fought to hold her gaze steady. Where had *that* come from? What gave a little white woman like her the balls to ask this big black—

His teeth flashed like pearls as his laughter filled the Caddie. "A woman who speaks her mind without mincing words! I like that, Miss Gamble."

She let out the breath she'd been holding. He knew damn well she wasn't really so brave or resourceful: he was playing along to see what he could get out of her . . . whatever that meant. Sitting so close to this powerhouse of a driver was becoming more of a challenge with every minute that ticked by. Where was that Rodrigo fellow, anyway? And why wasn't Spike whispering brilliant questions or answers to her?

No response, on either count.

So Cat decided to see just how much truth Ramon could take. What did she have to lose? She could head for home anytime and never see these people again. She would tell Trevor, Grant, and Bruce the estate didn't measure up to its advertisement. This overblown overseer might as well find out who she really was—because sometimes reality was far harder to believe than anything she could make up in her books.

"My husband overdosed six months ago," she began, pleased that her voice didn't crack on that subject, "and then I was confronted by more creditors than you can count, for debts he'd run up with his gambling habit. I lost my car and house in the process, Ramon. It was a stroke of sheer luck and a friend's generosity that landed me a Powerball lottery jackpot. So here I am, ready to start a whole new life."

His gaze hadn't wavered; his lips showed no sign of a grin. "Leilani was right," he murmured. "She saw you as a fugitive with a tragic past when she consulted her guides."

Another little shiver streaked up her spine. Was this island voodoo he was talking about, like the priestess Tia Dalma performed for Captain Jack and his pirates in the movie?

"I, meanwhile, Googled you," he went on matter-of-factly. "Along with the covers and reviews of your romance novels, I found your photograph, your Web site, the blogs you've posted, and several recent references to your personal tragedy in Midwestern newspapers online." His big brown eyes softened then. "I'm sorry for your loss, Miss Gamble. Sorry you learned such regrettable things about your husband and then had to deal with them."

"Th—thank you," she wheezed, determined not to bawl—not after all she'd endured to get to this time and place.

"And I'm damn glad your story matches up with my research!" He pulled a compact walkie-talkie from inside his jacket and flicked a switch. "Rodrigo? It's a go, man! Come and get us!"

Cat's jaw dropped. From around a protrusion of rocks where wild orchids and bougainvillea bloomed in profusion and palm trees swayed in the breeze, a dilapidated ferry boat chugged into view. A man in island-print shorts and dreadlocks waved his arm excitedly from the large round steering wheel, as though he were greeting a long-lost friend.

"Meese Gahm-bahl!" he called out. He steered the ferry within a few yards of the shore, dropped primitive anchors over the sides, and then shoved a makeshift ramp toward the Cadillac. "Meese Gahm-bahl, we be so very happy to see you, preety lady!"

Cat narrowed her eyes at Ramon as he put the car in gear. "Don't tell me," she muttered, peeved at her own naïveté, mostly. "Rodrigo has not only Googled me, but he attends the chats I do at the Novel Talk site and follows my blog."

"Does the screen name 'Ferry4U' ring a bell?" Ramon laughed and eased the car onto the ramp. "He's read every one of your books, Miss Gamble—borrowed them from the Contessa. We're all tremendous fans, and so honored to have you here!"

She let out an exasperated gasp. Then she spotted the photo from her Web site enlarged and posted on the ferry's grubby wall, with a scrawled sign that said WELCOME! "If this is how you treat honored guests—"

"Things aren't always what they seem," he crooned, squeezing her hand. "It's my mission—my duty to the Contessa—to investigate the dozens of prospective buyers we hear from each month, and to separate the gemstones from the cut glass. And as far as I'm concerned, Miss Gamble, you're the Hope Diamond."

Why would she argue with that? She swore she heard the popping of a beer can somewhere behind them—as though Spike were congratulating himself for pulling this whole thing off. What an ego that angel had! Why couldn't she have gotten the kind who spoke in reverent tones and glowed with a heavenly—

Hey, whadaya want here? At least I didn't smoke in the car, right?

3

When Cat caught a glimpse of the house, nestled high among flowering bushes and palm trees, she fell in love. *Had* to have the place, without even seeing inside. Its flamingo paint, trimmed in bright white with flourishes of Victorian millwork, made her heart sing. Never in her wildest imagination could she have conjured up such a fabulous home!

She sat forward, gawking through the windshield as they rounded the curve in the driveway. "Oh, Ramon, it's so beautiful! So different from anywhere I've ever lived—"

"Not so fast, Miss Gamble," he warned, although he was chuckling at her little-girl exuberance. "Best for all of us if you make an informed decision. For you see, Leilani and I are part of the package." His dark face remained utterly serious as he steered the Caddie into the garage at the rear of the house.

"How does that work?" she ventured. "I can't imagine being considered part of the property—like furniture or—"

"It was Miss Borgia's way of taking care of us, in appreciation for our years of service to her. Anyone who buys Porto Di

Angelo must love my wife and me—and *need* us—as much as we do him or her. This is our home, you see."

"And what a wonderful home it is." Cat barely had the patience to wait for Ramon to open her door. From a white brick wing wall that extended behind the garage, she had a breathtaking view of the sea . . . areas of deep morning-glory blue accented by turquoise and green . . . waves breaking like lacy petticoats against a white sand shore . . . gulls circling lazily on the breeze that ruffled the leaves of the trees. A rainbow of tropical blossoms welcomed her with their heady scents, inviting her into the back patio area.

Was she really here? Could this estate really be hers? She inhaled deeply, reminding herself to be practical . . . to compare what she'd seen and heard with what Ramon and his wife told her.

"Wow, the flowers here pack a punch," she remarked. Maybe she was jet-lagged, but the scent was reminiscent of marijuana smoke.

Ramon smiled, gesturing toward the hillsides covered with trees that had long bell-shaped white blooms. "Wait until this evening! These angel's trumpet trees perfume the entire island with their musk. We have to be on our guard, though, because the leaves and blooms can be smoked as an asthma remedy . . . or as a narcotic. Which sometimes attracts uninvited guests."

More pieces to this puzzle; more things to consider before she became Porto Di Angelo's owner. Could she really handle these details without getting taken advantage of? Who should she believe?

"How have you maintained the property so perfectly, if the Contessa has been absent nearly two years?" she asked, recalling the plane steward's story. "Where does the money come from to—"

"She has accounts in St. Lucia banks, as well as numerous trusts worldwide, which are managed by her attorney," Ramon answered. He stood so close his sleeve brushed her arm. "Leilani and I are provided for in perpetuity, as is the estate."

Cat pondered this, inhaling the brisk, clean scent of the sea and feeling more invigorated—more alive—than she had in years. "So you're saying you and your wife could remain here forever, taken care of, whether or not you sell the place? Why allow someone to intrude on your little slice of paradise?"

Ramon leaned on the white railing, so his smile was mere inches from her own. His eyes held her in a momentary trance in which she imagined all manner of wild, erotic things he wanted to do to her—before she blinked to clear that fantasy from her mind.

"My Leilani and I were born to serve," he murmured. "Porto Di Angelo needs a mistress—or master—to belong to, just as we do, if our life's purpose is to be fulfilled."

Cat saw not a hint of a mockery on his long, angular face. This man, dressed like a Fortune 500 CEO yet possessing the exotic mystique of these islands, was telling her he would *serve* . . . a concept so foreign to her, after being married to Laird King, that she had to mask her disbelief.

"Ah, but your mind is weary from your journey, and we speak of matters that can certainly wait, dear lady," he crooned, gesturing toward a staircase painted in bright white enamel. "Leilani has prepared tea—a custom Valenzia observed with us every afternoon, no matter what her schedule."

"And what sort of schedule did she have?" Cat mused aloud. "I don't mean to sound presumptuous, implying she led a life of leisure, but—" She stopped at the top of the stairs inside an open porch overlooking that magnificent beach and sea. "—Well, if I lived here, I'd be thoroughly tempted to just move from one vantage point to another, gazing out over the sand and the surf—"

"And write no more of those wild, exciting stories?" a female voice challenged. "The world would be a sadder, less sensuous place without Catalina Gamble romances. You've given Ramon and me many hours of pleasure! I feel absolutely giddy, getting to meet you right here in our home!"

Who could argue with that? Or with the lush, petite beauty who stood beside a colorfully set wicker table beaming at her?

"My wife, Leilani," Ramon said, extending his hand grandly.

As though drawn by some inner magnet, Cat closed the distance between them to clasp the woman's outstretched hands. Why did she feel she was coming home? What sort of magic did this couple practice, that drew her in before she pondered or analyzed her decision to buy this island? Leilani's ebony waves flowed past her shoulders, and the bright pink lily tucked at her ear matched the pattern of her simple dress. Her full lips and wide-set eyes captivated Cat, as did her richly tanned skin.

"Leilani, it's such a pleasure to—"

"The pleasure is mine, Catalina," the woman purred. "The Contessa wishes she were here to enjoy this historic moment, I can assure you! She used to read your books aloud to us in the evenings, as the rum punch took up where the sunset left off."

"My stories probably sounded much more inspired when you were sipping that punch," Cat said with a laugh. "But what a compliment! There's nothing so wonderful as hearing that people have enjoyed my books."

"And another will be out soon, I hope?" Leilani pulled out one of the three cushioned chairs at the table for her.

"Easier wished for than done, I'm afraid." People who weren't in publishing never really understood how things worked for writers, but perhaps this intuitive woman would get most of it. "My last two books didn't sell well—never mind that they were eclipsed by the September Eleventh disaster and an unforeseen distribution crisis. So my contract got canceled."

Leilani's lovely face fell in sympathy—and disdain. "What fools, to dismiss your talent! I hope that hasn't discouraged you from writing, dear."

"I'm working on another story. A pirate romance," Cat replied. Her voice rose with new hope—a sense that she could succeed again! "I found this fabulous island while I was re-searching—"

"No, Miss Gamble. Porto Di Angelo found *you*."

Her hostess pronounced this with the unflinching certainty of one attuned to higher realms. "We placed our ad again," she explained, "sensing the time was right to find a new mistress. While we knew this person would never replace Miss Borgia, she will take up where the Contessa left off . . . will bring a focus—a sense of direction—to the island again."

Leilani placed her hands on Cat's then, her smile mystical yet sly. "You might as well say yes, Catalina. I knew the moment you contacted us that we'd finally found the right earth angel for the job."

Was it the way Leilani used her full name that captivated her? Or the way this woman's eyes glowed a light, luminous blue in her deep olive face, framed by that cascade of sable waves? The bright pink lily at her temple drew Cat's attention to an ageless face that radiated serenity and a sense of purpose.

And when Ramon sat down beside his wife, smiling deeply at her, Cat understood implicitly that she could have her hot, edgy fantasies about this man, but hopping into bed with him was not an option.

And that was fine! What a pair they made, he in his high-powered pinstriped suit and she wrapped in a graceful pink sari that draped her shapely curves. The fabric whispered seduc-tively with each move she made pouring tea and passing Cat trays of sliced fruits, crustless sandwiches, and tiny glazed petit fours.

Cat's mouth dropped open and she couldn't choose. The Fi-esta dishes and tropical fruit made such a colorful presentation, it looked like they were throwing her a party! "Maybe it's jet lag or those stale pretzels on the flight," she murmured, "but I'm suddenly hungry within an inch of my life."

When Leilani laughed, her glimmering eyes urged Cat to really help herself to everything she wanted. Well, everything but Ramon, maybe.

"You've heard this before, but your blue eyes are such a . . . a novelty on someone with your tropical complexion."

Her hostess smiled proudly. "My father was an Englishman and my mother from Polynesia. Ramon insists I got the best of both their features, even though he never met them. You've no doubt discovered what a romantic side he has."

Cat paused with a small sandwich in front of her open mouth. How was she to answer that? "He—he had a very courtly air as he chauffeured me here, yes. Gallantry is hard to come by these days."

"It is." Leilani watched Cat's eyes for ulterior responses . . . secrets, perhaps. "I'm sure you understand why I'm a very . . . possessive wife. He's the only man on the island, and he's mine— to share as I see fit."

"As he should be." Cat nodded briskly, choosing more fruit and sandwiches. "Believe me, Leilani, after what I went through following my husband's death and the nasty surprises that came after, it'll be a while before I want to—"

"No, it won't. You're hot for it, same as any healthy, attractive woman." Leilani's smile broke through the wariness of their conversation. "I predict you'll attract a man in less than a week, Catalina. We may be isolated here, surrounded by the sea, but I feel your vibrations already beaming out."

"Like radar? Or sonar the dolphins communicate with?" It occurred to her then that Spike had been keeping his distance— or at least keeping his smoke to himself. Maybe he had some manners, after all. Or maybe he was already on his mission to find her a man.

Taking her hand, Leilani pointed over the porch railing. "Just like those dolphins frolicking in the surf, yes. They send out their joyful delight, and it returns to them in even greater abundance."

Cat stood up, mesmerized. While the ad for this island had mentioned dolphins at play, she'd never in her wildest dreams imagined living where she could watch them. Her heart pounded with an inexplicable yearning. Her body tightened with intense excitement. Bright red and white hibiscus bloomed in profusion amid dense, flowering shrubbery that appeared wild yet carefully tended. It was all so pretty. So perfect.

As the dolphins rounded the island beyond her view, she leaned against a porch pillar to take in the view toward the front of the house. The breeze caressed her cheek, and a pair of gulls swooped gracefully over the breaking waves, dipping down to catch their dinner.

Accompanying this dream was the surf, the rhythmic lullaby of waves breaking against the sand. Cat had the sudden urge to shed her black twin set and slacks to walk barefoot in the sand . . . to feel it ooze up between her toes as the ruffles of white foam lapped at her ankles.

"Perhaps we should see the house," Leilani suggested, "and then there's nothing like a sunset walk along the beach to clear your mind. While we talk as if your staying is inevitable or predetermined, you do have a choice. It's a life-altering decision, dear, so think on it well."

Cat breathed deeply and then exhaled what felt like a lifetime of stress and heartache and betrayal. "You're probably right. But then, you already know my answer, don't you?"

"Leilani knows everyone's answer, usually before they do," Ramon remarked. "And because I trust her intuition completely, I'll leave you ladies to your tour."

He rose, towering over them, smiling down like some beneficent chocolate god. "If you have questions, please don't hesitate to ask," he said in that late-night radio voice. "And if you need inspiration for this book you're working on, well, we can come up with something for you there, too."

Cat watched him duck slightly to enter the house, hearing his innuendo and knowing to leave it alone. On impulse, she piled more grapes and petit fours on her plate. "I'm so excited—and so hungry—I hope you won't mind if I nosh while you show me around."

The housekeeper smiled that mystical smile again. "Why would I mind? It's your house. And you're going to write a blockbuster, breakout novel before you've been here six months."

Cat nipped her lip. Maybe this woman, so very much a Caribbean lily, was more knowledgeable about the world of books and publishing than she'd thought. But then, at this point in her career, she was ready to believe anything, wasn't she?

From the doorway, Leilani extended her hand with the grace of a ballerina. "If you trust what I say about your new stories—and a new romance in your life—follow me, Catalina."

Oh, how Cat longed to believe. She slipped her hand into her housekeeper's and felt that shimmer of mysterious magnetism . . . a delicious invitation she didn't dare decline. Who was *she* to deny the power of positive seduction?

Cat stepped inside and entered another world . . . a world of ocean-blue shutters and sunshine-yellow walls, where the main floor of the house blended into one large, open room divided subtly into separate areas of a dining room, a living room, and a library. As she would expect from a mistress who was nobility, many of the furnishings were carved from glistening mahogany that bespoke old European elegance, yet the cushions on the couches and chairs echoed the bright island hues of coral and red and yellow.

And everywhere—from the high ceiling beams and the stair railings and the lamps—hung angels of all shapes and sizes. Dark-skinned Caribbean angels in island colors floated above the dining room table, tinkling as a wind chime, while larger angels fashioned from diaphanous fabrics drifted in the living room's afternoon breeze. From the skylight, tendrils of philodendron and pothos dangled down behind plants in painted pots on the floor, and smaller angels were attached to their long strands like ornaments on a Christmas tree.

While these decorations added a whimsical yet spiritual element to the large room, Cat was immediately aware of moving into another woman's domain. Did she dare ask about redecorating, once the house was hers?

"My angel collection," Leilani explained as she opened her arms to them. "Valenzia agreed that this island—Porto Di Angelo means 'angel haven,' you see—was a place where such entities favor us with their charm and wisdom. The light and vibrations here are unlike any we've felt elsewhere." The housekeeper grinned impishly at her. "The guardian who escorted you here seems to prefer the beach, where it doesn't feel so . . . girlie."

Cat laughed. "I met Spike right before I won the Powerball. He does seem . . . *unique*, considering my previous notions of how angels behave."

"Crusty like old concrete on the outside, cream puff on the inside. He's taking good care of you, dear."

How could Leilani *know* these things? Her psychic sensitivities would take some getting used to—a subject that would not be discussed until the exotic caretaker decided it was time. A *lot* of things revolved around this woman, it seemed.

"At the risk of sounding like a skeptic," Cat murmured, "would the angels allow the Contessa to come to harm? I'm still puzzled about—"

"Do not worry yourself over her fate, Catalina. I'm convinced our beloved Miss Borgia is alive and well! She is a free spirit, a childlike fairy with a flair for living well." Leilani gazed at the winged figures floating on their invisible strings and lifted her hands to them again. "This isn't the first lovely home Valenzia graced with her presence and then left behind when she evolved into higher places. I send her my love each time I smile at my collection."

Cat blinked. Some of this stuff was still beyond her—and she heard a response between Leilani's lines: if she bought this place, the angels stayed whether she liked them or not.

They moved on to the kitchen, a separate alcove where white appliances gleamed against ocean-blue walls. From louvered doors of sunshine yellow streamed rays of afternoon sunlight, with a breeze that felt cooler as the day came to a close. Cat looked forward to watching a glorious sunset from the porch they'd just left.

"Ramon and I have our quarters on the west side of the house," her guide explained as they ascended the graceful free-standing stairway. "We thrive in the heat of the day, while Miss Borgia preferred cooler rooms and the less intense light of morning."

"I'm with her," Cat agreed, and then she let out a low sigh. They were stepping into a suite of airy, pristine white . . . white tile floors and stucco walls, with more of that glossy mahogany furniture: a four-poster bed canopied in heavy cutwork lace of bridal white. The white comforter and pillows covered in blues and yellows invited her for a much-needed nap. A window seat looked out over the bay and the unbelievably beautiful water. A desk and bookcases filled an alcove that gave her a view of the gardens below, and her bathroom flooring and fixtures glistened bright white, with towels of the same ocean blue as the shutters throughout the house.

Cat gazed in awe at this space, so peaceful and perfect it looked like a page from the decorating magazines Trevor subscribed to. A room like she herself could never have put together with such simple yet sophisticated details.

"I . . . I feel like an intruder, taking over Valenzia's suite—"

"Fear not," Leilani assured her. "We've removed her clothing and the personal effects she left behind, along with the contents of her desk, knowing that whoever bought this home would bring her own belongings. I left your books in the case, however. She would want you to know how she enjoyed your work."

Unable to suppress a grin, Cat lovingly drew a finger along the paperbound spines she knew so well. "A complete collection," she mused, "starting with *Ride the Wild Wind* and the *Flame* trilogy. . . . I haven't thought about these characters and their stories for years! I was writing on an electric typewriter—assuming a computer would stifle my muse—when my first romance got published. How antiquated does *that* seem?"

"Perhaps their presence will inspire you, dear." Leilani gazed around the room with the pride of one who'd maintained it for years. "If you want or need anything—anything at all—please tug on this bell pull. Once for me, twice for Ramon. We live right across that hallway, and we hear the bells from all over the house."

"I—I can't imagine having servants at my beck and call, so I doubt I'll—"

"Get used to it." Leilani's eyes twinkled like the sunlit sea. "We'll feel superfluous if you don't summon us, Catalina. What good is being an angel if you can't bestow your blessings on those around you?"

Again Cat couldn't imagine any American domestic thinking that way . . . but then, Leilani was unlike any housekeeper she'd ever seen. Her sun-kissed body glowed with vitality. Her sari fastened at her shoulder with a simple knot: the breeze fluttered the fabric to reveal lovely legs and feet adorned with the simplest of sandals. She opened the balcony doors overlooking the ocean as if she were giving Cat the greatest of gifts.

Cat swallowed. When the sunlight silhouetted her, Leilani appeared naked in the gauzy dress. Not a hint of a bra or a thong. Her smile said she knew quite well what an enticement she was.

"I spent many a fine hour advising the Contessa on affairs of the heart and soul, and I look forward to doing the same with you, Catalina. Such intimacies are foreign to you, I know," she added with an arched eyebrow. "You are a loner and an introvert by nature. But your soul is like a lotus flower, just waiting for its time to blossom and bring its unique beauty to the world. I'm honored to be here for your awakening."

Her mouth opened, but Cat didn't know what to say—an unsettling experience for a writer whose words had always flowed easily. Or at least they had until she started her pirate project.

"I'll leave you now. You're tired, and you need to immerse yourself in Porto Di Angelo as you rest, to reaffirm your sense of belonging here."

"How do you know that? What do you mean?" Her questions sounded harsh and impatient, but damn! She could only handle so much of this talk from a higher realm.

"We'll talk of past lives and reincarnation some day . . . and I'll reveal the whys and wherefores of your deep feelings for this island. Meanwhile," she added with a coy smile, "don't forget to let those at home know you've arrived safely."

With that, Leilani drifted from the room like mist on a warm morning.

Cat knew she was too damn tired when she thought she saw the flutter of gossamer wings as the housekeeper descended to the kitchen. Not a drop of rum punch yet, and already she was a goner.

4

To: AttyCareyGrant@earthlink.net
CC: TTeagueDesigns, BigelowLandscapes
Subject: YES! Gotta have this place!

Guys, you will not believe this island! WAY more beautiful than the ads. Comes with Leilani and Ramon, live-in domestics—not to mention a mysterious Italian Contessa who has disappeared . . . into the Bermuda Triangle? Kidnapped by pirates? No one knows!

Why do these islanders speak perfect English? Why are angels dangling from every fixture and ceiling fan? Why do they all welcome me, and how did they know I was coming before I knew it myself? (insert Twilight Zone music here) But they've read all my books! They love me already!

Don't mind me—I'm tired. Sitting in a bridal-white bedroom with a canopied four-poster, overlooking the ocean and sand that shimmers in the sunset. Ready to walk that beach and think this over, but YES! It calls to me. Leilani predicts I'll have a love life within the week, so I have to stay at least that long!

More later. Thanks again to all of you! Miss you guys!
Love, CatWoman

She pushed back from the rolltop desk and marveled at yet another miracle of this isolated island: she could gaze out over moonbeams dancing on the Caribbean Sea while, thanks to satellite internet, she could e-mail friends in the States . . . a world she suddenly felt separated from by more than geography. It was a distance inside her; a sense that she had nothing to return to in St. Louis. Did she even need those clothes in her closet or the reams of blank paper and office supplies and research books she'd left behind with life as she knew it?
   On second thought—

To: AttyCareyGrant@earthlink.net
Subject: my stuff!

Grant—
Soon as you can, send my books and office supplies! Let's hope the mail drop is working like it's supposed to, because my pirate book is taking on a whole new life, like the sails of the Black Pearl swell with the sea breezes!

You savvy, mate? I feel like a whole 'nother woman! Ripe and ready! Too bad I'm not your type, eh?
   Kisses anyway, Cat

Satisfied, she shut down her laptop and lolled in the tilt-back desk chair. The twilight had crept into her room with delicate shadows, on a breeze that smelled sweet and musky and sensual. Those long white angel's trumpets caught the moonlight and glowed like lights on a whole forest of tropical Christmas trees . . . a magical sight.

On impulse, Cat stripped off her stolid black slacks and sweater set. Something called to her like a siren song and she felt compelled to step out onto her balcony. After all, who was there to see her? Her panties hit the floor, followed by her bra, and as she padded barefoot to her balcony, the deep coolness of the tile floor seeped into her soul.

Serenity. Tranquility. Total, blissful freedom here . . . not to mention a decadence that called from so far inside her she'd forgotten such a wild, romantic place existed. Never in her life had she ventured outside in the altogether—not even as a newlywed. Yet here she was, accepting the sea breeze's invitation, drawn by an invisible force to be at one with the universe.

And what a universe it was! A sky of midnight blue velvet spangled with diamond stars stretched into forever, while the waves below lapped at the sand in an endless, ancient rhythm that lulled her . . . made her believe she could walk through the house naked and unafraid, to stroll across sand that glistened in the moonlight . . . to let those waves tickle her toes and coax her to laugh and frolic along their frothy edges.

Laugh and frolic. Lord, how long had it been since she'd done that?

And never naked, that's for sure!

Why not? If not now, when? Spike whispered.

Cat gripped the balcony railing, torn between living out this fresh, brazen fantasy and staying here in the safety of her new home. Leilani would no doubt applaud her crossing of this boundary . . . perhaps even shed that sari to join her, which would no doubt bring Ramon along, as well. Tall and sleek and so damn sexy he'd be, as dark as the night and as potently mysterious.

But what was that on the horizon? Cat leaned forward, squinting. Something bobbed along on the water like an angular, pointy cork—

"Oh my God . . . oh my *God!*" She sucked in her breath and stared as the object sailed closer to the island. With its three tall masts and pale sails swelling in the breeze, it looked for all the world like a pirate ship!

Cat's nipples hardened, and goose bumps tingled over her entire body. It was like something out of the Disney movies, only better! Because it was real! As the minutes and waves brought the ship closer to Porto Di Angelo, Cat could only hold her breath and gape at the ship's antique magnificence. Not even in her wildest, most flowing imagination could she create such a vision . . . now close enough that she could make out the men on the main deck. They were looking this way—

Cat's hands fluttered to cover her bare breasts. Could they see her up here? Would the palm trees shield her, or should she duck inside?

So what if they see you? Spike teased. *You could do worse than have a pirate ship's crew spot you through their spyglasses and then pull up at your dock!*

"And I suppose you arranged this?" she whispered, her eyes fixed on the roll and sway of those people on the decks.

Maybe I did. And maybe I just wish I had. Lookin' fiiiiine, Miss Kitty!

Her nipples jabbed her palms as she stood, caught in the sudden knowledge that with the light from her desk lamp behind her, she was a very visible, very naked silhouette to anyone who'd caught sight of her.

She swore someone waved . . . no, two or three of them waved their arms above their heads in greeting!

And then she sucked air again: two figures sprinted across the beach, waving their arms in response to the crewmen. They were silent, but their bodies spoke volumes because they, too, were naked. Leilani and Ramon had doffed their clothes to commune with nature—and those sailors!

As though by an established pattern, the magnificent ship then swung around toward the sea again. For all she knew, the captain and his crew were decked out like buccaneers and swashbucklers of old, just out for an evening joyride, following their favorite currents around the sprinkling of tiny islands in this section of the sea.

Hell, for all she knew, Johnny Depp and Orlando Bloom were aboard, and their filming crew was checking out potential places to shoot the next *Pirates of the Caribbean* blockbuster!

The vision tantalized her imagination, and Cat knew it was time to start not a new chapter but a totally different book from what she'd been writing. Here, with the salt mist dampening her face and the whisper of the wind in the tropical trees, she could *live* the story as it unfolded. How cool was that?!

She gripped the railing, glancing down at the beach again. There in the glistening sand along the shoreline, with lacy waves running up around their ankles, Leilani and Ramon were kissing. Oh, it wasn't just the kiss of an old married couple, either—and maybe they weren't! Maybe Ramon had only said that to appease her civilized sensitivities today.

Does that matter, really?

Spike had a point, didn't he? Who was she to judge?

What struck her was their absolute beauty . . . their belief that they belonged on the beach on this perfect night in paradise, and that they wouldn't let this idyllic opportunity pass them by just because she had arrived. While Leilani's psychic powers intimidated her a bit, Cat realized she had a lot to learn from her ethereal housekeeper.

"Grab me!" Leilani challenged in a husky whisper. "You know you want to, loverman!"

Cat gaped as their bodies came together, in profile to her. Ramon, so tall and lean, stooped slightly to catch up Leilani's eager form as she reached for him. His cock jutted out at a right angle, just as her lush, rounded breasts bobbed lightly with her excitement.

"Make me!" he taunted after another feverish kiss. "Make me so crazy I'll have to fuck you again and again, witchy woman!"

Cat blinked, looking away. This was not only an invasion of their privacy, it was lewd and crude of her as a guest in their—

Hold on, missy! They're calling this your house, Spike reminded her. *Leilani suggested that you walk along the beach to sort out your thoughts. You might've walked in on them—and they might've planned it that way! They might invite you to frolic naked—*

She arched an eyebrow in the direction she thought his gravelly voice came from—although it was mostly inside her head.

"Let me guess," she whispered. "I don't smell your cigarettes because you've found other stuff to smoke!"

Don't knock it, doll. Puts a whole new spin on things. Maybe you could use a new spin.

Her eyes wandered back to the couple on the moonlit beach. Leilani's thick waves cascaded down her back, jerking like a curtain when Ramon wove his fingers into them. Leilani gasped with the force of his kiss . . . leaned into his tall, virile body and then shimmied against him, making him moan.

Hugging herself, Cat watched in envy. Damn, those two were really getting into it! Did they really intend to—

Of course they do! You're *the one who's hanging back, playing the voyeur!* Spike taunted. *You could slip out to another section of beach and wade naked, minding your own business, instead of gawking at—*

Would you stifle yourself? She waved him off, scowling.

A little burst of that angel's trumpet musk suggested he'd left her.

Meanwhile Ramon was kissing Leilani deeply, bending her back like a slender willow to do his bidding.

"Make me your slave!" Leilani rasped. "Force me to take every inch of your long, hot cock into my—"

"You'll be screaming for it!" he growled playfully. "Don't tempt me past more than your puss can handle!"

Their bodies writhed in rhythm, until their faces parted so their long tongues could duel in the moonlight.

Cat's insides tightened. She was fully aware of her wickedness . . . felt the come-on in the breeze that tickled her between the legs as she undulated to the same rhythm she watched below. Her legs parted, begging her fingers to satisfy the ache between them.

How long had it been? She twitched at the first flick of her fingertips. Leilani, too, seemed urgent as she backed away to look up at her dark lover and then turned to tempt him with her pert backside.

Ramon's rich laughter wafted around her on the sea breeze, making Cat squirm against the balcony support. If she shifted . . . bent at the knees just so, she could rub herself. No one would have a clue what she was doing . . . what the smooth, cool paint felt like against her hot, throbbing flesh.

Leilani was bending forward, bracing her hands on her knees, a midnight sprite so lovely it took Cat's breath away. Of all the tropical blossoms on this island, Leilani was the most delicate, the most sensual, the most stunning—and she knew it: assumed her place as queen of sensual realms Cat had had no previous dealings with.

But she was about to learn, big-time.

She knew damn well Ramon was going to take his wife from behind. She watched the lithe islander point his long cock and grab the lush hips offered up to him. Cat held her breath as he paused at Leilani's opening. She had no trouble imagining how wet and warm it would be because her own slit was brimming over.

Slowly and secretively, Cat moved against the carved cylindrical post, using a turning in the wood to best advantage against her clit. God, but this was dirty! She was beyond caring if Spike was watching her now. Trevor and Grant would *not* believe—

Trevor and Grant are probably in the same position as the couple you're watching, with Bruce egging them on.

But why entertain such images—why wonder if her guardian angel had spoken, or if those were her own thoughts—when she had a bird's-eye view of such a lovely couple making love? Cat held her breath . . . pressed herself more firmly against the balcony post when Ramon disappeared inside Leilani, inch by excruciating inch, until she whimpered and began to pump against him.

Ramon arched back slightly, his pigtail as stiff as his other extremity. Slowly, bending to achieve a better angle, the man who'd driven her home from the airport drove himself deep inside his woman, pulling out and then burying himself to the hilt. Again and again he thrust, as though he could control his own climax all night long.

Leilani's moans taunted Cat. God, how she wished Ramon was putting it to *her* that way! But for now, Cat gyrated herself to a very nice thrum that would soon bring the release she needed so badly.

With a little whimper, Leilani fell forward and caught herself, the prima donna in a breathtaking ballet during which Ramon eagerly followed her every lead and granted her every request. He moved with her, lowering himself slowly with those long corded legs until his knees dropped into the soft sand on either side of Leilani's.

They were grunting and rutting now, two lithe animals in heat. Cat heard Leilani's wetness, echoed by her own as she matched the speed of their primal dance. Her housekeeper's breasts jiggled with the force of Ramon's thrusts, and she met every one of them with an eager grace, tilting her head back in ecstasy.

When Ramon clamped his arms around her, Cat grabbed the railing and hung on for dear life. She could *not* cry out when she climaxed! Could *not* let the couple on the beach know she'd been following their every move so avidly. So brazenly.

She found it then, that sweet spot that promised the rush she needed. As Ramon's triumphant grunts punctuated the night, she curled against the railing and succumbed to a climax that went on and on. Cat bit back a scream that would've torn the night in two.

Leilani did it for her: she wailed like a wild creature surrendering to her mate, releasing cataclysmic forces that crashed inside her like tidal waves beating the rocky shore. On and on Leilani moaned, in a randy duet with Ramon, until Cat thought she might rub the paint from the post.

She couldn't stop. Her hips wriggled, and wetness spread down her thighs until her eyes flew open from the implosion below. She hugged the railing so hard she knew she'd have bruises tomorrow—

Then she realized the couple on the beach had stopped, still joined at the hip. They were watching her.

Had she squealed, too far gone to hear herself? She might pretend Leilani and Ramon didn't know what she'd been doing, but that just showed how naive her thought process was.

They'd caught her spying on them. If they quizzed her about it, she had no recourse but to confess—and to admit to herself they knew what *she'd* been doing while she watched them.

Life on this island would be more complicated than she'd thought. And a whole lot hotter.

5

After a night that alternated between erotic dreams and waking up so giddy she couldn't sleep, Cat slipped out of bed to watch the sunrise from her balcony. Ribbons of bright pink and peach wrapped around the island, to make her new world a glowing, cozy place she longed to explore today.

But what would she say to Ramon and Leilani? She felt awkward about spying on them and then getting caught in a compromising position—but damn it, they'd told her to go for a walk on that beach!

What to do? She had to go downstairs sometime . . . had to decide whether such encounters would limit her explorations and—

Hey, doll—who's the boss here? If it's gonna be your island, you've gotta get past this "what if?" stuff. Tell 'em how it is!

Spike's greeting made her smile into the sun, which rose like a vibrant red ball above the sea. Already she was behaving differently: hadn't seen the sun rise since she could remember; had met her guardian angel; believed *she* could be in charge again!

Life with Laird, and not selling a book for a while, had dampened her independent spirit more than she knew.

But those things were behind her now! If she never wrote another page, she could live out her life in paradise!

Cat went inside, still in awe of the white room with its shiny tile floor and cut-lace canopy . . . fluffy towels . . . walls like the sand beach. Who knew the color white could have so many textures? She felt not so much like a bride here, but like an innocent again. Alive in a childlike way, anticipating wonderful things that each and every day might bring her now!

She flipped open her laptop and waited for the satellite signal, grinning when she saw Grant's message.

TO: cmgamble@catwoman.net
SUBJECT: You go, girl!

We're happy you're so happy, Cat! Your money has been deposited at the Bank of St. Lucia in Castries, so if Porto Di Angelo is your heart's desire, you should have it! Proceed with caution, sweetheart: those island types may appear unsophisticated and primitive, but things aren't always what they seem.

"Amen to that," she breathed.

When she read the last few lines, about the latest pirate fantasies he and Bruce and Trevor had enacted, she knew it was time to turn her own sense of adventure loose, too. Shopping for clothes had to be a high priority today: in her fuchsia print overblouse with navy twills, she looked like a middle-class wife from the Midwest, and it was time to change that!

Cat banished the recollection of two nude bodies on the beach and went downstairs. Heavenly scents of sweet spices and bacon met her on the stairway, and those colorful angels floating from the ceiling put her in a cheerful mood. She followed voices out to the porch, where her two caretakers lingered over their coffee.

"Good morning, Catalina!" Leilani's blue eyes glistened like crystals in her bronzed face. She poured a cup of tea from the scarlet Fiesta pot while Ramon hopped up to pull out a chair.

"You slept well, I hope?" he asked.

Cat sat down. How should she say what was on her mind? "You know how it is," she hedged. "I was keyed up about coming here, and tired from—"

"Not to mention *aroused* after watching sex on the beach that had nothing to do with liquor?"

She blinked. Leilani's voice hinted at a challenge, *pride* in what they'd done! "Well, I *wasn't* expecting to see—"

"Pardon my French, but we have an entire island to ourselves, so we fuck like bunnies." Ramon's eyes steamed like the tea in her cup. "Adventuress that she was, the Contessa encouraged us to love freely wherever—"

"And did she share in that love?" Cat's cheeks flamed when such a blatant question slipped out before she could catch it.

"Most times she was entertaining her own lovers." Leilani smiled enigmatically and passed a plate of nut breads and pastries that looked homemade. "We all agreed that this would be the best way to remain on proper footing, far as relations between the owner and her help. If what you saw last night upset or disgusted you—"

"No, I just—"

"—we'll be more discreet." Leilani gave her husband a pointed look when he opened his mouth to protest. "We must all adjust to this new situation, because Ramon and I are overjoyed that you're interested in Porto Di Angelo. Several corporate and Asian investors want to turn our home into a gentlemen's retreat or a swingers' resort, and I'm not ready to go there!"

Cat laughed, relaxing. "Maybe—at least until we're better

acquainted—you could warn me when you'll be running around outside my balcony . . . fucking like bunnies. Especially if I can't have any."

How crude did that sound? Cat quickly bit into a slice of papaya poppyseed bread so tender it fell apart in her fingers.

Ramon's snicker prompted Leilani to laugh out loud. "Point well taken."

"Yes, you did take it well, my witchy woman," her husband teased. "But you ladies are right. Miss Gamble's . . . desperation . . . isn't what we should be inspiring."

Again Cat's cheeks flared, but the issue had been defused, hadn't it? Thanks to Ramon's lusty humor and Leilani's gentle yet head-on handling of the situation, she could enjoy this wonderful breakfast, and her other issues would be a lot easier to discuss, too. She reached for a pinwheel pastry with apricot filling oozing out of it while Leilani poured her husband another cup of coffee.

"You've come to a decision," the housekeeper stated with a faraway smile. "So how may we help you implement it?"

The pastry fell back to Cat's plate. Was she that easy to read, or was Leilani tuned in to her deepest frequencies?

"I—I've decided to buy Porto Di Angelo! My attorney tells me the money's been deposited at the Bank of St. Lucia, so I'd like to go there as soon as possible—"

"Today," Ramon affirmed with a grin. "This is the news we've hoped for, pretty lady!"

"—but first you've got to tell me why your English is so perfect!" It was an odd request, but now was the time to clear up all the discrepancies between reality and her expectations, wasn't it? "So many things here are too good to be true. I certainly never expected domestics whose command of the language exceeds my own. And I don't say that to just anyone!"

Leilani's blue-eyed smile focused more intently. "I mentioned, I think, that my parents were English. My mother was a teacher, and my father sailed in the merchant marine. Since my dark skin and wavy hair are so very different from theirs, my . . . *lineage* was always a matter of speculation. Even to me." She smiled ruefully and sipped her coffee. "I was a fanciful child with many imaginary playmates," she went on, "but when I learned I was the result of my mother's affair with a cabana boy, my invisible friends revealed themselves as my angels. They protected me from cruel remarks and the judgmental attitudes of Father's friends."

"Oh, my." The beautiful woman's thin voice told a more poignant tale than her steady smile let on. "I didn't mean to intrude—or be nosy—"

"No, no. I've come to terms with my mother's pursuit of happiness. I survived the teasing of the neighborhood children by immersing myself in my books—and my angels. I was earning my second master's degree when I met Ramon—savvy, dashing man that he is! That's when I knew I needed a life and a lover much more than I needed more time in school."

"She speaks seven island languages, as well as English, French, and Portuguese," Ramon chimed in proudly.

"And Italian, since Valenzia thought we girls should have a language all our own." Leilani grinned impishly. "Of course, you've learned that Ramon is very good with . . . tongues . . . himself. But you have more pressing issues on your mind than our love life, Catalina! If you have questions about this house— or how the island is maintained—please ask us!"

The housekeeper's dazzling smile derailed Cat's train of thought—another uncanny talent Leilani had. "Yes! I'd like to arrange the sale and payment for Porto Di Angelo today. And I'd certainly like to buy some appropriate clothes!"

"I'll prepare the yacht, then. We'll be on our way as soon as you ladies are ready," Ramon crooned. "If you'll allow us, we can make sure your transaction goes without a hitch."

"My cousin is a loan officer at the Bank of St. Lucia. He'll be sure no hidden fees or taxes get figured in just because you're American and wouldn't be aware of them," Leilani clarified.

"I, of course, will see that no one takes advantage of a pretty Anglo woman here alone," her husband added suavely. "You know by now that I'm not violent by nature—"

"But nobody messes with a guy who stands nearly seven feet tall! And who has very interesting . . . thumbnails." Once again Cat wondered where such a question had come from. Had Spike prodded her into saying that? Or were this witchy woman and her buck lover redefining her rules of engagement?

Ramon's coffee-colored eyes steamed as he gazed at her. He clasped his hands together so those unique nails were on the tops of his fists, pointed upward like swords. He looked very, very confident. Downright predatory.

"Do you have any idea how those feel when they flick my nipples?" Leilani breathed.

Startled, Cat looked over to see a simmering look lighting her dusky face. "I doubt anyone thinks about that when they imagine Ramon using them as weapons!"

"Exactly."

The man rose with a lazy, confident smile, unconcerned that his ivory robe had parted below the sash to reveal his spectacular privates. "Now, if you ladies will excuse me, Mr. Intimidation must dress for his day. Between falling all over themselves to assist you beautiful ladies, and seeing *me* as your escort, those loan officers and store clerks don't stand a chance!"

How much fun can you cram into one day? Cat mused with a huge grin. The breeze was brisk where she and Leilani sunned themselves on the yacht's flybridge, with Ramon in the driver's seat behind the windshield. Her spirits flew high and fast as the sleek white boat raced across the turquoise waters, and she suddenly realized that days like this could be her whole reason for living.

When had she ever felt such freedom? Such satisfaction? Maybe money couldn't buy happiness, but it certainly provided a lot of the props. Thanks to Grant's e-mailed docs and help from Leilani's cousin, Porto Di Angelo had become hers with a minimum of fuss.

Who else pays cash for a whole frickin' island? And then loads up her yacht with clothes? Nobody you know!

She grinned again and adjusted her shades. Those thoughts so mimicked her own that only Spike's accent gave away his presence.

"You look awfully pleased with yourself, Catalina," her whiskey-skinned companion murmured.

"Damn straight I am! I spent too many years wondering where my next contract was coming from," she murmured. "Too much time dealing with vultures who demanded the money my husband owed them. Living well really is the best revenge!"

Grinning, Leilani untied her lime bikini top and then held it up to flutter like a flag of victory. "It's your destiny, dear. My prayers were answered when our angels heaped prosperity on your pretty head. Just when you needed it most."

"Yeah, they must've whispered in Bruce's ear when he chose those Powerball numbers—and then they made sure *I* got that ticket, instead of our other two buddies."

You wanna give me a little credit, doll?

"You earned it, my dear," Leilani assured her with a serene smile. "The cosmic wheel of fortune is rotating in your favor now."

How should she answer that? Her Midwestern ethic and her parents had always preached that only money you worked for was its own reward.

But right now, she didn't really care. It just felt damn good to have a home again, free and clear. Not to mention this yacht with its four staterooms, and two estate caretakers who'd been her fans before they even met her.

From behind her large, dark sunshades, Cat stole a glance at Leilani. Her ripe, rounded breasts pointed to the sun and bobbed softly with the vibrations of the yacht. How old was this woman? Her thicket of wavy hair shone blue-black—not a trace of gray—and her face remained seamless and dewy, like the rest of her lovely body. Stretched out on her deck chaise, her eyes hidden behind her own shades, Leilani could pass for a college coed. Yet she spoke like a much older soul, with a wisdom that defied anything Cat had ever known.

Shopping with this woman had been quite a trip, too! Leilani had steered her to an out-of-the-way shop where native ladies sewed their unique saris, sundresses, and other simple yet stunning clothing. Along rack after rack, Leilani had yanked garments of bright lime and lavender and paradise pink—tropical prints and designs like Cat had never seen stateside—and insisted they were perfect for her.

And they were. While Cat tried them on in a dressing stall too tiny to hold them all, her housekeeper kept bringing more . . . and she'd succumbed to every last one of them. The three shop ladies had stood and applauded as they left, and she'd never even looked at the total. How much fun was *that*?!

"You're grinning again."

"Yep. Recalling our shopping excursion and how you picked out all the best stuff for me."

"You were generous to buy them all. Those families will live well for months on what you spent today."

"Which is why you guided me there. And I thank you for that." Cat looked over at Leilani full-on this time, envying the way that tiny lime bikini bottom tied at the sides of firm hips. A hint of tight curls whispered beneath its upper band.

"Like what you see?" Leilani lazily raised her sunglasses to peer under them. Her smoky blue eyes insisted on a straight answer.

"What's not to admire—and envy?" Cat admitted. "I have

no idea how old you are. It's a wonder Ramon can keep the yacht on course, you look so damn spectacular."

"Forty-six. And who says we're on course? One stretch of ocean looks pretty much like another, you know."

"The yacht has GPS," Cat replied promptly. "And enough rum punch and food to sustain us for days, should we truly lose our way."

Leilani chuckled. "You're already lost, Catalina. Lost and gone forever." There it was again, that all-knowing, all-seeing tone that spooked the hell out of her. Yet it held a challenge as sexy as the woman who awaited her reply.

"What do you mean by *lost*?" Cat protested. "I found you and Ramon, didn't I? And what was it he said about the Contessa? Something like, 'all who wander are not lost'?"

Low laughter bubbled up from her tormentor, and those perfect breasts shimmied until the nipples rose tall and hard, pointing at the sun.

And then they pointed at *her*.

"Take this off," Leilani teased, tugging at the hibiscus-print sari Cat had worn out of the clothing shop. "If you truly want to feel free, show yourself to this paradise you've just bought into! Become one with your new universe!"

Yeah! Take it all off, doll!

Cat blinked, hoping Spike took the hint. And then behind them, Ramon thumped on the windshield. He was grinning broadly, nodding for her to comply. He picked up a microphone. "What a pretty pair you ladies will make," he crooned. "Dark, succulent Leilani and Catalina the Sun Queen."

"Who's out here to see you?" Leilani prodded. She untied the sides of her bikini bottom and parted her legs to flick it off, baring herself completely. Then, thoroughly at ease, she walked over to the deck railing.

Cat couldn't take her eyes off that glorious woman—a decade older than she but so flawless. So comfortable displaying herself. And what a contrast her tropical body made against the yacht's blinding white sundeck. Her hair rippled like a sleek black banner in the wind, and she was nothing short of a goddess as she lifted her face to smile at the sun.

"I won't force you. Or touch you—unless you want me to," the sleek feline purred. She leaned back against the railing to extend her arms along it, totally unconcerned that Cat was watching her breasts sway . . . following the line of her sleek hips to where that black triangle of curls nestled between her slender thighs.

"Come on, Catalina," she coaxed. "Ramon was asking me if you were a natural blonde, harkening back to that clichéd line about how we would know. And seeing *is* believing."

"I can't believe I'm hearing—"

Thump-thump-thump! Ramon's grin was wide and white as he gestured through the windshield for her to rip off her sari. "We have a bet, Miss Gamble," he teased through the speaker. "You must settle our wager while we can both witness it!"

"After all, you've seen *us* without clothes," Leilani kept on in a soft, sly voice. "And we saw you, too. Rubbing yourself into a frenzy like there was a wanton, very horny woman inside who wanted *out*! Set her free, Catalina. What have you got to lose?"

Yeah! Whadaya got to lose, girlie?

What, indeed? Such a crazy-ass proposition, and she had little left to hide, now that they'd caught her bringing herself off. Yet coming from this prophetess, who stretched like a contented cat against the railing, with the endless cerulean sea for a backdrop, it sounded oh, so logical . . . oh, so tempting, to feel the sea spray and the Caribbean sun on all of her skin at once.

"I'll rub on your sunblock, if you want some."

I'd be happy to help! I'm all about protection, ya know.

Cat swallowed hard. Now was not the time to reprimand

her brazen guardian angel. Not when Leilani was gracefully extending a hand toward her, slowly teasing her over the edge.

"What the hell?" she exhaled, sitting upright. "What are they gonna do? Arrest me? *Fine* my ass for indecent exposure, when—"

"Oh, yes, Catalina, your ass *is* fine! Ramon told me so," her housekeeper teased. "And wouldn't the sight of it as he's driving be a nice tip for his services? It won't cost you a thing but your modesty. And where has modesty gotten you?"

As she reached up to untie her shoulder strap, her fingers trembled . . . her knees trembled . . . her heart thudded a reminder of everything she'd ever been taught about how good girls behaved. Even Laird, as cavalier as he was with his money, had expected discretion when it came to flashing her assets.

So what was she doing on this yacht, out here in front of God and everybody—including her housekeeper's husband— taking off her clothes?

Cat closed her eyes, exhaled her fearful thoughts, and let the silky hibiscus print sari slither down her body.

For a moment there was only the whisper of the wind and the pounding of her pulse. Her nipples pebbled just from imagining how Leilani and Ramon must be staring at her.

The woman at the railing cleared her throat to keep from laughing. "All well and good, Catalina, but the white cotton panties have to go."

Heat flared in her cheeks and her eyes flew open. Why did she feel more exposed in these little-girl undies than she had when these two caretakers caught her on the balcony? Laughing nervously, Cat tugged the elastic waistband down with her thumbs. God help her if the yacht swerved and she fell flat on her face right now.

"Now *that's* what I call a fine piece of tail," a low voice came through the speaker. "If you're taking requests, Miss Gamble,

I'd really enjoy it if you stood beside my wife there at the railing. So I can look you over like I've been wanting to. From the safety of this cabin."

Nipping her lip, Cat stepped carefully toward Leilani and then stopped. Those exotic blue eyes were locked on hers, pulling her forward—to what? Was her housekeeper putting the moves on her?

Cat turned to lean against the railing, looking up at Ramon— who at least had his clothes on. Or did he? A camera flash took her by such surprise she couldn't swear to what he might be wearing.

"Hey! I never said anything about—"

"No worries, sweetheart," her companion assured her. "We have some hot shots of Valenzia standing here in the altogether, too. They're tucked away in the scrapbook of memories made on Porto Di Angelo."

"But I—it was all I could do to peel off my clothes!" Cat sputtered. "It's a whole 'nother thing to be taking nude photos of me when—my God, I just met you people yesterday!"

"Oh, and don't I love it when you shimmy that way, pretty blond lady?" Ramon teased in a singsong voice. "Makes those nipples dance! Leads my eyes down between those luscious thighs—but we still can't settle our bet, can we, Leilani?"

Directing her gaze slowly down the front of Cat's pale, bare body, the priestess chuckled seductively. "Some things we just have to take on faith, Ramon. Would you like it if I shaved mine, too? Then we could be your two innocent girls. Your two smooth, naked pussies."

"I'll leave that up to you, my dearest," he replied with a little laugh. "You know how my fingers love to play with your fur."

"So come here and say that to my face, teaser. Don't promise what you won't deliver."

Leilani turned to her then, smiling. "Don't let all this bedroom banter frighten you, Catalina. Sex is how adults play, and Ramon and I are firm believers in letting our Inner Children lead us where they will."

"I'm dropping anchor, Leilani," came a hoarse whisper from the speaker. "You'd better be ready to stand and deliver yourself, woman! And if Cat wants to play, we might as well let her in on the game. It'll happen sooner or later."

Cat gripped the warm railing. How the hell had she gotten into *this*? Here they were out in the middle of the Caribbean, dropping anchor so these two dark lovers could frolic, and she was feeling very much like a third wheel. A rather wobbly third wheel. Leilani was looking her over, sizing up her attitude as much as her attributes, and her intensity came across as a crystal-blue challenge.

Cat cleared her throat. "My Inner Kid wouldn't want to interrupt your fun, so—"

"Chicken," Leilani whispered. "*Bwahhk-bwahhk-bwaaaaahhk!*"

Bwahhk-bwahhhk-bwaaaahk! came Spike's reply.

"That's not fair! You and Ramon are married—"

"Is that what he told you?"

"—and I'm the new kid on this block, and maybe I have *issues* with—with triangles!"

"Yeah, geometry wasn't my best subject in school, either," Ramon said as he descended the white stairway. "But I understand *points* and *curves*, and I know that three-ways only work when all three sides of that triangle are happy. And horny."

He stepped to the deck a few feet away from them, and yes, he was naked. All seven-foot-something of him paused before her, sporting at least nine magnificent inches.

Cat's breath left her, and she immediately focused on his eyes. Where would she put all of that cock if it *was* offered to her?

"I hear the whirlpool calling," she said, trying not to stare when Ramon walked up behind his gorgeous wife and cupped her breasts. He teased her midnight-pink nipples with those brazen thumbnails, and Leilani melted against him.

Her own nipples jutted out farther than she'd ever seen them, as if trying to lead her in the direction they pointed. "Take your time! We can start back for home whenever you're ready—tomorrow or the next day if you want!" she rasped. "Me, I'm going to enjoy a water massage and then stretch out in my nice, cool stateroom when my skin starts to sizzle."

She was backing away, giving them a little wave. Already off their radar screen, they were so hot into their kissing. She felt like a naive little goody-goody running scared, even though she'd just braved a whole new world and then *bought* it!

And you've bared yourself to it, too! Gettin' gutsy, girl!

"Some guardian *you've* been!" she muttered as she hurried to the back deck. "Seems to me you only help when the mood strikes you!"

You got it, doll. But, hey—did you ever dream things would go so well so fast? You can thank me later when you see the other miracles I've arranged.

Cat paused with her hands on the ladder of the hot tub. As the tropical sun warmed her back and the turquoise sea shimmered for as far as she could see in every direction—from *her* yacht—she saw his point.

"Thank you, Spike. If I sound ungrateful, it's just that talking with an angel I can't see—not to mention dealing with exotic lovers who drop their clothes a lot—takes some getting used to." She smiled at the sky, inhaling deeply. "And thanks for leaving your beer and cigarettes behind today."

He laughed, damn it. She swore she felt fingers riffling her hair and then caressing her breasts.

If I stay downwind, who knows what I've found to smoke and drink here, sweetie pie? Enjoy your dip in the Jacuzzi now. I will, too.

Would she ever get used to talking with this angel? So many

new experiences had come her way this week, Cat hoped she could truly appreciate each one . . . even if the uninhibited love sounds on the foredeck drove her a little nuts.

She twisted the dials and slipped down into the sparkling, pulsing water, a luxury she'd only enjoyed on trips with Laird. So here, on her very own big-ass yacht, stark-raving naked and totally exposed, it gave her a secretive thrill when the jets massaged her body. She immersed her shoulders, letting her mind unwind from today's world-altering events: she'd paid cash for an entire island; she'd bought more clothes than could fit in her closet; she'd been invited to play naked with her caretakers; she was floating totally exposed on her yacht in the Caribbean Sea.

It felt so good to drift . . . so damn decadent to offer herself to the slanting afternoon sun as though she didn't *care* if a small plane or another yacht might come within range. As her thoughts wandered, she heard the love play of that feisty couple on the deck in a foreign language an adult of any nationality would recognize.

Cat shut them out, awash in the fine sensations of the Jacuzzi. She turned on her stomach so the water pulsed against her breasts . . . thinking how positively outrageous that current would feel against her slit. Thinking that the twitch between her legs, brought on by Ramon in all his dark glory—Ramon, who was now buried to the hilt inside lovely Leilani—needed tending. She deserved a little mind-bending pleasure of her own, didn't she?

Her vibrations shifted subtly as her feet found the floor. Cat crouched with her elbows on the rim of the tub so she could maneuver herself up and down . . . easing herself into the full force of that pulsing, throbbing water jet.

"Ohhhhhhhhh gawd . . . oh my gawwwwd," escaped her as the sensations in her thighs gave fair warning of what her clit might expect. Before she lost her nerve, Cat slid sideways and opened herself—

And froze with her eyes clenched shut and her mouth open in a silent scream of ecstasy. A little gyrating to ease the force of that water had her convulsing without a shred of decency or self-control. On and on the sensations rocked her until she wondered if a climax could get so intense she'd pass out from it.

When she'd tested that thought as far as she dared, Cat sprawled on the rim of the tub. Had Ramon started the engine again? A subdued thrum told her she'd better get her rag-doll body inside before her caretakers found her this way and—once again—knew what she'd been doing.

The noise became a louder, more insistent racket. Just as she stood up, with water running down the length of her bare body, a small water plane swooped down for a closer look.

She groaned. The two occupants of the plane waved at her—or maybe at Ramon and Leilani because they knew them? Out of sheer desperation, and the need to appear as bold as the rest of these islanders—she waved back! Timidly at first, but then she gave those guys a big grin and waved both arms, swaying as though her Inner Kid was an exhibitionist rather than an introvert.

What'll you do if the plane lands and those two fly boys wanna come aboard, missy?

I haven't a clue, she replied silently. *But I'd at least have someone to talk to, right?*

Once the plane turned around and regained altitude, however, she chuckled. Wait till she told Grant and Trevor and Bruce about *this*! No point in playing the shrinking violet if her domestics were doing the deed right there on the sundeck. And, yes . . . they were still moaning. Then came the firm slap of a hand on a backside, followed by an outcry that sounded blatantly turned on.

While she secretly envied their freewheeling, free-loving ways, it was clear Leilani and Ramon had eyes only for each other. She might someday accept their invitation to play, but it wouldn't be for keeps.

Cat went to the railing then, to gaze out over the blue-green of the sea as sun diamonds danced on its surface. Solid and satisfied she felt—and wasn't that an improvement, considering her ordeal after Laird's death?

But she was, for all practical purposes, alone. She'd bought an island and this yacht and the mansion and the caretakers that came with it today, but how long could she wander through this wonderland all by her lonesome?

Maybe the Contessa left for that very reason. Found somebody to play with and never looked back.

So while she remained naked for the rest of the ride home, and strode boldly across the dock carrying her new clothes rather than wearing any, Cat no longer thought how horrible it would be if someone saw her this way.

She just wanted somebody to *see.* Somebody who'd entice her Inner Kid out to play and chase away the ghosts of a financial disaster. Somebody who wouldn't want her for her money. Somebody who'd teach her how to live uninhibited, without fears or boundaries or following someone else's rules.

She let her shopping bags hit the bedroom floor and then opened her laptop. When she'd first seen the links to personal ads on the Escape Artist website, advertising for sex and friendship seemed outlandish and, well—dangerous. Colossal lies abounded on the Internet, spawned by guys who listed various versions of themselves in matchmaking services when they were already married. Maybe to more than one woman.

She didn't need that! Didn't want a man who faked his way past all the security measures and submitted a photo of his best-looking friend. But how would she know who she might meet until she tried? It was for damn sure she wasn't going to find anybody here on this little paradise called Porto Di Angelo, no matter how much she loved her new home.

Cat glanced at the ads and let her mind play . . . tapped a few lines into the blank ad form and then deleted them. Created an alias address—just in case anybody responded—and then forged full speed ahead through her ad, modesty and caution be damned!

Heart pounding, Cat read through the lines again to check for errors. Then, before she lost her nerve, she hit SEND.

6

RUhot4it?

Got the villa on the private island, the 100' yacht, off-shore accounts out the wazoo, but nobody to play with? Me, too! Your privacy and pleasure are my top priorities! Cat@hot4it.com for pix, details.

Jack Spankevopoulos rubbed his eyes to reread the ad. It had jumped out at him with a power all its own—an energy that zinged through his system, even though it was four in the morning and he was dog tired from last night's madness. Here in his crow's-nest office, high above the decks of the *Captive Fantasy*, all was finally quiet after three female passengers got too drunk and too mouthy. He'd nearly had a mutiny! Even though it was *his* damn ship!

He blamed it on the full moon, still riding high, just as he blamed his restlessness on that fickle princess of the night. All the nut cases signed on around this time of the month. Should he call a halt to these pirate abduction vacations? A man could only stand so much. A captain shouldn't have to endure such foul language and manners, not to mention the stench that lingered on the decks after his passengers yarked up their rum punch. Then they blamed *him* that they weren't having a good time!

But this Cat woman must be a breed apart, to flaunt her financial status and still be looking for a man. Or was she just butt ugly? And where in the world was she? Those who knew about the Escape Artist sites might hail from anywhere—and then relocate to somewhere else very quickly, depending on who they were hiding from and why. Jack clicked her URL to take a look at her.

"Sweeeeet *baby*," he breathed, stunned by her windblown blond hair and arched eyebrows and that soft, sexy smile. "If this is really you, dear lady, it's time Captain Jack jumped ship. I could vacation in the paradise of your sea-green eyes for a looooooong time."

He clicked the e-mail link and then realized he needed a response as alluring as her come-on. No doubt he'd land in her box—and wasn't *that* a titillating thought!?—with hundreds of other famished men looking to ravish a tidbit like this one.

As Jack pondered potential witticisms, a techno-tinny version of "Sixteen Men on a Dead Man's Chest" made him reach for his phone. When he saw the name in the ID window, he set the infernal thing aside. Studied that ad again . . . *your privacy and pleasure are my top priorities!*

And when had *that* ever happened? Certainly not with the whiny-ass bitch who'd called him just now. Jack collected his thoughts, fingers poised over his laptop keyboard to—

The phone rang again, and he nearly tossed it out his window. Of *course* Maria Palaveras would call him in the wee hours during the full moon—which she'd no doubt been howling at naked from her lot in the trailer court. He thumbed the button to let her talk: he often set the phone aside while she ranted, and she never knew the difference.

"Jack! Answer me, damn it! I *knew* you were there, and you didn't pick up!"

He rubbed his eyes wearily.

"I was calling to see how you were, but *no!*" her shrill voice escalated, "you couldn't spare a few moments of your precious time playing pirate to talk to an old friend in her hour of need."

Sighing, Jack took the bait. To get rid of her faster. "And hello to you, too, Maria," he replied, caressing the words to irritate her. "What can your old whipping boy Jack do for you at four in the morning, my pretty?"

"Oh, stop it right there! Is it any wonder I walked out on you? All you ever thought about was—"

A woman who could have a good time. And who talked like she had a brain in her head.

"—business! As though I would ever consider those pirate ships and your stupid love-slave vacation a way to make a decent living! Why, I—"

I have manacles and a gag in your size, honey. Should've used them while I had the chance.

"—was hoping you'd seen the light," she said, stopping to gulp air, "and would consider coming home soon. I promised you'd always have a place with me. And while I might be a little scattered, I *am* a woman of my word!"

Jack stared at his phone as though it were an alien life form. He considered his answer: if he set his ex live-in straight about why they'd parted ways, she'd pitch another fit. And he *sure* as hell wouldn't consider moving in with her. He'd learned that lesson the hard way during the months she'd spent aboard the *Captive Fantasy. Big* mistake, letting her do that.

"While I appreciate your offer—and your integrity," he added with the merest edge of sarcasm, "I'm still the captain of my own ship, dear heart. I own a *fleet* of party boats along with the *Captive Fantasy*, so I couldn't possibly come to—"

"See there? I asked you nicely and you didn't consider my invitation for the blink of an eye! *Jack!*" she whined.

He closed his eyes, anticipating Maria's change of tactic. First came the lower, slyer, more suggestive undertones; the begging and pleading. Then she'd cry and threaten to do herself harm—the red flags that told him she'd gone off her meds again. He would never wish bipolar disorder on *anyone*, but damn! It left him in a helluva fix, feeling responsible for her even though he was sailing the Caribbean as a pretend pirate. Not the kind who'd intentionally ruin anyone's life.

Her sigh slithered out of the phone. "Jaaaaack," she cooed, "Spank, honey, you knooooooow how good we were together. You can't tell me you didn't enjoy every soft, sultry inch of this fine body—"

She had that part right, but he wasn't buying in this time. Footsteps made him swivel his chair, to be sure one of those mouthy passengers hadn't climbed to his crow's-nest hideaway. When Stavros, his cousin and first mate, stepped in, he rolled his eyes and pointed to the phone. Then he held it out with his hand over the mouthpiece so the wheedling filled the small office.

"Mad Maria?" Stavros muttered. He raked his sun-bleached sorrel hair into rough spikes. "What the hell does *she* want?"

"I'm guessing her latest boyfriend moved out, and she has no one else to rag on," Jack replied quietly.

"—and you know how good it was when we spent all night fucking and all day sleeping in each other's arms," she reminded him urgently. "We could have that again, Jackie. You could be *my* captain again, and—"

"You're not considering that, surely?" Stavros asked.

Jack scowled. "One of us is insane, but it's not me!"

"Then tell her you've got a life! Another woman! Hey— sometimes a little white lie's the loving thing to do."

"Jack? Jack! You've not listened to a thing I've said for—"

He ogled the photo he'd enlarged to fill his laptop screen, wondering why *he* hadn't thought of that plan! "Maria, honey, I know how you miss me—how you miss *us*," he added softly, "but there's someone else in my life now. We both agreed to move on, remember?"

When she sucked air he thought his ear might go through the phone. "Another woman?" she whined, shifting into her pathetic mode.

"Well, certainly not another man," he replied, even if it was overkill.

"So why didn't you *tell* me? But no! You had to let me humiliate myself by groveling—"

"And when have I had a chance to get a word in edgewise?" He pulsed with purpose now: his cousin's plan was the lifeline he needed! No lies, white or otherwise. "I'm going to hang up now, Maria. I wish you all the best—and if you're off your meds, I sincerely hope you'll get back on them," he advised in the fatherly tone he reserved for such times. "Not a man on this earth can resist your charms when you're in control of your game plan, Maria. But don't call me again, all right? I'm not your Jackie Spank anymore."

"But I—"

Snap. He folded his phone and let out a relieved sigh. "You're a genius, Stavros. I can't think straight once Maria gets going on—"

"And you *can* with that magnificent blonde gazing out from your computer?" The slender Greek studied the image, a sly smile stealing across his angular features. "So, you gonna introduce me, cuz, or do I have to—"

"Haven't met her yet, but I'm about to." Jack's gut fluttered as he said this. "Her name's Cat—"

"Yeah, right. Let's just call her Pussy Galore."

"—and she owns an island, a villa, a yacht—and is looking

for a playmate on that same level," he continued, reviewing these facts to spark his own creative response.

"She paid a model to pose for that photo, then! Don't *tell* me you're resorting to matchmaking ads for—" Stavros stared him down, incredulous. "Jack, those things are for losers! If this chick's got all the stuff she claims, why's she hunting for a *guy*? There's a problem we can't see here! Maybe something as serious—or just plain annoying—as finding out about Mad Maria's mental disorders."

"She's bipolar, Stav. She can't help it that—"

"She's using it to keep you on the string. She's *that* smart, anyway."

Jack gave his cousin a pointed look. "And she's behind me now. The longer it takes to get my reply e-mailed, the more fishes will be snapping at Cat's bait. Get it?"

Stavros muttered something and turned to go.

"I'm sorry." He sighed. "That was rude and uncalled for. Why'd you come up?"

The man whose features resembled his, but in a skinnier size, smiled with that European sense of sexy women flocked to. "Saw your light on. Wondered why you weren't sleeping, after our catastrophe last night."

"Thank you. But if I have my way about it, I won't be getting much sleep once I meet Miss Kitty here, either." He grinned despite eyes that were stinging with fatigue and a head that still throbbed from Maria's call. "But we must all make our sacrifices, right?"

"Whatever it takes to get laid, Captain. Let me know how I can help."

When the door closed and the crow's nest was his again, Jack drew in a deep breath. He tried to imagine the scent of this luscious woman . . . how those glossed lips would taste and then feel . . . as they closed around his cock. God, he hoped she was the kind who'd do that for him.

He was rock hard. Closed his eyes and coaxed his brain cells north again. Summoned some bravado and then let the words pour onto the screen.

Best not to ramble or get his hopes up. Best to answer to her lead, far as why he met her prerequisites, and hope to hell he didn't sound like some desperate braggart of a weenie looking for a fire to roast himself in.

7

Cat clicked into her e-mail box and gasped. The sun floated on the horizon like a fiery beach ball, lighting the sea with diamonds, and she'd received twenty responses to her ad! In less than ten hours!

You won't have to be alone! Unless they're all jerks and losers.

She cleared her mind, trying to pick up on each guy's attitude as she read. Hmmmmm . . . this one posted a photo of his yacht but not of himself. Said he was a consultant for a major oil company.

Sounds arrogant. She hit DELETE.

She clicked on the next message, smiling at the subject line: LOOKING FOR A QUEEN TO RULE MY CASTLE. When she clicked the link, however, she got a virtual tour of this guy's house—and the immediate impression that his queen would spend a lot of time cleaning and updating its rooms. DELETE.

Cat shifted positions on her rumpled sheets and burrowed back against her pillows. She could summon Leilani for a cup of strong, hot tea and something to tide her over until she ventured downstairs, but she wanted to check out these applicants first. Alone.

The next one was old enough to be her father—DELETE—and the next guy gave a lengthy commentary: *Miss Cat! Miss Kitty! Miss Pussy! And I'm gonna love licking your pussy because you're a woman who craves a man's tongue. Let me amaze you with the miracles I can perform with my avid, worshipping fingers . . .*

"Probably has erectile problems," she murmured.

She glanced up to see her housekeeper standing beside her bed with a tray. There was the cobalt Fiesta teapot and a scarlet cup and saucer—her favorites of all the Fiesta colors—along with a plate of warm muffins.

"My Catalina is hungry? I'm so pleased you called!"

"But I didn't! I *thought* about—"

"I tuned in, to see if you were awake." Leilani wore a pale peach sundress with a matching rose in her hair and a knowing expression as she glanced toward the laptop. "You've received messages from friends? You look . . . perkier than when we got home yesterday."

Damn! What should she say? Cat still felt uneasy about advertising herself to catch a man. Didn't want Leilani to think she and Ramon weren't the perfect couple to share this island with. But then, if this woman had tuned in about tea, she already knew what sort of e-mail was in the box, didn't she?

"On impulse yesterday, I composed a personal ad," she admitted, watching that honey-skinned face for a reaction. "Not because I'm desperate, but because—"

"Ramon and I remind you of what's missing in your life." Leilani's blue eyes twinkled like stars on a balmy night. "I suspect Valenzia got a little tired of overhearing our groans and—"

"Oh, I'm not tired of—you have every right and reason to—Ramon's really, really hung, isn't he?"

Leilani's laughter tinkled like wind chimes. "It's a challenge to take him all in, but so worth the sacrifice," she teased. "Let me see what you've got here. We can quickly eliminate those who aren't worthy to lick your sandals, Catalina. Far worse to be with a man who's unsuitable than to be alone."

"So right! But I posted my ad less than twelve hours ago, and already twenty—now twenty-four!—guys have replied."

Leilani handed Cat the tray and then slid onto the mattress beside her. She leaned forward slightly to study the laptop screen. "Why don't you open each one and I'll get a quick feel for him. This'll be fun!"

Chuckling, Cat opened the next message. She was as curious about how Leilani's psychic powers worked as she was about the men who'd sent these e-mails. This one's name was Derek—

"Not his real name. And he's married." Leilani hit DELETE.

Her mouth fell open. "How'd you know that?"

"How do I know anything?" she replied with a shrug. "My intuition whispers inside my head—or laughs out loud, like at *this* man! Who does he think he's fooling?"

Up popped a photograph of a nude man lounging on a rumpled bed, holding his impressive cock. "Why do you say that?"

"Who do you think took that picture, dear one?" Her pretty eyebrow arched, as though Leilani were playing teacher, awaiting her response. "If he's a model—which he'd like you to believe, from his message—he's much more interested in his own pleasure and performance than yours. And what if his girlfriend snapped it? Or his boyfriend? Too pretty by half, this Tyler is."

Cat hit DELETE and then opened the next one. "Oh, jeez—" DELETE. No need to consider a man who called himself King Kong and sent a photo of his erection with jizz running down it.

Leilani skimmed the list of messages with a thoughtful sigh. "Try this one," she said, pointing prettily at his name. "It's jumping out at me. I like his sense of play."

Like Pirates? the subject line teased.

Cat's pulse shifted into overdrive. *What if it's Johnny Depp? Looking for an island to film his next movie on?* She was beginning to like Leilani's vibrations—until she saw this guy's address.

"Jack at Captain Spank dot com?" she demanded. "You've got to be—we've just met so you don't know this, Leilani, but spanking is *not* what I consider play!"

Those dusky blue eyes focused deeply on hers. "What's it going to hurt to open it? You're getting trigger-happy with that DELETE key, dear."

Cat clicked on the message. A photograph unfurled like the sail of a ship, showing two guys dressed like pirates . . . very tan, sexy pirates in billowing shirts and bejeweled bandannas. Holsters hung low on their hips, and they held a gleaming sword between them.

This is my cousin Stavros (left) and me aboard my ship, the *CAPTIVE FANTASY*. While I don't own an island or a yacht like yours, Cat, I'm the proud proprietor of a fleet of Tall Sails pirate ships on which cruise passengers come out to play! We have great fun on a daily basis, but I saw your lovely face and craved coherent conversation. Among other things.

While I enjoy my work, most women who fancy themselves love slaves aboard my ship are *not* the type I'd spend time with if they weren't paying me. I'd love to swing by your island so you can sail away with me, Cat. Soon!

Cat cleared her throat, not sure why this guy's note was making her heart turn cartwheels. "You don't suppose . . . Could this be the guy who sailed by the other night? It was a magnificent antique-looking ship—"

"What'd I tell you? Isn't he a better bet than these others?"

Cat clicked on the link to the Web site he'd provided and began to giggle. "Pirates!" she breathed. "Look at the parrot—and the cat on his shoulder! And there's the room like Captain Jack had aboard the Black Pearl! And a pipe organ like Davy Jones played in—"

"Hit REPLY, Cat," Leilani said with a nudge of her elbow. "Easy to see you're already primed to—"

"Oh my God, look at this! It's the *Captive Fantasy*, and he—Captain Jack arranges for guests to be kidnapped by pirates and held as love slaves for their entire vacation, with like-minded adults—"

"Didn't I tell you he knew how to play?" Leilani patted Cat's knee. "I'll leave you alone to compose your reply. And if Captain Spank doesn't measure up when he calls you, you'll have twenty or thirty more to choose from by noon."

The housekeeper floated gracefully across the white tile floor, with all that shiny black hair swaying down her back. She turned at the doorway, smiling over her shoulder. "And of course, if Captain Jack shows up and you don't like him, Ramon will send him packing! No worries, Catalina. Your life's about to change in a big, wonderful way!"

Cat nodded, hope shimmering within her. Again she read Jack's message and studied the man in the tightly wrapped bandanna. That wicked mustache outlined lips parted in a come-on smile, in a face tanned by the tropical sun . . . a lean, handsome face framed by windblown brown hair. Cousin Stavros wasn't half bad, either. Stylishly thin and loose-limbed, like Trevor Teague.

But it was Jack her eyes returned to. She saw then where he'd signed his last name as Spankevopoulos.

"Which explains why he goes by Captain Spank." She quickly hit the REPLY button, but once the blank message was in front of her she had no clue what to say. Didn't want to say that out of dozens of replies, he was the only one who didn't wave his ego—or his cock—like a red flag. Didn't want to let on how much she adored pirates, for fear he'd never stop playing the swashbuckler: she also longed to know the man he was while dressed in normal clothes. Or not.

CALL ME! she typed and then gave her J2 phone number and hit SEND. Better not to second-guess him based on an e-mail and an intriguing Web site. Better to hear his voice on a phone he couldn't trace, if he turned out to be a creep who got off on spanking or a for-real kind of slavery.

Would I lead ya to a creep, sugah? Here's that miracle I said I was arrangin', and still I get no respect!

The room filled with the sweet, druggy scent of the angel's trumpets growing outside her window, except she noted a suspicious undertone of smoke. Cat grinned anyway. "Thank you, Spike. But you know me—I call 'em as I see 'em. This pirate's not a miracle until I say he's a miracle!"

Confident she'd done the right thing, Cat headed for her shining white bathroom. "Yo, ho, ho! It's a pirate's life for me!" she sang out. She grabbed the phone, on the off chance Jack might call her this quickly, and then chided herself for feeling so girlie and giddy. But gee, it felt good, didn't it?!

When she stepped into the pulsing massage of the shower, Cat closed her eyes in gratitude that here, on this remote paradise, she had the divine pleasure of a hot shower. Enough water pressure to make her body sing and tingle. Jack's face drifted into her mind, and Cat cupped her breasts beneath the invigorating spray. She squirted three times her usual amount of mango-scented body wash onto her scrubbie and watched the dense froth cling to her skin. Watched her nipples peek through the white suds.

Then she ducked her head under the water, still humming that sea chantey about the pirate's life. She felt really excited! Vibrant! Clean hair would be her crowning glory—just in case

Captain Spank could swing by on the *Captive Fantasy* to take her for a—

She jerked her head out of the shower spray. Her phone was ringing!

Cat hopped out onto the white plush rug, oblivious to the water running down her bare body. Grant would have no reason to call her right now—and indeed, that number on her phone screen wasn't one she recognized.

Had Jack been watching his e-mail? Waiting for her reply—just as she'd hoped for his call? She felt downright lewd pressing the ON button as she stood stark naked and dripping, but she closed her eyes. Prayed the right words came.

"Yes? Hello?"

Jack inhaled the soft sweetness of her voice and focused on her life-size photo—now his computer's desktop wallpaper. "Cat? This is Jack Spankevopoulos, and I can't tell you how pleased and excited I was to get your message! How are you, darling?"

"Uh—" Cat sucked in her breath. Ordinarily, the word *darling* sounded outdated or too cutesy, but this guy's luscious British accent might change it to her favorite endearment.

"I'm so glad you called!" she replied, wishing she didn't sound so gushy and—well, desperate. "After seeing your last name—Greek, isn't it?—I wasn't expecting a pirate with a Brit accent."

He laughed softly. She *could* carry on a coherent conversation! "Parents of Greek persuasion, yes, but we hail from Australia, and I was educated in London. How's that for an international pedigree?"

"Hellooooo, Cat! We're *sooo* glad to be talking to you!"

"Who's that?" Cat grabbed a towel and ran it one-handed over her wet body. Not one man but two, and here she was talking to them naked!

"My cousin Stavros. Always getting into the act," Jack explained, hoping his scowl and wave-off didn't come across to Cat on the other end. "He's my first mate here on the *Captive Fantasy*, and the chief engineer, as well. We look like a seventeenth-century pirate ship sailing toward a good time, but the *Fantasy* has all the modern technology and amenities of a first-rate cruise ship. Just on a smaller and more . . . suggestive scale," he added slyly. "Takes a top-notch sailor—a couple of us—to keep her on course and properly maintained."

"And are you properly maintained, Jack?"

His jaw dropped. Then he laughed, anticipation singing through his insides. "Oh, Cat, you can't possibly know how badly I need maintaining and—refitting and—this isn't coming across well, is it? I sound like a lecherous old codger who—"

"You sound very nice, actually," Cat said with a soft sigh. "Nothing wrong with admitting the need for some R and R or quiet time with good company. I need that myself."

Bless her. She wasn't the type to nag or insinuate or ask nosy questions. Jack looked down at the main deck below, wishing he could make that group of hip-wiggling women disappear so he and Cat could have the *Fantasy* all to themselves.

"I hear music," her voice caressed his ear. "So maybe you're not totally bereft of . . . entertainment?"

Jack laughed ruefully. "That, my dear, is our steel drum band. Perfect for setting the Caribbean mood, you know. And right now we're having island dance lessons on the deck. You caught me wishing I could wave my sword and they'd all disappear.

"They're Red Hatters, you, see—a lovely organization, and I applaud their positive outlook on life," he insisted, hoping he wasn't boring this beautiful woman to tears. "But when a large group of them reserved the entire ship, they forgot that few *men* would be aboard to carry out their love-slave fantasies."

Jack cleared his throat. He had to proceed carefully—couldn't insult her sensibilities before they even met. "My poor room stewards have been run ragged and cornered in the restrooms and—well, it's been a trying week, having a ship full of women with too much booze and too few males to meet their . . . needs."

Cat nipped her lip. The way he whispered that word, *needs*, in his low, flowing voice, prompted her to walk off some of the nervous energy burning inside her. She headed for her balcony.

"And you're saying Captain Jack can't service them all with his mighty sword?" she teased. "Why, I thought you'd be invincible and—indefatigable. Like Captain Jack Sparrow."

"Indefatigable," he echoed, grinning at her subtle insinuation. "Been many a year since I heard that term or met a woman who knew how to use it. And you *do* know how to use it, don't you, darling?"

"Oh, yesssss, Jack," she purred. That stretch of white sand below her balcony was calling her to stroll ankle-deep in the surf and greet him—naked— when he steered the *Fantasy* up to her shoreline. "But I'm getting a vibration that even with an entire ship full of wild, willing women, you're not happy, dear man. How can I help?"

"Sweet Jesus," he muttered before he could catch himself. "I—I have a vision of you and me aboard this magnificent ship, just the two of us—"

"And Cousin Stavros to navigate her?"

"Yes, but—I'd lock him in the engine room, damn it! I want you all to myself!"

"And I wouldn't have it any other way. So when can you swing by my island and pick me up?"

Jack paused. This conversation had progressed a lot faster than he'd anticipated. He hated to disappoint her, but he had reservations for the rest of the season, and—

"I didn't mean to corner you," Cat came back. "Fact is, I'm not usually this fast-forward or—"

"But you're caught up in it? Liking what you hear and wanting to give it a shot?" he breathed. "Me, too, sweetheart. Very much so. But—"

"But you can't just cancel all those reservations during your peak season, because the *Fantasy* is your livelihood—"

"A good part of it, yes."

"—and I slipped in under your radar before either of us realized how . . . needful we were."

"So right! So, so right," he mused, closing his eyes. "Tell me about your island, darling. I get the sense you haven't lived here long."

"Less than a week. But it struck me yesterday, as I watched my caretakers cavorting, that I have this magnificent villa on a tropical paradise—and a huge yacht to get me wherever I want to go—but no one to share it with."

"Hmmmmm . . ." Jack looked out over the bow, barely able to make out the next island his ship would circle today. "You don't happen to be on Angel Haven, do you?"

"Porto Di Angelo—"

"Which was named for all those angel's trumpet trees blooming there and the fact that Contessa Valenzia Borgia was into angels, big-time."

"You've heard about her?" How spooky was this, that Captain Jack not only knew where she was but knew the Contessa's story, too?

"Only that she went missing a couple years back. Oh, Cat, what a lovely home you have!"

"You've seen it, then?" She laughed, low and throaty. "So picture me on the balcony that overlooks the eastern beach. And since your call got me out of the shower, I'm—"

"Sweet Jesus. I—I could be there within the hour, but we can't drop anchor there because—"

Cat's heart thudded into triple time. She scurried inside to activate her laptop. "So sign me up! I want to be aboard your next cruise!" she cried. "I want to be kidnapped by pirates and forced to live as a love slave!"

"But you don't have to—"

"Yes, I do! It's only fair," she insisted as she brought up the Web site mentioned in his message. "It gives me a chance to see you in your natural habitat, taking care of business, while I take care of mine."

"And that would be—?"

"I'm a romance writer, Jack. And I'm working on a pirate story," she wheezed, holding the phone to her ear while she typed with one hand. "So even if—even if it doesn't work out for us—"

"I *so* believe it will, darling."

"—you can still keep your schedule while I do some wonderful on-site research, and—"

"And if either of us gets much work done, I'll be sorely disappointed."

She laughed, and it felt so good—so lighthearted and free—she didn't want to stop. "I've accessed your site, Captain Spank, and I see you accept PayPal. How much? You'll have it in minutes."

He chuckled. "Darling, I'd like you to be my guest—"

"*How much?* Does the fifteen hundred dollars I'm seeing here cover all the meals and taxes and—"

Jack closed his eyes so all those bright, sunny harmonies in her voice . . . all that beauty and energy . . . could wash over him in his claustrophobic crow's-nest office. "That includes air fare to selected pickup points, which you don't need. Seven hundred should more than cover—"

"Eight fifty," she stated, typing in the amount and hitting SEND. "It's already on its way, so your cousin—or whoever—can't say I stiffed you after you answered my ad."

Stiffed. Now *there* was an interesting verb! He sensed it wasn't the best path to pursue right now because it brought Mad Maria to mind rather than this lovely young woman he wanted much, much more.

"Thank you, Cat," he murmured. "I admire your sense of fair play. Your insistence that I not sacrifice my week's work. *Yet.*"

She melted. A couple weeks ago, she couldn't have been having this conversation or sending funds through cyberspace or . . . wanting a man so badly she could taste him. "Quite all right. I've done the sacrifice thing, and we're not going there, okay? For once, I'm just a good-time girl going with the flow."

"So tell me this again, Cat," he said softly. "You're standing on your balcony right now, naked? Looking out across the sea, like a woman watching for her man to come home?"

"Ooh. Now there's an image." She closed her eyes against sudden tears, desperate for this adventure to go well—and to start *now*!

"All right then, I've just added you to my roster for our next voyage, which begins on Saturday—that's tomorrow—evening."

"I'll be ready! What do I do?"

"Oh, how shall I orchestrate this?" he whispered. His whole body thrummed to the rhythm of this woman's inner melody. "Since others might already be aboard, you should probably wear at least a swimsuit. Wait for me on the beach with your bag nearby . . . always more fun when you follow the fantasy scenario by acting as though our pirate raid is a total surprise."

"Of course! That's the exciting part!"

"Oh, there'll be lots more excitement, Cat," he crooned. "But for now, dear lady, why not walk down to that stretch of beautiful white beach and wave at us when the *Fantasy* sails past Porto Di Angelo? About forty minutes from now."

"All right! I'll be there!"

"Naked?" he breathed.

Cat laughed low in her throat. "Hey, whose beach is it, anyway? Do I need a permit for nude sunbathing? But I have to confess," she added in a more serious tone, "that the whole idea of lying naked on a beach was totally unlike me before you answered—"

"Well, then! Here's to new ideas, my love! I'll see you soon, all right?"

"Yes! I'm on my way!"

8

What had she just done? Had she really told a total stranger she'd stroll on the beach—naked—to wave at his pirate ship?

And before that she'd signed on for a week aboard the *Captive Fantasy*, saying it was for research! Knowing damn well she'd be flirting outrageously with Captain Jack: succumbing to decadent, mindless lovemaking for an entire week, like some wench captured by those pirates of the Caribbean who cavorted in her imagination.

Had she just made a big, *blond* mistake, or what? This was *not* a movie in which Johnny Depp and Orlando Bloom would follow her script! Who knew if Jack was legit? What if he didn't bring her back to her own island—

"Better come down for some breakfast, Catalina." Leilani's knowing tone interrupted her mental lecture. "Can't have you passing out from low blood sugar while you're hailing your new pirate friend."

Cat closed her eyes. Of *course* her caretakers had overheard every word: the open porch where they ate breakfast was right below her balcony. Didn't take a psychic to pick up on the vibes *she'd* been sending.

"Let me comb my hair, and I'll be right down."

Cat slipped back into the bathroom, letting her towel drop as she looked in the mirror. Her eyes looked bright and clear and green. Her mouth—why couldn't it stop smiling? And her hair, well, it was half dry and hanging in a windblown halo around her face, yet it suddenly seemed perfect for today: carefree. Lighthearted. Given to whim and natural inclinations.

And wasn't she inclined to believe in Captain Jack's authenticity? To believe he'd deliver an adventurous week aboard the *Captive Fantasy*, even if nothing came of the romance that had whispered between the lines as they chatted?

She grinned, already planning her seduction. Cat slathered on a tropical-scented lotion she'd loved at home, yet it paled in comparison to the flowers here on Porto Di Angelo. She'd have Leilani identify the various bushes—something to do while she waited for Jack today, and again tomorrow night when he sailed away with her.

How exciting was *that*?!

Cat grabbed a new sundress from among the twentysome that made a rainbow in her armoire. This one was sky blue with orchids of pink and lavender and yellow, entwined in palm fronds. It suited her mood for eating breakfast with Ramon and Leilani, and it would be a better bet than waiting naked on her beach when the *Fantasy* sailed by. Those Red Hat ladies didn't need to see her naked. Nor did they need to watch Jack's reactions while he checked her out.

"You look lovely, Catalina!" her housekeeper proclaimed as she took her white wicker chair at the table. Today the napkins were a batik floral print that coordinated perfectly with the scarlet dish of fresh mango and pineapple. A platter of herbed scrambled eggs sat in front of her plate, with bacon arranged alongside sweet cornmeal muffins that smelled heavenly.

"How'd you know exactly what I was hungry for?" she asked the woman beside her.

Leilani grinned. "It's my life purpose to anticipate needs and meet them, Catalina."

Arching an eyebrow at Ramon, she helped herself to the food. "No doubt she meets *your* needs, eh? So what do you think of this pirate abduction idea? Did I make a major mistake, or will it be as exhilarating as I hope?"

The dark man beside her flashed a grin that made his pointed goatee look absolutely diabolical. His island print shirt hung open above his shorts, displaying a heavy gold medallion on a massive black chest.

"You, pretty lady, approach *life* with exhilaration," he replied in that baritone voice. "You'll have a good time with Captain Spank. He sails past twice a week, dependable as a planet orbiting around the sun. From what we know of him, he seems reliable. And of course," he pointed out, "you can phone me the moment something goes wrong. Our yacht can outrun anything in the Caribbean."

An excellent thought. So when Cat finished eating, she went upstairs to fetch her new J2 cell.

"Program your number into my memory," she told him. "I doubt speed dial will be an issue, so let's keep things simple until I'm more familiar with this little gadget."

As Ramon's long brown fingers closed around her phone, his lips quirked. "You'll forget you even have this," he teased as he tapped in some digits. "You're face is so aglow with excitement, Captain Spank doesn't stand a chance."

"We'll see about *that*, won't we?" she breathed. "Meanwhile, I'm going to wander out there and get a good look at his ship when he sails past. It's time to walk barefoot in the sand and let the waves welcome me."

She felt their eyes on her back as she started down the path through an Eden of trees and bushes that bloomed profusely.

How many shades of red and dark coral were there, anyway? Cat smiled up at the embankment where the angel's trumpets hung like white bells; from this angle, the flowers that perfumed her room looked like five-pointed stars amid leaves of green velvet.

These trees covered the ridge around the island, and from the beach she got a glimpse of just how many white trumpets swayed in the breeze. No wonder Jack knew exactly which island she was on! He probably told his captive passengers about the narcotic qualities of these plants, as a point of tourist interest. Maybe they inhaled incense made of dried angel's trumpet—or rolled their own smokes—to enhance their sexual adventures.

Cat let that idea drift in her mind like sweet, pungent perfume as she stepped into the waves that lapped at the soft, white sand. Her feet sank into its warmth, and as the clear water caressed her ankles she raised her face to the morning sun.

Was this a dream? How on earth had she landed on a pristine beach where the turquoise and aquamarine waters played? To the west she saw a school of dolphins arching up from the water in twos and threes . . . nearly two dozen of them, from what she could count.

And from here, the villa reigned over the island in all its flamingo-pink glory. Its corners and porches, adorned with white Victorian embellishments, blazed in the morning sunlight. It dazzled her to realize she now owned this paradise—if indeed anyone could lay claim to so much beauty. Her Powerball jackpot really had nothing to do with it. Porto Di Angelo had existed long before banks and real estate transactions, and the island would endure after she and Leilani and Ramon had passed on.

It was one of those light-bulb moments, one of those diamonds in time that left Cat gaping at the perfect blue sky and the island and the sea: she herself was just a miniscule speck amid so much tropical perfection. But she was a part of that providential perfection—which meant that, in her own way, she was perfect. Right?

She dug her toe into the pale sand . . . watched the hole fill and overflow, just like her soul was doing right now. Sweet, peaceful justice, after the life she'd left behind.

Her phone trilled, and she nearly dropped it.

"Hello? . . . Trevor! How nice to hear from you!" she gushed. "You won't believe what I'm getting ready to do! But first, is everyone all right?"

A sophisticated chuckle tickled her ear. "We're fine, Cat, but we miss you, dear. How's your new home?"

"I—I couldn't be happier," she replied. "You caught me in one of those mountaintop moments when I realized what a marvelous thing destiny is, to land me here on Porto Di Angelo. You guys really need to come see it! My description—those pictures on the Internet—really don't do it justice."

"Glad to hear it. And indeed we will."

"Oh—and if you don't get any e-mails for a while, it's because I've been kidnapped by pirates!" she said with a giggle. "Can you believe it? There's a guy here named Captain Jack—aka Captain Spank—who owns a fleet of those Tall Sails pirate party boats. But he also offers to kidnap you for a week of love slaving aboard his ship, the *Captive Fantasy*!"

"And you're going? Have a wonderful time!" He sighed then, laughing softly. "It was destiny that *you* won the jackpot, Cat. Had one of us held that ticket, we'd still be here working our jobs and sticking our money into investment funds and stock portfolios. But *you* jumped at the chance to live a dream—a wild, romantic dream—like we three can only envy."

"Invitation's open, Trev," she repeated with a sudden pang of missing him. "Lord knows I could support us all for the rest of our days, if you wanted to come and be beach bums. Although plenty of resort properties around here would be playgrounds for your architectural imagination. *Think* about it. Seriously."

He sighed, and his longing resonated deep inside her. "Don't give up on me, dear. You might talk me into that idea, even if Grant and Bruce stay behind," he confided. "Well—you have a wonderful pirate adventure, and we'll hear all about it in your e-mails when you get back!"

"Thank you, Trevor. Thanks for everything."

He made a little kissy sound, and then the line clicked. Cat sighed. the sound of that mellow voice—even though the man who belonged to it would never be hers—made her miss the company of those three swashbucklers and their antics in that cathedral of a house.

She was slipping the phone back into her sundress pocket when it rang again. "Good grief! I go for a week without any calls and now—hello?"

"Look over your shoulder, darling."

"Jack!"

Cat whirled around, ankle-deep in the warm water. A large ship, reminiscent of ancient days and seafaring movies, cut across the glasslike sea from about a hundred yards out. Even from here, it looked gargantuan! Truly a world unto itself.

"Oh!" she breathed. "Oh, Jack, she's spectacular!"

"Yes, she is, Cat," he breathed, "and I can't wait for you to experience every exhilarating inch of her."

"Spoken like a man who wants a piece."

"In the worst way," he confirmed with a chuckle. "And while I'd hoped to behold you in all your natural glory, you're the loveliest thing I've ever seen in that sundress."

Her mouth fell open. "Well, thank—you can see me from there?"

"In intimate detail, my dear. The wind has run its fingers through your golden hair—like I will soon do—and you were just minx enough to leave your underthings behind," he added with an edge in his voice.

Cat stood with the phone at her ear, gazing out at the glorious sight of the *Captive Fantasy*. Her engines purred powerfully, like a cruise ship's, while her masts stood proud and her square sails billowed in the wind like huge ivory sheets hung on three levels of clothesline. She had a buxom figurehead leaning out from her bow, and the scarlet flag flapping from the main mast proclaimed her name in gold letters that resembled . . . handcuffs and whips. As she sailed closer, Cat could make out people at the railing. When she waved her arm above her head, they all waved back.

"Where are you, Jack?" she whispered into the phone. "I don't have binoculars—or your pirate spyglass—and I don't want to miss you."

His chuckle made tingles of electricity skip down her spine. "Look high, love! My office is enclosed in the crow's nest. I've stepped out to its platform so I can send you a surprise!"

"A surprise? My—oh! There you are! I see you waving!"

Was this fun, or what? Like a buccaneer of the most dashing caliber, Captain Jack brandished his sword while leaning out from the frame of the crow's nest. His blade caught the sun and sent a bolt of light straight into her eyes—as though he'd planned that! Cat marveled at the rich drape of his silk shirtsleeves and the twinkle of jewels on his crimson vest. His knee breeches rode above sleek black boots, where a jeweled knife was sheathed, and beneath his royal blue bandanna a gold hoop earring dangled. As though on cue, the pirate flashed her the sexiest grin she'd ever seen: dimples on both sides of that rakish, thin mustache. . . .

"Oh my God," she breathed.

His chuckle reminded her that he was listening. "Like what you see, my love? Or should I refund your money?"

"Now! Pick me up *now*!" she cried. "We'll think of a way to get rid of those Red Hat ladies and—"

"Patience, dear heart. All will unfold in due time, and I promise you," he murmured in a husky voice, "it'll be well worth a week of your time, Cat. Now, I'm going to give this a good toss—"

Something flashed in the sunlight and then splashed into the water, not fifteen feet in front of her.

"—and you'll have a little something to dream about until tomorrow night."

Cat scampered into the waves, laughing loudly when she got wet to the waist. Just ahead of her, a corked bottle bobbed on the water! A bottle with a message?

"This is too much fun!" she gasped, rushing forward to grab her prize. "So now I suppose I'll have to come up with a surprise for you—"

"Oh, I'm already up, my sweet. I wish I were that dress, clinging to your body, all wet and warm. My fingers tingle with the need to touch your skin . . . to yank away the fabric and make love to you right there in that clear, swirling water."

Her breath left her. She raised her phone hand to shade her eyes, squinting up at him as she gripped the bottle. The ladies who lined the rail—some in their fanciful red hats with purple feathers—were clearly visible now, and they chattered in speculative tones as they gestured at her. The waves were rolling higher and faster in the *Fantasy's* wake, so Cat slogged back to the safety of the beach.

She watched the majestic ship swoop to follow the current that rushed around the island, agog at the glorious sight of it all.

"Until tomorrow, Cat," Jack whispered.

"I'll be waiting. Don't be late!"

9

"... and those tall yellow trees are yellow poui, while these red bushes by the house are bougainvillea. These lovely shrubs lining the walkway are oleander. Very poisonous, dear, so be aware if you cut some for a bouquet."

Cat nodded, her mind fascinated by Leilani's botanical knowledge while her body vibrated with anticipation as sundown drew near. Only another hour or so, and she'd be kidnapped! Held hostage by Captain Jack! She fully expected to be weak with exhaustion—exhilaration would be good, too!—by the end of her voyage with him.

"And that plant with the orange pointy flowers is a bird of paradise, right?" she asked, trying to stay focused on her lesson.

"You're learning! And this plant with the white waxy flowers is . . . ?"

"Madagascar jasmine. And these pink ones are torch lilies, from the ginger family. We'll see how much of this I recall after my adventure on the *Captive Fantasy*. My brain'll be mush by the time I return."

"And won't that be *fine*?" Leilani steered her toward the two white slatted chairs in the shade. "I want to hear every little detail! And I mean the nitty-gritty stuff, like how he's hung and what positions you did it in and—"

"You think I'll reveal such secrets?" Cat teased. She raised a tall glass to her lips, sipping deeply from the mango rum punch they'd made for her send-off. "Seriously though, if you want me to wait until Ramon gets back from—"

"You act like I've never been here by myself! Vile and dangerous creatures will *not* rush out of these trees to attack me." Leilani smiled fondly. "I want you to have the time of your life from the moment those swashbucklers storm the beach, Catalina. You're sure you've got everything?"

For the dozenth time Cat checked what she'd stacked beside her chair. "Laptop, phone, duffel with six sexy new sundresses— but no undies!" she crowed. "And I can't tell you how happy I am to be leaving my bras behind."

"An advantage of the island life," her housekeeper agreed. "Your assets are always accessible. None of those Puritanical panties or hose or even thongs. Makes my ass itch to *think* about wearing one of those!"

Cat glanced over her shoulder at the ocean. They'd positioned their chairs to face the house, so the element of surprise—the anticipation—would be more intense, even though she wondered how such a huge ship could sneak up on anyone.

But why ruin the mood analyzing details? Sometime within the hour, she'd be hustled aboard the *Captive Fantasy*! Her entire body quivered with the idea of greeting Captain Jack . . . kissing him for the first time—probably before they even left the beach—while his arms twined around her and his fingers found her hair.

"I can't believe he sent me a refund check after I insisted—"

"He likes to pay his lady's way. Not a bad trait in a man."

"True, but I didn't expect him to sacrifice my fare when—"

"He sees it as no sacrifice, Catalina," Leilani insisted with a chuckle. "And he's right. The pleasure this week will be his as much as yours."

Cat nodded, grinning again at the steamy note he'd enclosed around the check:

My darling Cat,

Words cannot express my utter lust and love after our initial phone chat and then sailing past Porto Di Angelo to get a closer look at you! Your photo drove me insane with desire, but seeing you on the shore, with the sun highlighting your hair and your beautiful legs in the water—well, it was a vision of paradise about to be mine!

I can't tell you when I've been so excited. I've made Stavros vow to leave us alone, at least most of the time. He can put in special requests to the chef and the sommelier on our behalf, as well as carry out any other wishes we might have, so I don't want to banish him from our presence completely. He'll be handling the other passengers while you and I frolic, after all.

For now, my dear lady, I wish you steamy dreams of all the fantasies you want me to bring to life for you. I may be the captain who kidnaps you, but I truly am your eager servant, here to please you in every possible way. Perhaps this won't turn out to be the love of our lifetimes, but I guarantee you it'll be a week we'll never forget.

Yours very soon, Captain Jack

Cat closed her eyes, visualizing his swarthy, handsome smile and the sturdy physique his stunning costume couldn't conceal. She was in lust with him already, so how much more could she—

"Don't look now, but here comes a johnboat," Cat whispered, quickly tucking the note into her dress pocket.

Leilani grinned at her, averting her eyes. "Jack must've anchored the *Fantasy* on the far side of the island. Have a wonderful time, dear! I'll be thinking about you!"

Cat's pulse was racing so fast she figured she'd never settle down—and wasn't that a fine feeling? She chugged the rest of her punch, trying not to tense up . . . thinking the johnboat must be on the beach by now. The two men she'd seen would be stalking up behind her chair soon.

She buttoned her phone into her sundress pocket and slipped her arm through the straps of her computer tote and duffel. Leilani was sitting as stiffly as she was, trying not to giggle. Her gaze was ripe with anticipation.

A loud yell behind them startled Cat straight up off her chair. A short man in jeans and a striped polo shirt circled Leilani's chair while his taller partner grabbed Cat from behind.

"Oh my God, you must be—"

"Pirates!" her captor confirmed as he snatched her up. His face was painted blue, and his long black hair flowed over his shoulders as he held her against his slender body.

"You don't *dress* like pirates of the Caribbean!" Cat quipped, partly to cover her disappointment at their T-shirts and jeans. Then Leilani let out a howl, and Cat glanced behind her. "No, no! Leave my housekeeper—Leilani's not part of this—"

"Arrrrrgh!" her kidnapper crowed. Before she could explain, the two men sprinted down the beach, carrying them. "The first rule of this game is to never trust a pirate, my pretty!"

The knot in her gut matched the dismay she saw on Leilani's face. Her housekeeper was struggling and kicking, as she was, but the two men were stronger than they looked. Something seemed desperately wrong, yet—

"Are you *sure* we're the women you want?" Cat rasped. "We were just sitting on the beach minding our own business—"

"Waiting to be abducted. And so you are." The man who held her flashed a grin made ghastly by his blue face paint and red lips. He dumped her on a bench seat in the johnboat, and before Cat could struggle away he wrapped a bungee cord around her arms. His partner, with spiked black hair and his face painted red, did the same to Leilani.

"But—Leilani isn't part of the charade—"

"Oh, this is no charade, cutie-pie," the shorter man said with a laugh. This time, instead of rowing, he yanked the string on an inboard motor and drove them around the island, out to sea.

"Gentlemen, if this is some sort of devious trick, my husband will have the coastal authorities—"

"No, he won't! Shut up and drink this." The taller guy thrust a plastic cup against Leilani's lips. "Don't worry, Goldilocks. You get refreshments, too."

Cat scowled, turning her face from the cup. She struggled against the tight cords around her arms, wondering how fast she might sink if she hurled herself over the side. "I don't know who you think you are, but I'm not drinking anything that resembles a urine sample until—"

The man swiveled her head to meet the liquid in the cup. "I'm sorry we don't measure up to your expectations, Miss Gamble," he said beneath the roar of the motor, "but you're the one who wanted to be kidnapped by pirates, and we're the ones making good. So drink up! The party's just starting!"

On the bench behind her, Leilani was kicking and struggling against the driver's arm, which made the small boat sway crazily in the water. "This is—I'm telling you, you're messing with the wrong women—"

Leilani made a gurgling, choking sound when the man with the blue face tipped the glass to her lips.

What the hell's wrong with this picture? Cat fretted again. The first taste of the strong, sweet liquor made her gag. Instead of the *Captive Fantasy* awaiting them, she saw a large sleek yacht. For a moment her heart jumped at the chance that

Ramon had returned from his errands and dropped anchor, to observe her abduction from a vantage point where he wouldn't seem obtrusive.

As the johnboat pulled up alongside the yacht, however, Cat realized it wasn't hers . . . just as the black-haired Asian man at the top of the ladder was definitely not Ramon. He looked to be in his forties; slim and grim with narrowed, assessing eyes.

Cat knew she should be kicking and fighting as her captor hauled her up onto the yacht, but her head was spinning in high, tight circles. She felt desperately scattered, and she wanted to be sick, and she wondered if she might shatter from the intensity of the burn in her stomach and the lights that flashed inside her eyes.

The last thing she saw before she passed out was the trio of identical smiles on faces of red, white, and blue.

"It's our lucky day, Miss Gamble," the oldest man said in a slightly accented voice. "You'll bring a fine price on the auction block. So nice of you to join us."

Cat went limp as all her lights blinked out.

10

"Yo, ho, ho—"

"It's a poi-rate's loife fer me!" Jack sang out. He and Stavros jogged around the hillside covered with white angel's trumpets that glowed in the dusk. The flowers' heavy sweetness wasn't the drug he needed right now: they'd had to wait on a few passengers this afternoon, so the *Fantasy* had arrived later than he'd planned. But now, as the stars came out to play, he gazed eagerly at the strip of white sand beach where Cat had said she'd be.

"Shit! She must've gotten tired of waiting, or—"

"Or she's pissed, thinking you stood her up."

Dropping all pretense of playing pirate, he advanced warily upon two white wooden beach chairs lying on their sides, at odd angles to each other. Two glasses, one half full, sat on the white table . . . as though someone who'd been here expected to come back. Except . . .

"This is fishy, Jack," Stavros muttered. He glanced at the dense bushes as though someone might be lurking there, ready to jump them. "Look at the way those footprints—"

"Suggest a struggle and lead back to . . ." Jack scowled, his gut tightening. "They go around to where we dropped anchor. But we could be jumping to conclusions, cuz. Maybe Cat had to use the lady's and went back up to the house."

"I hope you're right. I don't like the smell of this."

Jack stepped toward the stone pathway that led up the hill to the house. "Cat?" he called toward the balcony. "Cat Gamble, are you here, darling? So sorry we're late!"

Their boots squeaked softly, quickly, on the dew-kissed stones. It was so quiet even the birds had stopped their twilight trilling, which gave the place a very deserted feeling. Extremely eerie.

"Cat?" he hollered. "Our pirate ambush was delayed, darling—"

Once up the stairs, he gazed around the porch with its white wicker furnishings. Two places were set at the table, as though the caretakers would be eating their supper here. As though nothing were amiss or missing.

But where were they? His gut clenched like a fist as his disappointment turned to dread. "I feel very strange about this whole—"

"You don't suppose something unforeseen and awful has befallen—"

"—situation, and I think we should go inside," Jack continued in a muted voice. "Lord love us if we find bodies or other evidence of foul play."

"But we'd better look," his cousin agreed. "You go first, Captain."

Jack's lips quirked. He gently pushed the screen door, and they entered the unlit kitchen. "Cat? Anybody here?" he called out. "I'll understand if you're upset about us being late, love, but we really mustn't play games right—"

He sucked air when something hard jabbed him in the back.

"Don't take another step, gentlemen," a low voice ordered. "Just turn around slowly and explain all this to me."

Out of impulse, Jack's hands went up. Then he saw that Stavros had gone so quiet because a large hand was clamped around his neck . . . long, dark fingers with thumbnails filed to sharp points.

"Surely Miss Gamble mentioned our week's adventure aboard my ship, the *Captive Fantasy*, sir," Jack offered cautiously. "She was to be waiting on the beach, and—we've run late all day, so—"

"My wife, Leilani, was *not* part of the package." Still holding that pistol, the man looked far too lethal as a weapon himself: he stood head and shoulders above both of them and sported a devil-get-screwed goatee and a stiff, braided pigtail at the back of his head. "You'll understand why I called in the IMB. And of course you'll have answers for them, because here they come now."

Stavros looked relieved when their hostile host went out to the balcony to hail the men hopping down from a white coastal patrol boat with red lights flashing across its top. "Our passengers probably wonder what the hell—"

"We'll tell them it's an added bit of excitement—at no additional cost," Jack quipped quietly. He watched the two fit-looking fellows in white uniform shirts and shorts sprint up the walk—International Maritime Bureau agents whom he recognized, thank goodness. He wouldn't have to show his licenses and proof that Cat Gamble had paid to board a boat that resembled a bordello. And he wouldn't have to explain their seventeenth-century pirate costumes.

"Tell us again about this abduction, Ramon," the one he knew as Kurt said when he came inside. "The *Captive Fantasy* is anchored offshore, which suggests that—well, hello, Captain Spankevopoulos. What seems to be our problem?"

"Kurt, Ricky," Jack said, shaking their hands cordially. "Stavros and I came ashore for a little pirate play because Cat Gamble, the new owner of Porto Di Angelo, was to be waiting for us. But all we saw were the overturned beach chairs and a lot of suspicious-looking footprints leading back to the other side of the island."

"And no sign of your passenger?"

"Nor my wife—and she wasn't going on the trip." The man they called Ramon looked from the IMB agents to Jack. He'd relaxed his intimidating scowl, but he was still tightly wound. "I didn't want to *believe* Captain Jack had anything to do with Leilani's disappearance, since we wave at his ship each week—and since Leilani is highly psychic and wholeheartedly encouraged Cat to sail with him. But this means we have no idea where either of them are or who got to them. Or why."

He crossed his arms, looking out toward the sea—and looking downright worried as he considered the situation. "They couldn't have left the island on their own, because I was coming back in the yacht, and the car's still in the garage. I . . . I can't think they drowned, because they were excited about Miss Gamble's pirate rendezvous, and . . . my wife and I had planned for a little romance while she was away."

Jack smiled. While he never expected Ramon the Island Warrior to wax romantic in front of four men he didn't know, he still didn't like this one bit. After his suggestive chat with Cat Gamble—watching her wave to him from the beach and scurry after the bottle he'd tossed her—he couldn't believe she'd gone elsewhere rather than join him for the week. She was just as hot for it as he was.

"This may not be related," Jack said in a low voice, "but we all recall stories of how the previous owner of this island disappeared without a trace, as well."

"And to have it happen again," Stavros chimed in, "especially knowing how attractive Miss Gamble is—"

"Attractive and very, very wealthy. As Valenzia Borgia was," Ramon stated in that low, serious voice. "We can contact Miss Gamble by phone or an e-mail, but if she's in danger, the chances of her checking either of those is pretty slim."

Like gunfighters in an old Western, Jack reached for his cell phone at the same time Ramon did. He held his poised, letting Cat's caretaker have the first try. The man's chocolate-colored face lit up slightly when her message about leaving a voice mail came through. At least her phone was working.

"Cat—Miss Gamble—it's Ramon," he said urgently, "you must call me immediately, on the number I programmed in for you. Until I hear from you, we're very concerned about you and Leilani disappearing so . . . mysteriously."

Jack noted how Ramon's stiff upper lip was slipping. The fine lines around his eyes deepened, too. "I'll give her a try, as well," Jack suggested. "Perhaps if someone finds her phone, they'll contact us on her behalf. If both of us leave a callback number, we've doubled our chances."

He punched in her number from memory, waiting for Cat's silky, seductive voice to give him instructions about leaving a message. "Darling, it's Captain Jack and I'm so hoping you're all right, dear heart. Please call me, *right now*—"

He gave his number in a deliberate voice and paused, closing his eyes. "And if you are *not* Cat Gamble and you hear this message, you damn well better call me anyway! We've notified the International Maritime authorities, so don't do anything stupid."

Jack sighed as he clicked off. "Sounds like I've been watching too many espionage flicks, but Miss Gamble's wealth—and her unfamiliarity with the islands—make her a target. While Stavros and I stage a consensual kidnapping adventure, I've long suspected that real, modern-day pirates are operating in these waters."

"Me, too—even if the information on our Web site and maps

suggest the Caribbean is quiet," Kurt assured him. "Technology makes them very difficult to catch. The good ones have fast boats and enough computer savvy to fly under our radar. By the time we realize that calls and messages to our missing persons got intercepted, the thieves are long gone. On their way to their next lucrative target."

"Lucrative . . . how?" Ramon queried pointedly. "If I get wind of somebody snatching my Leilani to—"

"No matter what they say about slavery being abolished in the civilized world," Ricky replied, "plenty of underground racketeers shuttle attractive women and young men to buyers for a very pretty price."

"Slave traders?" Ramon murmured with a frown. "If you suspect for one minute that's what's happened to Leilani, you *call* me, understand? My wife and I share a very strong psychic bond—"

"Which means *you* will also call *us* if you get any brain waves," Jack insisted. "This is more than a compromise of my clientele and my livelihood, you see. This is about the women our lives revolve around."

11

Cat woke up with a moan and a killer headache that drove her to find relief—aspirin or caffeine or—God, anything! But when she sat up, she vomited before she knew what hit her, into a basin beside the bed.

She flopped back onto her back, sweating yet feeling chilled. What on earth had she eaten, to—

Her memory returned in disjointed pieces, jagged like broken glass from the pain throbbing in her head. She'd been forced to drink something very strong and sweet—something that had knocked her out. Before that, she and—

Leilani! Again Cat tried to sit up, but that awful queasiness flattened her. She gazed around the room from her bed instead.

Yes, she was in a bed . . . in a cool, dark room, thank God, because light would drive her absolutely insane. The walls and floor were a textured beige, but she was so unfocused she couldn't tell if it was wallpaper or rush matting or what sorts of fabrics and fibers were around her. The furnishings, too, were a pale wood, reminiscent of a bedroom set her grandma had. Blond, they'd called it in the Fifties.

Boring, she called it now, but didn't have the inclination to open her mouth and say it aloud. Just the thought of sitting up again made the beige, boring bedroom spin in beige, boring circles, but they were more excitement than she could handle, so she closed her eyes.

No luck. The room kept spinning, and she had the helpless, hopeless sense that she might not ever climb out of this strange bed.

Then came the hallucinations. Odd splashes of color and movement . . . swirls of neon pink that morphed into a gruesome face of an angel-turned-gargoyle leering at her with pointed fangs—

Cat's eyes flew open. If she couldn't *see* that imaginary monster, it couldn't attack her, right?

Once again the room took a spin, so she closed her eyes . . . felt a volcano of intense orange and violet yearnings spewing up out of—

She turned to vomit again. As she clung weakly to the edge of the mattress, feeling very green and shriveled, it occurred to her that the basin had been placed by someone who knew she'd be sick . . . someone who'd put her into this bed to sleep off that noxious stuff those . . . painted faces, red and blue . . . grabbing her—and Leilani!—and dumping them into a little dinghy with an engine that now whined shrilly in her mind. Would these weird sensations never go away?

Focus! Cat demanded of herself. *Find something real to center on until you can tell what the hell it is.*

She turned her head enough to see the far side of the room. After a few moments, the film cleared from her eyes, and she recognized a pitcher. . . . Ice water so cold that condensation ran down its shining glass sides. Ice water that would cleanse this sick-sour taste from her mouth and—

You'll land on your ass before your feet even hit the floor.

Who said that? Cat blinked, trying to reason. If she sat up, swung her legs over the edge of the bed, and then stood up . . . how would she land on her ass? Most likely it would be her face that hit when she fell forward—

What difference does it make? You're not getting up anytime soon, doll.

Her guts rolled. A hand fluttered to her stomach . . . her bare stomach. And as Cat's eyes flew open again, she realized she was lying here without a stitch of clothing on: someone— her captors, probably—had seen every inch of her body . . . probably took great pleasure in stripping off that new dress and leering at her. Maybe they'd touched her breasts or stroked between her legs because she could do nothing about it.

Her head throbbed harder. Her tongue felt like a dry, bloated sponge, and getting over to that pitcher of water became her life's mission.

Slowly she rolled to her side. She stared steadily at the pitcher until it stopped circling the tabletop. Heard the seductive shifting of the ice cubes as they melted and floated to the surface.

When she sat up, she took her time, still gazing at the pitcher as a point of reference to aim for—and because this sort of visual exercise seemed to be keeping those mental monsters at bay.

Tentatively Cat dangled her legs over the side of the bed . . . an ordinary double bed it was, with only the fitted sheet covering the mattress. Probably so she wouldn't puke on any other bedding—or be able to hide herself under it.

Were they watching her? Clearing the gunk from her throat, Cat peered intently at the corners of the ceiling, but she saw no cameras. When she felt relatively balanced, she eased herself to the floor . . . stood slowly, feeling the hard, tiny ribs of the rush matting indenting the soles of her feet, as if each little cylinder were a separate entity.

"Stop stalling," she whispered—mostly to see if she could

talk. Despite her pounding headache, the room's movement had subsided. So she took one shaky step ... another ... a third one ... until the nearness of that cold water propelled her forward with her need to gulp it all down.

When she lifted the pitcher to fill a glass, it took both hands to hold it steady. Was she really so weak, or was the damn pitcher made of lead crystal? It was a very pretty piece, with two poppies etched into its thick surface.

Poppies. Where opium comes from, right?

She closed her eyes in sheer ecstasy as the cold water slid down her throat. Gulped as though she could never get enough of the soothing liquid. Its coldness tingled all the way down into her stomach.

After a second glass, she felt steadier. Cat approached the closet so she could dress before anyone discovered she was out of bed. Did she recall two—or three?—Asian faces when they abducted her? All men. And all involved in this nefarious trickery, making plans to do—*whatever* to her.

She didn't dare define *whatever*. Remembering the ocean-blue paint on her captor's face—the poppy red on the shorter fellow who'd grabbed Leilani—didn't do a thing for her confidence.

Neither did seeing her dresses hanging here, free of wrinkles, as though some unseen maid had unpacked her duffel and—

Where was her other stuff? Her phone and laptop?

Cat reached into the pocket of the sky-blue sundress she'd been wearing. Something made her rifle around, searching for—?

"That was a touching note Captain Jack wrote you, Ms. Gamble. If you're looking for it—or your phone—you won't find them there."

Cat whirled around and then was sorry for it. A slender Asian man—or were there two?—stood inside the doorway.

His expression remained unreadable, except for an air of amused superiority.

"Who the hell are you?" she rasped, yanking the dress from its hanger to cover herself.

"I'm your host, Arthur Wong. We met last night aboard my yacht."

He was *wong*, all right! This whole frickin' situation was so *wong* she still felt imprisoned in a surreal dream. "Where's my laptop? And Leilani— what'd you do to her?"

"She's resting. Not here, in the house, so don't go looking for her."

That didn't set well, but Cat felt too agitated to analyze things just yet. "So where are my computer and phone? You have no right to take my belongings!"

His face remained a bland mask. "It's my home, Ms. Gamble, so I make the rules. And the sooner you begin behaving as a model guest, the sooner you'll receive answers. And breakfast."

Food was the farthest thing from her mind, but Cat sensed she'd better keep this man talking rather than *doing*. He wasn't a lot taller than she was; had his black hair cut conservatively and wore no facial hair. When he cocked his head slightly, she caught the glimmer of rimless glasses, which made him resemble one of those wise Chinese philosophers of centuries past.

She realized then that this was the man who'd driven the yacht—was it last night? He was wearing a black silk robe now, loosely belted at his slender waist. He looked ready to take that robe off, and she knew damn well he was nude underneath it.

"So what's going on here? Why did you snatch my housekeeper and me from our beach?"

He smiled slightly. "Because you are beautiful women who will bring a fine price—"

"You're going to *sell* us?" Cat's heart raced into overdrive and her head began to spin again, but she focused on this conversation to keep from getting sick. No way would she let this irritating man watch her lose control!

He stepped toward her, slowly but with a purpose in those onyx eyes. "Sometimes we keep the choicest women for ourselves, to train them in the ways of sexual servitude," he replied in a breathy voice. "My sons and I truly enjoy breaking a woman's spirit and then helping her rebuild herself. Reshape herself as a holy vessel in which her man's desires may reside."

Cat's jaw dropped. "You've got to be kidding. This is really a set for some two-bit Caribbean movie company, right? And—"

"*You* were the one who signed on to be a love slave, Ms. Gamble. Once Jack Spankevopoulos answered your provocative ad, and you learned of his exotic vacation package aboard the *Captive Fantasy*, you made the conscious decision to become his hostage."

"What's that got to do with *you*? And just how do you know this?" she demanded, although she wasn't sure she wanted the answers.

Her host smiled again, enjoying her clueless state. "We can intercept phone calls, e-mails—all manner of satellite transmissions," he replied with a little shrug. "We knew when you'd be waiting on your beach to be kidnapped. Our superior technology and marketing savvy keep us in business."

More stuff she didn't really want to know. "And that business would be?"

"We're pirates, Ms. Gamble. Smugglers." He waggled his eyebrows to torment her. "We don't dress like the swashbucklers in the movies, but we're *real*. And just as ruthless, if provoked."

"But—but this is so *stupid*!" she spouted. "Do you think Jack didn't notice I was missing? Do you think my estate manager hasn't notified the authorities that his wife is gone, too? "

There was that offhand shrug again. "They have no way of tracing us. Our technology is far superior to what these impoverished, understaffed island forces can afford," he said coolly. "And once we were onto the exchange between you and Captain Jack, and we saw your photograph, we knew you'd be worth a lot more to us than to him. Either for the ransom—which we know quite well you can afford—or for the money you'll bring on the slave market once we tire of you."

Cat sensed he was stacking stones of unwanted information around her to make her his mental hostage as much as his physical one. What he'd said about technological interceptions sounded like something out of a James Bond movie!

But it wasn't such a stretch, was it? In this era of identity theft and electronic bank robberies, having pirates who used technology and high-dollar yachts to carry out their trade seemed pretty reasonable. She just didn't like it much; was too much of a techno-nerd to understand how all that stuff worked.

"How much do you suppose Captain Jack or Leilani's husband will offer as ransom?" he asked in a speculative voice. He stood about six feet away from her now, his obsidian eyes shining like an Oriental trance master's. "How much are you worth to them, Ms. Gamble? Don't be stingy! We've located your new offshore accounts, so we know how much you have to bargain with."

Outrage scorched her cheeks. Arthur Wong was baiting her, working her into a state of frenzy so she'd reveal things she shouldn't. He was probably bluffing about this account stuff: what Americans *didn't* have offshore accounts in these islands, if the Escape Artist site reflected reality?

"I should hope Jack and Ramon have sense enough not to meet your asinine demands, Mr. Wong," she replied tersely. "And what makes you think either of them—"

"Stupid? Asinine?" he echoed archly. He took another two steps toward her, making her very aware that she had nowhere to go but the closet. "Those are not terms I appreciate, Ms. Gamble. My sons and I have worked much harder to build our empire—

and this island paradise—than you have. Those who win large lottery jackpots have no sense of their financial strength because their work ethic is flabby. They piss away their windfalls, buying islands on impulse and—"

"And your point would be?" Cat demanded. Although she still held the blue dress against her body, she felt far too exposed.

Arthur Wong's infuriating smile told her he'd put her where he wanted her. "Never mind," he whispered. "You're probably right about the ransom because when Captain Jack saw you weren't waiting for him, he assumed you changed your mind. Stood him up. Figured you could afford to pay for a vacation and then not take it."

She refused to answer to that. Tried her damnedest not to follow that train of thought to its hopeless destination.

Again Arthur's lips curved. His eyes lingered on the breasts her clutched dress wasn't quite covering. "Of course, if he or Ramon were really trying to contact you, I'd think they would've left voice mails by now. But no," he added with a sly shake of his head. "No e-mails on your laptop, either. We removed your theft-prevention software, by the way."

Her head was throbbing hard now, and she wanted to hurl the pitcher of ice water at this infuriating man. Was he hazing her? Trying to worm even more information from her than he'd apparently gleaned from her phone and computer, and those message interceptions?

As Wong kept staring at her with an interrogator's expressionless expression, a deep, dark anxiety swept over her. Cat felt so alone—so vulnerable from the drugs—she feared she would never see her beautiful Porto Di Angelo, or Leilani, Ramon, and Jack, again.

Did Captain Spank believe she'd stood him up? He'd refunded her money, so he wouldn't feel as responsible for her pleasure—or safety—right? He probably used that same sexy sweet talk on all of his attractive clients—

Arthur Wong seemed to be reading her thoughts, so she stopped thinking. Looked him in the eye with the coldest expression she could muster.

"When you apologize for your rudeness—for the ingratitude I won't allow in this oasis of serenity and grace that is my home—you may dress. Then you will be escorted downstairs for breakfast," he said in a low, no-nonsense voice. "When I've deemed your apology to be sincere, we will begin your training."

12

Apologize?! Like that's going to happen!

Cat turned her back to Arthur Wong as he left the room, closing her door without latching it. *Such* an old-school Asian he was, with all that "women should know their place and obey" crap! Well, these Wongs could take their training and cram it up their tight little asses!

There. That felt better.

She chugged another glass of water, pleased that this encounter with Papa-All-Wong had cleared her muzzy head. The monochromatic beige room had more dimension and texture; certainly more stability. Now that her head wasn't spinning from the drugs, Cat realized her room was *round*: the walls curved all the way around her, with four large floor-to-ceiling windows. From what little she knew about feng shui, she figured they'd faced the bed toward whichever direction would bring the most chaos upon her.

But then, since she didn't *know* which direction would set her emotionally off-balance, she didn't have to believe in that crap, did she? She tossed her sundress on the bed so things would look messier, and to relieve the monotony of all the *beigeness* that surrounded her.

Feeling bolder, Cat went to the nearest window—a French door, it was—and stepped out to a very small balcony. There was only enough room for her to stand and look out over the ocean and this side of the island that was apparently the Wong stronghold.

She inhaled the fresh morning air, gloating: although this little spot of Caribbean paradise was lovely, it wasn't nearly as lush as Porto Di Angelo. She spotted a waterfall to one side, flowing into a pool surrounded by very orderly, very precisely arranged shrubs and flowering plants.

Curious, Cat stepped back into her room and crossed to the opposite French door, which also had a step-out balcony. From here, she saw a low-slung structure enclosed in a high wall. While it was also landscaped nicely, the area gave her the feeling of a . . . concentration camp.

Turning inside again, she walked out a third door, pleased that this one faced the sea and had a larger porch with a slatted maroon chair and matching table. The railing here was lower and afforded a fine view from the chair—and it also gave her a wonderful idea about climbing *down*—

Except *down* was a long, loooong drop into a chasm lined in large jagged boulders. These rock formations probably looked spectacular at the ground level, but from here they looked like sudden, certain death.

Which explains the lower railing, doll. You have a round room because you're being held hostage at the top of a tower.

She looked in either direction, and sure enough—just like the legendary Rapunzel—she was sequestered very high and away from any means of escape.

"So much for my getaway, eh, Spike?" she murmured.

Don't jump. I may be an angel, but the laws of gravity still apply.

She sighed wistfully and then glanced in the direction his voice had come from. "So where've you been? How come you allowed those paint-faced pirates to snatch Leilani and me—"

The ways of human nature still apply, too—free will, and all that. I can only work with what you people give me. But I am working!

Small consolation, but it made her feel better. Maybe.

Sighing, Cat went back into her room and gasped.

Standing in the center, beneath the ugly bamboo chandelier, was a tall, slender man with hair that shone blue-black as it tumbled over his shoulders to the middle of his back. He wore a short red and black silk robe printed with dragons and Asian symbols, and when he turned, with a slow, ethereal grace, she recognized him as the pirate who'd hauled her off the beach.

This morning he wore no blue face paint. His features resembled those of Arthur Wong, as did his unblinking obsidian eyes, but he was noticeably taller and exuded a less . . . chauvinistic air.

"Good morning, Catalina," he murmured. And damned if he didn't press his palms together in a prayerful pose and bow.

"How'd you know my full name?"

The man smiled enigmatically. "I have many ways of knowing many things, my dove. I am Thomas Wong, elder son of the man you insulted with your . . . disregard for his authority, as the master of this island. It is my mission to guide you along a nobler, gentler path, so you will blossom like a lotus and open yourself to clarity and light."

"So I'll see things your way, you mean? Don't count on it."

His smile remained benign. "You have a lovely body. With my tutelage, you will become a temple befitting the dignity and light that will radiate from within, once you find that gentler, more appropriate path."

Should've packed your hip waders, sugah.

"*Your* path, I assume," she replied, crossing her arms.

He nodded once. "Enlightenment will come, Miss Gamble. Sooner, if you surrender to my physical and spiritual teachings."

"But even if I become your highly enlightened temple full of lotus blossoms, I'm still your hostage, right? So where does any of this surrender shit get me, really?"

His lips flickered with amusement, but then he resumed his Maharishi-Oh-So-Glowing attitude. "I see you have chosen to remain naked for your first lesson, and this is a positive sign. It shows me you are giving yourself into my control—"

She stepped forward to grasp the prominent ridge in the front of his robe. "How's *this* for control, Thomas?" she asked, tightening her fingers around his erection. "How about we come to terms real fast, about why I'm naked and how I feel about your magical, mystical bullshit? I'm not dressed because I've been looking around this nifty little prison. Sort of like the Tower of London or reminiscent of where Rapunzel was locked up, eh?"

Thomas exhaled very slowly, his eyes locked into hers. "Towers are very phallic, are they not?" he asked in a silky voice. "And, since in most of life, form often follows function, we shall surmise that this tower you are housed in is much like the tower within your grasp: it will keep you within my reach, at my disposal and discretion. And it *will* dominate you."

Cat found herself at a disadvantage because she had to stoop to hold this Asian's cock . . . which meant he was gazing down at her from a superior position. He'd won this round.

She let go of him. Tried to deny how the feel of his long, solid cock had made her temperature rise. Where had she found the nerve to grab him that way? Ordinarily she had *some* sense of decency—especially around men she didn't know.

Oh, but this one's appointed himself your Most-High Guru,

girlfriend, Spike whispered. *You're gonna know him in every sense of the word. He'll turn ya every which way but loose before it's all said and done.*

She swallowed. That idea appealed to her, damn it. How many long, lonely months had it been since she'd had a man?

Thomas Wong, without his face paint, was attractive in a slender, wiry way that was by no means weak. He was all about discipline in mind, body, and spirit, and if she bolted out the door he'd have no trouble overtaking her. After all, he'd lifted her from her beach chair last night—from behind—and carried her effortlessly to his boat.

He focused intently on her. His dark eyes drifted from her face to her bare breasts . . . slowly down the curve of her torso. He untied his robe. Let it fall open, so she could see what she'd just had hold of. He shrugged, to let the silk ripple down his body and pool around his slender feet.

Cat clasped her hands at her chest and then wondered about the wisdom of this. Had she positioned herself this way to fend him off—or to appear open to his teachings?

That's exactly what he wanted, wasn't it? He intended to show her, right from the get-go, who would be Tarzan and who would be Jane.

"You have nowhere to go, but you have several choices," he murmured, forcing her to listen intently. "You may stand outside, on any of the balconies or on the larger porch. You may remain where you are, standing. You may lie down, on the floor or on the bed. You may stand against a wall. You may turn away, or you may face me. You may open yourself, or you may resist my teachings. In other words, you may exercise your free will, or you may succumb."

This was no longer about who would be slave and who would be master: it was all about *sex.* Position possibilities.

While he'd slowly named her options, a wild surge of heat had taken her to each of his places, each of his positions, in her imagination. And she hadn't been there alone: this guy might be high on Spirit or strung out on something else, but when he kept his mouth shut, he was *way* too sexy. Hot for it in a higher way that made her head spin.

Cat's throat clicked when she swallowed. Thomas Wong remained silent and purposeful—and very, very hard—as he challenged her from the center of her room. No doubt he believed this gave him the place of central power, around which all other entities orbited—or some such celestial hoo-hah.

And as long as he stares at you in silence, he has control, doesn't he? Take a stand, missy. Tell him how it'll be, or you could be standin' here all damn day.

She had that sense about Thomas, that he was persistent and powerful in a most persuasive way, rather than being an arrogant bully like his father. And gee . . . if she remained here with him, testing his power—playing with him—she didn't have to apologize to Arthur yet, did she? It seemed like a win-win situation, even if her hunger pangs told her to go downstairs for breakfast to keep from passing out. From hunger of one sort or another.

Two can play this game, she reminded herself. Cat turned on her heel to head for the largest porch. The fresh morning air proved how warm she'd become, and how . . . wet with anticipation. It seemed perfectly normal now to be standing in broad daylight, looking out over the brilliant turquoise sea without a stitch of clothing on, letting the breeze caress her hair and skin.

"A wise choice," Thomas intoned behind her. "Here we will absorb the sun's energy and warmth, and we will move in rhythm with the eternal sea. A breathtaking view, is it not?"

Cat smiled. "Nice, yes. But not nearly as breathtaking as the view from my window at home."

Home! Had she really said that without a moment's hesitation? Her heart longed to be back in that pristine white room, so clean and bright, gazing at *her* flowers—inhaling the sweet, druggy scent of those angel's trumpets while gazillions of tiny diamonds danced on the surface of the sea.

He came up beside her, to stand just close enough that their elbows brushed. She felt acutely aware of his body heat, his powerful presence, his lean, graceful stature—and that silky hair that stroked her own shoulder when it blew in the breeze.

She was aware of that cock, too. It jutted out over the low railing and rested on it. Propped into position.

He smiled serenely—looked out over the water, pretending he didn't know how she stared at his erection. How she wanted it, in spite of what it represented.

"Do you see that ship, Alina?" he asked, gracefully extending his arm to point. "Keep your eye on it. Tell me what you notice as it approaches."

Was this an oddball Oriental slave-training tactic? As Cat found the distant speck he referred to, like a dark, angular cork cutting through the water, he moved behind her . . . placed his hands above her shoulders by half an inch . . . exactly the distance to make the little hairs on her body stand at attention, either from static electricity or just out-and-out excitement.

Keeping his palms curved, he followed her body without touching it: slowly down her shoulders and the length of her arms . . . slowly back up them, to let the tips of his long fingers meet in front of her breasts. Then he just stood there behind her with his arms around her space. Yet he touched her nowhere.

God, this is nerve-wracking! Cat held her breath, remaining rigid within her cage made of air. Her nipples peaked and stood straight out. They strained brazenly toward his touch, but he eluded her. Gooseflesh blossomed all over her bare body—not from cold but from sheer *need* and the energy that radiated from his palms as he began to move them again, about half an inch from her tingling skin.

"I'm caressing your aura." His warm breath tickled her ear.

"You are very excited, Alina. So stimulated that bringing you to orgasm would be extremely easy. Would you like me to do that?"

Her breath came in rapid gasps, and she was afraid to answer. Afraid this new nemesis would prove himself right in *seconds* if he touched her down there. She shifted at the thought. Felt very warm and wet.

"How fortunate for both of us that we are attracted, my dove. That our yin and yang are interwoven as though by destiny."

He was baffling her with bullshit, wasn't he? Yet the warm caress of his breath was impossible to ignore. Cat closed her eyes, thinking the sensations would feel less blatant that way—but *no*. His low laughter, so triumphant yet so teasing, reverberated through her body with the pounding of her pulse.

"Open your eyes, my Alina. Tell me about that ship you saw a few moments ago."

It was a trick—she just knew it! And what the hell could he do to her if she refused to look? But his words were compelling, his voice as low and flowing as a hypnotist's, so her eyes fluttered open of their own accord without her permission.

Cat stifled a cry. This was no ordinary Tall Sails pirate ship that cruise passengers cavorted on—it was the *Captive Fantasy*! Even if she hadn't read the painted lettering beneath the busty figurehead at its bow, Cat *felt* the ship's identity—just as she had when she'd waved to it from her own beach.

Thomas knew that, of course: Ramon had told her Jack's ship circled Porto Di Angelo like clockwork each week, and the magnificent vessel would make a pass around the Wongs' island. Right now, while she watched.

Every nerve jangled within her. She leaned forward with a longing so strong—an urge to holler at the top of her lungs, even though the ship's engines and the breaking waves would drown her out. Maybe Captain Jack would see her in his spy-glass! Maybe he'd drop anchor and rush ashore—

When Thomas closed his hands around her breasts, reality returned in a rush.

"She's a beauty, is she not?" he murmured, coaxing her body against his. "Such a romantic notion—such a voyage!—with those sails billowing in the wind and the dip and sway of the sea . . . the salt breeze blowing your hair back from your face, lovely Alina. Ah, you are *so* close to—"

"Don't think for a minute you'll keep me here!" She focused intently on the *Fantasy*. Within moments it would sail close enough that she could distinguish individual passengers. Maybe even Stavros or—she searched out the crow's nest among the fluttering sails—the captain himself.

"Your determined spirit will be a challenge for me. But I shall triumph."

For a few breathless moments he stood with his erection pressing her spine. He kneaded her with it, reminding her how hot and solid it had felt in her hand . . . how hot and solid it would feel inside her. He matched his breathing to hers, giving her the silent treatment again.

How would he haze her next? How would he prove—in his uplifting, enlightening, inspiring way—that he had her under total control?

Cat knew better than to talk. Knew better than to cry out—or cry. The ship's sails rippled in the wind, and the low roar of her engines made Cat's hopes cave in with desperation.

In one smooth movement, Thomas pivoted and then lifted her so she was seated on the narrow balcony railing. She was balancing only on the padding of her ass, with her legs flailing on either side of his body. His hands were at her waist, but he was holding her very loosely.

"This is your first lesson in trust and in following direc-tions," he informed her with an easy smile. "As you're well aware, it's a long way down to those rocks. Only one foolish woman has defied my advances—my attempt to teach her about sublimation of will and release of control. She didn't live to tell about it."

Cat was too damned scared to argue: if he released her—one simple, sudden movement—she'd fly backward in a fatal free fall. From this angle she saw that the roof of her tower was pointed like the top of a pagoda, and that the sky above them was a fine, clear blue with a few feathery white clouds floating by.

Not that any of that mattered. Behind her, the waves rushed around the *Captive Fantasy's* bow . . . a steel drum band played a perky Caribbean dance tune . . . and Cat was suddenly sucked away from all the extraneous details into Thomas Wong's bottomless black eyes. He was prodding her with that gaze, the way a sheep dog controlled a flock. Cat had no doubt whatsoever that she was now the sacrificial lamb.

She went absolutely still. Stopped struggling and kicking. Remained riveted by that glittering obsidian gaze, knowing it was her doom but her salvation, as well. For if she really *thought* about what was happening right now, she'd die of fright.

She teetered, and his arms slipped around her. Cat lay cradled in his embrace, leaning out over the precipice . . . totally at his mercy, in more ways than she cared to think about.

And then she knew what he was about to do: read it in the ripple of passion that flashed like lightning in the night of those eyes. He licked his lips, holding her gaze. Even as he lowered his head, Cat could only stare, senseless. Speechless.

My God, he's not really going to—

The first touch of his tongue on her bare mound made her whimper and suck air. Thomas chuckled, warming to his task of torture. He extended his dark pink tongue to an unbelievable length and wiggled it, to make her laugh.

But that would mean letting down her guard—letting go and maybe falling—

He bent to his purpose, still watching her face. Slowly he lowered himself at the knees until his face was between her legs, with that wicked tongue extended a blasted half an inch from her pulsing, aching, dripping slit. He stopped to inhale her . . . to moan low in his throat.

Something inside her snapped. "You're giving my aura a tongue job, right?" she quipped nervously.

Thomas's guttural laugh sounded like a snarl. He drove his pointed tongue deep inside her and then thrust against her clit, high and hard. Cat screamed with the sudden impact of heat and need, writhing with her body's traitorous surrender. For fear he'd lose his grip—he stood in a grueling crouch, supporting her suspended weight—she clamped her hands around his head.

His hair was warm silk, and his tongue was an insistent piston. Never had a man gone down on her with such merciless purpose, thrusting and licking her sensitive skin with impassioned abandon.

And now he shook with laughter. After all, grabbing his head, forcing him to drive her wild this way, was the ultimate sign of surrender, wasn't it?

So she stopped caring about his head games. Cat speared her fingers into his luscious long hair and opened herself to his glorious, thorough attention. Her body bunched and curled like a cougar about to pounce, and she let the sensations blow her away. As the first spasms grabbed her, she realized that succumbing to her magical, mystical instructor might have its advantages.

And if she fell to her death, well, at least she'd flown to heaven first.

13

When Cat could see again, she was on her bed, sprawled where Thomas had apparently tossed her. He stood at her left, like a dark angel whose intent she couldn't read: even when this guy was pissed, he hid his emotions behind that mask of serenity and quiet control.

He sat on the edge of the mattress, looking tender, like a lover. "You nearly flew the coop, my dove," he murmured as he stroked her hair from her damp face. "But now you have returned to me, and you have another choice. We may continue with your lessons, or we may go downstairs for breakfast and meet my younger brother, Charles. He's a trained chef, and he cooks for us here on the island."

Cat listened as though from a distance, or from behind a translucent wall that separated her from Thomas. And that sense of detachment would serve her until she figured out what he was up to. He'd so obviously staged that display on the balcony, at just the moment when she might have called to Captain Jack, that he would use every little incident to teach her some sort of lesson. Everything he said or did would have ulterior motives, and her new mission was to unmask them. Unmask *him*.

She closed her eyes so he couldn't gaze into them. "Breakfast sounds lovely," she rasped, surprised her throat was so dry.

How long and loud did you scream, anyway? Did everyone on this island hear you come?

"Breakfast it is. But first we'll cleanse ourselves."

"You first," she murmured. Her arms and legs felt like soft-cooked pasta, and she just wanted to sprawl on the bed for a while.

"We shall wash together, Alina. As our captive and student, you must accustom yourself to being in the presence of your masters at all times."

Cat quirked an eyebrow. "But I slept last night without any of you—"

"Did you?"

His angular face relaxed in a quiet smile. She'd been so far out of it from that drugged punch, they could've held an orgy in her room and she wouldn't have known.

"Did you enjoy removing my clothes? Knowing I was powerless?" she demanded. "Does that make you feel strong, Thomas? Potent and in control?"

"It was Father who stripped you. Charles and I—"

"Charles was the one who grabbed Leilani, I assume?"

Thomas nodded. "My brother and I secured your belongings and positioned you so you'd awaken relaxed, rather than stiff. He was quite taken with your blond hair and creamy complexion—and the fact that you're already shaved between your legs. He usually has the honor of performing that ritual."

He's hazing you again. Trying to make you protest.

Cat took a deep breath, to focus on the Wong who sat so close he touched her lightly. Perhaps she *could* learn a few things from Thomas about containing her emotions—so he couldn't use them against her.

But what did she have to protest, really? Deep down, the idea that three powerful Asian guys had handled her body . . . looked at her most intimate parts . . . stolen her for their own nefarious purposes . . . appealed to some dark, lurid facet of her imagination.

But if she kept thinking that way, she'd never get home, would she? These Wongs impressed her as men who would use her up and then pass her along to the highest bidder.

She sat up slowly, still rubbery. "Shall we wash, then? It's been too long since I had anything to eat."

"And Charles will delight in feeding you. But you will always be my Alina."

Cat *almost* challenged him about that annoying nickname. It gave him too much power—felt too intimate when he renamed her as his own.

But *intimacy* took on a whole new meaning when she stepped into the small bathroom behind a pocket door in the wall. Its sink, stool, and shower were wedged into the rounded room, and beside the toilet stood a fixture like she'd *never* seen before.

"Do you know how to use this, Alina?" Thomas asked with a trace of condescension. "You Americans get squeamish about such things, but you'll find this bidet most convenient during our time together."

Cat bit back her irritation. He'd spoken in that soft, goody-guru voice, but he'd still insinuated she was totally clueless!

She straddled the white porcelain basin—which put her face-to-face with an imitation of Michaelangelo's statue of David, except his hands were the faucet handles and his enlarged cock directed the water flow. She'd be here all damn day if she challenged every little thing Thomas subjected her to, so she turned it on.

"Now, wash your genitalia—"

"Genitalia?" she blurted. "How clinical is *that*?"

Thomas's lips quirked as he handed her a bar of soap shaped like a phallus. "So what's *your* name for it?"

Cat blinked. This was getting *really* intimate, to divulge such personal terminology while rubbing herself with a cock made of soap. But the rumble of her poor, hungry stomach reminded her of her mission. "That's my puss you invaded," she replied, and then she wet the soap in David's stream of warm water.

"Your legs were open, my dove. You were holding my face and tongue hard against your wet, heated flesh. Is that what you call invasion?"

With the light aroma of lemon wafting around her, Cat decided to rub his nose in it again—by refusing to be a weenie.

She stroked herself with the suggestive soap, gazing at the slender, naked Asian not two feet away from her. If she hadn't been so hungry, she might've worked herself into a real lather, just to see how long he could watch without participating.

He focused on her fingers and the soap froth. His arms remained loosely crossed over his flat, firm chest as he leaned against the wall.

To tease him further, Cat held the soap like a dildo, so it appeared to be penetrating her. She rocked in a suggestive rhythm, squeaking against the bidet's slick, wet rim.

Nothing, damn it. Thomas's cock remained limp between his slender, muscled legs. "You may rinse now," he instructed.

Small consolation that she heard a rasp in his low, controlled voice. She set the lurid soap on the small shelf built into David's neck, and then—again to torment rather than be tormented—she swiveled the cock faucet to direct the water where she needed it. Had she been alone, she might've indulged in some sex play with this classical, curly-haired David—whose cool, removed gaze mirrored Thomas's—but rinsing seemed the more expedient thing to do. She turned off the tap, raising an eyebrow.

He handed her a small towel and then watched every flick of her fingertips between her legs.

"If you had hair there, I could watch you dry yourself longer," he said in a thin voice. "But I must settle for the sensations you evoke when you rinse your orgasmic secretions from my lips and chin."

She smirked and took the wet washrag he handed her. "You can't tell me you didn't like it when I came in your face, Thomas. Tell me what a sense of power it gave you, to make me scream with my climax while the *Captive Fantasy* sailed away."

When he opened his mouth to respond, Cat rubbed his lips with the wet cloth. Black eyes snapped above white fabric, and she knew better than to laugh—but it felt pretty damn fine to shut him up for a moment.

And he was no longer leaning nonchalantly against the wall, was he? Thomas stood directly in front of her now, in kissing position. He rested his hands on her bare hips while she washed his smooth-shaven cheeks.

Cat looked up into those onyx eyes and immediately regretted it. While Thomas Wong might've been a master at controlling his physical reactions, those eyes burned with a dark fire that threatened to consume her in less time than it took to drop the washcloth.

Which she did. Because as he gazed at her, lowering his face to hers, Cat felt that weak-kneed sensation of giving in to him again. The prospect of him kissing her mouth, plundering it as mercilessly—as skillfully—as he'd taken her puss felt like even more of an invasion than having him tongue her while she balanced on the porch railing. His face tightened. His dark hair fell forward over his shoulders, and then over hers like a silken curtain to shut her away from the real world once again.

Even in the shadow created by his jet-black hair, Thomas glowed like hot coals. His fingertips pressed into her hips, branding her with his heat. He stepped against her, rubbing his chest against her breasts . . . sighing when her nipples rasped against his skin. His lush lips parted mere inches above hers, and without thinking she closed her eyes and opened her mouth to receive him.

But he stopped. Stood there in that damning position for more heartbeats than Cat cared to count.

She'd caved. Silently admitted she wanted to kiss him. Thomas had won again, and he was making sure she knew it.

Cat closed her mouth. Made her face a bland mask that matched his.

"Shall we go to breakfast?" he asked quietly.

"Yes, let's." She waited until he stepped away first, and then went into the bedroom. Picked up the sundress on the bed, aware of his gaze on her backside.

"No, my Alina, you'll go downstairs without your clothes. We need to acclimate you to nudity, no matter with whom you find yourself."

Why hadn't she guessed that? The Wongs intended to teach her so much more than she could learn in clothes: after they'd held her hostage for a while, she would exchange her humiliation for humility. Willing surrender.

Right.

She stepped into a crescent-shaped hallway to descend the spiral staircase ahead of him. With each step, Cat saw more of the lower level of the house and was surprised: the tower had seemed *so* much taller when she was perched on the railing, poised above those pointed rocks! From here, the rest of the island stretched away from French doors on the far side of the kitchen. This level, which also housed a large living room that opened onto a porch, told her that the base of the building was much wider than her penthouse prison.

Not that this really mattered, but who knew when such information might be useful? Like, when she escaped.

"Ah, good morning, my pretty!" the man at the stove crooned. When he turned to grin at her, Cat recognized the pirate who'd manhandled Leilani into the johnboat. " 'Come into my parlor,' said the spider to the fly."

More head games. At least this one has some laughter in his voice.

She gazed around a kitchen that would put Martha Stewart's to shame. Pots and utensils gleamed on their ceiling hooks. Everything here was either a burnished shade of stainless steel or shiny black countertop. Silver and black . . . a potently male combination that reminded her again whose turf she was on. "Whatever you're cooking, it smells wonderful."

Charles bowed slightly, still grinning like a kid. But then, why wouldn't he? He had a naked woman walking into his kitchen. A blonde with a shaved pussy, no less—and Thomas said that excited him.

We'll have to keep that in mind, won't we?

Cat sidled over to the stove to stand beside the other Wong brother. He wore a palm-tree-print shirt and white shorts, and as he cooked he swayed to the catchy song playing on a high-tech sound system. His black hair prickled in a longish spike above a band of orange and green print fabric he'd tied around his head like a chic sweat band. He resembled a Navajo porcupine—but a *happy* porcupine—as she peered into his skillet.

Cat inhaled ravenously, ready to fork up the food directly from his pan. "So we're having sausage?" she asked, nodding toward a platter on the warming shelf. "And this luscious stuff is—?"

"Pineapple, papaya, and mango spears sautéed in a reduction of sangria," he said as he removed them to a serving platter. "We have nut-crusted crepes, too. All created especially to welcome *you*, Miss Kitty."

His eyes sparkled with a boyish mischief that made her bite

back a retort about yet another nickname. Of the three Wongs, he was at least pleasant and approachable. She could actually *like* this guy—

And where will that lead? Watch out—you're surrounded by them now.

Arthur Wong, gravely dramatic in a black karate-style shirt and pants, nodded formally at his sons without even glancing at her.

She could play that game, too! Cat returned her attention to chef Charles, who hummed along with that cheerful, syncopated song as he playfully flipped two featherlight crepes about a foot in the air.

"All will soon be ready, angel cakes." He caressed her bare breasts with his gaze as he poured more crepe batter into the hot pans. "Why not watch from over there, where I won't step on your pretty toes? Hoist yourself up on the island! We can chat while I finish."

Thomas had joined his father at the table on the porch, which suited her fine. The island Charles gestured toward was cleared off, but she felt a little funny sitting on it, well, *naked*. "Are you sure you want me to—"

Before she could blink, Charles lifted her to the cool, hard countertop. Then he stood between her legs and wrapped his arms around her.

"Ambrosia for the gods," he murmured. And damned if he didn't suck one of her breasts into his mouth!

As his tongue teased her nipple to rapt attention, his long black lashes brushed her skin. His spiked hair tickled her neck when he leaned into his task. Still humming, he shifted his mouth to give her other breast equal time.

"Your—your crepes are burning!"

"Nah, that's your hot, naked pussy we smell," he rasped. Then, with a breast in his mouth again, he gazed up at her with adoring brown eyes. He let her nipple slowly slip over the tip of his warm, rough tongue. "I hope you'll allow me to serve you breakfast in a very special way, Miss Kitty. I've waited a long time for my turn."

Still gazing raptly at her, he untied his headband and looped it around her eyes in one easy movement. Then he tied it snugly with one snap of his wrists.

"Now!" he exclaimed. "I will serve you, my sweet, while you savor the flavors and textures with heightened senses. Don't be shy about oohing and ahhing over this exquisite meal, Miss Kitty! Your passionate purring will be highest praise to my ears."

What the hell was he up to? She sat too high to scoot down—couldn't see where she'd land—and once again Cat felt caught in a compromising position. Would he tease her with her food while Arthur and Thomas watched from the porch?

"Charles, what are we—"

"Call me Charlie, angel. It's much more *me*." He hummed happily as he placed a plate on the countertop beside her bare butt.

He's cute, yeah, but he's still all Wong for you, she reminded herself.

But when he coaxed her mouth open for a bite of sweet, saucy fruit, how could she protest? The sangria reduction gave the mango a sassiness that made her giggle as she chewed.

"You like?" he murmured.

"I like a lot!" She licked stray sauce from her lips, grinning. "You could wrap some of those fruit spears and a sausage in a crepe and—"

"That would be a delicious thing to do, wouldn't it?" The warmth of his whisper made her nipples peak. "So here you are, Miss Kitty. Purr over this one."

Feeling like a baby bird, Cat eagerly dropped her jaw. She

was rewarded with a bite of spicy sausage wrapped in soft, sweet crepe he'd drizzled with sangria sauce—which dribbled down her chin when she bit into it.

"Mmmmmm!" she rhapsodized. But when her fingers fluttered to her chin, Charlie beat her to it.

"What a lovely morsel you are," he crooned, delicately tonguing the sauce from her chin. "And now I'll sample some more of that mango—oops! It landed on your—"

Cat squirmed and laughed when the warm, sticky fruit splattered on her chest. Charlie was on her in a heartbeat, pressing his lips into her skin, kissing up the sauce.

"Can't let this sausage sit idle," he teased. "Especially since you're simmering up a sauce all your own . . . just for me."

She wasn't surprised when a crepe-wrapped sausage found its way to her slit, but she hadn't expected its soft, spongy texture to feel so velvety when he stroked her with it.

"Spread 'em, Miss Kitty. Gonna make you yowl for it."

She sucked air when the sausage entered her. Cat fell back on her elbows, aware that she was probably setting herself up to be—

Oh, my God, he's fucking me with—that sausage is between his teeth—

She yelped and moved with him, shamelessly meeting his thrusts. Charlie's chuckle came from between her legs, along with the exuberant sound of his chewing. As Cat anticipated what came next, it occurred to her that captivity among these horny Asian men wasn't exactly the worst thing that could happen to her—if she held herself above the slave mindset they expected of her. With a little attitude adjustment, she might come to *enjoy* this iffy situation.

Fabric swished quickly down skin . . . something scooted across the floor . . . and then Charlie gripped her hips to pull her toward him, to the edge of the island's granite top.

Unable to see, Cat struggled. "I—might fall off—"

"Not a chance." He stepped up—onto a stool, she supposed—between her legs and took her hands between his. "Slip this on me, you hot little kitty, and we'll play hide-the-sausage. I'm sure you know how. I bet you break all the rules, too."

He gave her a ring of rolled latex, and then his tip prodded her palm. Cat cleared her throat, amazed—slightly appalled—at how eagerly she sheathed him . . . how willingly she stroked the condom down his hot, solid cock . . . how desperately her insides clenched with wanting him, the first man who'd approached her this way in many a moon.

He wasn't Captain Jack, a man she truly wanted to meet and make love to. But there wasn't a thing she could do about that, was there?

Maybe she'd earn points for compliance—convince the Wongs she was becoming their slave—if she leaned back slowly along the length of the island, displayed herself as a feast for Charlie's avid eyes, still grasping the cock that throbbed in her hand. A platter fell to the tile floor and shattered, but he didn't seem to notice.

"Yeah, baby," he murmured as he positioned himself on top of her. "Wrap those long, perfect legs around me and let's do some *cookin'*."

When he slid slowly inside her, Cat couldn't stifle a moan of pure pleasure: Charlie filled her tight-full. For a long, lovely moment he held still within her, catching his breath.

"Squeeze it," he breathed against her ear. "Milk it out of me, sweet thing." He slid in and out . . . in and out, balancing his weight on his elbows . . . moving with exquisite precision against her clit.

This may be all Wong, but he sure as hell's hot for—Jesus, I'm gonna rush too fast and finish before—

"I can't hold it any longer," he rasped. With a grunt he surged into her, driving them both to the brink. Cat wished she could watch his face pass beyond cuteness into a tight, intense need—a need that ripped into her from out of nowhere and made her rock up to meet his thrusts, high and hard and fast.

With a strangled gasp, Charlie buried himself. Cat triumphantly wrapped her legs around him and ground against him until she, too, writhed in mindless release.

For a few breathless moments they lay in each other's damp heat. Then Charlie shifted off her, sighing blissfully. "We're off to a lovely start, Miss Kitty. Can't wait until our next cooking session." He grasped her hands to help her sit up.

Cat straightened. Found the edge of the island with the undersides of her knees. Let her head settle. On impulse, she reached back to untie the blindfold—

Her hands got slapped! And when the cloth was yanked off her head, she faced Arthur Wong. He stood a foot away. His face resembled cold stone the color of browned butter.

"Foolish *slut*," he muttered calmly. "How dare you partake of my food and seduce both of my sons without first apologizing for offending me? For insulting me with your high-toned arrogance."

She knew better, but she scowled at him anyway. "Wait just a damn minute! Neither of your sons can honestly say I seduced—"

"My sons know their place. They will say nothing that contradicts my opinion." Wong crossed his arms, looking ready to begin a martial arts demonstration.

Indeed, Thomas stood with his shoulder against the doorjamb, following this exchange with an otherworldly detachment while Charlie swept up the shards of china and breakfast that had landed on the floor. Easy to see that neither of them would come to her defense; easy to assume they'd set her up for this little scenario so Papa Wong could play Lord and Master over her.

Cat took her cue from them: she returned Arthur's gaze but

remained silent. Not being obedient but obstinate, forcing him to deal with her.

"I have contacted Captain Spankevopoulos and Ramon, informing them that you are well—and worth a spectacular ransom," Wong informed her. His lips quirked. "The fact that neither of them has responded tells me your fate means *nothing* to them. That you are *worthless* in their eyes, even though both men have access to accounts that make my demands seem a pittance in comparison. Don't they, Miss Gamble?"

Cat clenched her jaw to keep from wincing. How did she know he'd even contacted them? It could be another head game—a tactic designed to demoralize her. To shove her one step closer to submission.

So she folded her arms. Imitated his stance, mute and unmoving.

"Since money will not be forthcoming, I have no choice but to train you for slavery with the highest bidder. Not always a pleasant situation, like you have here," he added with a slight rise of an eyebrow. "Once you've been bought and paid for, I have no control over how your new owner will treat you. Do you have any last words? Any questions?"

Like they would do me any good, she thought, her face mirroring Wong's cool detachment.

"Very well, then." He turned to his older son, Thomas. "It's time she met Ebonique."

14

As they blindfolded her and tied her hands behind her, Cat stifled a sigh. This was *so* like a bad movie script! So bizarre it seemed unbelievable.

And yet . . . Ramon and that airline steward had mentioned pirates on these seas, and Trevor had tried to protect her from those who'd steal her computer. So here they were. In a business suit, Arthur Wong would pass for a Fortune 500 executive—and probably had the smarts to perform at that level. Charles was a trained chef, and Thomas could be broadcasting his New Age enlightenment to a radio following of millions. So why were they pirates?

Yo, ho, ho! It's a pirate's life for me! sang in her mind, but it lacked the luster Captain Jack Sparrow displayed on the big screen—and the riot Jack Spankevopoulos had incited inside her during their call. She should be lolling on soft, rumpled sheets right now . . . probably red satin ones . . . maybe while tied to Captain Spank's bedpost as he had his way with her.

But no, Thomas was escorting her across the porch and down a path of smooth paving stones. He'd slung his arm around her shoulders, and probably enjoyed the way her boobs bounced out in front of her because her arms were pulled back.

So much for that magical mystical guru shit, she mused. *He delivered you into the hands of Number Two Son so you could dig yourself a deeper hole. Fine mess you're in here . . . and where's Spike been while all this happened?*

"Step carefully onto the golf cart." Thomas's low voice cut into her thoughts. "It's a short ride to the training compound, but I could be persuaded to take a lengthier route, should you care to discuss alternatives."

Her mouth quirked. "Like I believe that, after the way you and Charlie served me up on a platter."

"Had you not taken matters into your own hands—"

"Your cock, you mean?"

"—we would have progressed down a harmonious path toward your enlightenment," he went on in an unruffled tone. "I hope you've learned the futility—the foolishness—of assuming control, sweet Alina."

"Get real," she muttered. Then she turned her face toward him more pensively. "I *would* like to know that Leilani is safe, however."

"All things will be revealed in their time, my turtle dove—or at Ebonique's whim, anyway," he added with a chuckle. "I hope you've learned the consequences of lust and arrogance and insisting on your own way, because Mistress Ebonique will set you straight, where proper behavior and mindset are concerned. Far more demanding than Father, she is."

"Why does that name conjure up images of black leather and whips?" Cat murmured. The sea breeze teased her, and on her right she heard the waves breaking and flowing along the shore. What a beautiful morning for a ride on the beach—under any circumstances but these.

A few moments later, Thomas brought the cart to a jerky halt. When he came around to guide her, she winced at the way her bare ass stuck to the leather seat and made a gross sound as she peeled herself away from it.

That, however, was nothing compared to walking barefoot across small, jagged pebbles and then through a doorway, where the pungency of incense nearly overpowered her. The room felt cavernous yet stuffy. Crying and whimpers of desperation drifted to her from a distance, yet she sensed those who suffered were in this large room.

Was this the low building she'd seen from her window? It seemed to fit the feel of "slave compound," and as a tattoo of steady, powerful footsteps approached, Cat feared her fate had indeed taken a turn for the worse.

"Good morning, Thomas," came a throaty voice she couldn't place as male or female. "And who have we here?"

"This is Catalina Gamble, the specimen we picked up off the beach—"

Specimen? He's making you out to be bird shit, sugah!

Thanks so much, Spike. What're you going to do about it?

"—last night when we acquired her housekeeper, Leilani, as well," Thomas said. His fingers found the knot of her blindfold, although he took his time, fondling her hair as he loosened the ties. "And how is Leilani progressing? Alina is most interested in her welfare."

Cat heard a derisive snort as the band was whipped off her head.

"Leilani was so belligerent and combative we tranquilized her," came the gruff response. "She's in solitary confinement in a windowless cell, so she can ponder her displays of aggression and realign her attitude, once the drugs have worn off. Because—"

A slap on her cheek made Cat open her eyes and gasp.

"—*I*, Ebonique, am the only one entitled to an attitude here. Understand that, missy?"

Cat blinked back startled tears. The Amazon before her

stood so tall that her breasts, upheld by an elaborate bustier of black leather laces and metal grommets, protruded into Cat's face. Ebonique's body radiated a disciplined physical strength that warned of dire consequences for smarting off to *this* woman . . . this ebony-skinned vixen with the voice that didn't seem to fit.

"And what're *you* staring at?" Ebonique challenged in that low, reedy tone. "Your punishment and training will bring me many hours of pleasure, Miss Puss. For starters, you will greet me as your mistress."

Cat studied the no-jiggle waistline with its pierced navel exposed below the black contraption Ebonique wore on top, as well as the long muscular legs extending from a steel-studded G-string. Thigh-high black boots with lots of studs, along with black leather gloves flaring wickedly at her wrists, completed the ensemble. Ebonique's jet hair swirled in tight ringlets around her head, looking almost alluring—until she stared Cat down with python eyes ringed in black mascara. A cobra, poised to strike, was tattooed on one sleek, brown shoulder.

Cat knew better than to laugh or ask where her whip was: despite Ebonique's interesting costume, this was no Halloween party.

"Good morning, Mistress Ebonique," she purred. After all, with her hands bound, her breasts remained the most prominent—and vulnerable—part of her naked anatomy. No sense in getting them slapped before this introduction was complete.

Thomas bowed. "I'll leave you ladies to get better acquainted," he said, gazing steadily at Cat. "Perhaps, if I hear good reports, a reprieve can be arranged, sweet Alina. It will be my pleasure to continue your soul's instruction in the tower penthouse."

"But don't count it!" Ebonique's reedy laughter echoed in the cavernous room. "You're at the point of no return, missy. Our slaves leave this compound only because they've been bought and paid for. So say good-bye to the outside world and your cushy private island life, Miss Gamble! Here, there be monsters!"

As Thomas left, Cat almost called after him. Might've gone down on her knees and groveled—or given him a very convincing blow job—if she thought it would change his mind. But Thomas Wong, Eminent Luminary, followed his own enlightened path. He would insist she stay here to clear up her cluttered karma with Mistress Discipline.

So Cat stood quietly, awaiting her orders. She endured the suggestive, leathered stroke of Ebonique's single finger as the dominatrix drew it along Cat's cheek . . . down her neck . . . across her clavicle to dip and circle each quivering breast.

She hated it that her nipples poked out. Despised it even more when Ebonique stepped behind her to fondle the curves of her ass.

"Grab your ankles."

Cat's eyes widened. Yet another line reminiscent of some old decadent film about—and couldn't Ebonique see her hands were tied behind her?

"You deaf?" the bitch barked. "I told you to assume the position! It's time for your first lesson about who's the predator and who's the prey."

No point in telling her she'd learned that three times over in the Wong household, was there? Cautiously, because she couldn't balance with her arms, Cat placed her feet shoulder-width apart and slowly leaned over.

"Farther! Kiss your knee!"

Closing her eyes, knowing damn well Ebonique was staring at her exposed slit, Cat folded herself down over her shaking legs.

"Pussy!" the slave mistress taunted. "You're the poorest excuse for a bimbo I've ever seen! Got the blond hair—got the flawless skin—got the Brazilian wax job—and all the personality of a cardboard box. Well, we're about to fix that! We're about to make you scream for it, Kitty."

Cat gasped as a rude leather finger poked inside her.

Ebonique chortled, removing the finger quickly—but re-placing it with two. "You like that, don't you? What a slut!"

Then it was three fingers, which bore *no* resemblance to the Scout's Honor sign Cat had learned as a girl. She suddenly had to pee—badly. That trio of stiff leather fingers rotated with enough pressure to make her stumble forward.

So she thrust back to keep her balance, knowing she'd again compromised herself. Hot liquid was dribbling down her legs. Despite the humiliating welcome this bitch was giving her, Cat was panting . . . inhaling with shallow, needy gasps.

Ebonique withdrew her fingers and placed her damp hand on Cat's back. "Squat! Relieve yourself on the floor!" she or-dered with a shove. Then she looked toward the far recesses of the hazy room. "Celina! Baptiste! Come here and clean up this mess!"

Mortified, Cat froze in her awkward position. Every nerve tightened with the effort of not pissing this way. Surely there was a bathroom—

"Go now, or hold it for a long, loooong time—and be en-tered in tonight's golden showers competition!" that reedy voice challenged at her ear. "Let me help you, Miss Persnick-ety."

A loud *smack* made Cat cry out. Her ass stung as though she'd have a red mark in the shape of a hand for several days, and just as two hollow-eyed waifs arrived with rags, she let loose. Her face flushed a dozen shades of red when Celina and Baptiste, a tormented-looking young pair of perhaps sixteen, watched the puddle flowing around her bare feet.

"They're enjoying the show," Ebonique said with a snicker. "Probably because we don't see many blondes on this island."

I'm sure that's the reason, she retorted in her mind.

"Is that *all*? Surely you can give a better performance than that!" Ebonique reached around her to press her hands into Cat's abdomen—and then gyrated against her bare hips with that studded G-string.

Whimpering, Cat gushed another thin stream.

"All right, show's over," Ebonique proclaimed. "And because you've already made a mess someone else has to clean up, Miss Gamble, well, we'll have to find a suitable means of atonement, won't we?"

15

When the door locked behind her, it sounded like the closing of a casket. Cat sensed she wouldn't stay closeted long, however: Ebonique was already devising other torments designed to humiliate her. And that required an audience.

Slaves. The moans and whimpers she'd heard from the hazy end of that huge room came from others who'd been snatched; who wondered what they'd done to deserve such a fate.

I do not deserve this! If Arthur Wong thinks he's prepping me for some warped sort of buyer, he can go fuck himself!

That's the spirit, kid! Spike cheered. *Resist their lies while I work on them from other angles. You will get out of this mess!*

Cat smiled in the darkness. Her butt still tingled from that smack, but she was past that now, wasn't she? Being closed up in this cell wasn't much different from her ordeal when Laird abandoned her to his creditors, was it?

It felt more peaceful, in fact. And now that she had a chance to *think*, away from the Wongs, she might find a way out of this quandary.

Cat let her eyes adjust to the thick dimness. She touched

walls on either side of her, and as she stepped in a slow circle she scraped the dry roughness of unpainted wood. Her bare feet felt nothing slimy or crawly on the floor. As long as she didn't think of it as an oversized coffin, she might get some rest here!

She inhaled the silence and solitude. Then she noticed a small shelf, about shoulder level, where objects were labeled with little signs.

EAT ME, the first packet said, and the bottle beside it said DRINK ME.

Her jaw dropped. Wasn't this straight out of *Alice's Adventures in Wonderland*?

Cat snickered as she put the items back on the shelf. Naive Alice might've followed such instructions, but she wasn't falling for them! She knew how Alice felt, though, being ordered to do something and then suffering the consequences— only to meet up with the *next* quirky antagonist.

"Mad Hatters and Black Queens," she mused aloud. "Plenty of those on this island."

Then she gazed around in the darkness. Microphones might be catching her remarks, so she could incriminate herself further when Ebonique returned.

Silently Cat looked at the remaining items on the shelf: LIGHT ME, said a stick that resembled incense, and SNIFF ME was written on a vial with a screw top, but she wasn't that desperate for entertainment yet. These objects would probably put her in a delusional state—and who knew what Ebonique might try then?

On the wall nearby, a small sign said SLIDE ME. It had a peg for a handle.

Did she really want to see what was behind Door Number One?

Cat lowered herself to the floor by sliding down the rough wall. She closed her eyes and sat cross-legged. If she let her thoughts wander while she regrouped mentally, chances were good she'd come up with an escape plan. Her best writing ideas always came to her that way.

And think of all the adventures you can write about when you get out of here! This is how Destiny—also known as Spike—has provided you with ideas you could never dream up yourself!

Cat blinked. Were those voices coming from the other side of the wall? Other hostages, perhaps?

Pressing her ear to the wood, she listened intently. Sighs of pleasure rather than pain . . . and damn, that had to be skin slapping against wet skin!

Were a couple of prisoners going at it in the next cell? She nipped her lip, eagerly assessing each rise in pitch, each suggestive murmur. Once such eavesdropping had seemed beneath her, but she'd learned a lot about herself since she won the Powerball jackpot, hadn't she?

A few minutes later she rose slowly from the floor. The sliding section felt about eight inches wide and three inches high, and would make a peephole the size of a brick.

Do you really want to do this? her thoughts warned when she gripped the peg. *If you suspect all these other goodies are tricks and traps, why wouldn't this be one, too?*

She'd learned to trust this still, small voice of intuition over the years: Cat sensed this potential opening was just one more way to get herself into a bind so Ebonique could humiliate her further.

She heard the voices more distinctly then . . . definitely a male and a female. Definitely doing the deed on the other side of her cell.

"Yes . . . yes, Valenzia, you know precisely how to please me!"

Cat froze. How many people named Valenzia could there be in this part of the Caribbean? What if the previous owner of

Porto Di Angelo had *not* wandered off but had actually been snatched by—

"Arthur, you sly dog! That is *not* your finger!"

Cat's mouth dropped open. Arthur Wong knew way too much about her accounts and who should be looking for her, so *this* was too good to resist! Was she really about to discover the missing Contessa's biggest secret? Perhaps see firsthand how Arthur Wong treated the women he kept on his island?

She slowly slid the panel sideways, hoping it didn't set off an alarm. Cat covered her mouth to keep from crying out: the next room was small yet elegantly appointed, festooned with beautiful silk in a paisley print of deep jewel tones. Huge velvet pillows dotted the merlot-colored carpet.

Looks like a sheik's harem, she marveled—although Arthur Wong, naked, did not call forth those bold, manly images of Rudolph Valentino or Omar Sharif she'd ogled on the big screen. But he was in command of the room and of the gorgeous woman who hugged one of those floor pillows so her pert, pretty ass pointed at him in invitation. She wore a laced ivory blouse, like a gypsy fortune teller, and her flowing print skirts were tossed up over her back for Wong's viewing pleasure.

By the looks of his erection, Valenzia pleased him a *lot*.

Her angular face radiated lust and a sly feline confidence Cat admired; this woman, slave or not, wasn't one bit afraid of the pirate she played with. Her dark, flowing hair set off an olive complexion highlighted with just enough rouge and eyeliner that she looked slutty . . . and damn proud of it. A starburst of silver hair above her left brow gave her the distinctive air of a high-class courtesan. The longer Cat gazed at Valenzia, the more she knew the Contessa was here because she *wanted* to be.

How incredible was that? Had she really left an island, a fine home, and her two loyal caretakers behind for *this*?

Does she know Leilani is here?

Cat stifled the impulse to blurt out this question, because Valenzia was busy obeying Arthur Wong.

"Roll over, so your back is arched up over the cushion," he ordered in a husky voice. "Spread your legs like the whore you are, so I can give you the fucking you so richly deserve, Contessa."

Cat covered a cough. Wong addressed Valenzia as nobility, yet he demeaned her as a whore! Ordered her around as though she were a mere—

Slave.

She pondered this revelation carefully. Did he still plan to sell the Contessa, after all this time? Had Ramon and Leilani refused to pay her ransom—or had he even demanded such money? Or was it a mistake to believe what her caretakers had told her about the Contessa's disappearance?

Or . . . was she second-guessing what Arthur Wong the pirate *said*, when he looked so much like Arthur Wong, a successful technological entrepreneur? She was so accustomed to creating characters, her imagination might've filled in the wrong blanks about him.

Valenzia's response made her eyes widen.

"Ha! You think to bully *me*, little man? Do you forget who I am—you with your cock come a-begging?" Valenzia plopped onto the cushion then, her breasts bobbing out of the blouse's laced opening. "Come here and order me around to my face! I'll show you exactly where to stick that little dick! Why, it's so skinny I should light it up and smoke it!"

Wong's expression took on a desperate intensity. Prick in the lead, he approached Valenzia's lush, lounging body like a man entranced—as though it took his utmost restraint not to fall all over her and kiss every inch of her lovely skin.

"Is that *all*?" she mocked, swatting at his cock. "Why, that tiny thing will get lost in my crack, and we'll never find it again! You can't tell me you *come* with that?"

Wong's legs quivered. Cat felt his anxiety rising . . . sensed his trepidation and humiliation as the Contessa glared at his erection—which looked about average, from her vantage point. His body was slender and smoothly muscled and hairless: Wong wouldn't stop traffic with his looks, yet he commanded an island and a yacht with a power that refused to be denied.

"Pray, Miss Borgia, spare me your disappointment," he pleaded. "All I have ever wanted was your unconditional love. Your overwhelming approval. What must I do to earn it?"

Now *that* was a new wrinkle! Cat leaned against her cell wall, peering unabashedly through the peephole to catch every nuance of this lovers' exchange. Who could've guessed Arthur Wong would switch so rapidly from being the ruler of a slave empire to a humble slave himself? A *woman's* slave, no less!

"You go, girlfriend!" Cat murmured as Valenzia arched an eyebrow and beckoned him closer. "Get in a lick or two for me!"

"I suppose you want me to lick your lollipop?" the Contessa taunted. "Suck the cum out of that little hole as though I'm sipping through a straw?"

Wong nodded desperately as he offered his cock to her with an air of a penitent at confession. He was standing in profile now, so Cat saw every gesture quite clearly.

"I think you're being very impertinent, Arthur. First you call me a whore and now you're pleading for sexual favors!" Valenzia jeered. "I might have to *spank* you. To clarify who rules and who will be the servant of all."

Cat clenched her fists in anticipation. This was getting *good*!

"Assume the position, Arthur. You know the drill."

To Cat's amazement, Wong turned his tush to her and then leaned over to grab his ankles. It was a side of this bully she'd never expected to see—and who knew what might come next?

"How many shall we start with?" Valenzia asked slyly. She

rose slowly from the floor pillow; took several moments to straighten her skirts and blouse and smooth her hair, while Wong remained bent over. Then she rubbed the spot she intended to whack, to be sure not a single hair or fleck of loose skin came between her palm and his ass.

Arthur sucked in a nervous breath. "I—I probably deserve at least four or five swats—"

SMACK! SMACK! came the Contessa's crisp response. She raised her hand again but then paused coyly.

"You know, you're such a worm I'm not sure you're worth the effort, Arthur. The way my hand stings after I—"

"Oh, please—don't stop! Don't *stop!*" he wheedled. "Use your shoe, or—your hairbrush! If you don't punish me enough for slighting you, you know I'll do it again—and again!—until you spank me so hard I have to come."

Cat blinked. While she realized the spanking thing had a huge following, she'd never seen the fascination. Had never considered it sexy to get her ass smacked by someone who presumed to control her. It brought to mind times when her dad had paddled her, and sexually that was one big *ewwwwww*.

But seeing a *man* beg for punishment . . . watching him not only submit but plead for more, until he lost control of himself . . . well, this put a whole new spin on spanking! It put the woman in control, and that appealed to Cat immensely—even though it would take a major renovation of her sexual repertoire to carry it off with the Contessa's aplomb.

SMACK! SMACK! Valenzia's face radiated sheer glee but something else, as well. Satisfaction, it was! A sense that she was giving Arthur what he had coming—what really was in his best interest.

"Almost there," he rasped. "Please, Valenzia, I've been a *very* bad boy, calling you a whore and then telling you I was going to fuck you senseless when—"

He can't get off any other way. Oh, my God. Wong's admitting he couldn't have penetrated her—for whatever reason—and needs to be spanked and put in his place before he can—

SMACK!

With a low groan, Wong grabbed himself and began to pump. Valenzia, obviously a longtime player in this game, plopped back onto the huge velvet cushion and whipped her skirts up. As she spread her legs, Wong turned to gaze intently at her slit: she made a vee with her fingers to raise the patch of black hair so her dusky pink cunt opened, fully exposed to him.

"If you don't screw me till I scream, I'll to have to spank you again, Arthur!" she challenged in a raspy voice. "How very rude, to satisfy yourself and leave me in the lurch!"

As he stroked himself into a frenzy, Wong stared mindlessly at her fingers, which strummed her inner lips and clit.

"If I have to bring myself off, you'll be a very sorry man, Arthur," she went on in an edgy voice. "Look at you! Hard as a gun barrel—ready to shoot! Yet you're too selfish and pigheaded to shove that cock up my—"

Arthur lunged, landing between Valenzia's open legs with such force they nearly teetered off the pillow.

The Contessa curled inward to meet him. As her hips met his every thrust, she let out a feline hiss of victory. "Now!" she yelped. "Shoot your hot cum into my cunt! Take me harder! Harder!"

Wong writhed like a madman, and as his grimace became so tight Cat had to look away, his cry filled the room. It was a low, guttural moan that made her insides tingle with need—a need that shamed yet fascinated her. How low had she sunk—again!—that she got hot from watching such a scene?

She shut the trap door and turned away from what she'd just witnessed. Pulse pounding, Cat slid down the wall to sit on the floor with her arms wrapped around her bent bare legs. Even in the dimness of the tiny cell, the lurid images played out again and again in her mind, like a really raunchy X-rated film.

Maybe I should've done the eat me or sniff me and left that slide me thing alone. If Wong had any clue I was watching him—

As though on cue, the peephole slid open above her head.

"You really love to be punished and humiliated, don't you, Miss Gamble?" Arthur's voice sounded raspy from his exertions.

How should she answer that? No matter what she said, this maddening Asian would twist her words to his own purpose. Cat pressed her forehead to her knees, waiting for the other shoe to drop.

The cell door flew open, and in stepped Valenzia Borgia. Her presence filled the small cell: her flounced skirts tickled Cat's calves, and from the floor she looked very tall—*statuesque* was the better word. Her lush breasts bobbed beneath her flowing ivory blouse as she held the trap door shut, laughing at her lover's protests from the other side.

"So—how do you like my island, Catalina?" she purred. "I'm so pleased to make your acquaintance! I'm Valenzia Borgia, by the way. The Contessa, they call me."

"Yes, I—"

—began eavesdropping like a lowlife voyeur when I heard your name—

"—I'm pleased to meet you, too," Cat said in a hurried whisper. "In the short time I've spent there, I've come to *love* Porto Di Angelo! But why are you *here*? Leilani and Ramon believed you left of your own free will—"

"Something like that," Valenzia cut in mysteriously. Her glance flickered to the peephole, as warning Cat they had little time to chat. "I have indeed made my home here now. What is it about a pirate a woman just can't resist?"

Cat's eyes widened. "But why—what on earth do you see in—"

"Arthur?" The Contessa chuckled slyly. "Ours is a strange and wonderful love affair, dear. He's strange, and I'm wonderful! He makes me feel *needed*, and I fulfill him in ways no other woman can. Life without passion is . . . truly unforgivable."

Where had *that* answer come from? "But—they kidnapped Leilani, too! I haven't seen her since—"

"*So* sorry to interrupt," Wong snapped as he swung open the door, "but it seems Miss Gamble can't behave herself even in solitary confinement. Perhaps, since you found our love games so fascinating to watch, *you* would like to be on display, as well."

He pulled the Contessa from the small cell so he could step inside. The flowing silk of Arthur's black robe whispered against his legs as he leaned down to put his face level with Cat's. "Since you Americans insist on fair treatment and the democratic way, I'll give you a choice, Miss Gamble: you may stay here in the slave compound, at Ebonique's mercy, or you may take your chances on what *I* have in mind."

Like that's really a choice.

Cat kept her expression carefully composed as she considered these options: Wong had *misery* in mind for her, no matter what she decided. She recalled the aura of anguish in that huge room she'd first entered . . . the moans of countless hostages, and the haze that smelled like more than incense.

Coyly, she extended her arm for help up from the floor. "Your wish is my command, Mr. Wong," she murmured. "If I'm to be a captive, I might as well bow to the higher power."

16

In his crow's-nest office high above the deck of the *Captive Fantasy*, Jack Spankevopoulos frowned at his computer screen. All damn day he'd been dogged by the sensation that Cat Gamble was hidden in plain sight—the pawn in an unfortunate game where his opponent ducked around the edges of his awareness but refused to show himself. Here it was again, the same ransom note he'd received in the wee hours when he'd been too worried about her to sleep:

> We have your Cat, Captain Jack! And such a pretty puss she is, too! Deposit a mere $100K in the PayPal account below, and maybe we'll give you a peek at her.

Jack picked up his walkie-talkie. "Stavros, have you got a minute?"

A burst of static faded to the sounds of dinner being prepared in the ship's stainless steel galley. "Yo, boss. Better come on down for your steak and lobster. Surf and turf like only I can prepare it!"

"There's something on Cat Gamble you need to see. Whenever you can get away—"

"Like *now*, right? So you can stop pacing and get some sleep? Be right up, cuz. Hey, Lorenzo! Gustaf!" he hollered to his sous chefs. "You're on, guys!"

Thoughts of steak and lobster, his favorite temptation during these cruises, hung heavily in his gut until nimble footsteps ascended the cross-board ladder to his inner sanctum.

Stavros stepped in, his mustachioed grin subdued. "You found her?"

"Well, she's out there and she's got a price on her head—just as I figured," Jack grunted, gesturing at the message on his monitor. "But I tried to trace this PayPal account earlier—"

"Meaning, you've seen this ransom note before?" Stavros angled an eyebrow at him. "What is it with you, cuz? Riding in like the Lone Ranger instead of asking Tonto to translate the smoke signals? Lemme sit down."

Sighing, Jack relinquished his chair. He stretched stiffly, startled that the sunset scorched the horizon and had set the sea on fire. Last he knew, the afternoon limbo contest had been in full swing. . . . His cousin's rapid-fire typing was a song he couldn't dance to. The moon's golden glow made him think about what he'd hoped to be doing with the gorgeous Ms. Gamble by now. . . .

"You figured right, Jack. There's no way to access owner names or banks or any other connection to this PayPal account."

"So no guarantee that if I make that deposit, we'll really see her. Damned if we do, and damned if we don't."

"Notified Kurt and Rick about this? Maybe the IMB's got some fake accounts set up to handle ransom situations."

He grunted. "Pirates who play this kind of game can fly under the virtual radar with dummy corporations and untraceable phones and e-mails. Unfortunately, Cat's J2 phone and computer sites were set up the same way—not that I believe for a moment they'd let her have access to them."

Stavros scratched the stubble on his narrow chin, which to Jack looked scraggly, but it acted as a chick magnet. "Are you sure she *has* her phone and laptop? Most women waiting on the beach to be kidnapped wouldn't—"

"Women don't leave their cells behind for *anything*. And because Cat's a writer, she would've had her computer along. I just know it." He let out another disgusted sigh and reached for his own phone. "Let's see if Ramon has heard anything."

Jack tapped in the number and listened to the first ring . . . the second ring . . . wondering if that tall, dark, and intimidating caretaker had gone looking for his woman. He was mentally composing a voice mail when he heard Ramon's low, intense hello.

"Captain Jack here, wondering if you've heard anything from Leilani or Cat? . . . Sounds like the same message I received, and I'm thinking that PayPal deposit they've demanded is just another form of piracy . . . .Rick and Kurt have nothing new to report, either?"

He wished Ramon didn't sound so secretive. Wished for an ingenious way to cut through this invisible wall of technological protection. "Did she take her laptop to the beach with her? . . . Yes, I thought as much. Well, I'll keep you posted if I hear anything new. Thank you so much, Ramon."

He clapped his phone shut. It sounded a lot like the snapping of his last nerve. "And thank you, Stavros, for sharing your expertise when you should've been cooking. Carry on."

"There's a kiss-off if I ever heard one," the slender man in kitchen whites teased. "I'll keep the best steak and lobster tails back for you. Better get 'em while they're hot."

Jack nodded wearily. He waited until his first mate was halfway down the ladder and then clicked REPLY on that damn ransom note.

You'll see your $100K when I see Ms. Gamble alive. Even exchange, to be made in person, he tapped rapidly. Just you and me—no police. Name your time and island.

He sent the message and then gazed at her lovely smile on his monitor. Would he ever see her again?

Miles away in St. Louis, Trevor Teague scowled at his screen. While he expected the address messages from Cat's security software to change global positions when she did, he didn't like it one bit that he hadn't received anything in a couple of days.

"She's on that pirate ship, remember?" Grant Carey said from over his shoulder. "After all the shit she went through with Laird's death, I'm glad she's having too good a time to contact us."

"It doesn't feel right." Trev clicked the URL for the *Captive Fantasy*'s Web site. Together they watched the waving sails unfurl on the screen, along with the photo of those two costumed pirates.

"From all I've checked, Captain Jack looks legit," Grant remarked, although his voice betrayed some concern. "His sailing papers and licenses are in order. He's a member of umpteen cruise line associations—and not a one has registered a complaint. And didn't you tell us her software would send messages if her laptop was taken?"

"She has to report it stolen before the software company sounds the alarm." Trevor shrugged, scowling again. "Which tells me she either didn't take her computer along—and I don't believe that for a minute—or she went to this last location in the log and hasn't gone on-line since. I find that odd, because she's been so quick to inform us of her discoveries and adventures."

"Envious because she's found herself a professional pirate to play with?" Grant flashed him a rueful grin. "It isn't the same around here without her, is it?"

"Got *that* right. Even when she was down and out, leaning on all of us, she had a radiance."

"A gentle presence that made me glad you took her in."

"More than a client, was she?" Teague clicked out of his mail program with a sigh. "Maybe you should call her—if only to see that her box of books got there. If she doesn't answer, we'll figure she's having way too much fun—"

"No, Trev, you'll go on assuming something awful has befallen her." Carey squeezed his shoulders, working it into a firm massage . . . firmer than usual, because, yeah, he was seeing red flags, too. "Cat's a grown woman with a mind of her own. Maybe not one to share her sexual adventures, now that she's having them."

When the attorney picked up his phone, however, Trevor noted with unspoken satisfaction that he had Cat's J2 number on speed dial . . . was listening intently as the rings went by. . . .

"Cat, dear, it's Grant," he said in his smoothest courtroom voice. "Just checking to see if your three boxes of books arrived at your mail drop. . . . Hoping you're having a splendid time with your dashing new pirate! Trev and Bruce send hugs and hellos. Let us hear from you soon, so we know how the *real* buccaneers do it!"

Carey folded his phone into the pocket of his dress shirt. He arched his thick eyebrows. "Satisfied?"

"No. But you gave her a compelling reason to reply, without sounding like a mother hen." He rose from his desk chair in the loft office he'd reclaimed after Cat left. The leather still smelled of her . . . Images in his mind of her romping naked in bed with the shorter, stockier guy in that Web-site photo had their way with him.

"Think I'll buckle on my sword," he remarked huskily.

"Think I'll see if Bruce is up for a sail aboard our *Black Pearl*. Care to play captain this time, Grant?"

Arthur Wong smiled as he closed her phone and then locked it back into his desk. "Your friends Trev and Bruce send their love. And Grant wonders if you received your boxes of books," he added archly. "Too bad you can't reply. I detected a tone of concern beneath his casual inquiry."

Cat narrowed her eyes at the slender Asian. It became more difficult with each day not to show her frustration. She held on to the faint hope that Arthur had been hazing her when he claimed they'd disabled her theft-detection software: why would they have reason to mess with her laptop anyway? She'd spotted computers in the kitchen, and here, and in this small office, and in the slave compound when Ebonique escorted her to solitary confinement—and the units were far more sophisticated than hers.

She suspected her computer was hidden in this odd office, which, with its mismatched furnishings and walls of different colors, looked like anything but a business center. It would take a minor miracle to get her hands on her Mac, much less send Grant a reply. These Wongs watched her like hawks.

"I'll assure you—again—that we've disabled your theft-detection software, Miss Gamble," her captor said coolly. "Until we see a deposit from Captain Jack or your island caretaker, you won't need that laptop anyway. The only messages you'll heed will be mine."

Her fingernails itched to tear into his face, but Cat mimicked the unruffled superiority beneath Wong's taunts. Should she believe even half of what this man said? And which half would that be? It was good that Grant and Trevor were getting suspicious, however—even if they were thousands of miles away. Even if the software Trev had installed was useless now.

"What have you done with Leilani?" she blurted.

Wong's mouth flickered. "She's in good hands—"

"Ebonique's?" Cat let out an unladylike snort.

"—although we've had to sedate her. To control her violent outbursts after she awoke in the slave compound."

Like I believe that! Cat turned away from him. She suspected they'd drugged her housekeeper when they learned of Leilani's psychic powers. No way would they let her contact Ramon via her brain vibrations to guide him here.

Did the Contessa know where Leilani was kept? Would she have shared this knowledge if Arthur hadn't interrupted their brief chat—or kept her mouth shut as part of this bondage situation? Cat tended to believe Valenzia Borgia would pander to Arthur Wong's wishes, no matter how strong the bond she'd shared with her caretakers. She had too much to lose if Wong suspected duplicity.

Cat glanced at Warden Wong, thinking he'd be almost attractive if he weren't such a jerk . . . and if she hadn't witnessed his spanking fetish. Today he'd brought her to this small room at the back of the house. The poor paint job suggested murals or symbols had been covered over, and the two windows were an intricate stained-glass pattern. A bed with a puffy quilted comforter protruded from a small alcove where an altar might've been—although this felt like anything but a bedroom or a chapel. Too many lights with pale umbrella-style shades on the ceiling—

Like a photographer's studio.

Cat blinked. Wong had opened a louvered door near the bed, to wheel out video cams, plus equipment like she'd seen in a radio station, for recording and mixing sound.

"Yes, this is what you think it is!" Arthur chirped as he adjusted the tripods. "I had the brilliant idea to capitalize on your love of *watching*, Miss Gamble. We'll film you playing sexual games and then send out Web cam samples to prospective buyers to drive their bids higher. I should've thought of this before!"

She closed her eyes to keep from rolling them. A man who sold slaves in this Internet era probably filmed every woman he put on the auction block. How else would he tantalize buyers without inviting them to the island—which increased the chance of port authorities tracking the transaction?

Cat turned to look out the single clear window, a porthole that faced the Caribbean Sea. As a large yacht cruised by at a leisurely speed, she saw passengers on the sundeck working on their all-over tans. . . . A handsome young stud muffin delivered drinks and snacks to the captain and his chesty companion. *She* could be enjoying such amenities right now, if the Wong pirates hadn't grabbed her first.

And yet, Valenzia Borgia had given up a stunning island home to stay on with this warped Asian egomaniac and his sons. Or that was her story, anyway.

"Yes, Miss Gamble, I'm going to make you a star!" Arthur nattered. "Attractive as you are, why, your new master could rake in millions making porn films! That'll be my hook when I write the remarks that accompany this Web cast."

His arrogance curled her lip, but she camouflaged it with a benign smile; she stood taller and thrust out her breasts to prove she wasn't bested yet. Not by a long shot! She, Catalina Gamble, hadn't survived those long, awful days after Laird's death without cranking up her actress persona with a panache that kept his creditors off-balance—and kept her sane. She could do it again, even without clothes.

It was a head game—one she'd played on herself. And it would work here, because if she could turn Arthur's "exposure" of her to her own advantage . . . if she saw the Contessa again, or reconnected with Leilani, she might find a way to contact someone. With all the ships and yachts that sailed around this island, there *had* to be a way to send a signal. . . .

"We're ready for our first session," Wong announced. Then he picked up a phone. "Yes. Thomas!—"

His chatter became whichever Asian dialect his family spoke, to keep her clueless about what would really happen once the cameras rolled.

Doesn't matter, she convinced herself—or was that Spike's voice whispering in her ear? *You're a hot commodity, doll, If you flash your assets so they think you're complying, you'll buy some time . . . find a way to get the hell outta here. Hey—you're a Cat, and you'll land on your feet. Right, baby?*

She smiled, stronger already. Yes, indeedy! She could do that!

17

"All right, here's the plot for our fantasy film today."

Arthur Wong looked pretty damned pleased with himself as he gazed at her and his two sons, who stood on either side of her. "I call this *The Enchantress*. Our heroine is so bewitching, so beguiling, she will satisfy both men in the story while displaying herself to best advantage for the cameras. Understood?"

Cat nodded, her pulse pounding. She was costumed in a body stocking of transparent purple, and her gossamer tunic, spangled with gold moons and stars, glimmered with the slightest movement. An exotic gold mask covered the upper half of her face; it flared into mythological wings on each side, in a way that made her feel very wicked and wanton. She carried a gold wand topped with a star. Cat felt like she had in her childhood dance recitals—except back then, her body stocking hadn't had a split crotch!

"Thomas," Wong went on, "you are the priest who marries this divine creature to our King Charles, on this side of the set, which represents the cathedral."

Wong had bisected the wall with an Oriental dressing

screen, so a stained-glass window gave the area a holy glow—if the viewer had a really good imagination.

"And then you, King Charles—"

Charlie bowed to her with a flirtatious grin. His gray body stocking resembled a suit of chain mail, set off by a red velvet cape fastened over his shoulders and a jeweled crown. His slender black mask made Cat think of the Frito Bandito, but she knew better than to laugh at it.

"—will escort your bride to the other side—your castle bedroom—and consummate your marriage. I know you'll take her in a graphic yet artistically pleasing way that leaves no doubt of your delight in her. Meanwhile, on the other side of the screen"— Arthur gestured to his left again, obviously caught up in his fantasy—"Father Thomas casts his spell, lures the Enchantress to be *his* lover. Which she will, once she has thoroughly exhausted the king. Unable to resist his silent call, she shall slip back to the cathedral and service the priest by seeming to go to confession, performing her sexual magic on him until he, too, is sated and exhausted!

"Then, my Enchantress, you shall bow to the camera. Smile and entice prospective buyers who will be viewing this as a Web cast."

Wong steered them to the stained-glass side of the divider and blocked the first scene as if they were enacting a wedding ceremony.

"The beautiful thing about silent film is that you communicate with your bodily movement and expressions, rather than distracting your viewers with words. *Nothing* comes between you and their libidos, Miss Gamble." Arthur paused to give her a purposeful look. "The more effective you are, the more likely I'll keep you for our personal enjoyment. Just as I retained the Contessa as my courtesan."

Cat resisted the urge to decline or argue: her brief chat with Valenzia Borgia rang truer than anything this Asian would say.

And why should she believe him? He was directing a fantasy, after all . . . something he seemed extremely adept at. He'd probably cast this same story with dozens of different Enchantresses.

Yet this scenario had its advantages, didn't it? She was disguised with a mask and more clothing than she'd worn in days! She could pretend to be an Enchantress—a witchy woman who cast her spell on men and in the end had *her* way with them. It was a pleasant departure from Wong's male-dominant mindset.

So she positioned herself beside King Charlie, whose hand was on her ass. Father Thomas stood before them in his loose cassock of dove gray, tied with a rope at the waist. Never mind that the priest's white mask looked like a leftover from *Phantom of the Opera*.

Wong started some organ music—classical and high-minded, perhaps a Bach chorale, to make it sound like church. He adjusted the lights and then stepped behind the video cam.

"We have set our scene. . . . Camera is focused. . . . ACTION!"

Father Thomas raised his hand in a gesture of benediction, silently mouthing words as he looked from his brother to Cat. His raven hair was tied back, and in a monastic sort of way he looked dangerously sexy . . . like forbidden fruit as he gazed at her breasts from behind the white mask.

He gestured for them to kneel. As they gazed up at him—Charlie's wayward hand was still feeling her up for the camera—Thomas made a sign of the cross above their heads.

King Charles helped her to her feet and pulled her into a clinch. With a long hungry look at her face—so the camera could catch the lust in his sparkling dark eyes—he left nothing to her imagination as far as what he intended to do to her. His hands roamed her back, and her skin tingled with their heat and the friction of the skintight costume.

When was the last time she'd had this much fun? It was even

better than playing pirates with Trevor, Grant, and Bruce because *this* man intended to ravish her!

He started with her lips . . . teased her into a kiss that made her quake all over. Charlie speared a hand through her hair, establishing his dominance as he lavishly explored her mouth. His lips were warm and smooth, pressing and then releasing. In the space between them, his tongue came out to play.

How many hot scenes in movies showed it this way? A kiss orchestrated so the audience could see every nuance, every thrust of tongue and flicker of hungry lips?

Cat responded with an abandon she didn't have to fake, for Charlie Wong was as passionate about kissing as he was about cooking. He came at her, holding her hips to his; his dark eyes dared her to top each gesture, each tongue thrust. Their mouths met again and again as they gasped with hunger and need.

He writhed against her then; dented her backside with insistent fingers that coaxed her to move with him . . . to rub the ridge in his tights.

Father Thomas clapped his hands, exhorting them to take their lust out of the sanctuary. Like a bride and groom facing the congregation, she and Charles stood side by side for the camera. His randy grin made her giggle and tap his crown with her wand. As he escorted her away from the altar, Cat gazed over her shoulder at the priest, waving flirtatiously with her wand . . . a magic wand that empowered her to play like she hadn't in a long, long time.

The hot look Father Thomas flashed at her left *no* doubt how the script would play out.

But meanwhile King Charles was catching her up in social dance position to waltz with her. The soundtrack had changed to something dreamier, and, yes, in a three-quarter beat that guided them around the bed in the King's fantasy castle.

Charles was barely taller than she but a skilled dancer whose lead felt sure and confident. After a couple turns around the small room, he began to strip off his clothes—first his crown, then his cape, all the while gazing at her as if he intended to burn off her costume with the fiery eyes behind that mask.

This might be a fantasy, a silly little script . . . but it sure as hell feels real.

Cat, inspired by her wand and the King's lustful gaze, called up her long-ago dance class moves. She raised her arms to pirouette, which felt much more provocative now that she had breasts to thrust at her audience. Then she gracefully touched her toes, to shake her tush at him.

He grabbed her! Charles was hard and horny, so he ground his erection against her. With an arm around her hips, he fumbled between their bodies . . . his knuckles brushed her slit as he slipped his privates out of the front of his costume. Then his fingers found her open seam—he stepped back slightly, because the camera had to catch every detail—and Cat gasped when his fingers slipped inside her.

Slowly he began to pump her. She caught his rhythm and moved forward and back . . . forward and back to receive his attention. Her costume restricted her yet added to the sense of being violated while fully dressed. The O of her mouth widened and shut with the contractions of her muscles around his fingers. . . . Again, she didn't fake a thing, because this fellow was spot-on.

Then he grasped her hips in both his hands and inserted his cock inside her from behind. Cat curled upward, forming an open-mouthed moan. He exaggerated his thrusts so the camera could catch every inch of him as he moved in and out in a quickening rhythm.

She quivered, and for something to do with her hands, she grabbed her breasts to caress them lewdly. Then, with a sly smile, she teased herself with the butt of her wand. Charles thrust hard then and held her, writhing as though he were shooting her full of cum . . . except this was just a movie climax.

Cat smiled to herself while she mimicked a grimace of orgasm; just like in the porn flicks, Charles intended to take her again and again for the sheer show of it.

He pulled out then, to show her his huge, shiny-slick cock in all its glory. Even sheathed in a skin-pink condom, it was an inspiring sight. Cat leaned down to kiss it and then bless it with her wand.

Charlie gestured toward the bed and then led her there, his gaze red-hot in that wicked black mask. He was clearly enjoying this, and as he lay down he pulled her on top of him.

"Stay high," he whispered without moving his lips. "Then ride me."

Cat grinned. Again inspired by the wand, she stood with her feet on either side of his hips so his cock pointed at her crotch. Squatting to open her seam, she placed the wand between her legs to stroke herself while he watched. His sleek body arched up with her rhythm. He was really getting into this!

And it was no secret that the wand worked magic on a slit already warmed up by his fingers. Cat pressed harder, inflamed by bad-girl urges to play with herself while a rampant man watched.

Charlie grabbed himself. As he pumped and she pumped, both of them gazing at each other's sex, the bed rocked with them. The music had segued into a song with the quick, suggestive beat of a sultry sax and tambourine. She didn't recognize the tune, but the song they shared was as old as time—as fresh as this little game they were playing for Wong's camera.

As though he'd watched the same dirty movies she had, Charles shut his eyes, ready to spurt up at her spread slit.

Cat threw out her arms in a gesture of delight and lowered herself onto his cock. They writhed like wild things. She rode him hard, feeling the way he throbbed as he spent himself in a very dramatic way—for real this time.

His head fell sideways on the pillow, and his body went limp. Time to heed the call of that sorcerer priest on the other side of the screen! Cat gazed toward the chapel like a woman entranced as she left the king's bed.

For effect, she waved her wand over Charlie's spent body—kissed its star and touched it to his lips—before raising her arms in another ballet movement. Her body took wing as she gracefully propelled herself around the screen.

And Father Thomas was waiting. His arms remained outstretched, like magnets beckoning her to where he sat in a shallow frame that represented a doorless confessional. He was flexing his fingers, gazing raptly at her as though *he* were the enchanter. Cat paused in the center of the set to stare . . . to enact a battle of sexual wills. She raised her wand as though to override his spell with her own.

But then the priest parted his cassock with a flourish, to reveal yet another high-flying cock. His was longer than his brother's, just as his angular face had a more wicked, irresistible expression despite his Phantom's mask. He truly looked the part of a sorcerer with his jet hair flowing over his shoulders. His eyes sparkled with a black magic that pulled her nearer . . . nearer . . . until she knelt before him in an attitude of penitence and prayer.

He slid his hips forward on his bench, opening his legs in invitation. As she moved between them, Cat heard the tripod's whisper as it rolled closer, but she again set aside all thought of Arthur Wong watching her through his lens.

She had eyes only for the priest who waved his own potent wand, a silent demand that she satisfy him.

Forming her mouth in an O, she leaned forward . . . lightly fingered the base of him to bring the tip to her lips. She teased the little hole with the point of her tongue.

Thomas sucked air. His thighs flexed on either side of her, and Cat felt fully aware of her power over him. Just as she was aware that she'd better not stray from the script.

This time.

With a sly smile, she ran her tongue around his reddish head—again, giving the camera full advantage of every lick and tickle, just like in the porn flicks she'd seen. Then she trailed her tongue down the impressive length of him and back up again. Cat caught his midnight gaze and watched him strain to control his climax. Felt his long, lean body tense all over with the effort of accepting pleasure when he could do little to enhance it, or to pleasure her.

And what's wrong with this picture?

Cat drew her lips firmly up over him one last time and then slowly rose to her full height. Grasping the sides of the shallow confessional's doorway, she stepped up on the bench with her feet a slight distance from his quivering hips. Slowly, carefully, she crouched. . . . By God, it was time for this mystic to dip his wand in her waters and initiate himself at *her* command, after the way he'd kept his distance in her room!

Thomas understood this: his gaze darted between her eyes and her slit, which was bared when she opened her crotch seam in this crouch.

He looked ready to devour her again with that wanton tongue—yet ready to grab her hips and impale her on his tall, throbbing cock, too. She watched it pulse with a life force all its own, inviting her—no, begging her!—to partake of the magical mystery of Thomas Wong's wand.

Without shifting his dusky gaze from her eyes, the priest reached inside his cassock for a foil packet. He sheathed himself in latex the color of his onyx eyes; dark and dangerous, it towered beneath her open puss, a startling contrast to her pink skin and inner lips.

Silently he mouthed his command. "Fuck me. *Now!*"

Cat didn't have to read lips to understand his order. And, sensing the camera had zoomed in on her yin and his yang, she played it for all it was worth: lowered herself just to his tip, to tease him into submission—to make Thomas the one who lost control.

His lip curled. He shoved her down on his cock, and it wasn't play-acting that made her throw her head back and gasp. She despised him for taking the upper hand again, yet she'd been primed twice with his brother and this time her puss demanded its own satisfaction. Angling back, so he'd rub the right spots, Cat bounced while he held her steady. Her thigh muscles would kill her tonight, but she was too hot to care.

Father Thomas gritted his teeth and shoved himself inside her, holding her hips against his so he could grind out his pent-up frustrations and cum. Of its own accord, Cat's cunt squeezed him. She spun into inner space with the shattering impact of her orgasm.

When she could breath again, she realized the camera was still rolling and that Wong wanted a final bow from the Enchantress. Carefully—aching from that intensified squatting—she raised up and stepped back out of the fake confessional. With her back still to the camera, she raised her arms and wand, drawing her powers back into play with a deep breath.

Then she turned toward Arthur Wong and flashed a foxlike smile at his camera. Slowly she drew her wand down in a shimmering gesture of benediction as she bowed to her audience.

"It's a wrap!" Wong crowed.

When he stepped from behind the camera, he looked as ecstatic as she'd ever seen him. Had her performance really been so inspiring? She'd simply let herself go with the flow: it was a helluva lot better than being locked away in that closet in Ebonique's slave compound, after all.

She should've known Arthur Wong had his own arrogant reasons for such a wide smile.

"Excellent, Miss Gamble! And such fortuitous timing," he added slyly. "I received a response from Captain Spankevopoulos concerning the payment of your ransom. He has refused to consider it until he sees that you're alive and well, and this video drama will provide the proof he needs! Now we'll see if he antes up. Once I put this out for my usual buyers, he'll have to pay more than I've requested if he wants you back!"

It took enormous restraint not to spit in his face or show any emotion. Should she even believe him? What if he was baiting her again?

He smirked. "Take her to her room, Thomas. We'll film again tomorrow, since Miss Gamble is a natural actress and her own best selling point. I'm thinking that for our next episode, we'll perform for her caretaker, Ramon. Maybe *he'll* find a way to buy her back."

18

Jack read the terse, unsigned message and cussed himself for checking his e-mail before he went to bed. After a long day of peevish passengers—why did women sign on for a love slave experience without bringing any men?—and searching for a way to rescue Cat Gamble, the last thing he needed was another taunt from her captor.

At least she was a marketable commodity, so the fiend would keep her alive and healthy. But what a frightening thought! What was this guy up to, sending him a link called "The Enchantress?" He should damn well leave it alone—

But that enchantress had already bewitched him, hadn't she? Feeling as much a slave to Cat's captor as to his own frazzled emotions, Jack clicked on the link.

"Oh . . . my . . . God," he breathed. The actress in the skintight purple suit and star-spangled cape wore an alluring winged mask that covered half her face, but it was Cat Gamble . . . lovely, lithe, and so damn playful. He gritted his teeth as he watched a wedding scene, complete with a mocked-up cathedral and organ music, a fake priest in a bone-white mask, and another guy decked out in a velvet cape, a crown, and a black mask. Members of the pirate crew, no doubt, concealing their identities to cavort with this woman—*his* woman, damn it! She should've been here with *him*, in this bedroom aboard the *Captive Fantasy*!

And oh, what a fantasy. . . .

The seam of his pajama pants cut into him as she waved her wand and made her magic. That bozo fondling Cat's ass played his part to the hilt—aware that this little scenario was being filmed for *him*, probably. They frolicked off to the other side of a room divider . . . not in a big-time porn studio, as low-budget as the sets were, but the quality of the color and sound suggested a crew who could afford top-notch Web cam technology. The picture on his screen was so real, he could've *been* there—

And if he were, heads would roll! These sons of bitches left nothing undone: that guy in the crown was kissing Cat like he hadn't tasted a woman in years!

And by the way Cat was playing back, King Bozo was getting really, really lucky. Their mouths dueled in a dazzling close-up that showed her wet, slick lips and playful tongue, not to mention the feline smile on her face when he whirled her around.

Oh, Cat . . . God, what a woman you are, sweetheart. I am so fucking sorry we ran late the other night.

His hand slipped to his aching cock to ease it from his pajama pants—which he wore in case an emergency erupted among the passengers in the night. The fake King slipped his prick out of those tights, already covered in a condom the color of skin. . . . Cat gasped as he pumped more for the camera than her enjoyment.

"Bastard," Jack muttered. He should just turn the damn

thing off, but he had to watch Cat's body respond . . . the way she moved, as silky and free as a contented, stretching cat . . . that zoom-in on her pussy when King Bozo pulled out, which sent her wetness dribbling from that decadent, open-crotched costume.

"You wouldn't need to mask yourself for me, darling," he murmured longingly. "Nothing so artificial would come between us. . . ."

They were flitting over to the bed now . . . not nearly as large or inviting as his own. And he sure as hell wouldn't have landed on his back with his cock jutting up—

Oh, yessss, it is. Oh, yessss, it's needy and hard and—

God almighty, she was teasing him now, standing above the king at an angle where he looked right up her hot, slick snatch.

And then she took him, *hard*. Riding the tiger, she was. And then she slipped off the bed, because the priest was casting a hokey spell—rendering this drama as bad as any low-budget porn flick he'd seen. But holy shit, Cat was stepping up onto the bench of that confessional and—

"Would you look at the sweet, sweet ass on that woman?" he moaned, grasping himself.

Then she straddled the priest, her knuckles white with tension as she lowered herself . . . onto that second cock, the color of midnight with another condom. At least they were protecting her from disease, but they were sick! *Sick*, the way they used this Web cast to torment him into paying up. If he had a lick of sense or decency, he'd fork over—

But how many desperate fools are these guys playing against each other? Who's to say they'd really turn her over to you?

When the priest grabbed her and shoved her onto his tall cock, Jack nearly shot all over his desk. Up and down the bastard bounced her—*her legs will be so sore!*—until he ground up into her, his grimace of release clearly visible below the white mask.

She got off him. Drew in a graceful breath as she raised her arms.

And when Cat Gamble, the enchantress, turned to wave her wand at him, Jack squeezed his eyes shut and gritted his teeth to keep from climaxing. Those pirate bastards might be controlling Cat, telling her how to perform—but *he* would not. Much as he detested watching her this way, at least she was whole and healthy.

The best way to keep her that way was to call in the IMB and hope Kurt and Rick located these guys before they sold Cat to somebody on the auction block. Or on eBay, God forbid.

Angrily he clicked out of the Web cast and opened his e-mail program.

NICE TRY, he tapped rapidly, BUT YOU'LL HAVE TO DELIVER HER TO ME BEFORE I CONSIDER EVEN A PARTIAL DEPOSIT. NO COPS, IF YOU'LL TELL ME WHERE AND WHEN TO WAIT FOR YOU.

He signed it and clicked SEND, knowing in his desperate, lonely . . . horny heart what their answer would be.

Late that night Cat rose from her bed to look out the window. Ever since the triumph of her filming episode got trounced by Wong's pronouncement about tomorrow's Web cast, she'd had a lot to wonder about.

If he was targeting Ramon this time, did that mean Leilani would appear in it? Damn! She wished she knew where her laptop was, and whether she could trust *anything* that conniving Asian pirate told her.

Holding herself, she ached with the beauty of the moonlit sea below. . . . The soft flow of the surf along the sand sang a sad lullaby, because now that she was alone with her thoughts, they once again centered on what she did *not* have: her rendezvous with dapper Captain Jack and his British accent. Had he really asked to see that she was alive? Did he care about her predicament, or did his weekly love slave adventure occupy all his time and attention?

She held her breath . . . followed the muffled rumble of an engine, from around the side of the island where the trees and flowering shrubs blocked her view.

Then she saw it! A large boat—a fishing vessel, or maybe a private cruiser—putted slowly along the coastline without any lights on! Why would anyone endanger themselves along that rugged, rocky section of shore? Or risk getting hit by another boat?

She stepped out to her balcony to watch it. Its engine went silent, and two figures tossed ropes over the side . . . hopped nimbly to the moonlit dock to secure it. Then movement from farther inland caught her eye, and she sucked in her breath: a parade of people, being hurried through the darkness from the direction of the slave compound! They hobbled awkwardly be-cause—because they were roped together at the ankles! Were these slaves, being smuggled to—?

"Never mind what you think you see," a low voice mur-mured behind her. "The less you know, the fewer questions will plague your mind, my dove. I so want you to feel at peace with yourself and the universe as we continue to acquaint our-selves."

She whirled around, scowling. "It's not enough to put me in this tower where escape is only a suicide leap away!" she rasped. "Oh, no! I have to have a fucking guard so I can't even pee without someone knowing it."

Thomas's slender face eased into a dreamy smile. "I suppose today's performance *does* qualify me as a fucking guard—and what a fucking it was, my lotus flower! But you injure me deeply," he continued with a warning edge in his voice. "You disappoint me with your bitterness and cynical outlook. As though you'd rather be left to my father's whims during the night."

Cat stifled a retort. He had a point, but she wasn't going to admit it. This secretive sorcerer already had far too much power over her and what happened on this island.

"This is how you trade out your hostages?" She pointed toward the secretive activities at the pier. "You demand payment, and then the buyers must come to fetch their goods? What if they bring along the police?"

"Not likely, my dear Alina." He smiled again, in a slightly disjointed way that made her wonder what he'd been smoking. "We sell only the finest serving girls and whipping boys, trained and subservient. So eager to leave Ebonique's domain they'll do just about anything. Our buyers know better than to reveal our identities because they'd expose their own illegal activities, as well."

Is this what Leilani's enduring? What if she's among those poor souls on that boat?

Cat didn't dare ask. Didn't want him to twist her worry into his next enticing trap. So she leaned against the balcony railing, which reminded her how he'd held her there in a breathtaking, death-defying assault on her slit and her senses. His face appeared paler in the moonlight. His eyes looked slightly unfocused.

"What's that I smell?" she quizzed him softly. "Were you outside my door getting high?"

His giggle started low in his chest and sounded almost girlish. "Angel's trumpet," he murmured as he lightly stroked her arms. "Enables me to see visions while the universe enlightens me with its . . . eternal wisdom. That moon up there is my priestess! I feel properly worshipful when I elevate myself to this state of religious bliss."

She coughed to keep from laughing. Now she realized why

those angel's trumpet trees on Porto Di Angelo had filled her room with such a deep sweetness: however he'd smoked or injected or imbibed it, the drug was potent. Maybe, if things got horrible enough, she'd coax him to share some. Right now, though, she wanted to be stone-cold straight.

"The parts of the tree are poisonous, you know," he informed her with a disjointed nod. "In the wrong shaman's hands, the drug could kill rather than cure. Very effective against asthma and other respiratory disorders."

Doesn't have much effect on magical, mystical bullshit, though, does it?

"I'll remember that next time I'm tempted to pick those gorgeous blooms," she replied. "And for now, I think I'll go back to bed."

His eyebrow flickered wickedly.

"*Alone*, Thomas. You got yours today—and we're saving up for tomorrow, remember?" she said pointedly. "Never forget how hot I become. The same body heat that scorched off my pubic hair could roast your weenie in a flash."

He backed away. He was lucid enough to believe what she said, and up here away from his father and brother, he was at her mercy in more ways than he realized.

For a fleeting moment, she envisioned pitching him over the balcony rail and into the abyss. But that wouldn't help her case, would it? Better to behave herself while these Wongs allowed her the relative freedom of this boring beige penthouse. Things could be a whole lot worse.

"Good night," she whispered. "If I'm to be my scintillating, photogenic self tomorrow, I need my beauty rest, Thomas."

"All well and good, but you must promise to be *mine* tomorrow. Leave my little brother begging for it while I take my pleasure with you."

"As you like it, sir," she replied—as if she had any control over that! But what else could she say? If she cut him any conversational bait, he'd pester her all night!

"I'll be outside, should you need anything," he assured her in his mystical voice. He bowed in that Asian way that grated on her nerves. "As long as I'm your keeper, my fair Alina, no harm shall befall you."

"I'm holding you to that! Now good night!"

19

When Thomas shut the bedroom door, she listened to be sure he'd settled himself in the hallway again, so she could further observe that pierside scene and decide what it meant.

As she returned to her balcony, the loud *thud* of a door chilled her. It sounded very final, like the closing of a tomb.

What if Leilani's on that boat? What if they really did drug her? She's so beautiful and agreeable, she'd sell quickly to some twisted, perverted . . . And the Wongs would get her off the island so she and I—and maybe the Contessa—couldn't conspire against them.

Cat nipped her lip, watching the white cruiser pull away from the shore. Her temples throbbed, and she felt queasy with dread. By tomorrow night, *she* might be on the same sort of boat.

So what're you going to do about it, doll? Spike queried near her ear. *Life's just one little test after another, and I can't give you all the answers. That's cheating.*

She inhaled the warm night air. Forced herself to think logical thoughts about how to escape such a fate. Without her phone or laptop, she was dependent upon what the Wongs chose to tell her—and what a load of crap *that* was! Being watched so closely meant she had no way to signal to ships sailing past, whether it be Captain Jack's or the police or—

The movie tomorrow! What could she do to catch a viewer's attention? Ramon's attention?

Cat gazed into the sky, wishing upon the stars and the moonlight that glimmered on the midnight sea. How could she possibly relay her location, or her captors' identities, to the caretaker on Porto Di Angelo? As she concentrated, drumming on the varnished railing, it sounded like she was typing a hell-bent-for-leather action scene in one of her books.

When she glanced down at her pale fingers in the moonlight, it came to her!

She slipped into the bathroom. Shut the door and turned on the night-light so she could practice in the mirror. Again and again she shaped her hands and fingers; even if she perfected the motions, she'd be dead meat if Wong caught her at this. But it sent a surge of hope and sly triumph through her as she perfected the gestures she'd flash at the camera tomorrow.

Finally Cat switched off the light and climbed back into bed. She lay there a long time gazing up at the ceiling, listening for Thomas in the hall, mentally rehearsing her plan and hoping she'd have an opportunity to use it. Because once she got hauled onto a boat in the dead of night, chained to other slaves, who knew what horrible things might happen?

Who knew if she'd be lost and gone forever?

When Thomas escorted her to the churchlike room to make their next movie, Cat studied the set more carefully. While Arthur and his son discussed details in their rapid-fire Asian gibberish, she looked for a place to enact her plan—realizing that the Wongs' plot might not pan out the way she figured. What *had*, since they'd plucked her from her beach chair?

But if she gave up—if they believed she was their victim—her cause, and Leilani's, would be lost.

Music began to play, a soft, suggestive piano piece with mysterious undertones that felt more somber or . . . dangerous than yesterday's mood. When Arthur had adjusted the mix, he turned to acknowledge her presence.

"Good morning, Miss Gamble," he intoned pointedly.

Cat nodded. She was naked, fresh from her shower—and she hoped her clean scent wouldn't inspire some perverted story twist. Thomas, meanwhile, fetched a costume from the closet: black leather straps that resembled a dog harness or a piece of S and M fantasy garb from a raunchy movie.

She remained quiet as the long-haired mystic slipped the leather contraption over her head. When she looked down, she swallowed hard: the ebony leather bisected her midsection and cut between her breasts to accentuate them.

"Absolutely beautiful," Thomas breathed. "Such a stark, startling contrast to your lovely skin, Alina. And tell me—what is this I've just put on you?"

Cat clenched her jaw. Arthur watched them, loving the way she had to spell out her degradation. "It seems to be a harness," she muttered.

"And of what use is a harness, my dove? You've been the perfect slave, so why would we resort to such a blatant form of control?"

She closed her eyes. "Because you think I'm a dog?"

Arthur laughed behind her. "Well, yes, a female dog is a bitch—and we've seen that side of you. But in this case, Miss Gamble, we'll secure you as part of your role in today's drama. Before we bring in the rest of the cast, Thomas will hook you to the wall so you can . . . *watch*, without missing a thing. I know how you love to watch."

Why did those words curl her insides? Cat was struck by the deft expedience of Thomas Wong's movements as he cuffed her and then steered her to where they'd enacted yesterday's church scene. The stained-glass window cast a purple shadow on her as he snapped a clasp into a ring on the wall. He'd done this before. And he loved every minute of doing it to *her*.

"Now then," Arthur said gleefully. "Thomas, while you fetch the others I'll set the cameras. Another day, another fine film from the Wong Studio!"

Cat nearly choked on the irony of that, but when two other actresses entered the room she clammed up. The lush figure in front, clad in a colorful wrapped tunic and a tacky auburn wig, flashed her a grin. The slender woman behind her, guided by Thomas's firm hand, had long wavy hair. She wore only a red velvet blindfold and matching bindings around her wrists.

Leilani! Cat bit back the name, not wanting to appear agitated or eager—*or find out she's doped out of her mind.*

Yet her island's caretaker walked upright with an ethereal grace that suggested full mental acuity. Maybe Leilani had adopted the same psychology she herself was using: outward acceptance of her captivity to disguise her focus on escape.

And when the woman in the red wig smiled at her, Cat recognized the Contessa. Why would this marvelously wealthy woman take part in a shoddy production to showcase her former caretaker—and good friend!—for potential buyers?

It was just one more mystery surrounding Valenzia Borgia. One more reason to keep her mouth shut and play along . . . and find a way to gesture at the camera. Would viewers be savvy enough to get her meaning?

"Today, ladies, we shall explore the role of the love slave—something near and dear to *your* heart, Miss Gamble, since you signed on for such an adventure aboard the *Captive Fantasy*," Arthur intoned. "And of course Valenzia here has made a whole new *life* playing such a role. With such talent as the Contessa's at my disposal, I'd be remiss to deny her training time with the most promising new captives in my compound."

He smiled like a snake oil salesman or a TV evangelist. Cat reminded herself not to react—not to respond—until she knew precisely what was expected of her. It was a hopeful sign when the blindfolded Leilani perked up at the sound of her name. She, too, quickly disguised her excitement as the elder Wong further summarized his plot.

"Thomas has requested the role of the buyer today—although men of his exquisite sensitivity and sensuality are rare in this business, ladies." Arthur nodded, and his older son went to the costume closet. "For the sake of our promotional Web cast, however, he'll be perfect."

What could she say to that? She stood in a partial crouch, attached to a wall ring, while a black leather harness outlined her bare breasts and spanned her abdomen to draw attention to her sex. She hadn't had time to style her hair this morning because that exquisitely sensitive Thomas had barged into her room. He'd told her to go heavy on the eyeliner and mascara—to make a wanton contrast between her natural peaches-and-cream complexion and the artifice of face paint.

So much for being his lotus blossom. Cat had imagined Thomas Wong working himself into a lather over a slutty piece of trailer trash, which produced a hard, heavy-handed look that made her smile even now.

"The Contessa will play the part of the trainer who wants to display her wares—you, her charges—in the most positive light," Wong went on cheerfully. "So when she tells you how to perform, or how to pose yourselves, it's to your benefit to obey. She and Thomas will follow a scripted dialog, but you two slaves are to remain silent. Understood?"

Cat nodded, noting that Leilani did the same. Had she and Valenzia collaborated on this little gig? Or was Leilani as much at their mercy as she?

"Any questions?"

Now there's a trap if I ever heard one. Cat gazed pointedly

at the little man, who paced and gesticulated with his anticipation of today's scenario. In his red satin shirt and black pants,
he resembled an exotic-breed rooster.

"You may answer if you wish, Catalina," Wong replied in a
silky voice. "I require your silence only after the filming begins."

She didn't answer. Just looked at him, attempting an exquisitely enlightened, sensitive expression, even though her hair felt
skanky and her makeup looked lewd.

"Fine, then! Thomas! Let's get this show rolling! I've told
our viewers we'll be Web casting live at nine, which is in five
minutes!"

Web casting live! Cat's pulse revved into high gear: presum-
ably Arthur Wong had notified Captain Jack and Ramon of this
presentation, so by the time these Asian pirates caught her ges-
ticulating, it would be too late! Her message would already be
on the Internet! Arthur could get his revenge—and punish her
he surely would—but her island caretaker and the captain
could be decoding her information in the meantime.

She sighed. Her plan depended upon having her hands free.

She'd have to entice someone to release her. The silent gestures she'd practiced still seemed like a much better idea than
blurting out the Wongs' identities—risking their retaliation—
while the camera rolled.

When Thomas Wong returned in a Mandarin-style jacket
and pants of ebony silk, with his jet-black hair streaming over
his shoulders and a black patch over one eye, Cat tried not to
grin like a little kid with a big secret. His father stood behind
the camera on its wheeled tripod, focusing, while the Contessa
smoothed her henna wig. She obviously relished her role as the
slave trainer, and was determined to give quite a show for the
camera—and for her Asian lover.

Off came her colorful tunic, which revealed a camisole and
boy-cut panties of white lace so sheer it showcased the white

push-up bra and thong beneath them. A white garter belt and lace stockings with clear stiletto heels completed her virginal attire.

Cat gawked. Valenzia Borgia may have been wearing more clothing than either she or Leilani, but even in that ridiculous wig the Contessa was the most provocative of the three of them. And she was damn proud of it! Her olive skin glowed, and her dark eyes snapped with her amusement.

"Action!" Arthur cried. The soft music now sounded like a cheesy soap-opera theme song.

"You have brought the slave girls I requested?" Thomas demanded in a brusque accent that sounded totally unlike him.

"Of course I have, sir," the Contessa purred. She shimmied her breasts to make that lace cami whisper against her bra. "Only my finest ladies are fit for your service, and you'll want them both by the time our presentation is complete. This exquisite creature—Polynesian by birth—is Leilani. I myself have trained her in all the sensual arts."

Cat watched closely for signs that Valenzia played little games like she did. Did she think Ramon was watching and would come for them?

It was impossible to tell. As the Contessa ran her hand down the curtain of Leilani's sleek black hair, Thomas peered avidly at her bare, honey-colored body. Cat knew her housekeeper was a looker, yet she watched in awe as this alluring woman straightened her shoulders to make her lovely, pert breasts protrude toward a man's touch.

And touch her he did: Thomas circled the blindfolded woman to cup her breasts from behind. His hands followed the curve of her waist to her lush hips, which he caressed in provocative circles as he lightly rubbed himself against her. Arthur moved closer with the cam to capture the arousal on Leilani's lovely, expressive face . . . the lips that parted like petals of a flower opening to the sun.

But instead of kissing her, Thomas crouched to put his eyes level with her sex, which was adorned with a triangle of black thatch that pointed toward her slit. He slipped a finger between her thighs. Leilani opened to him with a little gasp and then moaned invitingly when he angled the finger up inside her.

"Very responsive, I see," he remarked, sounding coolly clinical.

"Oh, yes! Leilani was born to please a man! She specializes in sucking cock," the Contessa confided with playfully arched eyebrows. "You may have a sample of her skills—at no extra charge!—if you'd like, sir."

As Leilani obediently knelt and opened her mouth in an O, Cat wondered how Ramon would react—if indeed he was watching. Such a devoted couple they were, and Valenzia knew it! Surely the Contessa wouldn't torment her home's caretakers with sexual blackmail!

But as Thomas whipped out his long, lean erection and met Leilani's lips with its tip, Cat forgot her concerns. Even blindfolded, with her hands bound behind her in those red velvet cuffs, the exotic Leilani moved forward and back . . . up and down. Her mouth caressed his cock with the grace and fervor of a skilled prostitute hungry for more than money.

Thomas sucked air between his clenched teeth. His head lolled back, which sent his hair whispering down the back of his silk jacket. Cat held her breath. He was far too sexy and sultry . . . far too enticing when he was aroused. When he speared his long fingers into Leilani's hair, she felt him handling *her* hair . . . moving *her* head up and back, up and back, as she sucked his long cock.

As though he sensed her fascination, Thomas turned to gaze at her. Leilani continued attending his member, but the alluring Asian watched *Cat* now . . . letting that onyx gaze linger on *her* breasts . . . the black leather straps that bisected her body . . . the way she stood so awkwardly, with her hands fastened to the wall. So helpless against anyone who came up to her.

Gently but firmly, Thomas moved Leilani's mouth from his shaft. Cat marveled at the hard, swollen length of manhood that jutted toward her as it issued the ultimate challenge.

"I think I'll try this other slave now," he rasped. "I don't often run across a blond, fair-skinned angel like this one. She looks so brazen in her harness."

"Yes, sir, she's a feisty one," Valenzia agreed as they approached her. "We haven't had her long."

"And why is she shackled?" Son of Wong stopped in front of her, as though to give her the full measure of his manhood.

"Oh, this one has tried to escape!" Valenzia replied gleefully. "We have to watch her every moment. Where she thinks she's going—or how she thinks she'll get there—is anyone's guess."

When Thomas caressed her messy hair, Cat pressed her cheek into his palm. With her most innocent smile, she looked up into that lean face, so exotic with its one dark eye and that ominous patch. Sure it was an act for the camera, but she longed for a taste of that damp cock, which still glistened from Leilani's sucking.

"What if I turn her loose to see how she moves and responds?" he queried. "She won't be getting away from *me*. Not that she'd want to."

Valenzia laughed prettily. "If that's what you'd like best, sir, by all means loosen her from the wall ring and have a look."

Was this really happening? As tall, slender Thomas leaned over her to unfasten her cuffs from the iron ring, his silk jacket brushed her skin. So seductive and male he smelled, as if he'd shot some of his wad into Leilani's mouth to relieve some pressure.

At last her arms were free! Cat rolled her shoulders to get the feeling back into arms too long restrained. She flashed him a grateful smile.

"Ah, an appreciative woman!" Thomas crooned, although

his theatrical accent sounded harsh. "How often does a man run across one of those?"

"I worked very hard to teach her submission and gratitude," Valenzia said with a smug smile. "This one would've sold the day after she came, except she was too rough around the edges—too willful by half—and we couldn't risk letting her go until we tamed that runaway spirit. I think you'll find her to your liking now."

"I'm sure of it." He gave Cat another of those languid smiles, rendered more roguish by the patch over his eye with its string that angled diagonally across his forehead. Such a dangerous devil he was, in the jet-black costume that made him look leaner and meaner. Bad to the bone—including that boner extending from his open fly.

But she had to keep her plan uppermost in her mind. Couldn't get carried away by fantasy and the edgy novelty of performing for the camera. Ramon and Captain Jack might be watching, and her message to these viewers remained her first priority.

Her body thrummed with nervous anticipation. How would she know the right time to make those moves she'd practiced? What if Arthur Wong caught on before she finished and—

"Turn around. Lean over," Thomas commanded. "Show me your ass. Spread your legs so I can see your cunt, as well."

She swallowed hard. Lowered her torso slowly, so Thomas had full view of the rippling muscles in her legs. Without turning her head, she assessed her position as far as where Arthur Wong and his camera were. If she allowed Thomas to distract her, or if he faced her in another direction, she'd lose her chance—maybe forever—to signal for help so someone could capture these slave traders.

From her folded-over position, she saw the older man's bare feet beneath his black silk pants . . . watched him walk around her, toward Thomas, while the tripod remained in place. Cat could only guess where he was focusing, and didn't dare raise up, for fear of arousing their attention.

"Excellent . . . quite possibly the loveliest slit I've ever seen," Thomas remarked in that rough voice. "Pink and moist, with pouty lips waiting to be parted by a cock that means business. And I just happen to have one!"

While he rolled on a rubber before a powerful, proper introduction to his technique, Cat drew in a breath . . . gathered up her nerve . . . flexed her fingers and mentally reviewed her plan.

Then she quickly formed letters by moving her two hands in sync: W . . . O . . . N . . . G, she spelled. And then, since Arthur seemed to be watching his son's cock disappearing into her back there, she flashed the finger letters again: W . . . O . . . N . . . G.

Good thing she'd done it when she had, too: Arthur then rolled the camera slowly toward the angle where male was claiming female, making wet slapping noises as Thomas pumped her.

Cat gasped. When she caught herself, her palms slapped the floor.

"Like that, do ya?" he asked in a tight voice. "Before I consider buying you, my pale, perfect lotus blossom, I must know you can handle the full length and strength of me."

When Thomas thrust deeper, Cat thought her eyes might pop out. Her mouth dropped open: out of the blue, she was ready to come. She bunched inside, clenching the length of cock that slowly entered and then slid out of her . . . slipped farther each time, and then pulled away—

He thrust hard and deep, grasping her hips while he vibrated inside her. Her breaths came in short gasps as desperation overrode all thoughts of how her viewers might react. After all, Ramon and Jack, if they were even watching, were miles away. She had to do something *now* about this ache that clamored to be satisfied.

Gritting her teeth, she squeezed him hard.

Thomas let out a sudden groan. "Jesus! Sweet—God Almighty—"

"Oh, yes! Yessss!" Valenzia fluttered around to catch Cat's shoulders so she wouldn't fall flat on her face. "I can see this girl pleases you greatly, sir. In fact, watching the two of you fuck has made *me* so hot, I hope you'll jump *my* bones before you go, sir! Or at least you might tongue me to take the edge off before we strike our bargain?"

Brazen lady! The Contessa rolled on the floor to spread her shapely stockinged legs in invitation, showing off the tiny white thong beneath those lace boy shorts. Her breasts heaved in exaggerated lust, to overflow the low-cut bra. She made an alluring picture spread that way on the floor, with her white garter straps straining against her bronze thighs. Those clear stilettos winked at him.

Thomas watched her, his cock in his hand. Then he looked at Cat again, narrowing his eyes. "I want *you* to lick this woman while I watch," he commanded. "Start with your mouth on her mound, outside the lingerie. Let's see how long it takes her to yank the thong aside so your hot tongue can lap at her skin."

Valenzia sucked air. "Oh, I don't think that would be—"

"Do we make a deal for this harnessed mare, or do I walk away?"

Cat's pulse thudded. Long seconds ticked by, until the Contessa ran a teasing finger up her thigh in consent.

Did he really expect her to lick Valenzia's snatch? Had she reached the point of refusing aloud—or was this a line Thomas thought she couldn't cross? Another chance for the Wongs to punish her for disobeying?

Needing to prove to him—to herself—that she could do *anything* in defiance of her captors, Cat moved between Valenzia's quivering legs. She held those muscled thighs down with her hands . . . closed her eyes and pressed her mouth hard against the tiny white triangle of the thong. As she rubbed, the lacy shorts rasped against her lips, egging her on.

"Oh, my—"

"Yes!" Thomas rasped. "Be relentless with her, Alina! Nibble her through her clothing—"

The Contessa wailed and began to writhe, but Cat held her harder.

"—and then rub her nub with the bridge of your nose, right where the nerve will drive her straight to the ceiling!"

Cat had become aware of how sheltered she'd been sexually—and how much she enjoyed making her fictional mistress squirm. Valenzia's fingers flitted around her ears while her hips wiggled crazily.

"Please—please! Take off my—"

"Yes, lick her till she howls like a bitch in heat!" Thomas urged. He knelt beside her so he could watch every heated detail. "You can't give it to her hard enough, brazen whore that she is."

When Cat grabbed the waistband of those white lacy shorts, the Contessa raised her hips, eager for release. Now she faced a pair of dusky, rose-colored lips on either side of a little white cord, and she went after it. Tugging the thong so it pressed the wet skin between those nether folds, she wiggled her tongue below it.

The response was gratifying: Valenzia's cries rang in the little room, and Cat kept after her—more intently because a long male finger was teasing her own slit from behind. Her nerves a-jangle, she hung on to her sanity by driving the Contessa to a high, wailing climax that seemed to last forever.

When Valenzia went still, except for panting, Cat collapsed on her thigh. Had she really just done what she thought she had? Had Wong's challenge driven her to tongue another woman while he watched and fingered her?

"When you get your head together, we'll make our deal."

Thomas sounded coolly in command now, standing above them. He offered Cat a hand up, and when she could get her legs under her she caught his expression of wry satisfaction.

"You'll do quite nicely, my fair-haired dove," he said. And damned if he didn't kiss her long and deep. Like he meant it.

When he released her, Cat shook her head to clear it. The myriad sensations she'd just experienced still spun in wild, wobbly circles in her mind. Had Thomas Wong actually praised her? Or was that just a part of the script?

But there was no mistaking Arthur Wong's wrath as he glared at a monitor beside him. "Look at this! You were signaling at the camera—and that will *cost* you, Miss Gamble! If you think you'll get away with—if you think our prospective buyers will be able to decipher such a feeble attempt—you're more foolish than I thought!

"Get her out of here!" he ordered, pointing toward the door. "Lock her up where they'll never find her!"

20

"Sonuva *bitch*! Would you look at the way he's—you can't tell me Cat's doing this to spite me for being late!"

Jack Spankevopoulos fought the urge to delete this Web cast, because he sensed Ms. Gamble—and that honey-skinned angel who'd just performed a stellar blow job—were in deeper trouble than he'd first believed. But how could he *not* watch her? God, she was luscious—bad-ass *hot* in that black leather get-up, which cut between her bouncing breasts as she knelt with that horny bastard—

"Say—isn't that the same guy who played the priest in yesterday's clip?" Stavros, too, was glued to the computer monitor, taking every halting breath with Cat on the screen. At least he sounded somewhat sane. Rational, rather than overblown with anger and . . . lust. *Need.*

Jack leaned closer, trying to behave like an adult capable of intelligent thought. "You could be right . . . might've had that long hair tucked into his cassock. We can compare that later."

"Because of *course* you didn't trash the previous flick—even though you were so pissed, I thought you'd jump from this crow's nest?" Stavros shook his head, but his eyes followed every move of the couple doing it doggy-style. "And today's message said this was the real deal—that this dude in the black suit was trying her out, to buy her as a slave? And that they filmed all their transactions to be sure nobody got screwed?"

"Fine way to put that, cuz, considering what we're watching. Hey, wait a minute . . . what's that she's doing with her fingers?"

They watched closely as the gorgeous blonde who should be screwing *him* struggled to keep her balance, she gestured at the camera—twice. Meanwhile, that horse's ass in the eye patch entered her from behind.

"Do you suppose she's trying to spell . . . Hit the reverse arrow!"

"No way! We'll see this through to the bitter end," Jack rasped. "It'll be archived, so—holy mother of God, would you look at the camera angle on—"

"She's got him comin' and goin'," his lanky cousin said with a hoarse sigh. "Damn shame she's not aboard the *Fantasy* doing that with us."

"*Us?* You thought I was going to share—shhh! What'd that bitch in the bad wig just say?"

"Holy moly, she's hittin' the floor! Spreadin' those thighs for the same guy!"

"He can't do it three times! This whole scenario looks as fake as his—" Jack's mouth dropped open. The man in black demanded that *Cat* give the trick in the white skivvies a licking. "Do you think she's really the type to—"

"Oh, Jesus. I'm creamin' in my jeans." Stavros shifted quickly in his chair. "Just does something to me, watching a girl-girl . . . Oh lordy, she's rippin' down those tighty-whitey lace panties—"

"Not that her thong's going to be any protection from— shit! Shee-*yit,* the tip of Cat's tongue is flickering over—"

Jack clenched his eyes shut against the harsh, hard ache where his jeans threatened to emasculate him. But he peeked at the screen sideways, noting the vivid color and detail . . . the alluring contrast between that slave trainer's olive skin and her not-so-angelic garter belt. Cat's quick, pink tongue made those hips wiggle uncontrollably.

"Shit! Her tits just popped out!" Stavros rasped. "If this doesn't end soon—"

"Wait! The cameraman's pissed!" He cranked up the volume, sensing this segment wasn't supposed to be on film. Was this part of their game, or had the videographer forgotten the mike was on? He ranted at Cat about—

"Lock her up where they'll never find her!"

Jack blinked. The image on the screen blanked out. "Now wait a minute. The e-mail message said this was an actual transaction, showing how Cat had been purchased by—"

"But somebody off-camera just ordered her to be hidden where she'd never be found," Stavros mused. "So they're leading us by the nose—"

"Or whatever else is sticking out."

"—which suggests the whole thing is a hoax. Maybe to make you *think* she's been sold, so you won't try to find the guys who snatched her. Make sense?"

"As much as any of this does." He reached for his cell phone, thumb-nailing the number he practically knew by heart. "Yes—Ramon? Did you just see the Web cast with Cat and those two other hot mamas?"

Ramon almost smiled. Yes, indeed, those three women were so hot they'd scorched the clothes right off him, although the Web cast's assault on his senses had left him pissed and worried and way too vulnerable. But he would get himself together. Would *do* something before this new lead got cold.

"These bastards show nothing by mistake," he replied when

Captain Jack remarked about that last off-camera line. "They intend to pull our strings with every breath they take and every damn film they make. They'll keep us off-balance as long as they believe we might pay the ransom.

"And that guy with the long black hair?" he echoed as he considered the captain's question. "Yes, he *was* the priest yesterday! And he's got to be one of the kidnappers. I'll call IMB to show Rick and Kurt these clips. To see if they recognize him or that guy who played the king yesterday."

Spankevopoulos ranted then, about how Cat and that other luscious honey must've been forced into this lurid filming of—

But he'd seen the ladies' faces, too, hadn't he? His Leilani, even bound and blindfolded, hadn't exactly turned her head when that guy's cock came to her lips. And that fallen angel in white, playing the slave trainer. . . .

Should he tell the captain everything? Would his woman come home sooner if he swallowed his pride and told the whole truth?

"Captain, you probably don't know this," he said in a muted voice, "but that woman with the velvet blindfold?"

"The one with the long black hair and lips that—"

"Watch out now. She's my wife."

The abrupt silence gratified him. At least Captain Jack had the decency to let out a shocked, appalled wheeze.

"I—Jesus, I'm sorry, Ramon. I—" A pause indicated he was thinking about what he'd seen . . . what he knew from sailing past Porto Di Angelo the past few years. "Please accept my apologies for being so damned dense and insensitive. Of *course* I've seen your wife with you on the beach, but I—"

"You sail past us at night, usually," Ramon offered.

"—assumed these pirates had other women to play the parts of—"

"At least she's healthy. And alive," he added quietly. "Cat seems to be faring all right, as well. And that other woman—"

"In the red wig and the white lace?"

"—is Valenzia Borgia. The previous owner of this island, who disappeared a couple years ago."

Another moment of dead air. "You're shitting me."

The Captain's precise British accent gave that line a whole new spin, and Ramon snickered. Better to laugh than to lose hope, after all. "No, I'd recognize those legs and that voice anywhere. At least she hasn't met an unfortunate end," he remarked with a rueful laugh, "but she didn't exactly look like she was suffering, either. Did she?"

"Seemed to me she was in the driver's seat . . . in cahoots with the kidnappers. If we just knew how to reach her, we'd know *where*."

Ramon cleared his throat, trying to recall other things he'd seen: he'd been so intent on finding signs of mistreatment, other details of the Web cast could've flown right past him.

"Did you catch what Cat was signaling with her fingers?"

"Ah, that was it!" Ramon thought back to his initial impressions, trying to recall the details. "I need to watch that part again. Was she spelling something?"

"Yes, but what?"

"I'll have the IMB agents work on that," he replied firmly. "Let's both watch her hands again—call each other if we figure it out. It all happened pretty fast—"

"While something on her other end was distracting us?" the captain mused sadly. "Let me know when Kurt and Rick plan to show up. If the *Fantasy* is anywhere near Porto Di Angelo, I'll get there soon as I can. I'd cut this current cruise short, but my passengers would have my ass for that."

"I understand. But you know," Ramon said thoughtfully, "now that I've seen Valenzia's part of this, I'm confident that neither Leilani nor Cat will be sold. Or harmed. The kidnappers are just after our money. I also think the Contessa will do something to get our girls home, even if we don't catch the bastards who snatched them."

There was a longer pause this time.

"I hope you're right, Ramon. This escapade's getting dicier by the day," Jack replied. "The cameraman and that guy in the eye patch might retaliate, now that Cat's sent those signals. And who knows how many other guys received this Web cast? Could be hundreds. And could be her captor sent it to only you and me. Let me know about the IMB boys, all right?"

"Will do. Keep your spyglass handy, Captain. Watch out for pirates."

"Pirates ahoy! All hands on deck—we got another one!"

Grant Carey clicked links connected to the e-mail, but as Bruce and Trevor huffed up the loft steps he cussed under his breath. Damn it, he couldn't reply to this one, either, or trace its sender. He opened the attached file entitled Fair-Haired Slave.

Trevor leaned over his shoulder to glare at the computer screen. "You can't mean we've gotten another one of those fuckin'—"

"Looks like it. The message was very cryptic. Said we might want to watch the *'transaction'* that took place this morning." Carey clicked on the FORWARD arrow, half afraid of what he'd see. "Seems whoever sent yesterday's enchantress thing—holy shit, who's this babe in the velvet blindfold?"

On his other side, Bruce moaned. "If she needs rescuing, I volunteer! Would you look at the way she's playing that organ—"

"But that's Cat there in the background! What the hell—?" Grant sensed he didn't want to know why she crouched at such an odd angle to the floor—while that hot little mama in the blindfold sucked cock like there was no tomorrow.

And maybe there wasn't. Did the e-mail message mean this "transaction" was a done deal?

"We've got to watch for clues about . . . I've had a bad feeling about Cat's pirate kidnapping vacation from the get-go, so—"

"Shhh! Listen to that bitch in the red wig! She's—"

"She's convincing the Asian dude to *buy* this chick," Trevor muttered. "But isn't that the same guy who played the priest yesterday?"

That made sense to him, unfortunately. But it gave Grant a glimmer of hope that this was only playacting. "Yeah . . . same facial shape and—shit! Now he's unfastening Cat from the damn wall! What kind of creeps would clip her to an iron ring—"

"But you gotta admit she's got a great bod for bondage. For a girl." Bruce's thigh jiggled in anticipation, yet he looked really worried. "This is all my fault, for givin' her that Powerball ticket when—"

"Yeah, right! You just wish you were down there in the Caribb—"

"Shhh!" Grant waved them off in exasperation. "This has gone beyond fun and games, guys. The message made it sound like this sale thing was for real! She doesn't look like she's been knocked around, but—wait! What's she doing with her hands?"

The three of them moved in closer, focused on the monitor.

"Spelling . . . damn, I dunno! Go back! Go back!" Bruce demanded. "She must've known she'd be on video stream today, so she practiced—"

They held their breath as the images blurred backward. Then they watched again, in slow-mo.

"Looks like a . . . W . . . and then a—"

"Is that an O or a—"

"G! It ends in G, and she's doing it again!"

"Yep, that's a word all right, and if we knew—"

Carey gasped as Cat took it from behind. "What difference does it make? She's down there—somewhere—while we're up here getting worried sick about—"

"Slave trading. Now *that's* sick—"

"I say we head south on the first flight outta here."

"Jeez, that dude in the eye patch is—"

"Just my type, but that's not why I plan to get my hands on him!" Trevor stood at his full height to watch the olive-skinned woman in the risqué white lace play *Let's Make a Deal*—except it was Cat's life on the line. "We might be the best friends Cat has right now, guys. Who knows? Maybe those new caretakers on her island set her up for this."

"So they could live on Porto Di Angelo with everything paid for? A credible motive, now that Cat's accounts are activated." Grant took in an eyeful of that slinky bitch in the bridal-white lace. Nipped his lip when Cat obeyed that Asian dude's command to lick her thonged pussy.

"Holy shit. I didn't think Cat was the type to—"

"Maybe she didn't, either—until she had something to prove to whoever's filming this."

"Like, maybe she was told if she followed orders—behaved herself—"

"They'd set her loose? I'm thinking she knows better. It took some forethought and practice to make those finger letters."

"Get outta that damn movie attachment and find me a plane ticket!" Trev insisted, grabbing the mouse. "I can't watch what these sickos are doing to her—"

"I'm with you, Trev!" Bruce chimed in.

"All for one and one for all!" Grant watched Trevor click over to Travelocity, sounding a lot more gung-ho than he felt. "We'll need to take plenty of cash, and copies of her U.S. citizenship docs and—"

"Gotta pack the daggers in the checked baggage. They'll never get through security."

Trev and Grant gaped at their younger housemate, whose fists were clenched at his sides. "You can't think we'll take our—"

"Pirate gear. Yessir." The blond yanked an invisible sword from an imaginary sheath at his waist and brandished it like they did when they played their roles. "We've got to be ready for anything! Or at least *distract* those bastards so Cat can break away when she sees that her real ship has come in."

21

Cat bubbled toward the surface of consciousness ... drifted up through layers of mist and dense, hazy images that didn't quite make sense ... as if her mind suddenly felt lucid and the rest of her had been submerged in a deep, cool gel that progressed from teal into turquoise and upward into aquamarine that sparkled like a sunstruck gemstone.

Almost there—almost ready to figure out—

Instinct made her lids quiver over eyes that didn't dare open yet. Intuition told her to bide her time, to get a feel for where she might be before anyone else knew she was awake. Whatever they'd drugged her with had been soooo smooth and sweetly hypnotic, she was in no hurry to rejoin the real world. What she'd seen in her mind lingered like wisps of mist ... felt more enticing—and safer—than the ordinary light of day.

She sensed it *was* day ... and she was outdoors. Very near the sea, which ebbed and flowed with its mystical whisperings. ...

But hadn't Arthur Wong ordered her locked away where no

one would find her? So why was she outside, where she felt the ocean's soft spray on her face?

She took stock of her situation: yes, she was still naked, but in the shade, surely, since she wasn't squinting. Nor did her skin feel ready to fry.

Puzzled, she exhaled very softly. For all she knew, three Wongs were leaning over her to monitor her breathing. . . .

It was breathing she heard, in counterpoint to the whisper of the waves . . . breathing that sounded rhythmic and deep, as though some sort of physical exertion went along with it.

Open your eyes just a slit, missy!

No! *They might be waiting for me to move, and—*

Chicken! You gonna hover here in limbo all day? Get a grip, girl!

Before she could resolve her conflicted conversation with her guardian angel, Cat's eyes popped open.

She was indeed on a beach—saw the cerulean sea arching up into a large wave that toppled over itself and rolled toward the shoreline of white sand, just beyond the shade of these palm trees, where she—

She was caged.

The black iron bars rising on all sides of her scared the beje-sus out of her, until she realized it could keep the beasties away as effectively as they could keep her in sight.

And that breathing? Without moving her head, Cat caught sight of a tall, slender male with jet-black hair flowing down his bare back. He moved in slow, controlled motions, like a kung fu fighter who didn't kick or jab. Instead, his arms flowed in graceful arcs and pushing motions while his legs flexed in steady, measured stances.

Thomas. Her eyes remained on him, drinking in his grace and agility without revisiting her resentment over how he'd led her into temptation and trouble.

Yes, he'd kidnapped her. And, yes, his father had supposedly sold her on eBay or some such crazy thing. Yet she could muster no bitterness toward him. No stress. She just watched the slender Asian's smooth, repetitive motions . . . heard his deep intake of breath as he drew his arms toward himself and then felt him exhale as he scooped his hands up from his knees, past his chest, and then pushed them into a starburst above his head. His loose silk shirt and pants moved with him, adding to his allure.

He looked so serene. So . . . focused. Cat envied him, here in this paradise where he seemed at one with the shining sky and the deep green of the leaves and the rhythm of the sea as it lapped the sand. So sharp and pinpoint lucid she felt, she suspected it was from the drugs. Didn't give one little damn about it, either.

Then, just offshore, a dolphin leaped straight up into the air, flicked its tail, and chittered at them as it arched headfirst into the sea.

A little *ohhh* escaped her. Thomas's slow lunge didn't miss a beat: he followed his moving hand in her direction and stopped in a palm-pushing motion to glance her way.

"Welcome back. Don't get up too fast or you'll fall."

Like I wanna get up, came her mind's reply.

She felt quite content to lie on her side and watch him step back into a closed stance. Then, with breathtaking control, Thomas bent so his palms brushed the air above his knees—

Caressing the aura of his thighs, ya know.

—and then brought them together with prayerful reverence. He bowed low. Then he slowly rose to his full height, his hands still pressed together as he focused on her.

"Ah, my dove . . . my wondrous lotus blossom awakes to behold her master performing his morning tai chi meditation."

All sorts of smart-ass retorts came to her, but Cat felt no compulsion to blurt them out. Let herself flutter in the breeze like a silk flag, drinking in those dulcet tones of his low voice . . .

letting the sounds caress her ears. Why quiz him about her whereabouts? Or this very visible hiding place? He'd give these answers sooner than she really wanted them, so Cat let him take the lead and have his way. Or let him believe he did, anyway.

"You slept well?" he inquired.

Had she? She blinked at him, content in her silence.

Thomas walked slowly across the secluded beach, sending sand backward in the wake of each footstep. His hair swung like a rich, ebony cape, catching the sunlight in its luster. He gripped the iron bars on either side of his angular face.

"When you're more fully awake, you'll thank Charles and me for hiding you where Father himself won't find you!" he said with a quirk in his smile. "We couldn't see leaving you to Ebonique's whims, or in the bowels of her slave compound for God knows how long. We believe you'll show your appreciation in . . . appropriate ways . . . for our creative leniency."

As her mind gathered itself, Cat sensed no one had purchased her after they made those two films—

Not Captain Jack or Ramon? Damn. . . .

—or Thomas wouldn't dare hide her—

Like Papa Wong couldn't find me on his own damn island!

Her bullshit meter began to register . . . but, as Thomas had said, she might well be rotting away in Ebonique's stronghold instead of feeling the sea breeze and watching the dolphins play. There went another one, leaping high into the morning-glory sky, wiggling its tail, terribly pleased with itself. Damned if it didn't look right at her and laugh!

She giggled.

Thomas glanced toward the ocean. "Yes, my dear, even our dolphins flirt with lovely ladies," he remarked breezily.

Cat suddenly suspected those playful dolphins were no freer than she was. Did the Wongs kidnap Flipper for a price, too? Nothing would surprise her at this point.

"Have you ever swum with a dolphin, my lovely?" her warden mused aloud. "Tourists pay big money to step into a swim tank with twenty others, trussed up in life jackets, to bob in the water while the dolphins swim between them."

He flashed her one of his magical, mystical smiles. "But I can give you goggles and a freestyle encounter with Romeo. You may hug him and ride—or dive with him, if you feel that confident," he said in a rising voice. "Whatever you wish, my blossom! It'll be my delight to watch you discover his warm, slick skin and the bulk of him as he rubs against you like an oversize kitten. Perhaps Juliet will join us. She's shyer but just as tame."

Excitement sizzled through her. She'd always wanted to swim—in controlled circumstances—with dolphins, and yet . . .

"Not very together yet," she murmured. Her head spun into a loop-de-loop when she sat up, so she collapsed into the warm sand again. "Might drown. Might just fall asleep and slip away—"

"Not on my shift you won't!" he replied slyly, yet he seemed anything but the big bad-ass pirate as he gazed at her. "I'll have Charles bring you something to eat—fresh water to revive you. Don't go away!"

She stuck out her tongue at his back as he ran, but to her rubbery muscles it felt like the leer of a deformed jack-o'-lantern. What was it with her head? Cat rather enjoyed this sense of drifting in and out—not being responsible for the state she was in—but how long would it last? What if they kept her doped to control her from here on out?

What if you never get to go home???

She fought it then—shook her head to clear her muzzy thoughts. Slowly Cat sat up . . . crossed her legs to balance herself . . . absently stroked the sand from her legs . . . and recalled old jokes about it getting up your crack when you sunbathed naked.

The thought of exactly *where* sand might've gone propelled

her toward the nearest wall. When the Wong brothers returned, she was standing against a warm iron bar wiping sand from her puss as discreetly as she could—considering she was naked in a cage on the beach.

"Hot for it already!" Charlie crowed. "What a woman! Never gets enough and needs the both of us to keep her satisfied!"

Cat gripped the bar to fight her nausea. Didn't have her legs under her yet, and already they expected her to drop and spread. Men were alike no matter what their nationality, weren't they? The serenity she'd felt while Thomas performed his tai chi had flown like a crow, and she wanted to lash out at his younger brother for being too damned perky and presumptuous. Among other things.

Charlie offered her some ruby-red liquid in a tumbler damp with condensation, but she just looked at it. "Don't tell me. Now you're giving me that rum punch we got on your yacht."

Charlie feigned shock and astonishment. "How can you think such a thing, Miss Kitty? We enjoy an occasional round of Cat in a Cage, but we would *never* add insult to injury. This is fruit punch, my love. It'll bring your blood sugar and hydration level back up. We love it when you're sweet and wet, you know."

Cat in a Cage? These cheeky bastards had made her situation into a new game! Another way to mock her! Thomas and Charles had promised to protect her from their father . . . which sounded like a pretty good idea, if she could believe *any* of this manure they were spreading.

Who else do you have, doll? Besides me?

Spike made a good point: even when she had only dubious things to choose from, the choice was still hers. And Charlie's bright red fruit punch looked like the most delectable decision she'd made in days.

She snatched the glass and chugged it down without stopping for breath. Looked straight at him as she plunked the tumbler back into his hand. "Gimme more," she rasped.

"What a woman! *Yessss!*" The younger Wong scurried away with his lime shirttails fluttering behind him. That pathway of mosaic tiles looked too, well, *planned* to lead anywhere but the house, which meant Arthur Wong might stroll out here at any moment, didn't it? But what did she really know about these pirates . . . the motives behind what they said and did?

"Doesn't take much to excite Charles," his brother remarked in a low, hypnotic tone. It was a voice he could easily use to control her because she reveled in its richness. "I, however, actually *care* that your functions return to normal before we take that swim. Would you still like to go?"

He gazed with bottomless black eyes that seemed to suck her into their depths. He looked serene, even from between the bars of her latest prison.

"Yes. I'd like that," she breathed.

Thomas smiled softly. Lowered his face like a lover, cupping her head in his long, lean fingers. Then he kissed her with an exquisite delicacy that nearly made her faint. "We'll give you a little more recovery time. Or is it my affection making you weak at the knees, my fairy princess?"

For just a moment that's how she felt—like a princess in a Disney movie being swept away in the arms of her true love. The rapid slapping of bare feet on tile brought her out of her fantasy.

"I thought you might be ready for—well, ex*cuse me!*" Charlie jeered. "I see we've already set the mood for *love*—or sex on the beach—or whatever you're after, Thomas. It's my turn! You promised, when you told me I wouldn't be in yesterday's movie!"

Thomas flashed him the most condescending smirk she'd ever seen. "Miss Gamble is mine for as long as I care to entertain her."

"But you *said*—"

Fine! Now they'll fight like puppies over a bone. What a great way to lose an afternoon—

Pay attention, sugar. What brothers fight over can be used against them.

Cat blinked. While Spike always showed up *after* the fact, his gravelly voice reassured her. She listened more attentively as the Wong brothers escalated into an upscale version of "did not—did too," as if she didn't even exist. When she slowly reached out of her cage to grasp the new glass of fruit punch, Charlie never missed a beat.

"You said part of the deal—part of our hiding Cat from Father—was so I'd get another go at her, so—"

She turned away from a man whose fists were planted on his hips and the brother who stood firm, with his arms folded across his chest. Sipping the sweet, fruity concoction this time, Cat realized how tasty it was—an original recipe, no doubt, for Charlie seemed much more talented in the kitchen than he was on the field of brotherly battle.

How irritating, that he'd spoken of having a "*go*" at her. No consideration whatsoever for her feelings, as though she were some cheap tramp at his disposal! She *was* at their mercy, but at least Thomas pretended to give her choices, even if he had his way in the end.

Cat smiled slowly. Someday, yes, she'd remember that these two Wongs could be set off by the denial of her favors—if Arthur didn't hear their squabbling first and condemn all three of them to some sort of punishment. *That* Wong was turned on by demeaning others. To him, everything was a power game.

So strip him of his power.

She blinked again. Glanced over her shoulder as one face grew redder while the other appeared more distant. What would it would take to strip Arthur of his power? Valenzia Borgia certainly knew.

He can't get it up, remember? Has to play fetish games—have a fantasy where his power is usurped by his lover.

And speaking of fantasy: out on the ocean, a large ship came into view. Cat *so* wanted it to be the *Captive Fantasy*—so wanted to holler out as it sailed past so Captain Jack would hear her cries for help. Of course, having *any* ship's captain realize she was a prisoner here would be a positive thing.

Cat couldn't believe the two brothers were still arguing, now about something unrelated to having sex with her. As she stepped to the opposite side of the cage to watch the huge cruise ship sail closer . . . closer, her desperation took over.

What were the odds, if she threw her glass high into the sunny sky, that someone at the ship's railing would see its flash and then recognize it as a cry for help? Could she send a mental message, like Leilani? Or should she scream at the top of her lungs and take whatever punishment the Wongs doled out? At least she would've alerted the outside world of her predicament.

Her hand trembled as she gripped the empty glass, studied the spaces between the top bars of her cage, so she wouldn't throw the tumbler against one. Behind her, two male voices raged. The magnificent vessel came close enough that she could make out individual dots as heads at the railing: it was a Royal Caribbean ship, and awfully far away for a yell to be heard above its engines. She had an ice cube's chance in hell of being seen and then rescued, but if she didn't try, how could she live with herself? Wouldn't *not* trying to escape mean she wanted to remain a slave?

As her arm cocked back over her shoulder, Cat inhaled mightily. The cruise ship was moving fast enough that she had a very brief window of opportunity to—

"Nice try, Miss Gamble. But it disappoints and saddens me."

Thomas stepped around to block her view of the ship. All

she saw now were those two eyes like fathomless black pits. Lips that had just kissed her pressed into a tight line.

"Give me the glass and no one gets hurt."

Cat fought the urge to laugh; Thomas Wong was deadly serious. Would he get nasty now that she'd tried to attract outside attention?

He reached inside the cage, and then his hand stopped. His thoughts changed direction, and he withdrew his arm. "If you'll give me the glass, Alina, we'll forget this little incident happened," he said softly. "We'll prepare ourselves to swim with Romeo and Juliet in the idyllic realms of the deep—"

Is he going to drown me?

"—where few mortals know the beauty and bliss of the silent sea, accompanied by peaceful, intelligent creatures who crave our affection."

"So do you Wongs smuggle dolphins, too?"

His lip quirked. For just a moment that magical, mystical facade slipped and she glimpsed the capitalist beneath it. "We're in business to make money, my lovely," he murmured. "Thanks to my father's various enterprises, we have an elegant penthouse for our privileged guests to enjoy."

Cat knew better than to pursue this thread of conversation, since he'd backed away from his original wrath. The only sign of that cruise ship now was the surf pounding against the shore in its wake. She was still a hostage on this island. Had three captors to contend with until her next opportunity sailed by.

"A swim sounds wonderful, Thomas." Her gaze lingered on the sparkling turquoise sea as she swallowed her disappointment. Relenting—getting real—she extended her arms between the bars in a gesture of appeasement.

"Thank you for offering me such a sensual temptation," she continued softly, fighting fire with fire. "While experiencing the dolphins and the water in my naked state sounds extremely alluring, I tingle with the anticipation of my warm body drifting into yours, Thomas. As the afternoon sun ignites our passions, it will free us to love with all the abandon of Nature herself."

His eyes held hers. "You're pretty good at that, my dove. Couldn't have said it better myself."

"Occupational hazard, when you're a writer."

What she wouldn't give to be back in Trevor Teague's loft, letting her pirate fantasy flow into her manuscript with the hearty exclamations of her three fun-loving friends inspiring her from downstairs. Did they have any idea why she didn't e-mail them? Any inkling she could really use their friendship and legal influence about now?

With a sigh, Cat grasped his hand. "I've never been swimming naked. Never made love in the ocean, either."

His Adam's apple bobbed as he swallowed. "Then I shall be delighted to initiate you into those pleasures, my Alina. Shall we?"

22

Where had Charlie gone? Probably back to his kitchen with his tail between his legs, to whip up some Ex-Lax fudge for the brother who'd pulled rank on him.

Not that it mattered. Cat inhaled the scents of sea salt and hot sand and flowers that bloomed in lush abundance; they'd caged her in a small grotto garden she hadn't seen from her room. A waterfall burbled down the hillside into a pool that glowed morning-glory blue, where a huge Buddha sat in prayerful repose. She sensed this was a sanctuary where Thomas meditated or made plans to control his captives.

But she was free now—held only by Thomas's hand, anyway—as they strolled across the soft beach. An inlet protected the bay from the wakes of oceangoing ships and gave the grotto a sense of serenity. Ahead of them, orange buoys bobbed in a rectangle.

"So even your dolphins live as captives?" she queried. Then she wished she'd chosen less challenging words.

Thomas smiled with that Zen-like patience. "If we didn't confine them, they'd be at the mercy of poachers. Romeo and

Juliet are our pets, Alina. I'm their trainer and mentor, so they'll welcome you lavishly. You'll be glad you swam with us, lovely lady."

Yes, he was her warden, but Cat was as susceptible as the next woman to a compliment. He stopped on the wet shoreline, where the waves lapped at their bare feet, to gaze at her with unadulterated lust. Slowly he untied his pants and shrugged from his shirt. The shiny fabric of black and purple and red rippled in the sunlight, baring him as it whispered down his arms and legs.

"Do you find me attractive, my Alina?"

With the wind playing in his long ebony hair, and his whiskey skin and fit physique, how could she deny it? "You know I do, Thomas."

"*How* do I know?" he prompted in that hypnotic voice. "You withhold your innermost thoughts from me, my love. I'll adore you even more if I share in your fantasies . . . if I can be the only man you want, from here on out."

He sounded ready to commit—to *care* for her. Or was this just another of his ploys? His father had probably used the same sly, sexy lines to entice the Contessa. . . .

Yet, as he gazed soulfully into her eyes, Cat knew there could be worse fates than to bask in the gentle light this man would shine into her life, if she allowed herself to love him.

What are you thinking, missy? Tell this thief whatever he wants to believe—just like he's been bullshitting you!

She had a brief flash of male faces: Grant and Bruce and Trevor . . . Captain Jack as he appeared on his Web site . . . .tall, dark Ramon with his crocodile smile. Odd that she should think of them all at this moment when she was about to skinny-dip with Thomas Wong.

Or was it a sign?

Cat smiled. She radiated peace and bliss at her Asian attendant full-force, hoping he fell for it. When she had time alone, she might try the telepathy thing with Ramon and Captain Jack, but right now she was on a mission: to woo this Wong. He *was* all Wong for her, like Spike implied, but it wouldn't do to rub his nose in it.

"So what do we do now?" In the clear water, she could see orange plastic fencing beneath the buoys. Two dolphins, submerged side by side, watched them with anticipation that made the water wiggle around their bodies.

Thomas drew her against his warm, taut body. Caught her chin in his palm . . . guided her into a lush kiss that waxed passionate. He moaned softly as he pressed his erection into her abdomen. "Do you swim?" he whispered.

"Yessss," she replied, letting the hiss tickle his ear.

"Good. Charles does not."

Now wasn't *that* interesting?

Thomas's smile took on a smugness she wouldn't have associated with his mystical mindset. It meant the brothers would have one more thing to squabble about—and that was to her advantage, wasn't it? They could exasperate each other while she thought of other things. Like escape. Or connecting to Captain Jack.

"You are mentally preparing yourself for this special dolphin encounter, I see. That's wise," her companion intoned. "Romeo and Juliet will sense your affinity to them—or your aversion. Or your utter ignorance about Universal Wisdom and the souls we all have in common."

Ah, there it was again, that higher-realm, cosmic BS. Cat smiled serenely; when Thomas Wong waxed philosophical, he was easier to tolerate.

She tipped up her mouth for another of those kisses that scorched her from the soul out. Too, too wonderful he was, when his lips were involved. Such a shame that he was into selling women—as though she could be owned!

"Wade in slowly with me," he instructed, his hand wrapped

around hers. "Send them your love and they'll swim right up to you, Alina. Once we tread water in the tidal pool, they'll know we're ready to play."

Fascinated, Cat watched the two dolphins approach in the crystal-clear water: one split off to the left and one to the right, as though they were choreographing this visit. The water swished around her with enough current that she grabbed Thomas to remain standing.

"They—they're huge," she murmured.

"Better than four hundred pounds apiece. But such gentle, loving creatures." Thomas reached out, and the nearest dolphin swam eagerly alongside him, insinuating itself under his hand to be petted.

Cat chuckled. "Which one's this?" The other dolphin cut silently through the water to rub her leg like a giant cat.

"Romeo, of course. He's quite the ladies' man."

"He's so . . . slick and warm and smooth," she marveled.

"That's what they say about me, as well."

Cat chortled and shot him a knowing look. "You have that long raven hair in your favor though. Poor Romeo is hairless—"

"The better to glide through the water, my dear."

"—but goodness, he looks so—so motivated."

"As he is. His main purpose is to please, however he can. A useful mindset, don't you agree?" Thomas glanced at her for a reaction and then clapped his hands twice. Juliet, a few yards away, rose out of the water to flap her flippers at them. "Wave back."

When she did, the female yipped and scooted backward in the water, still upright.

He made a kissy noise and tapped his cheeks then. Both dolphins swam to him, placing their shiny gray snouts on either side of his face as he slipped his arms around them.

"You see? The Beatles had it right, my Alina. Love is all you need."

Cat watched in delight and then tapped on her own cheeks, making that same kissy noise. A moment's hesitation . . . and then one followed the other away from Thomas, to smooch on her. Her laughter echoed around the little grotto.

As though they delighted in her happiness, the two dolphins grunted softly as they nuzzled her neck. Then, at a whistle from Thomas, they raced each other to the far side of the buoyed enclosure. The demonstration ended with their dramatic leaps into the air.

"Very playful and affectionate, much like their trainer. Do you believe that, Alina?" The sunlight dappled his bronze skin, and those obsidian eyes sparkled at her.

"They were wild, and you trained them?"

"Romeo, Juliet, and many others. And while you may regard me as a thief or a poacher," he continued with an arch of his eyebrow, "believe as well that when we sell our trained dolphins to encounter centers, *millions* of people experience their intelligence and affection each year."

He paused, waiting for her to acknowledge his humanitarian efforts—or just the sheer talent he had for training his charges. Maybe even the kind who walked on two legs—for, indeed, Cat had learned a lot since she'd met this alluring wizard.

You're only pretending *to be under his thumb, remember?*

"Very impressive," she murmured. She gazed beneath the clear water. "And so is *that*. Your most powerful teaching tool, I bet."

"See something you want, sweet Alina?" Thomas narrowed his eyes and lowered his provocative voice. "Come after it. Claim it as your own."

She heard two challenges there: taking that magnificent erection for her body's pleasure, or possessing it—and the man attached to it—on a more emotional level. Cat smiled sweetly. She would keep this encounter strictly physical, since he'd probably influenced countless other captives this way.

As she stepped within reach of him, however, Thomas retreated. He dared her to follow, gazing intently at her to lure her into greater depths . . . in the water and in their relationship.

How deep did the sea get within this enclosure? Would he tempt her over an edge so she'd grab him to stay afloat? It looked like another way to establish himself as her savior, the man she depended on for pleasure and protection on this island.

Or would he drag her underwater and hold her there?

Instinct told her that, just as he'd balanced her on the edge of that balcony while he tongued her into orbit, he intended to lure her beyond her limits again . . . beyond her comfort zone in a very sexual, sensual way no other man had. After all, it wasn't in his best interest for her to drown, was it?

As she fixed her eyes on his, Cat reminded herself that here, in this tropical grotto, where a waterfall danced and sang its way down a rugged cliffside to be with Buddha, she could explore her body and its reactions. Explore her psyche, too, in the capable hands of this tantalizing Asian.

Think what you'll be able to show Captain Jack! her thoughts teased. Or was that Spike? Either way, it sounded like a yes.

Cat stepped forward. Reached for him, his willing victim again. He read her reply—her surrender to his will—even if she knew it was just another facet of her facade he saw.

Slowly stepping backward, Thomas opened his arms in invitation. His cock pointed at her as the sparkling sea swirled around them.

And then he was gone!

As Cat had speculated, there *was* a ledge. Thomas had led her there, to drop beneath the crystal water's surface and swim like one of the dolphins he'd trained. Romeo and Juliet surged over to romp with him.

She gawked. The dolphins caught Thomas in the current they generated between their powerful bodies, so he effortlessly joined an underwater ballet that left her breathless. His black hair flowed around him like a magician's silk cape, swirling in the currents as if it held universal mysteries of life and love in its inky richness. Then it wrapped around him like a cocoon as he spun, until he raised his arms and surfaced a few feet to her right.

Cat's breath caught at the sight of this sleek Asian adversary with his midnight hair clinging to him like a second skin. He treaded water to catch his breath, watching her. Wanting her.

"Come after it," he repeated softly. "Come and get it, my Alina. Claim it as your own and let it spirit you away on the wings of another mind-altering climax."

He reached for her. And as those long, lean fingers beckoned to her heart and soul, her feet had already accepted his challenge.

Carefully she felt the lip of that underwater precipice with her bare foot. The inlet's warm current swirled softly around her chest, making her breasts bob on the sunlit surface. Inside, she felt hotter than this tropical day: Thomas was so long and hard she remained focused on him, allowing her curiosity and hunger to overrule her head. He was slowing, to let her catch up to him . . . to let her reach beneath the water and grasp that splendid erection.

Thomas pulled her against his willowy body, lifting her effortlessly so her chest was level with his face.

"Beg for it, Alina," he crooned. Then he noisily suckled her wet breasts, making her laugh aloud. "Let me be your merman. We'll make love beneath the sea like dolphins who frolic in the water with their passion."

How could she refuse such an invitation? Cat closed her eyes and let her head loll back. Surrendered to the longing he stirred within her.

"Yesssss, Thomas," she sighed like the fickle wind, "make me your mermaid! Take me into your underwater world, King Neptune, and crown me your queen!"

Sounded ridiculous—unless you were a wayward woman caught in a mystic's spell. Thomas let her slide very slowly down his strong, slender body. She held her breath when her breasts felt the water. Opened herself to him, above and below: to his exquisite kiss . . . to the maddening anticipation of his cock insisting on entry.

The kiss, as wet and silken as the sea, made them squirm with rising need until he broke away with a gasp. "Breathe deeply," he instructed, "and hang on!"

Obediently Cat filled her lungs—and then he filled her from below with a single, purposeful thrust. He pulled them under the water, using the thrust of his hips to propel them as he made smooth, crystal-blue love to her. On either side of them, the dolphins swam in sync: they kept their distance, yet the flow between their huge bodies put an additional spin to this incredible tryst.

Awed by these novel sensations, Cat forgot to worry about where her next breath came from. A veil of raven hair flowed around them, to envelop them in its mystery as Thomas spun her in slow forward rotations. His body moved rhythmically into hers, with the added suspense—the dangerous realization—that she might not draw another breath in time. Might burst with the need for air as much as for completion with him.

Her hips wiggled feverishly. Cat was ready to implode, and Thomas sensed exactly when he needed to thrust to suspend her in his surreal magic once again. For a few more heart-stopping moments they twirled in ever-slowing rotations, as though he were seducing her with the threat—no, the *promise*—to take her into the next world with him.

Just when she thought her lungs might burst, Thomas spun them upward as one.

When her head broke the surface, Cat cried out into the bright sunlight, craving air as much as the climax that rocked her body. On and on she rocked against him as he probed deep to seek his own release. He'd found his footing. His thrusts overrode her need to think or react or even breathe; Cat wrapped herself around him, awash in yet another world of sensations she'd never dared to imagine. Totally spent, she clung to his wet silky skin and satiny heat . . . a paradise they'd created between them.

His lips found the sensitive shell of her ear. "Alina, my love, tell me we can share this always!" he whispered.

With her legs wrapped around his strong body and their final shudders still tingling within her, Cat could have gushed her acceptance soooo easily.

You got bigger fish to fry, honey.

She blinked. Was that Spike or her intuition that sounded so edgy? She rested her head against Thomas's wet hair while she focused.

Charlie was seated on the beach. He looked right at her as he talked on a cell phone—*her* cell phone, which was a bright, shiny pink!

Cat surged, nearly toppling Thomas backward in her fierce need to reclaim that J2 phone. She had to tell the talker on the other end where she was and to *come get her*!

"Charlie, damn it! Give me that—let me *go*, Thomas!" she shrieked. But the more she struggled, the harder he held her.

The rumble of his laughter told her that yes, once again, she'd been had.

23

"Yes, this is Jack Spankevopoulos! And who the hell are *you*, telling me Cat Gamble has drowned!" His breath came in ragged gasps. He wiped sweat from his forehead as he struggled for rational thought. "You're the same crackpot who sent me that Web cast of her, aren't you? Well, by God, if she's dead, you'll hang for it, bastard! Tell me where—"

Click.

Jack stared at his cell phone in disbelief. Unbelievable anguish. God, he'd never even met this gorgeous creature, Cat Gamble, yet his entire being felt like it had been snuffed out.

Like this jerkball claimed Cat had been.

"You think it was them? The pirates who swiped Miss Gamble and my Leilani?" Ramon's eyes widened with concern; his body went tight like the expressions of the uniformed men who sat at the patio table with them.

Bad enough these two IMB agents had ogled their women while they'd all tried to decipher the word Cat spelled. Now they all bristled like pit bulls with the need to catch these culprits and serve up their just punishment—or not so just, depending on who got to them first.

"Lemme see that phone," Rick demanded.

Jack sighed as he handed it over. "I'll wager they've confiscated Cat's cell phone and made this call with it," he muttered. "If so, you'll find absolutely nothing to trace her whereabouts. No callback number, *nothing*! Stavros searched for connections through my computer, too, after those Web casts. All this high-end technology is worthless! I've been hanging by the balls all week *and I'm fucking tired of it*, gentlemen!"

The porch vibrated with his frustration when he slapped the table, a clear sign he was way too wrapped up in this woman.

But it was more than having a potential passenger in danger—it was a deep need to reclaim what had so nearly been *his*. He'd sensed, from the first sound of her voice, that Cat Gamble was destined to be his mate long before her week aboard his ship was over.

"Sorry this is happenin' to you, man," Kurt muttered. "We've got our boats out and got our investigators trolling the Internet for leads, too. We're *so* close! Just one lead away."

"But it's gotta be the right lead," his partner pointed out.

"It's like they know exactly when to call. Which strings to pull," Ramon remarked darkly. "Do you suppose this guy *knew* we were all together, talking about how to rescue her?"

"Nothing would surprise me. They keep leading us down the primrose path with little tidbits of truth buried in their bullshit. What can we believe?" Jack smacked his fist into his palm. "For two days they display Cat and Leilani at their hottest—for potential buyers, they say—and now this guy claims she's dead!"

"And hangs up before you can ask where to claim her body," Ramon added with a scowl. "I didn't think they'd let any harm come to her, because—"

"What if she drowned while trying to escape them?" *Because I let her down*, his overwrought brain added.

For a few moments he silently reviewed the images they'd seen on Ramon's computer . . . Cat making her gestures a little too hurriedly—and in front of lovely, pert breasts that jiggled from the thrusts of that long-haired asshole pumping her from behind. Once rational thought had time to dispel the shock of that phone call, he didn't really believe she'd drowned—didn't *want* to believe it, anyway—but what a shame it would be if such energy and cleverness and beauty were lost forever.

Jack looked away, to get past this morose mood so he could *do* something. But what would that be?

The sputter of an engine—a badly maintained engine—interrupted the stillness. Ramon sat taller to look over the porch railing.

"Ferry boat," he murmured, sounding half hopeful that their women were aboard. He stood up when the whine died and a rope thumped against the pier. "Rodrigo's delivering something. Excuse me."

Jack stood up, as did the two agents. "No way is there a body in any of those boxes," he muttered.

"These jokers are pulling your strings, Jack. Your *purse* strings," Rick reminded him quietly. "Just watch. If you won't pay their ransom, they'll work on her family from the States next, if they haven't already. Or they'll feed you some other line with loopholes built in. Too many desperadoes out there to keep track of, and their high-tech gadgets let them get away with crap like that."

Jack sighed, watching tall, dark Ramon close the distance from the house to the dock in long, leggy strides. His gaze wandered farther out on the water, where the *Captive Fantasy* was anchored.

"I truly appreciate your help," he remarked wearily. "I'd

best get back to my passengers before they shanghai Stavros and sail away without me. They were peeved that I made this unscheduled stop."

"We'll be in touch as soon as we find something." Rick glanced at Kurt and nodded toward the IMB cruiser in the dock slip. "We'd better be on our way, too. The weather service is predicting a storm later today, which always keeps us busy afterward."

Glumly, Captain Jack nodded. A storm was *just* what he needed, now that his passengers were already on edge. Any other day he'd bask in the beauty of this island Cat had acquired . . . the flowering trees that swayed in the sun-swept breezes, and the cool serenity of this haven of angels, this house he longed to explore for more clues of her—not that she'd lived here long enough to leave anything of benefit behind. He just wanted to get a feel for the woman who'd gone missing at the wrong time.

As he approached the dock, the rapid chatter of island patois flew between Ramon and the ferryman as the shorter man wheeled three sizable boxes from his boat. The loud *whump* they made when they hit the wood suggested that they were extremely heavy.

"Need some help with those?" he called ahead. Then he glanced at the men in whites on either side of him. "Wishful thinking on my part, but maybe the arrival of these boxes is in our favor?"

"Can't hurt to check, can it?"

The ferry's engine roared to life again, and then the rickety old boat sputtered away. Rick and Kurt waved to the man in dreadlocks as though they were well acquainted with him.

"Boxes for Cat," Ramon remarked. "Her attorney was to send her research books and writing supplies here, after she bought the island—"

"And look at this!" Jack crowed. His heart thudded as he

pointed to the shipping label on the top box. "Does the name Grant Carey ring any bells? Even if she never mentioned him by name, there's his phone number!"

He flipped open his cell, thumb-nailing the digits. He was overreacting—grasping at straws—but anyone with any connection to Cat Gamble was fair game now. It was a very long shot that this fellow in the States had heard anything from Cat since her abduction, but—"

"Yes, hello? Grant Carey? This is Jack Spankevopoulos, captain of the *Captive Fantasy*," he crooned, trying to sound conversational rather than crazed. "I'm wondering if you've heard from our girl—from Ms. Gamble, that is—in the last few days?"

Grant's heart hammered. What were the odds of this very guy calling him at this very moment?

"You tell *me* where she is, buddy!" he blurted. "The last message I got from Cat, she was ready for you and your dubious crew to kidnap her for some outlandish slave vacation!"

He gestured frantically for Bruce and Trev: here in this cavernous waiting area filled with Caribbean tourists, it was hard to hear himself think, let alone follow a phone call. The last thing he needed was to lose track of these other two swashbucklers—or lose this connection.

"By the way," he cut in before Captain Spank could answer, "how'd you get *my* number? You must be using Cat's phone, or you have her laptop, or—"

"Matter of fact, I'm standing here on *her* dock, looking at the boxes of books *you* have shipped her," came the terse reply. "Your number's on the shipping label, remember? Shall we waste time circling and pointing like junkyard dogs, or shall we figure out who the hell captured Cat?"

Trev grabbed his elbow. "What's going on? If somebody's—"

"Is it Cat?" Bruce chimed in, his boyish face brightening.

"Shhh!" Grant pressed the cell phone against his ear, wishing several hundred other people weren't milling around in this holding area.

"I beg your pardon?" the voice in his ear demanded coldly. Like maybe this guy thought *he* was responsible for Cat's disappearance.

"Look, I'm sorry," Grant replied. "We're at the San Juan airport, and it's a madhouse because several flights have been delayed by stormy weather—ours among them. I recently received a—a *disgusting* Web cast of Cat and some other woman—"

"That would be Leilani, her island caretaker, whose husband is standing right here beside me," the captain said pointedly. "And believe me, big as this fellow is, we want to keep him on *our* side! So what're you doing in San Juan?"

Grant's lips quirked. This guy might run a questionable business, but he darted and nipped like a bulldog in a conversation. Interrogated like a district attorney, too—or like a man who actually *did* have Ms. Gamble's best interests in mind.

"Cat's my client and close friend. So naturally, when I saw how you pirates had exploited her—had supposedly put her up for *sale* and had an eBay auction running—"

"*Don't* confuse me with the scum who abducted Cat! Just give me a straight answer, or we might as well hang it up."

Carey's eyebrows rose. This guy sounded stressed . . . and very protective. His gut told him to cooperate—if only so Trevor Teague didn't grab the frickin' phone from his ear and take over, the way he was chomping at the bit.

"Point well taken," he demurred. "You sound as worried about her as I am, so I'll give you the benefit of the doubt, if you'll reciprocate. You savvy?"

Bruce and Trevor rolled their eyes at his movie talk, but the guy on the other end chuckled.

"Fair enough." The captain paused a moment to cool down. "Ramon and I called in the International Maritime Bureau the moment we realized what went wrong last week, so they're here, too. Baffled by our lack of leads, even after we've received those same Web casts."

Grant considered how much more to reveal; he and his housemates had spent the long flight plotting out a sneak attack that would've done Captain Jack Sparrow proud, but coming from the States put them at a geographical disadvantage.

"I understand your frustration," Grant replied, "because right before she left, we installed theft-detection software in her laptop for just such an emergency. And we've heard nothing from her since right before she was to sail with you."

"We assume the pirates took it from her. As technologically keen as they seem to be, they probably disabled or removed your software as soon as they found it."

Grant grinned: *he had the missing link!* It would be sooooo tempting to leave this guy hanging! But then the loudspeaker crackled and a reedy foreign voice announced that their flight would be boarding at a different gate in fifteen minutes.

"Look—we need to meet our flight," he replied urgently, "but when I gave the software service rep the last location her laptop sent us, she shot us back a latitude and longitude. She said it was a blank message with a different point of origin from the e-mails Cat had sent from Porto Di Angelo."

There was a pause and some talking on the other end, between ominous bursts of static—probably from that storm. He and Bruce and Trevor slipped into the throng heading toward the concourse for their flight.

"All right, I've got a pen now. Shoot." Spankevopoulos sounded calm and competent, like—well, like the captain of a first-rate ship. Spoke with a killer Brit accent, too, and a mellow voice Cat would've fallen for in a heartbeat.

He couldn't very well back out or give false information that might delay her homecoming, could he? Grant set aside his proprietary tendencies and heroic rescue scenarios and fished a slip of paper from his pocket as they hurried along in the crowd. "Seventeen degrees north latitude—"

"Seventeen north—"

"—and fifty-one degrees west longitude. And say—"

"—fifty-one west—"

"—just to keep everybody on the same page, maybe you could pick us up when we land in St. Lucia?"

"How many is '*us*'?" the captain fired back.

"Three. And if you try anything underhanded—like rescuing her before we can help!—I'm an attorney," Carey asserted. "I can put the *Captive Fantasy* in dry dock until hell freezes over. Not that I think you'd bamboozle us, of course."

Was that another burst of static, or had the Brit stifled an off-color remark?

"If you think I've not given this location to the IMB, you're insane! They're checking their maps as we speak." The captain muffled the phone with his hand for a moment. "And of *course* we'll send a driver for you."

Grant swore he heard a sly chuckle ducking between the captain's lines. "Look for a very tall, very dark gentleman in a wicked goatee with a braided pigtail. And beware his pointed thumbnails," Spankevopoulos added ominously. "He tells some hair-raising tales about who he's used them on. And where."

Grant let out an exasperated sigh and trotted to keep up with Trev and Bruce as they grabbed their boarding passes. "Fine! I have to go now! And if we don't make this two-thirteen flight, tell what's-his-thumbnails to wait!"

A snicker came over the line, which was starting to crackle with a wavering connection. "Get ready for the ride of your lives, Mr. Carey. The *Captive Fantasy* has never lost a passenger, and I guarantee you we won't start now, sir!"

"What've you found?" Jack called as he approached the IMB cruiser. Compared to the sleek white yacht that bobbed in the slip beside it, it looked like a bathtub toy; that fine vessel and this island paradise were just two more reasons to find Cat before anything else happened to her. Once he took her for a spin on *his* ship . . . he envisioned them soaking in the spa together . . . hiding away in one of her posh staterooms—or his. Naked. For days.

But he shoved those thoughts aside. At least he *had* such fantasies again, now that Fate had whispered inside his head and helped him place that phone call to Cat's attorney. Carey sounded like a sincere sort, even if he took himself way too seriously.

Rick looked up from a large map of the Caribbean, which was speckled with more islands than the average person—like Carey—knew about. If Jack wanted to play dirty pool, he could rescue Cat and already have her aboard the *Fantasy* as a legitimate passenger, since—

"Here it is!" the agent said. "But you're not going to believe this, Spank."

He and Ramon stepped to either side of the map stand, scowling. From this vantage point, they saw dark, heavy clouds churning on the horizon.

"It's an island on the far side of Dominica, where there's a Buddhist monastery. The kind where the monks have no contact with the outside world, except to receive supplies."

"Monks?" Ramon sputtered. "Those were no *monks* screwing around with—"

"No, but there were stained-glass windows! We've got them now!" Jack crowed. "I sail past there every week. That pagoda structure fascinates my passengers. Let's go—"

Rick grabbed his arm, his grin purposeful. "Fools rush in, Captain. Before you go invading their turf, treading on holy ground—or at least private property—you'd better have the law on your side."

"And a search warrant or two," his cohort Kurt chimed in.

"From the sound of that conversation, Cat's friends wanted to be in on the—"

"They'll hold us up! They haven't even left San Juan yet!"

"—and from the looks of those storm clouds, we'd do well to plan our strategy while that weather blows through," Rick finished. He was a wiry man but stronger than he appeared. "Ever heard the term 'safety in numbers'? Who knows how many of those guys we'll encounter? And what they might be armed with? They're slave traders, remember?"

Jack's shoulders sank. "Yes, I suppose that's the more rational plan," he said with a sigh, "but—oh, by the way . . ." He glanced at Ramon. "I said you'd meet them at the airport."

"So I heard." The tall man with eyes like scalding coffee didn't sound any too pleased about being pulled away from the search for his wife, now that they'd made the right connection.

"I'm sorry if I acted presumptuous, promising your services without asking you, but you're the perfect bouncer for us," Jack insisted. "You'll know right away if they're legitimate, because you're an *astute* judge of—"

"Cross me, sailor, and *your* ass'll toot. You savvy?"

Jack smiled up at him. "Damn straight I do, sir. Just as I know you'll send those three packing—or just drive away—if something's screwy there."

Ramon straightened to his full, impressive height and then pressed one of those thumbnails into the center of Jack's chest. "I'm holding *you* responsible for whatever happens to Leilani and Cat while I'm gone," he said in a growl of a voice. "No funny business, or you'll learn *exactly* why my nails are filed this way."

24

"Here, kitty kitty kitty . . ."

Cat flipped Charlie Wong the bird and glared at the tidbit he held above her head. Never mind that it was a freshly baked triple-chocolate mocha cookie, so warm the fudge frosting dribbled onto his fingers! She was back in that damn cage, only this time it was in the kitchen where the other Wong brother had taken over her care and feeding.

"Who were you calling on my phone?" she demanded for the fourth time.

Charlie watched a large glob of the frosting fall between the bars and land on her bare shoulder. He aimed the next one better, so it plopped on her breast.

"Let me lick that off and I'll tell you. Promise."

Cat's arm shot between the bars to collar the jerk who was *so* stomping on her last nerve. "What is it with you people? I ask a simple question, and then I get the run-around, or answers so obviously designed to upset me—"

"Then why do you keep asking, my tender lotus blossom?" he mocked in his older brother's tone. "I told you, Miss Kitty—

I called Captain Jack to inform him you'd drowned, so there's no reason for him to search for you. Thomas and I adore you so much we've decided to keep you for ourselves!"

When the whimsical Asian kissed the hand that grasped his collar, Cat shoved him away, totally pissed. Lies upon lies they'd heaped on her—Arthur saying he'd put her up for auction, and now this joker proclaiming her their permanent plaything!

And all that hoo-ha when Arthur ordered her shut away, never to be found? More bullshit! He'd walked in for his dinner half an hour ago, saw her in this cage in the middle of the kitchen, and acted as though everything were hunky-dory.

Of course, for these Wongs, it was. They still had control, and they had pulled other strings than hers—had probably fed conflicting messages to Ramon and Captain Jack and everyone they'd found in her computer's address book. Then they laughed their tight little asses off because everyone was in a dither.

Or at least, she hoped they were. . . .

So now Charlie thought it was a big favor to lick her boob in exchange for another stupid nonanswer. Glaring at him, she swiped at the warm chocolate with her finger and then licked it off—closed her eyes and pumped that digit in and out of her mouth, trying not to moan with how damn good the chocolate was. She was hungry and tired and pissed and—

She jumped to grab the cookie through the top of the cage, but Charlie raised it just beyond her reach. He watched every bob and jiggle of her body, like an obnoxious boy would taunt a dog in a carrier. Then he popped the whole damn cookie into his mouth and bit down, so the edge that didn't fit crumbled softly, delectably . . . oh-so-tenderly down his chin. It bounced against his chest before it hit the floor.

Cat could only watch it with a desperation that sickened her. The kitchen reeked with the rich scents of their steak dinner, and gourmet coffee, and chocolate and brown sugar, so even if this exasperating chef ate every last cookie, the aroma would linger to torment her.

And that's what this was all about: torment. The Wongs might be among the sexiest guys she'd ever seen, but they were dogs circling a doe; each intended to have his steak and eat her, too. And Cat was damn tired of it.

She sat down cross-legged on the kitchen floor with her back to the oven and the man who took another tray of cookies from it.

"Such a pretty, pouty lip you're sticking out, Kitty," he remarked with a chuckle. "As if that will get you what you want."

She nipped that lip, determined not to reply. No more rising to his bait. She would sit here like a lump . . . concentrate on how Jack and Ramon would pool their resources to find her, and *soon*. She could only wonder what poor Leilani might be enduring—wherever she was. Cat hadn't seen her or the Contessa since they'd made that last movie.

"Of course, it's those other pretty lips I'd like to taste," he continued behind her. "Those dark pink lips between your legs, Miss Kitty. That pussy with its slick skin, where the pearls of your *need* pool at your opening, like the warm, dark chocolate I'm drizzling on these cookies. Soooooo delicious."

She did her damnedest not to visualize what he was doing—refused to humiliate herself again by begging for another taste of his outrageously rich fudge sauce and the soft, chewy cookie beneath it. How did this man know of her craving—her absolute enslavement—to the pastries he so lovingly labored over? Or was she an easy mark because she hadn't eaten all day? Next she supposed the Wong trio would gather around her cage for warm cookies and cold milk while she could only watch.

She sat up straighter: Charlie had walked around in front of her, his boyish grin bright. It was useless to turn away from him.

"I know you want one of these, sweetie." He knelt in front of her, to implore her with his sparkling brown eyes. "And if you'll open your legs—if you'll scootch over here and stick your feet between these bars—I'll show you sweetness that'll make you swoon, Cat. I'll make you moan and howl and forget all about mere cookies while I explore your clit with the tip of my tongue.

"But *you* make the first move," he murmured in a voice she strained to hear. "Offer yourself to me. Lie on the floor and . . . hold your lips open so I can gaze at you. Is that so much to ask?"

Damn it, it was! And his sexy, suggestive words wore her down as effectively as those cookies did. With his dark, spiky hair accentuating a dimpled grin, and his hands open in a conciliatory gesture, Charlie Wong was a difficult man to deny.

"I see your puss getting hot and wet," he whispered, settling his gaze between her legs. "I smell your juice, tangy and ripe, and my tongue tingles with the thought of delving inside you, Cat. Please—let me in!"

She shifted and then realized he knew why. It would be another stupid move to press her closed eyes to her bent knees, because Charlie Wong wasn't leaving his domain any time soon.

"When I took my turn at you before, on the kitchen island, I was totally selfish." His eyes widened with feigned sincerity. "But this one's all for you, pretty puss! See—I don't even have my fly unzipped. I'll keep it in my pants."

Charlie licked his lush lips. His expression turned sultry as he ran a finger the length of his front seam. He was thick and hard . . . longer than she'd imagined, blindfolded, when he'd shoved it up her on the island.

Is it us or that oven making it so hot in here?

Cat let her breath seep out like steam from the top crust of a pie . . . a very bubbly cherry pie about to overrun the pan as the pressure built up. She *was* pissed at him—didn't trust Charles any more than his father or his brother. But he talked a pretty line. The oven wasn't the only thing this Asian chef could turn on.

She listened to the hiss of his accelerated breathing, a subtle parallel to the rising winds that announced a storm.

That had to be it. The drop in barometric pressure, temperature, and all those other atmospheric things were at work as much as Charlie Wong was, leaving her physically and emotionally off-balance. She hardly needed to throw herself open to him; she'd had more than her share of hot, wayward sex since she'd been here. But something in his low coaxing . . . something in the way he softly stroked the arch of her nearest foot . . . made Cat ponder a tongue job.

Charlie would withhold her food until she gave in to him. He could do that, couldn't he? And if she didn't eat, she'd be too weak to make a run for it if Captain Jack showed up to rescue her. And *that* would be inexcusable!

Toy with him! Make him *beg for it!*

Words to live by. A way to make him ante up in the humiliation department.

Her smile slipped into sly gear. She spread her legs slightly but scooted back against the bars rather than toward her tormentor. "Charlie," she cooed, "Charlie Wong, you wicked thing. Watch while I stir myself up. You're not the only cook in this kitchen, you know."

His pupils dilated. The bulge behind his zipper twitched.

"You see this looong middle finger?" she asked coyly, wiggling it in front of her nether lips. "It's good for something other than telling you how I feel about being . . . *so* taken advantage of. As you can see, this pretty pink fingernail knows just how to flick this little hot button—"

"But how am I supposed to eat you if you're—"

"You'll have to stay hungry for a while, big boy. We'll see

who gives in first." Cat leaned back to open her legs wider, shamelessly spreading the slickness that had indeed pooled inside her.

A moan escaped him. He licked his sexy lips and speared his fingers through that spiky hair, looking like he'd already romped in the sack but wanted more. *Much* more. He'd started a mustache and beard, and that few days of growth of dark hair on his upper lip and chin gave him an edgier look that really kicked in, now that he was turned on.

"You want a taste?" She held her arm out to him, wiggling her wet fingertips.

Charlie's arm shot into the cage, but Cat was faster. "Sorry! It's not quite ready yet. I'll stir it some more."

He wheezed. His dark eyes followed every circle she made around her slick rim. She let her knees drop farther apart and began to breathe in a ragged pant.

"It feels so dirty—so down and dirty—having you watch me do this," she rasped. "I'm imagining this is your tongue . . . that rough, hot tongue you're shoving in and out of me. You can't get enough of it, Charlie. My sex juice is flowing so hot and free, you can't lap it up fast enough.

"See?" she added, spreading herself wider. "It's dribbling out—just like that fudge sauce on your cookies. It's running down my crack onto the floor."

He clenched his teeth and his hand went to his crotch. "Come here and let me—"

"Do I hear 'please, Miss Cat? May I lick your pretty kitty'?"

Charlie sucked air and glared at her. His knuckles went white as he gripped the iron bars.

Cat raised an eyebrow. "What? No manners? I thought you Asian boys were so big on the respect thing! I'll just do it myself, then."

Her finger returned to its business, and while she was

mostly getting her licks in watching him suffer, this little game had her more excited than she'd anticipated. Her pulse fluttered and the muscles in her thigh flexed . . . strained toward those inner spirals of heat he inspired with his unwavering gaze.

"Charlie," she breathed. "Ohhhhh, Charlie, I *so* wish you'd ask to lick this kitty. She's *so* hot she's gonna explode if you don't—"

"Please, Miss Cat," he rasped. He unzipped quickly to scoop himself out. "Please, Miss Cat? May I lick your pretty kitty?"

Cat smiled. Now that he'd done what she required, was it enough?

This Wong was young and randy: he could keep this game going well into the night—storm or not. She felt light-headed from lack of food . . . and, yeah, need.

"Thank you for asking," she purred. She slowly scooted forward. "Sounds like we've got quite a storm howling outside. I know you'll have me yowling even louder. *Won't* you, Charlie?"

"I can do that, yes," he rasped. He slithered down on his stomach then, with his eager face framed between two bars. "Come here, you naughty cunt! If I make you howl, you've gotta let me fuck you, too."

Cat sat upright, feigning indignation. "That's not part of our deal! You said this time was to be all mine because—"

Charlie grabbed her ankles and tugged her toward him, guiding her legs up the bars of the cage so her slit was wide open in front of his face. As he slipped his hands under her hips he thrust his tongue inside her.

Cat curled in on herself. While she tried to remember that she was in control here—she was making *him* beg for it—her body went its merry way. She was panting now, and those hot spirals intensified inside her with each thrust of Charlie's agile tongue. When she glanced down at him, between her spread-eagled legs, those sparkling brown eyes were gazing right back at her.

Daring her. Driving her. Gloating over how he'd once again made her play this game his way. Devilish intent written all over his face, he teased her slit with those stubbly hairs on his chin. His foxlike grin made her want to spit, but she didn't have the strength.

The first spasm made her cry out. She was vaguely aware that outside, waves crashed against the shore and the wind was howling through the trees—

And so was she. Damn it, she had to ride out the fire this younger man incited.

And then he raised from the floor before she'd recovered enough to scoot away—not that the cage allowed her to go far. It was the *choice* of moving that gave her the psychological edge.

But Cat had lost all her edges. Her limbs felt loose and fluid with that wet-noodle sensation. She couldn't even lower her legs from the vee they made against the iron bars.

Charlie sheathed himself with a quick snap of black latex that spoke a language all its own. Then, without preamble, he lifted her hips to his.

"Beg me to take you," he rasped. Her wetness gave his three-day stubble a diabolical shine. "Beg me to finish you, Cat, because I know you're not nearly done coming."

She whimpered. Implored him with heavy-lidded eyes. His cock pointed at her between the bars, looking like a lethal weapon in that black condom. "Take it. Take what you want, Charlie Wong. I'm in no position to deny you."

"Tell me you how *bad* you want it, Cat. I refuse to play if you're just gonna lie there."

She sighed at how damn weak and willing she felt. That cock

pointed at her like a finger, for being so easy. *So* easy . . . every fucking time.

"Yes, I want your cock," she breathed, her voice nearly drowned out by another forceful gale. "Bury that thing inside me and have it your way—hard and fast. You're evil, you know that?"

Charlie grinned. He entered her relentlessly—gripped her hips as he stroked himself and plundered her already sensitized passage. To further put her in her place, he rubbed his tip repeatedly against her G-spot, which was so, so vulnerable from this angle.

That loud, keening cry she heard was coming from *her*—it was not the storm. Cat fluttered rapidly, in the throes of another climax that brought Charlie out of his Mr. Superior mode. He grimaced and rocked madly against her ass.

When he slipped out of her, Cat slid away from him . . . flexed her aching thighs . . . noticed how the lights flickered. What happened if the island lost electrical power in the storm?

You make a run for it, missy, came the pointed reply.

Right, Spike. Like she could just disappear into the darkness, where unfamiliar rooms and a storm-torn island would trip her up or disable her.

Purposeful footsteps crossed the tile floor not three feet from her head. "Get her upstairs. Fasten her window guards and secure her door," Arthur ordered. "I'm engaging the backup generator. According to the radar, we're in for a monster storm."

Too late to batten down the hatches, she thought with a sigh. *I've already shipwrecked and shattered.*

25

After a noisy night alone—damn glad she'd always enjoyed the awesome interplay of lightning and thunder—Cat stood on her balcony. The sea was calm now, all its angst and upheaval a memory, except for branches and litter strewn over the beach. Sequestered here in her pinnacle, she had no idea whether the Wongs were awake or sleeping late after a busy night.

In the distance, a ship sailed sleekly across the aqua water, backlit by the coral sunrise. Its three masts and billowing sails distinguished it from a cruise or cargo vessel, even at first glance. Cat *so* badly wanted to believe it was the *Captive Fantasy*, she bit back tears.

But Captain Jack would have another batch of passengers by now, wouldn't he? If he sailed around these islands once a week on his tours, did that mean she'd been here seven days? Seven days with no sign of release or wearing down her captors. Seven days of giving in and wishing she hadn't.

As though they knew what she was gawking at, the Wong brothers entered her room on silent, secretive feet. The aroma of fresh coffee and warm, sweet pastry announced the arrival of her breakfast.

"Miss Kitty—"

"My Alina," they chorused, bowing as though she were their queen.

At least she was dressed this morning. It surprised her that these Wongs had hung her clothing in the closet—

To give you a false sense of control, her intuition whispered.

But she nodded and smiled. Too early in the day to let them know they'd whipped her. "Breakfast smells wonderful. Thank you for thinking of me."

As Charlie set the tray on her bed, his brother smiled furtively. "Ah, yes, my lovely lotus blossom, we have thought of you ceaselessly through the night, locked away up here all alone. The storm didn't frighten you, I hope?"

Cat picked up a coiled roll so fresh and tender it unwound in her hand. Her eyes closed at the first taste of pineapple and cream cheese. "I love storms. I absorb their power."

She peeked through the slit of one eye to watch their reaction. Somehow she managed not to snarf the whole roll in one bite, ravenous as she was after going without dinner.

"I thought as much," Thomas replied in his low, lyrical voice. "You look refreshed and ready to meet this new day."

"And we have a new activity. Something you'll love, Miss Kitty!" Charlie's eyes sparkled like carbonated cola as he ogled her pale pink sundress and all the assets beneath it. "Knowing how you've been deprived of exercise—"

"And believing you must spend time in the sun and fresh air, to honor the temple of your body," his brother cut in, "we'll take you for a walk around the island today. You'll be amazed at its loveliness, which you haven't yet had a chance to see."

"And you'll look stunning yourself—in this!" The younger Wong went to the door to retrieve what they'd left out in the hall.

Cat nearly choked on her sweet roll. "That's a damn . . . I will *not* wear a harness outside! And—and a *leash*, like—"

"Like the captive cat you are? Like our kitty on a string?" Charlie chose the biggest grape from her breakfast plate. He placed it between his teeth and bit down to make its insides squirt out.

She knew that feeling. Had been squished so many times here, she didn't ask Charlie to elaborate.

She hid another smile, however, as she helped herself to a second pineapple danish. If that *was* the *Captive Fantasy*, and she went outside, her chances of being spotted increased exponentially. If she played along with their stupid kitty game . . . even if it wasn't the *Fantasy*, she could signal to the passengers, couldn't she? She had to do something! Such attempts would get her into trouble again, but what was "*trouble*" again? After a steady diet of it this week, she'd learned to swallow and digest it pretty well.

When she finished eating, Charlie removed her dress and slipped the black leather harness over her head and arms . . . the same one she'd been filmed in, which cut between her breasts and under them. She didn't resist him. Only curled her lip a little when her captors hooked a long leather leash to a ring in the center of her back.

"Let's start at the grotto by the dolphin enclosure," Thomas proposed. "I've been thinking how lovely your body will look, bathed in sunshine and the mineral springs that tumble down the hillside into our natural pool. Back when the island was a monastery, the monks used it as a baptismal font. A place of cleansing and healing."

"And what happened to those monks?" she mused aloud.

Charlie chuckled. "Father bought off every last one of them! Financed their new locale, because the place was just too perfect a hideaway to let scruples or religion stand in our way."

That pretty well says it all, she thought as they went down-stairs.

The daylight made her squint, as if the storm had washed all impurities from the Caribbean air. The mosaic tile path felt cool and damp beneath her bare feet. Cat silently agreed that this is-land was *almost* as exquisite as Porto Di Angelo, now that the palm trees were swaying in the breeze and the gentle singing of that waterfall reached her ears. The grotto formed a little alcove in the island's hillside, sheltered from the winds that had wailed in the night, yet open to the sea . . . and to the view of that ship.

Cat's heart thudded harder. Was her imagination working overtime, or *was* that the *Captive Fantasy*?

While she was trying not to gawk at the letters painted on its hull, the youngest Wong suddenly swung her long leash around the huge statue of Buddha that sat in the center of the shining pool. Cat gasped, forced to walk backward into the cool, shal-low water because Charlie was pulling his end of her string. *Smiling*, as he always did.

She wanted to slap that glee from his impish face, but she had to balance herself with her outstretched arms as the water deepened.

"What the hell kind of game is this?" she protested when the leather leash drew her backside against the statue's rough belly. "Don't you know how cats hate water?"

Her humor was lost on them. Charlie stretched the leash across her abdomen and then slipped its loop around the fin-gers of Buddha's open hand. Both brothers stepped back to ad-mire their handiwork.

"God, she's hot," Charlie rasped. The front of his baggy shorts twitched. "Look at how the cool water makes her nip-ples beg for attention. How she arches out so gracefully over that stone stomach."

"Truly an offering worthy of a god," Thomas crooned reverently.

Charlie shifted his weight like a little kid who had to pee, while the breeze riffled his spiky hair. "Since this was my idea, I get first go at her."

"On the contrary, my dear Charles, since I am the firstborn that privilege is mine," the taller man responded. "Even if I were not the elder, Father has placed sole responsibility for Miss Gamble in my hands."

"That's a crock of shit, and you know it."

Thomas let out a derisive snort. "Fine, then! Go ask him yourself."

"You think I'm gonna fall for that one? I'm so damn tired of you pulling rank—and it's high fuckin' time you learned how to take your turn, Mommy Tommy!"

Cat pressed her lips together to keep from laughing out loud: sibling rivalry was such a telltale thing, wasn't it? What had happened to Tommy's mommy? Had she perhaps left this Wong madness behind when he was a child?

Cat couldn't imagine Arthur letting any woman cross—or escape—him. But then, who was to say these two sons were born in wedlock? Arthur could've had his way with different slaves—or wooed two love-struck women solely to have sons. As their argument accelerated, she saw distinct differences in their facial structure and physique—

Not that any of this mattered. That Tall Sails ship slid gracefully through the diamond-studded sea, its crimson flags and ivory sails a-flutter like her heart was at the sheer glory of such a sight. But it cut a wide, wide swath as it sailed around the island. She didn't show her keen disappointment, even though the Wong brothers were too engaged in brotherly warfare to notice her despair.

Damn! She'd *so* hoped to holler at passengers along the rail, or spot someone in the crow's nest with a spyglass focused on her—in which case, she was ready to spell out WONG with her fingers again and wave widely at Captain Jack. After all, how many Tall Sails ships would be cruising this part of the Caribbean?

"Why is it so damn hard for you to *share*?" Charlie demanded. His hand had passed through his spiked hair so many times he looked like a manic porcupine.

Thomas, the stoic, stood with his arms crossed loosely at his chest. So superior and refined; so attuned to higher vibrations he could float like a bobber on his brother's rebuttals, remaining cool and detached. "This is beneath you, Charles," he said with a weary sigh. "You could be taking your turn by now if you hadn't started this asinine—"

"You're calling *me* asinine?" Charlie retorted. "You're slinging so much bullshit even Buddha has to stay in the pool to keep clean!"

"And speaking of *clean*," came a raised female voice, "your father has requested a word with you both."

When the Contessa stepped into the grotto to address them, Cat blinked. Valenzia Borgia wore a bright yellow sundress that skimmed her ample assets; her hair was wound into a twist around a matching scarf, so its ends fluttered prettily in the breeze. Enviably gorgeous and classy she looked, in a Jackie Onassis kind of way. But then, Cat was beginning to think anyone who was fully dressed could make the supreme fashion statement here.

The Contessa batted her fake lashes when she got no response from Arthur's sons. "If he learns you've been squabbling over Miss Gamble again—"

"Oh, no, you don't!" Charlie interjected, pointing rudely at her. "Can't play *me* for a fool,'cause I know for a fact that Father expects *me* to keep track of Cat's whereabouts—"

"Then we'll get that issue ironed out, too, won't we?"

Valenzia lifted her gaze to Cat then, taking in how the

leather straps cut lewdly between her breasts. Then, very subtly, she glanced in the direction that ship had sailed. Damned if
she didn't *wink*.

Oh, great, now she's working me over, too. With a fleeting
image of Leilani bound in black leather—who knew where?—
Cat reminded herself to control her emotions. They were the
only things that truly remained her own, in the end.

"Let's go," Valenzia insisted tersely. "Your father doesn't
wait well."

"How can we leave Miss Kitty tied to Buddha's—"

"We'll be back. Very soon," Thomas replied, as much to Cat
as to his brother. "It'll be worth it to hear Father say—with
both of us present—exactly how Miss Gamble is to be handled.
And by whom."

They were still bickering when they turned their backs to
head for the house, followed by the glamorous Contessa.

Cat panicked. "Wait!" she cried, struggling against the tether
that held her to the statue. "You can't just leave me here to—"

Valenzia turned to look at her, and this time she batted her
long, thick eyelashes three times. Obviously a signal to—

Obvious to her, *maybe, but how the hell am I supposed to
climb down from Buddha's lap?* she ranted to herself—or to
Spike, if he was listening. He'd kept a low profile through this
whole ordeal. Or maybe he'd flat-out abandoned her. *Not even
nine o'clock, and this day's gone to hell in a handbasket.*

"All right, mates, you know the plan."

Captain Jack grasped the jeweled sword hanging from his
belt, hoping he didn't have to use the damn thing—and hoping
this new trio of pretty pirates would hold up their end of the
bargain. While it was noble of Cat's American friends to come
all this way to rescue her, who would take them seriously?
Would they ruin the element of surprise—refuse to run

through water or sand—when push came to shove? Her attorney now stood on the *Fantasy*'s deck wearing a purple velvet vest over a flowing silk shirt, with a tricorn hat, knee breeches, and tight boots, while his two friends sported the same sort of showy, theatrical costumes.

But then, he and his cousin wore this historical garb every day, didn't they? It was part of the fantasy they provided, and Jack knew how inspiring a costume could be—how exceptional clothing elevated moods and got them out of tight spots with crabby passengers. They didn't wear eye patches this morning, however. Useless—and potentially hazardous—while on the run.

Rick and Kurt waited, along with Ramon in his imposing dark suit and tie, in the white IMB cruiser. They'd shadowed the *Captive Fantasy* on the opposite side of the ship from the island, and they planned to move in for the serious business while Jack and their three guests provided distraction.

"If I saw things correctly," he continued, "Cat was sitting on the lap of a large Buddha—"

"Wearing that same leather harness from the Web cast," his cousin Stavros wheezed. "You'll have to be careful where you grab her!"

"Which will be *my* job, as we've previously agreed," Jack reminded them all. "Since Ramon will be with the IMB agents, I'm the tallest and the most able to physically transfer her—"

"Yes, well, shouldn't we be heading for the island instead of yammering here?" Grant Carey grunted. "I can't think any good will come of Cat being bound to a damn statue with those two slave traders in charge of her."

"Point well taken. Let's go." Turning to his cousin, he gestured for the other men to precede him onto the white cruiser. "Sail the *Fantasy* out of sight as best you can, and keep the passengers occupied, cuz. Keep the complimentary champagne and mimosas flowing with brunch, and they'll never realize you're circling, awaiting our return. But who knows what sort of surveillance system these Wongs have?"

"Watch your back. What we found out about them wasn't good," the slender Greek reminded him. "If they've masqueraded as monks these past several years, they might have more backup men and escape routes than we can anticipate. I do *not* want to buy you back!"

With a terse nod, Jack crammed his hat on and stepped nimbly down the rope ladder to where his colleagues waited in the cruiser. While his heart was pounding with the *adventure* of it all—a chance to do something more heroic than posing for pictures with snockered passengers—he was aware of how *Wong* this whole scenario could go. And how brilliant Cat Gamble had been to spell out the name he'd guessed and then Googled with Rick.

This family's portfolio—rap sheet, actually—was far too frightening for him to believe they could just storm the beach and carry Cat away unchallenged. And once they opened this can of worms, a lot of other hostages had to be dealt with, as well.

This was no game. Johnny Depp and Orlando Bloom weren't here to win the day for them with Disney movie magic. Someone might get hurt. Or killed.

Kurt steered the white cruiser around the *Captive Fantasy*'s bow and then throttled it to cross open water. The inboard engines ran quietly, designed for such stealth operations, yet as Jack felt the sea spray on his face he also sensed they were being watched. That pagoda tower seemed the perfect lookout for the entire island and miles of the Caribbean Sea around it. No doubt these thugs had security cams and radar everywhere, and full-time guards on duty. As the engines died and they coasted into an empty slip in the Wong's dock, everyone became silent.

He watched for the slightest movement from the pagoda temple and the trees that rose up the hillside from the beach.

"This doesn't feel right," he whispered to the pirate named Trevor, who stood nearest him. "Maybe I've watched too many movies, but I didn't think we'd set foot on their property without alarms or gunfire popping off."

"Place seems awfully quiet," Carey agreed. "If I've kept my bearings, Cat's statue is just on the other side of this hill. Of course, if they've spotted us, she might not be there now."

"Have to be ready for anything." Jack gazed from one earnest male face to another. Only the lapping of their wake against the dock broke the intense silence. Rick nodded tersely to signal the beginning of their mission. The two IMB authorities formed the front line with their stun guns, followed by Ramon the Intimidator in his dark suit, who carried the search warrants and Cat's legal documents in his briefcase. The rest of them were merely diversionary.

Merely? You fully intend to grab Cat and make a run for the ship—the rest of them be damned!

Rick and Kurt advanced with Ramon at a purposeful walk, looking cool and in control as they rounded the tall hillside. The flicker of a flat hand halted Jack and his pirates, which warned him there might be a problem.

"Good morning," Rick called out. "We've come to talk to Arthur Wong and his sons, Thomas and Charles."

Jack's heart thudded once . . . twice . . . thrice.

"You must be mistaken," replied a very cultivated Asian voice. "This entire island is a religious retreat for Buddhist monks and their—"

"With all due respect, sir," Kurt cut in, "there's a naked woman strapped to that statue. I have it on good authority that—"

"The only authority here is Spirit," came that Zen-like voice again, "and this young woman has requested a cleansing of her—"

"Like hell I have! Get me *down* from here!"

It was all Captain Jack needed to hear—all he could stand, after watching Web casts and receiving ransom demands and threatening calls. Jack surged around the hillside, sand flying behind his boots and a battle cry on his lips. "HY-ahhhhhh-hhh!" he hollered fiercely.

Carey, Teague, and Bigelow were on his heels, brandishing their daggers and joining in the outcry.

"HY-AAAAAAHHHHHH!!!!" resounded in the grotto as they all rushed in.

He hadn't expected three Asian monks in gray cassocks—

What difference does that make? This spiritualistic bullshit is their cover. It's all an act.

Who'd said that? Jack glanced around, but he knew better than to stall or question that spot-on observation. With a dramatic wave of his sword, he motioned the other three pirates to storm the monks while he himself headed straight for Cat.

His heart thundered so hard, he willed himself not to pass out—not to do anything stupid to botch the legal process for IMB. Behind him he heard a struggle . . . grunts and perhaps some martial arts moves. But all he could see was the lovely blonde in the black leather harness, squirming against her bindings as though she sensed their window of opportunity was brief.

"Cat!" he rasped. He crossed the pool in two long, splashing steps and clambered onto Buddha's lap. "I've been out of my mind with—"

"Captain Jack! It's really *you*!" she gushed. "God, I could only *hope* you'd see me and—I *knew* that was your ship sailing past, but—"

With his sword he slashed the long leather cord wrapped around Buddha's belly. "They've got you on a damn leash like a—"

A gunshot made him drop his sword. He covered her body with his . . . her very soft, very warm, very . . . bare body.

"The games are over, gentlemen!" came an accented female voice behind him.

Jack held his breath. Didn't dare raise his head from the luscious neck and shoulder that cradled it. What the hell was *that* supposed to mean—*the games are over*? Was there a gun pointed at his back? Had his other pirates surrendered?

"I can't see, darling. What's happening?" he murmured. He tried very hard not to notice how silky her hair was . . . how she smelled like she'd just gotten out of the shower.

Damned if she didn't begin to quiver beneath him, but it wasn't fear or a sexual reaction. She was *laughing*!

"Oh, you've got to see this to believe it, Captain. I'll explain it all later."

Cautiously Jack turned, apprehensive about the silence behind him. He was *not* expecting an updated version of Sophia Loren, dressed in a chic yellow dress with rhinestone sun shades and a scarf tied into her hair, to be holding the three monks at gunpoint with a pistol in each pretty fist.

"Valenzia, don't be ridiculous!" the oldest one in the center muttered. "This is no time for—you said we were preparing to—"

"Well, I *lied*, Arthur."

Jack blinked. Thank God Cat was snickering instead of getting upset, but he was clueless about the scenario playing out beside the waterfall. That must be Arthur Wong, the head of this slave trading ring—the man who'd tormented his poor Cat by filming those—

"I've had enough of your high-and-mighty chauvinistic pig superiority, and I'm going home now," the woman with the pistols continued calmly. "Game's over."

The monk with the spiky hair piped up. "If you think this is a game—"

"Charles, stifle yourself," Arthur barked.

"You're so right, Charles! There may be several players here in costume, but this is an encounter with the *law*, concerning your family's trading of slaves and smuggling of dolphins," the canary in yellow continued ... as though she were chirping those lines directly to Kurt and Rick. "And since these gentlemen in the natty white uniforms are here with warrants for your arrest—because you got *greedy* and *stupid* enough to Web cast Ms. Gamble all over the Internet—I'm preserving your dignity by handing you over to them. Someday you'll thank me for this, Arthur."

A snort escaped Cat. And Jack had to admit he'd never seen anything more unlikely—or more gratifying—than these three fake monks' vain attempts to remain calm and godly. The youngest one, with the spiked hair, piped up again.

"You've got no proof!" His glare flickered between the two IMB agents and the woman who stood steady, holding those pistols. "You can make your accusations and pull all the little stunts you want to, but—"

"Ramon, would you please show Charles your search warrants and the information the International Maritime Bureau has collected about the Wong family's criminal activities?" the woman asked with a knowing smile. "That's all in your briefcase, is it not?"

The tall black man in the dark pinstriped suit stepped forward with a purposeful grin. "Yes, ma'am, I'd be happy to."

When he stopped in front of the three Wongs, he took a moment to tower over—and glower over—them before unsnapping his black leather attaché case. "I have in my possession—"

"I don't give a rat's ass what you've got," Arthur Wong snapped, and when he stepped around Ramon, his eyes could've bored holes into the woman who'd orchestrated this little scene. "Valenzia! After all we've ... this is the most absurd, ridiculous—"

"Who're you calling *ridiculous*, Mr. Wong?" A very long black hand with sharpened thumbnails shot out to collar the Asian. "Seems to me the lady's made some *interesting* observations, and we should all *respect* those weapons in her hands. Because *I* taught her how to use them."

"And I thank you for that, Ramon—and for assisting us today," Valenzia cooed smugly. "It's damn fine to see you again."

He turned to flash her a wide white smile. "Damn fine to be here, Contessa. Wouldn't have missed this for the world."

Jack's eyes widened at this interplay . . . which suggested Ramon hadn't revealed all his cards, when it came to finding Cat and his lovely wife.

But he could get the details later. Valenzia shifted subtly, as though she expected that silent Wong with the long black hair—the one who'd played the priest and the buyer in the Web casts—to do something rash.

Damned if she didn't smile at the IMB agents then. "If you brought along cuffs, whip them out, boys!" she crowed. "Arthur *loves* hostage games—don't you, dear? He'll even beg for a spanking if you threaten him like you *mean* it."

Kurt looked flummoxed, but flashes of silver in the sunlight brought the eldest Wong to attention.

"This is not . . . I'm an American citizen!" Arthur huffed. "And I have a right to an attorney!"

"That would be me!" Grant Carey stepped forward with a flourish of his silken sleeves. "I fully intend to see that you get due process, Mr. Wong—but sending me those two Web casts of my client proved highly incriminating, sir. We've been following your activities ever since you stole Ms. Gamble's laptop."

The oldest Wong grunted when Rick pulled his wrists together behind his cassock. "Don't feed me that! I personally disabled the security software program when—"

"Not soon enough," Teague gloated. "The last message I received gave the security company a global positioning—"

"And once we knew Cat was in trouble, we were on our way!" Bruce crowed, flashing his jeweled dagger. "We helped her buy her island, so we couldn't let a bunch of double-crossing cutthroats—"

"I beg your pardon, but I am a priest," the one with the long black hair spoke up quietly. His hands were pressed together in a prayerful position, but his patience was clearly wearing thin. "Whatever charges you might bring against my brother and father are *your* concern, but my position as an Ascended Master—"

"Sorry, Thomas!" Cat called out. "Looks like all your bad karma's caught up with you, big boy. Maybe these guys in white will let you off easier if you take them to wherever you've stashed Leilani. We won't leave without her."

Thomas raised an eyebrow. "You won't do one fucking thing, Miss—"

"Well, there we have it," Rick muttered as he clicked cuffs around both sons' wrists. "Mighty nice of you all to be home, at the scene of your most recent crime together."

"You can thank me for that later, boys," the Contessa said breezily. "I'll bring Leilani out and then show you whatever you need, once you've secured these pigs in your boat. Tie them together at the ankles with that long leash, just like they bind the slaves they sell. Poetic justice, don't you agree?"

Jack still wasn't believing this, but why waste time on doubts? He tossed them the pieces of the slashed leash. happy to be rid of them. Then, at long last, he turned his full attention to the beautiful . . . utterly nude woman pressed between him and the stone Buddha's belly.

"It's time for us to disappear, darling," he whispered. "Would you like a ride on my *Fantasy*?"

26

Cat nodded eagerly. The breeze riffled the soft brown hair beneath his kick-ass bandanna, and his gold loop earring winked at her, so she gave in to impulse—threw her arms around him and gave him a big, boisterous kiss! Here she was in the arms of a pirate! The right pirate this time! How cool was that?

Captain Jack crushed her in a hug. Soft laughter rumbled in his chest, and he held her against his warm, muscled body for long, lovely moments while they released the tensions of the past week. He was grinning like a kid, and his delight was contagious—and he was so much cuter than the photograph on his Web site! Looked far more dashing and debonair in his seventeenth-century pirate attire than Johnny Depp did.

And he was taking her away to his ship. He'd really come to rescue her!

How hot is that? Could you love a guy like this or what?

As if he could read her thoughts, Jack waxed devilish—or at least he looked that way, with that sly, sexy mustache curving around a grin accented by dimples. And a chin cleft. God, he didn't miss a trick.

"Cat, darling, I can't tell you how many eternities have passed by this week," he murmured urgently. "First wondering what happened to you—and then seeing those damned movies—"

Her face fell. "So Wong really did send them out? While I was hoping he did—so my hand signals would alert—"

"Genius, that. Sheer genius, love."

"—it was so, well—" Her cheeks went red hot, and she glanced away. "I hope you don't think I'm always so . . . promiscuous."

His lights dimmed a little, but he kept his arms around her. Those blue eyes took on a more secretive glimmer. "What I saw shocked me, yes," he replied, "because, while I worried that they'd really sold you, I also saw how they aimed to *degrade* you. Strip you of any pretense of power—"

"You got that right," she muttered. Was he disgusted? Too disappointed in her to—

"—but hot damn, Cat." He exhaled loudly and allowed his gaze to wander lower. "I couldn't help wishing *I* were doing those things to you . . . taking every advantage of your wicked, wayward—*playful*—inclinations! This leather harness about sent Lancelot through my zip."

"Lancelot?"

The captain chuckled as though his self-control was costing him. He stroked her bare shoulder with one finger. "Lance is that fellow between my legs, you know. And you'll meet him soon, won't you?"

Jack turned around then, and they watched the two IMB agents lead the the Wongs away. One section of leather strap linked them all at their handcuffed wrists, and Kurt had attached the leash as a finishing touch; in their long cassocks, retreating down the beach with their arms behind them, the three slave traders made a satisfying spectacle indeed.

But she had better things to concentrate on, didn't she? A lot of lost time to make up for! "How soon?" she whispered.

Jack looked at her, and she melted. His eyes softened and

lingered on her lips—and then he slowly moved in for a *real* kiss. The kiss she'd longed for since she first heard his British accent on the phone.

He was even better than her expectations: his mouth made love to hers confidently, without any first-time hesitation. Cat gave in to him, the way she'd wanted to surrender to all the startling sensations Thomas Wong had introduced her to.

But this! This was sincere! This wasn't playing the willing slave or any of those other head games she'd used to stay sane this week. Captain Jack Spankevopoulos was the real deal. And he was real sexy, too.

And really horny, by the feel of that . . . that cock named Lance that nudged her thigh.

With a lingering sigh, he eased up. Closed with a couple of butterfly kisses that made her giggle.

"I'd best spirit you away before anything else happens, my dear," he said softly. "Hold tight while I get my footing."

She watched his every agile move as he clambered down the statue to stand in the pool, oblivious to the water filling his boots. He reached up for her, flashing that debonair smile, and Cat simply let herself free-fall into his strong, waiting arms.

How cool was that?! He caught her without so much as a grunt, and then curled her against his massive chest for another one of those mind-altering kisses.

"We've got to stop this madness until I get you into my room," he muttered against her ear. "Here—we'll wrap you in my vest. Such a shame to scratch your lovely skin with the harsh wool—"

"But you're such a gentleman to offer it. I'll wear it like a queen."

She watched his muscles ripple as he slipped out of the vest. He held it open for her as if it were a mink coat and she were royalty. And except for a detail or two, she was beginning to feel like it.

Cat nipped her lip. "Would you please unfasten this damn harness first? I know you said you liked it, but—"

"No more being treated like anyone's dog." Looking slightly strained, Jack reached behind her to unbuckle the leather contraption. He slipped it off her and then folded it tightly, stuffing it into the back waistband of his pants. "Should you feel compelled to wear it for me someday, that would be wonderful, love. And if not, well, you're totally wonderful without it, too."

She stood absolutely still as he gazed at her, basking in the admiration that shone in those eyes . . . along with many other things. He coughed then and held up his vest again.

Cat slipped her arms through the gaping holes and wrapped the large, manly garment around herself. Then she turned before him. "A perfect fit, considering it's about the only piece of clothing I've been allowed all week."

"Well, then, what if we return to the ship without any of your clothes?" he teased. "I won't know how to behave with a nude woman at my beck and call for a whole week, but I'd damn well love to learn—if you're still interested, after all you've been through, dear lady."

Dear lady. Had any man ever seriously called her that? Certainly never a man with Jack's blue eyes and compassionate expression. She smiled at his continental mindset; at the chivalry behind his Brit mannerisms and accent.

"You won't believe how interested I am," she whispered. Her eyes filled with tears, damn it, yet Cat sensed this gallant captain would find that endearing. And understandable.

And how many years had it been since she'd felt truly understood?

She raised her arms, and Jack embraced her tenderly. Cradled her to his chest as if she were a child . . . his little girl lost, rescued from unspeakable trauma and degradation.

Well, she could let him think that until something better came up, anyway. Something named Lance.

He headed for the shore, focused on her face . . . her hair . . . the vee of her bare skin beneath his oversize vest. "I—I've truly hit the jackpot," he murmured in awe.

And awe looked so damn good on this man.

"That's exactly how I got here, Jack—I hit the jackpot." Cat exaggerated her diction so he'd watch her lips even more closely as she spoke. "And after we play aboard your ship for however long I have left on my reservation—"

"As long as you like, love. Please stay a long, loooong time."

"—I'll show you around the island I bought with my Powerball money. If—if you'd like to come."

"I feel ready to come at the least provocation," he admitted with a randy grin. "I've been to your island, Cat, and I accept your lovely invitation. Sea legs may be a fine thing for a sailor like myself, but time away on that white sand beach . . . in your gorgeous home . . . well, my *third* leg's telling me it's his time to shine."

"Ohhh, I know just how to make that happen."

"Yes, my dear, you do." He looked out to sea, scanning the horizon like a mariner of old—tanned and weathered and so damn masculine as he held her against his chest. "There she is, Cat—the *Captive Fantasy*. Be a dear and flail your arms, since mine seem to be full of woman. Stavros is watching for our signal, you see."

Heedless of the way his vest gaped open, Cat raised up to wave her arms in wide arcs above her head. The *Fantasy* leaned into a graceful circle to sail toward them.

"What a sight she is!" Cat breathed. She felt like laughing and crying at the same time with the wonder of those ivory sails billowing in the wind from tall, majestic masts. "I'm so excited I might pee my pants, just waiting—"

"You're not wearing any, dear heart."

She burst into a laugh that started low inside her and erupted like a cork popping from a champagne bottle. Had she ever felt this damn happy?

"Captain Jack, sir, it's truly an honor to be boarding your pirate ship—"

"We'll see how honorable you feel when I sequester you in my bedroom for days on end, making merciless love to you," he growled.

"—to play and sail and live at sea and—" She gazed at him, awestruck. Aware she was gushing. "I can't tell you how excited I am about riding a pirate ship!"

"You don't have to say a word. It's written all over your lovely face."

Lovely. Not a word most men used well, and yet, spoken in that sexy accent with Captain Jack's blue eyes twinkling at her, *lovely* was something she hoped she'd be hearing for at least the next week . . . and then while he was sharing Porto Di Angelo with her . . . and then—

And then what? Cat licked her lips. Here she was, planning out a happily-ever-after with a man she'd just met.

"Thank you, Jack." She sighed like a movie heroine and then grinned up at him.

He blinked, as though he wasn't accustomed to a woman's gratitude. "For going to Porto Di Angelo to grill your caretaker, Ramon?"

"For being my hero! For calling in the big dogs! For believing I was in trouble even while I was . . . giving myself to every man in sight."

"And woman," he breathed. "You really hit me betwixt the legs when you . . ."

"Went down on Valenzia?" She shuddered slightly and then turned toward the whine of a fast-approaching speedboat. "I wasn't ready for that one. She's not really my type, you know."

"From what I could see, you had no choice, my love."

My love. Didn't that sound sweet—and sincere? It was too soon to believe such a sentiment from a dashing man who pandered to a ship full of love slaves every week, yet what was the harm in enjoying his endearments? She'd heard precious few of them from Laird—

He's dead and gone, doll, And this whole new life stretching before you looks as bright and shiny as the sunstruck sea, Spike whispered in the breeze.

Cat's lips quirked at how poetic her angel sounded. Spike was another subject entirely—one she'd mention to Jack later, when they both felt more sane. And sated.

The sleek, metallic silver boat slowed several yards from shore. Its engine purred quietly until the tall, wiry driver killed it and then steered the boat toward the beach. As though he felt perfectly comfortable holding her this way forever, Jack gave her a squeeze—and then nuzzled her lips into a long, luscious kiss.

"Yes, Cat, I'm a dog marking his territory," Jack admitted, "because that's my cousin Stavros. Cuz would snatch you away to his own bed in a heartbeat, now that he's seen you . . . in action."

Cat sighed. "Has the entire world watched me with those Wongs?"

"Dontcha worry 'bout a thing there, pretty lady," the angular sailor called out as he hopped from the beached boat. "Captain Jack's out to right all your wongs, and I'm here to help."

"This is my cousin and business partner, Stavros Spankevopoulos," the captain crooned in a businesslike voice. "And while he and I share almost everything, you won't be one of them, my darling. Let's get you onboard now. You can tell me what *really* went on back there, when that reincarnated Sophia Loren held those slave traders at gunpoint."

"She *what*? *Who*?" The slender Greek gawked back toward the pagoda as he ushered them to the boat. "Are we waiting for her?"

"We'll wait for the three musketeers and Ramon to return with his wife, yes. Which might take a while."

"And the Contessa, too," Cat insisted. "That marvel in the sundress and shades was Valenzia Borgia, who used to—"

"The woman who disappeared without a trace two or three years ago?" Jack's cousin looked stunned, while the captain smiled quietly. When the three of them had clambered up the ladder into the boat, Cat rewrapped the oversize vest around herself and sat down on the padded bench behind the driver's seat.

"The very woman, yes—and, would you believe, the former owner of my island?" Cat paused. What might happen, now that the Contessa was locking up her lover and leaving the Wongs behind? All she could really predict was that Valenzia Borgia would do the unpredictable. "I don't know much of her story, except that she figured out Arthur Wong's . . . *need*—"

"To be spanked? Humiliated? Controlled?" Jack queried teasingly.

Stavros snickered and yanked the harness from the back of Jack's pants.

"—and she cunningly made herself indispensable," Cat continued. "I still find it *very* odd that Leilani and Ramon, her loyal caretakers, didn't know where she was all that time. An odder coincidence still, that Leilani was captured when I was—and then reunited with her former boss and close friend. But we'll hear about all this in good time, from Valenzia herself," she said with a decisive nod. "I'll insist on all the details!"

"We certainly will. I'm just grateful to her for taking matters into her own hands when it counted." Jack cleared his throat, glancing from Cat to his cousin. "Ramon mentioned Miss Borgia might be involved, yesterday when all the facts finally came together. Still, I expected all manner of resistance—backlash from the Wongs—that might put Cat in jeopardy. But this classy Italian contessa blindsided those three fellows by holding them at gunpoint—a pistol in each fist!—so Rick and Kurt could cuff them."

"There they go now." Stavros nodded toward the IMB cruiser that was pulling away from the pier. He waved, but only the two guys in white smiled and waved back.

"This is only the tip of the iceberg, though." Cat watched those three robed figures grow smaller by the second . . . taking a boatload of stress and degradation with them. "I didn't see nearly all of the slave compound, but I sensed dozens of people were held hostage there, by this dominatrix type named Ebonique—"

"Oooh, I like her already." Stavros held the harness in front of him as if he could envision the spike-heeled slave trainer wearing it.

"—and now, after who knows how long, those prisoners will have to find their way home and—" Cat shrugged, shaking her head. "Surely there must be files and—videos!—to prove how Arthur Wong snatched innocent victims and then sold them as slaves."

"And that's a job for the Bureau, my sweet," the captain assured her. "Once Ramon, Leilani, and your three friends return to us, we've nothing further to worry over."

"Except how much heat you can cram into every moment, and how much Lancelot you can cram into—"

"Enough already, Stavros!" The captain's voice remained teasing, but he looked pointedly at the man in the driver's seat. "Lance is listening . . . thinking Zorba should mind his own fricking business—if you'll pardon my French, Catalina. I must use language my partner understands to get his attention sometimes."

Lancelot . . . and now Zorba. Cat chuckled at the way her full name rolled so prettily off Jack's silver tongue in the same sentence he mentioned his manhood, and his cousin's, as though they were part of this cozy conversation.

It *was* cozy, wasn't it? None of those first-date jitters, even though she sat here naked, wrapped in Jack's vest, with two men she'd barely met. Two men who'd set aside their business—risked their lives—to rescue her. It would make a helluva plot for a book someday. . . .

"You're absolutely bewitching when you get lost in thought."

Jack's low, buttery voice had Cat watching his lips . . . the flicker of those dimples alongside his wicked mustache. It was the skinny kind that cut a savage semicircle of dark hair around his lush mouth, rendering him absolutely hot. Absolutely sexy, in a Clark Gable sort of way that *so* appealed to her.

"I'll try not to wander into my thoughts too often while I'm your captive, Captain," she murmured. "So many other things to see and explore."

"And you'll be privy to every inch of them, soon as we get back to the ship." He gave his cousin a pointed look. "I'm putting you in charge of the *Fantasy* and our passengers while I'm locked away with Cat, you know."

"Aye, aye, sir!" The wiry Greek gave him a mock salute. With a subtle smile he slipped the harness to the floor beneath his seat. "Here come those three other pirates, so between the four of us we'll occupy those passengers—"

Cat cleared her throat pointedly and leaned closer to them. "While Grant and Trevor and Bruce are the most . . . accommodating companions you could ever introduce your ladies to, they're also—"

"Gay," Jack finished with a wink. "And I assure you our guests will love them all the same. Just as you do, darling."

Cat's heart fluttered as she watched the three costumed men cross the narrow strip of beach. What a jaunty trio they made—especially since Bruce hadn't worn his dress today. When they caught sight of her, they hurried to the boat and dashed up the ladder.

"Cat! I was beginning to fear—"

"Damn, but I'm glad to see you!"

"You've *got* to let us borrow your harness, hon! It was so almighty hot I thought—"

She stood up. Let them mob her and grab her and kiss on her, marveling at how wonderful it felt. She'd missed them more than she thought possible this past week, and as she clung to each of them in turn, she felt pieces of herself coming back into place. All the Wongs' indignities and head games and lies disappeared, as if thick green scum had been cleared to reveal a pool as blue and shining as the one Buddha sat in.

"Let me introduce you to Captain Jack and his—"

"We've already met, sweetheart," Grant said with a gallant smile, "and I feel greatly reassured that he's on our side, with your welfare in mind."

"Along with other parts of you, of course," Trev chimed in. "When we saw those Web casts, where you were being told to—"

Her face fell, and her insides shriveled. "He sent those damn movies to you, too? God, I never dreamed—"

"Well, it's over," Grant assured her with a warm hug. "We were aware from the first that you were being coerced into—"

"That harness! I could not believe how smokin' *hot* you looked in that harness, babe." Bruce's blond hair rippled in the sea breeze as he helped himself to another hug. "At least it was also clear that fake priest and the king weren't roughing you up, or—"

"And I knew *exactly* what you were doing, flashing those secret signals," Trevor cut in. "What a woman! Signaling to us from the front while that long-haired, no-good Asian was putting it to you—"

The press of Grant's hand against his chest cut him short.

"I'm sorry, Cat," he wheezed. "That was thoughtless of me, to—"

"No, no, it's all right now." Should she tell them about the mixed enigma that was Thomas Wong . . . that spiritual, high-minded pirate who'd taught her things about herself while being a partner in his father's criminal empire?

She thought better of it. With all the lies and misleading information they'd fed her, why make it sound like she'd enjoyed even a moment of Thomas's company? There were issues she might not fully understand herself, until she'd had time to sort them out.

"I have to thank you guys from the bottom of my heart for coming all this way to rescue me," she whispered with a teary-eyed smile. "I wanted you to come see me, of course, but I never dreamed a kidnapping situation would bring us together again."

They looked a little misty-eyed themselves as they grabbed her hands and patted her on the back. Then Captain Jack cleared his throat.

"It would be my honor to welcome you aboard the *Captive Fantasy*, gentlemen, for as long as you care to cruise with us. While your dear friend Cat will be in capable hands—and out of sight," he added with a devilish grin, "your pleasure is my highest priority, friends."

"Or you could go to the house," Cat suggested, "and explore my island until I return. Ramon and Leilani will take excellent care of you. I won't be a bit surprised if Valenzia returns with them."

"Valenzia?" Grant's brow softened. "You mean that divine creature who held the Wongs at gunpoint—"

"She was the previous owner of Porto Di Angelo. The one who mysteriously disappeared a few years ago." Cat smiled at her recollections of this unique woman. "She's like an exotic cat who's lived a variety of lives all over the world. I bet she'll stay only long enough to reacquaint herself with the island and her friends, and when another fascinating opportunity comes her way, she'll be gone."

"Not a bad way to live one's life," Grant remarked. "She

told us, by the way, that she would see to the release of those hostages in the slave compound—however long that takes— and then bring Ramon and Leilani home. And she sends you her best wishes for a wonderful time aboard the *Captive Fantasy*, Cat."

He and his housemates shared a knowing smile, and then he flashed it at Jack. "So if it won't be an imposition—"

"If you won't feel we're excess baggage," Bruce tagged on.

"—we would *love* to come aboard your ship, Captain Jack!" Trevor cried. "What a beauty she is, with her tall masts and sails! And since playing pirate is our favorite pastime—"

"And since you're certainly dressed for the part," Jack pointed out, "I'd be honored to have you three scoundrels along! If you're so inclined, you might entertain the other guests as though you were a surprise brought on board for their delight. Why, if you do a stupendous job at it, I might even pay you! Keep you on retainer!"

Cat laughed along with her friends, pleased that all these men were getting along. When had she ever been among five such wonderful males who had her welfare in mind? Who wanted nothing but the best for her? The thought made her quiver with gratitude.

Captain Jack slipped an arm around her shoulders, glancing back toward the pagoda. "If the others have their own ride back, then we'd best return to the ship. Before the passengers think they're in charge."

Stavros stepped to the boat's ladder and began his descent. "All right, mates!" he teased his three new pirates, "it's time to earn your keep! We've gotta give this honey a shove before we start her engine."

Grant, Trevor, and Bruce eagerly clambered down after him as Captain Jack stepped to the wheel. Amid their grunts from below, he pulled Cat close for another of those kisses that held such hot promise.

"Soon, my love," he whispered, waggling his eyebrows at her. "I hope you'll pardon Lance for wanting to take an edge off before we show you around the entire ship. He's been a very worried boy."

"You don't know how much I appreciate that."

When the boat had drifted away from the beach and into the current, he cranked the key. "Perhaps you'll have to show me how much, my darling, while I prove how concerned and exasperated and—well, we've missed you terribly, love. We have so much to tell you."

Cat was aware of the other four scurrying aboard again—and of Stavros taking the wheel—but she got too caught up in the captain's kiss to care.

27

"Ladies and gentlemen! As he returns to the *Captive Fantasy* after rescuing a damsel in distress," Stavros called out over the crowd on the deck, "let's welcome Captain Spank and his fair lady with a *big* round of applause! Give it up like you mean it, folks!"

The response was deafening. Cat, still swaddled in Jack's vest and cradled in his arms, waved and smiled at the sea of people like a queen might greet her loyal subjects.

"Thank you so much!" Jack replied in a jovial tone. "And while you will surely understand how I must see to this lovely lady's welfare, I'll leave you in the company of the three *pirates* we've shanghaied, as well!"

Brandishing their swords with a bravado that made Cat giggle, Grant, Bruce, and Trevor rushed up over the side and struck fierce poses for a crowd who cheered them on immediately. They engaged in a neatly choreographed sword fight that showed how much time they spent carousing together this way—and how much fun they had at it.

Jack's chuckle rumbled in his chest as he slipped away from

the crowd and through the nearest door. He fell against it to shut out the noise and the afternoon heat; to let Cat slip gently down the length of his body until her feet found the floor. They stood alone in a cool, dark room that smelled of liquor and smoke, but Cat didn't look around. She was too busy drinking in the captain . . . watching the flicker of that mustache . . . wondering what he planned to do next.

Like you don't know.

"While it would be the grand, swaggering thing, to carry you all the way to my suite, like a caveman with his conquest," he murmured as he stroked her hair, "I must confess that I have the energy to either do that or to make you properly welcome aboard my domain . . . and in my bed. You choose, my lady."

Cat chuckled, adrift in his low, delicious voice. She let his heavy vest slip to the floor and then wrapped her arms around his neck for another kiss.

He groaned. Launched into her hungrily, now that they were finally alone. He devoured her mouth as his hands followed her bare curves to her ass, which he fondled with a low growl. Then ran his lips lightly over the sensitive skin of her throat.

"Come along then," he whispered, taking her hand. "We can slip out through the other door of this cocktail lounge and into the elevator. If we meet up with the housekeeping staff or other passengers, have no fear, my sweet. They've seen a lot of skin on these voyages, so you'll fit right in."

"Just part of the furniture, eh?" she quipped. They hurried along the carpeted aisle and then ascended some back stairs like mischievous, unwatched children.

Or like lovers. Wild, impassioned lovers who can't get enough of each other.

When the staff elevator door opened, he steered her inside ahead of him. Jack punched a button, and then he was on her again. He pressed her against the leathery wall with her head in his hands as if he intended to wolf her down in one bite yet believed her to be fragile, like a figurine made of fine china.

Her laughter filled the small cubicle with its wayward sound. "Just grab me," she rasped. "I can't *wait* to be ravaged by a man who can't get enough of me. Or acts that way, anyway.'

"Oh, it's no act. I've been a goner from the get-go, my love." He escorted her off the elevator and to a door a few yards down the narrow corridor. "When I saw your face on your Web site and heard you on the phone, I knew we'd get along—"

"As if we've met before? As if . . . we've loved in another time and place?" she ventured. It sounded like one of Thomas Wong's high-minded lines, yet the man beside her stopped in his tracks. Gazed at her with those blue, blue eyes.

"Precisely what I was thinking, yes."

Should he babble on about love at first sight and kismet and destiny? Or should he give this delectable woman a chance to know him first? To get her head together again after an abduction that was probably more excruciating and degrading than he dared to ponder.

"I've been all lust and bustle and lacking in manners," he said with a sigh. He slid his key card into the lock on his door and gestured for her to enter. "If you'd like to shower, or relax in the sauna, or even sleep after the ordeal you've just endured, it would be my greatest privilege to meet those needs, my love. Lancelot's a more chivalrous chap than he's led you to believe."

Her mouth fell open. Had she ever been so totally enchanted with a man? Even Laird, in his finer moments, had never swept her away with such kindness. Such sincere concern.

"A shower sounds really good," she confessed, "but only to wash away the remains of my stay with the Wongs—a ceremonial cleansing to prepare myself for you, Jack. And if you don't join me, I'll be awfully disappointed."

"Well, now." His gaze wandered freely over her bare body. "It would be most impolite to disappoint you before I've even gotten to know you, wouldn't it?"

"Precisely what I was thinking, yes," she mimicked, and his dimpled grin made her laugh out loud. "May I request the pleasure of watching you strip down, Captain Jack? After all, I've been without clothes for most of the time you've known me."

He laughed richly. "Shall we proceed into the bedroom, darling? The housekeepers come and go here in the parlor, but my closed door will assure our privacy."

Privacy! Didn't *that* sound nice? Cat glanced briefly at the bold, masculine colors of his suite: the deep blues and greens of the sky and sea in his sofa and chairs and carpet, with artful swirled paint in lighter shades on his walls. Splashes of yellow, in pictures and pillows, made this room warm and welcoming yet capricious.

"You like it?" he asked as they entered a large bedroom that echoed these same colors. "So much of the ship is done in the reds and blacks of the slave theme—lots of heavy metal and Goth—I wanted my own quarters to feel homier. More natural."

"As bright and cheerful as an island hideaway," Cat agreed. On impulse, she took a running leap and landed in the center of a huge round bed.

When she turned to him, flushed and ready to apologize, Jack drank her in: the pale perfection of her rosy skin . . . the blond hair now drifting in disarray around a face he wanted to gaze at forever.

You're sounding far too serious too soon, he reminded himself. But who wouldn't love the look of this woman frolicking on his bed?

"Have your fun, my pretty," he teased in an ominous pirate voice, "for once Lance is on the loose, the game takes a different turn."

She nipped her lush lower lip, looking like the little girl she must have been . . . a child who turned heads merely because she was walking from one place to the next with the sunlight dancing in her golden hair. As she settled back against his pillows, placing her hands behind her head to watch him strip, *he* got quite the show—those pert breasts bobbed with her movements, looking so fresh and delectable as her elbows pointed away from her like the wings of a playful angel. She bent her legs, blissfully unaware of the seductive show she was putting on between them.

Or was she? Her childlike demeanor made the perfect foil for more adult inclinations. He got even harder because Cat Gamble wanted to *play*! Wanted to be his plaything.

"You're stalling, Jack," she observed.

No child talking there! That was a woman who insisted on being filled! Jack yanked his shirt from his pants, watching her watch him. Lance was reacting like the randy, needy cock he was when she focused on the bulge he made. She crossed an ankle over one knee, and her sly expression undid him.

As he unfastened his belt, Cat made a circular motion with her hand. "Turn around. I want to watch your backside when you step out of those trousers."

His eyebrows flew up. "You'd rather I'd moon you than flash my Lance?"

"I'll get a nice shot of him when you face me again," she replied coyly. "Behave now, or you won't be getting any."

Jack laughed, feeling a new lightness. Those watchful green eyes did things to him—brought out the exhibitionist, even though he wasn't shy about showing himself off; he spent half an hour a day working out, keeping himself fit so his bawdy guests got a reasonably good eyeful. So as he turned his tush to her, he wiggled it a bit . . . leaned down sloooowly to step from his trousers. Slipped his fingers into his bikini brief to bare himself fully.

Cat just gawked. Jack Spankevopoulos had long, looooong legs that flexed alluringly as he bent over. And then there was that sleek, muscled ass of a man who didn't spend much time sitting on it. His skin glowed with the golden allure of a cabana boy's, yet he had no tan lines in the back—

Or in the front.

"Ooooh, here's what we've all been waiting for," she wheezed. "Lance looks ready to play."

"And so he is. Still want him to join you in the shower?" Jack walked with an easy grace to the side of the bed, extending his hand . . . looking at her with such lustful intent, she almost pulled him into bed.

But this opportunity to play—to prolong their coming together—was a finer thing by far, wasn't it? Now that she was no longer caged or leashed, she could take things—or leave them—at her own whim.

So she took Jack's manhood into her mouth. Just one quick sheathing of her wet lips, and then up she came.

"Jesus, woman!" he rasped. "I thought you wanted—"

"Oh, I want it all," she breathed. "It just seemed like the right thing, to kiss him hello."

"Like this?" Jack drew her up and fully against him, savoring the sensation of her skin again. Holding her by the shoulders, he held back the kiss her eyes begged him for. When the tip of him nudged her soft abdomen, he resisted the urge to raise her up and impale her . . . so *many* urges she inspired, and he didn't want to waste a one! But enjoying her sweet, steamy slickness in the shower was a temptation, too, wasn't it?

And indeed, with those eyes so wide and green, Cat Gamble opened to him like an exotic tropical blossom in the shower. Her arms twined around him as the steam thickened. When her head fell to his shoulder, Jack kissed her hungrily. Did his damnedest to make this last, and to woo her for at least a few moments before he entered her.

Her tongue swirled lightly around his, inviting it to dance. With a moan, he leaned her against the glass shower wall, answering her call and upping the ante. He cupped her precious face in his hands so he could drink more deeply of her. Cat tasted of surrender, and summer nights naked beneath the stars, and long winter evenings before the fire.

These long-term thoughts terrified him so Jack kept kissing and caressing, losing himself in her tenderness so he wouldn't say something to break this marvelous spell. He broke away then, but only to squirt body wash into a net scrubbie and then lather her body with it. The white froth swirled seductively around those breasts, where her nipples peeked—and peaked— at him like flirtatious girls.

Cat undulated, caught between the slick shower wall and the tall, muscled man who held her there in a fog of steam like an equatorial forest after a noon rain. Very much like a tree, he was, strong and stalwart. And the farther she went out on a limb, teasing and testing, the more he invited her to dare. To dream.

"Jack," she whispered, "I've never been taken in a shower, and I . . . I can't stop quivering, anticipating Lance. Pretty please, will you make love to me now?"

While part of him questioned that—*really, had no man ever taken her this way, or was that part of Cat's game?*—he'd be a fool to ignore that plea, wouldn't he? Jack slid her easily up the wet wall, until her eyes were even with his, which put Lance at entry level.

"Opportunist—optimist—that I am," he murmured, "you'll find a little package to unwrap there beside the soap. Yes?"

"A present for *me*?" Cat spied the foil square and chuckled. As she ripped it open with her teeth, she challenged him with her gaze.

God, but she was brazen and beautiful! Jack closed his eyes against a tremor that nearly made him come. "I've been waiting more than a week to see that. Lance *so* wishes you'd hurry!"

With one smooth swoop she sheathed him in the thin latex—Caribbean blue, it was, and it glowed with a fire all its own. Gently she guided him between her thighs, spread herself wider . . . heard only the *hisssss* of the shower and the pounding of her pulse, and Jack's panting in sync with hers.

"Thank you for believing in me—for finding me! Hope I'm worth your wait," she breathed. Then she angled herself and thrust downward.

Her cry fed into his. He balanced her against the wall, with her hips suspended in his strong hands, and began to slide in and out of her. With the water pelting his shoulders and his dark, wet hair hanging loosely around his tight face, Jack Spankevopoulos looked like a man on a mission.

And wasn't it splendid that pleasing *her* was his chief aim?

"Splendid, yes," he echoed, his voice hollow with need. "You're every bit as luscious as I'd hoped, my love."

"Back atcha, Captain." Never mind that he'd somehow known her thoughts. Her hips did things their way now; she writhed to give herself the best depth—the best of everything about this randy captain and his Lance.

"You first, darling."

"It's not a race," she rasped against his wet ear. "Go after it—just as I am. We'll both get our share." She kissed him wetly and willed him to look into her eyes. "Once you get me started, Jack, I'm going to make demands! I'm going to catch up on a week away from you—talk about deprivation!—because I know you're worth my wait, too. Does this make any sense?"

He held her hips to his, laughing carefully, as though it might make him lose control. "Perfect sense, love. I understood your desires long before you ever said a word. I'm going to take the edge off now, before Lance shatters."

Cat grabbed his shoulders, slick with her suds and the water and his own internal heat. When his blue eyes found hers again, she couldn't blink—just gazed back to urge him into the final steps of this dance.

When she squeezed him, Jack inhaled raggedly. Slowly eased himself deeper . . . deeper, until her mouth fell open. Still those feline green eyes held his gaze, daring him—no, *demanding* him—to climax. It was his way, however—simply good manners and sexual politics—to let his lady come first. So he nudged her, high and hard. Gritted his teeth . . . rocked her and rubbed that sensitive nub that would turn her loose any moment now—

And when Cat wailed, no one was more surprised than she! Her hips shot into overdrive, and desire spiraled within her to override all rational thought. She wanted to slap him—to hear wet skin clapping wet skin—because he'd bested her.

Except then he, too, grimaced and sucked air. He was there on that peak with her, and they writhed and grunted their way to completion, free-falling over the edge together.

For several seconds there was only the *hissssss* of the shower and hearts banging each other as Jack rested against her. When he could raise up to look at her again, Cat saw more of that awe and amazement in his twinkling blue eyes. Something much more serious, too. Something that scared her.

After all, what did she really know about this pirate of the Caribbean who'd just stolen her heart and soul?

What more do you need *to know? Hang on, doll, 'cause this one plays for keeps!*

28

"Do you believe in love at first sight, darling?"

There it was, the question that had swirled in her mind ever since she'd first heard Jack's deep, delicious voice on the phone. And as they leaned against the crow's-nest railing overlooking his opulent, amazing pirate ship, with the evening breeze caressing their faces, Cat could no longer avoid the issue.

Nor did she want to: two days of Jack Spankevopoulos, being with him every waking—and sleeping—moment had convinced her to believe in him and in the issue he'd asked her about.

"Yes, I do, dear man." She closed her eyes to rub against him like a contented cat as he kissed her temple. "While I've always thought love at first sight was a romantic notion—something I *wanted* to happen to me but believed was fairy-tale material—I'm right in the thick of it now. You think so, too, or you wouldn't have asked. Right?"

He exhaled, and even this ordinary sound took on extra-ordinary connotations as he hugged her close. "I, too, believed it was a matter for fantasy—not something a man admitted to, for fear of committing to the wrong woman too soon," he explained. "But here you are. And here I am, wanting to be with you forever, my love."

"And what a life, sailing aboard your *Captive Fantasy*—as a pirate's wench!" she finished with a giggle. "What a book there is in that. If I could pry myself out of your arms to write it, that is."

He chuckled. Loved the way her voice sang in such harmony with his when it was their hearts conversing. "Since I must occasionally show myself and command my ship, you'd have those same opportunities to work on your book," he assured her. "We could make this work, darling! You may sail with me whenever you choose, and when you need to write—or oversee your island—I'm but a phone call away. You could be my port in a storm, even when it's a storm we create with our passion. We could have a home together on land and on sea."

He smoothed the windblown blond hair from her forehead, studying her lovely skin and those green eyes in which he saw himself mirrored. "This is entirely up to you, love, but I can envision dropping anchor to let my passengers frolic on your beach for an afternoon as part of their slave experience." His voice rose with a new excitement. "A scenario like *Survivor* perhaps, where they'd be dumped on a tropical island—yours—and left to fend for themselves."

Cat chuckled dreamily. "I can already see Ramon dressed as a fierce war lord to keep them out of the house—"

"With a minimal barricade, we could ensure that," he agreed.

"—while the beautiful Leilani appears with island potions for them to drink . . . or smear all over themselves."

"Concessions. Souvenirs. Excellent way to make your island pay for itself, if we do it right."

He paused, hoping he hadn't overstepped. He'd known this woman only a few days, after all. He'd jumped in feetfirst, hoping she'd go along with his wild-ass fantasy expansions—plans he hadn't even discussed with Stavros because, well, being with Cat inspired new ideas. She was a breath of fresh air blowing into his life, and he knew better than to ignore or abuse that.

"If I'm rushing ahead here, or acting presumptuous—"

"Not at all," she whispered. She gazed into those eyes that sparkled like crystals; reveled in that devilish mustache that tickled her in all the right places. "You're the first man who's ever discussed his dreams with me. And you've invited me to share in it—already assuming I could make it a successful venture! And you affirm my need to write."

Cat blinked. She'd just said a mouthful, hadn't she? "I—I've never had this kind of validation from a man, Jack. And it feels good. So damn good. . . ."

He gently thumbed away the tear on her cheek. "I *live* to make you feel good, my love. I had my unsatisfactory past, too, you know, with a woman we now call Mad Maria. The relationship was unbalanced—extremely draining, as she was clingy and dependent and so damn needy.

"But you, dear," he murmured. "Not only are you reinventing yourself as a writer, you chose the road to adventure! You bought an island and began a whole new life where you didn't know a soul—just on the gut faith that you'd make it! I can't tell you how I admire that."

His words made her heart swell, yet Cat gazed off into the moonlight. While they were dumping old emotional baggage, they might as well set everything out in the open—especially during this first full hour when they weren't naked and going after each other.

"Jack, I need to know how you feel about . . . things I did while I was held hostage by the Wongs."

His brow furrowed. "Darling, no one could blame you for anything they coerced you into—"

"Surely you could tell I wasn't being *forced* to have sex with them—or to enjoy it—during those Web casts," she wheezed. "I put myself in that mindset to make them *believe* I was compliant, true. Yet I . . . I was astounded at what I learned. What I liked about the way Thomas and Charlie . . . handled me. I'll totally understand if you think that makes me a whore or a—"

His kiss wooed her into a silence that spoke volumes. Jack's lips claimed hers with an insistence that left no room for her to evade him—and no room for doubts about his true feelings.

"Cat, I was so—*so*—turned on by those films! By the way your body moved and how you responded—"

He paused so he wouldn't sound as beastly as those men who'd stolen her and then fed her a diet of threats and lies.

"It works both ways," he finally declared. "There are some who'd regard your compliance as obscene and immoral, and those same souls would berate me for *watching* your films. Again and again because, well, you fascinated me. And because, yes, you made me so damn hot I couldn't *not* watch you."

Jack paused to consider the rest of his answer, for Cat had asked a difficult question: it put their fine new relationship at risk, and she deserved a fully thought-out response.

"I knew, from talking to you, that you weren't the sort of woman who'd engage in such ventures voluntarily," he assured her. "But what a joy, to watch you embrace the sublime and the down-and-dirty and everything in between! Some women regard sex as duty, you know," he continued in a lower, slower voice. "Some women shrink away from intimate contact—or from emotional attachment—so I knew right off I wanted you, darling. It never *ever* occurred to me to consider you a whore."

Cat sighed as he brushed a couple more tears from her face. "Thank you," she breathed. "I was horrified when I heard they were putting their little films out on the Internet. And yet, that was my ticket to salvation, wasn't it?"

"And you capitalized on that opportunity instead of wallowing in a victim mentality," he said with an emphatic nod.

"My kind of woman! Were something to happen to me, I could entrust you completely with the *Captive Fantasy*—whether it be managing the business with Stavros or finding the right crew to keep her afloat in our absence. I—"

"Don't talk about that!" Her heart thudded as she stared up into his handsome face. "I . . . can't stand to think about something awful happening to you! And I've never felt that way about anyone in my life. Not even Laird," she whispered.

Jack's eyes widened. "And I've never given a thought to allowing anyone but myself to command the *Fantasy*, Cat. It just came out, as though—"

"As though our hearts and angels were speaking for us?"

"Precisely. You said it all."

Cat wrapped her arms around him, loving the feel of him even fully clothed. Jack smelled of the wine and the shower they'd shared before they'd emerged from his quarters. And he smelled of the sea . . . while his pulse steadied hers into the eternal rhythm of the tides, the ebb and flow between lovers destined to share their lives.

Don't get too comfy yet. There's this other little thing ya gotta tell him about, missy.

Cat chuckled to herself, wondering how to discuss this subject. And yet . . . it had inserted itself into her thoughts and words, and Jack Spankevopoulos had gone right along, hadn't he?

"Would you think I'm wacko if I told you I've recently met my guardian angel, Jack?" she asked softly. "While most writers hear characters' voices in their heads, it's an altogether different thing to hear—and follow—divine guidance. Even if Spike often smokes and drinks and swears a blue streak."

"Spike, eh?" The captain teased her with a wink. "Makes more sense than my listening to Lance, doesn't it?"

Cat laughed, and the sound slipped around the sails and

down to the deck below, where passengers were playing games like Twister and Spin the Bottle—naked—while Bruce, Trevor, and Grant emceed. Here they were within sight of so many others, yet so sequestered together . . . nesting. Happily. Without doubt or apology.

"Lance does speak with a conviction that's impossible to ignore," she said. She kissed his cheek playfully. "At least I know you're every inch a male—"

"And every inch of me craves *you*, dear Cat." He ran a finger through her gossamer hair, separating a few strands to watch the moonlight play in them. "It's clear to me that you're an angel in your own right. An angel who's come to save me from my busy-ness . . . to set things in perspective as far as what's really important and what's been missing in my life."

He gazed into her face, freshly scrubbed and lovelier for it, and hoped he would remember her this way forever. "If the *Fantasy* and my entire fleet sank tomorrow," he pondered aloud, "I'd be upset, to be sure. But not devastated. Because you've brought me a whole new life, Cat. A life of endless, delightful possibilities I've not known before."

To hear this man, a world traveler and entrepreneurial pirate, call her his whole new life made something stir within her. Something sacred, yet so wayward and playful she laughed for the sheer joy of watching Jack's eyes catch fire. "So you'll understand if I listen to Spike's guidance, even if I sometimes ignore yours?"

It was a double-edged sword, that question, to a man accustomed to commanding his own ship. His own empire. Yet Jack saw it for its honesty and potential.

"I suspect Spike first led you out of mourning, and then out of the house of bondage into my arms. So who am I to question his power?"

He was clearly giving this some thought, yet he seemed

comfortable with a subject she'd never mention to most men. "It feels providential to me, our coming together, Cat. I've never doubted that. And while we're sharing heart and soul here, sailing the magnificent seas of an omnipotent Creator, perhaps I could use a little instruction about listening to angels myself. Would you teach me, dear lady?"

Cat's eyes widened. Who else had ever presented her with such a profound request? "It's all very new to me. Mostly an intuitive thing—maybe reflected in the way I gravitated toward an island named Porto Di Angelo, where the caretaker has a strong connection to angels. Leilani exudes an attitude of gratitude. A willingness to listen and follow."

"Rendering oneself submissive without becoming passive."

"Precisely." She laughed because she was imitating him again, but he didn't seem to mind. "My relationship to Spike hasn't always been what I'd call . . . *heavenly* . . . but he got me through the rough spots last week. If we ask him, he might introduce us to more angels—your angels. Never know until you try."

Jack hugged her, letting out a low "Hmmmmm . . ." that rumbled against her ear.

"Yes, dear man? What's on your mind?"

He held her closer, to savor the night breeze that felt like a gentle wind of much-needed change. "Do angels listen best if we seclude ourselves from the everyday world? If we, say, remove all barriers between our world and theirs?"

"Like clothes, you mean?"

He snickered. "You are *so* entuned to my thoughts it's scary, love."

"Just listening to Lance. He wants to get a word in—or himself, by the feel of it."

"Are you hot for it, Cat?"

She grinned, tingling from his breath tickling her ear and

from another buzz of anticipation. "That *was* an effective head-line and Web address wasn't it?"

"It delivered me to you. Who's to argue?" Jack clasped her hand and opened the gate from the crow's nest. "Let's submit ourselves to another session of divine climax—and then see what our angels say about *that*, eh?"

29

"There she is, darling. There's no more wondrous view of Porto Di Angelo than from right here in my office."

"Oh, my. You're absolutely right."

Cat's heart thundered as the *Captive Fantasy* sailed toward an island lush with palm trees and colorful flowering bushes. Compared to others they'd seen this week it was small but so much more gorgeous! She swore she smelled those shimmering white angel's trumpets on the breeze. And then the house came into view!

"That flamingo-pink paint and white trim really make a statement, don't they?" she said with a chuckle.

"Indeed, my love. They speak of a woman who ventures boldly into life, bright and shining like the Caribbean sun."

"Well, from what I know of Valenzia Borgia, that's certainly true." She smiled, her gaze fixed on that island paradise—*her* paradise now. "I wonder how she's progressed with releasing those other slaves? It was good of Rick to e-mail you about the Wongs being proven as slave traders."

"Sounds like all three will be convicted, yes." The corners of his eyes crinkled as he caught her head-on in a suave yet thoughtful smile.

What was it about that bandanna and earring that made him look *so* damn hot? They'd just come up from his bedroom, and already she was thinking about what she wanted him to do to her next. But if she was this close to home . . . she'd wondered how Leilani and Ramon were doing. . . .

"Have you any concerns about the Contessa returning to her home—*your* home now?"

He'd done it again: read her thoughts at the exact moment they occurred to her. There was something to this angel connection thing—not-quite-coincidences they delighted in talking about.

"I'm not surprised she wants to come visit, after two years of being with Arthur," Cat mused, "but something tells me she'll be hungry for another adventure before long."

As Jack raised the spyglass to his eye, she watched the flexing of his arms in that flowing poet's shirt . . . the tightening of his thighs in knee breeches that left nothing to the imagination. "Could be she's already arrived. How many yachts do you own, darling?"

"Just the one."

"Here. Time to practice at being my pirate wench." He stepped behind her to guide the spyglass to her eye. "It's much the same as binoculars. Close the eye you're not looking with, and then twist the end to bring things into focus."

Cat held her breath. Not in her wildest dreams had she figured on being in the crow's nest of a magnificent pirate ship, peering through the captain's spyglass! Talk about firsthand research for her book!

"You're right," she said when her docks came into view. "The larger yacht—the one with the hot tub—is mine, and the other belongs to Wong. Which means the Contessa has commandeered it for her own use now."

"No doubt to return your caretakers. I'm sure Leilani's glad to be home—and *damn* sure Ramon's relieved." Jack chortled, recalling those edgy phone calls and strategy chats with the tallest, most intimidating man he'd ever met.

"Yessss. . . ." Cat's voice trailed off as she took in a panoramic view of her dock and the island . . . the pathway leading to the house and the porch—

"My God, Ebonique's with them! You can see *everything* with this—" She swiveled to quiz the man behind her. "Tell the truth, now! That first night I was there, standing out on my balcony—"

"Naked? While Leilani and Ramon frolicked on the beach?" Jack laughed so hard he couldn't stop, for he'd never seen such a flummoxed expression. "Yes, my darling, you were nicely backlit by a lamp in your room, and I was totally tantalized. And now here you are, the woman of my wildest fantasies come true."

He lifted her chin for a kiss and then gazed into her deep green eyes. "Do as you wish, my love. You're welcome to stay aboard and play with me, but I'll certainly understand if you need to go home and check on things."

"You'd do that? In the middle of this cruise?"

"Certainly. We'll drop anchor—just as we would if we were initiating our Island Survivor scenario—and Stavros will take you ashore in my speedboat. Your friends, too, if they care to go." He shrugged, doing rakish things to that pirate outfit. "I'm the captain, after all. I hold absolute power, dear one. Care to test that theory in my quarters?"

She grinned. This guy never seemed to run out of want-to, which made her feel pretty damn powerful herself. While it was a dream come true to remain here—she had no trouble imagining herself aboard the *Captive Fantasy* for weeks on end—she felt pulled toward Porto Di Angelo, as well.

"As you know, Captain Jack," she began, gazing again at her island, "there are things one simply has to oversee for oneself. Even if it means foregoing extreme pleasure in the arms of the man I love."

Jack's grin warmed his entire face, making those dimples wink wickedly. "I shall never tire of hearing you say that, my dear. And I so understand when duty calls, and—"

A little *beep* from his computer made them both glance at it. "New e-mail." He clicked it open and scanned the message quickly. "Rick's informing me that all those who were held in the Wongs' compound have been delivered to St. Lucia for dispatching back to their homes. More than three dozen of them, all told. From five countries and three islands."

Cat let out a low whistle.

He opened his arms, and she stepped into his kiss. "I hope you feel good about how many poor, helpless souls have benefitted from your hand signals on that Web cast, dear heart."

"Well, that's one positive thing that came from a nasty situation, yes." She gave back his spyglass, letting her hand linger on his. "How soon will you come back for me, Jack? I'm not nearly tired of—"

"One phone call—one e-mail—and the *Fantasy* can turn in place and head straight for your island."

Was that a power surge or what, knowing she wielded so much influence over this handsome captain? She glanced down to the deck, where three familiar pirates were staging a demonstration of swordsmanship for an admiring crowd of ladies laid out along the pool. "I'll ask the guys what they'd prefer. Looks like they have a . . . captive audience."

Jack groaned at her pun and then smacked her soundly on the backside. "I've been taken captive myself. And you know—it's not half bad! I'll be eagerly awaiting your return, my love. Keep me informed, all right?"

* * *

"Thank you, Stavros. I'll see you again soon."

"Not soon enough to suit Jack," the slender Greek teased. In his way, he was every bit as alluring as his cousin, but in smaller, subtler details that suited his wiry physique. "You've made a world of difference—a difference in his world—this week. And trust me, any woman who can get Mad Maria out of his life is a good friend of *mine*."

Cat considered this as Trevor, Grant, and Bruce stepped from Jack's personal boat onto her dock. "How do you mean, out of his life? Was she—"

"He hooked up with Maria on the spur of the moment—a very horny moment. And by the time Cuz saw the bipolar manipulator and man-eater beneath her beautiful surface, she already had her hooks in him. Took him a while to figure out he couldn't '*fix*' her because she wouldn't help herself."

Stavros shielded his eyes from the sun, to gaze at her with gratitude. "Maria called again last night, very late. Expected Jack to drop everything and help her out of her latest—probably manless—predicament."

The Greek shook his head as though he'd witnessed such a situation many times. "Jack informed her that he was engaged to a wonderful woman and had no more time for her emotional bloodsucking. It was an inspiring sight, to see him dancing on the bridge! Laughing as he hung up the phone!"

Cat smiled as she imagined such a scene. "Thanks for telling me that. He mentioned her once but never let on—"

"He was trying not to mention her name in your presence, for fear he'd jinx what he's found with you." His grin looked boyishly endearing. "He's talking about angels now—you, mostly—rather than Maria's demons. You've turned his whole life around, Cat."

Talk about another power surge. Stavros sounded totally sincere, which meant that somehow—without knowing how or why—she'd been in the right place at the right time. Had found herself a new life and rescued the playful pirate who'd been her salvation, as well. They'd marveled over this syncronicity many times this week, she and Jack.

"Cat! Cat, you've got to see what they brought back with them!"

With a wave to Stavros, she walked across the beach toward the house. *Home*, and a welcome sight it was! As she looked over to where her three pirate friends caroused, surrounded by a profusion of primroses and oleander, her mouth dropped. "Where the hell did you get that cage?"

Grant, Bruce, and Trevor—who was inside the damn thing—all stared as if she'd pronounced a curse on them. Even to her own ears, she'd sounded like a tight-ass teacher scolding naughty boys. Her attorney sheathed his sword, his expression wary as he approached her.

"Let me guess," he murmured. "Those Asian beasts used this to torment you, didn't they? We're only conjuring up a bondage game for later, Cat. If the cage bothers you, we can—"

"See? It's already history!" With a couple of strong yanks, Bruce lifted one side out of its iron hinges and tossed it to the ground. With a single shove, Trevor made the rest of the cage collapse on itself.

When the clanging of those fallen iron bars washed away in the whisper of the waves, Cat blinked. "You mean that thing was—"

"Collapsible?" Grant's irresistible grin deflated her nasty mood. "That's the beauty of it, sweetheart. We pirates immediately saw the gaming possibilities in such a contraption—"

"And had we known it would upset you, we wouldn't have asked the Contessa to bring it back for us." Bruce wrapped his arms around her, swathing her in his silken sleeves and the scent of his tropical cologne. "Now tell me all about this, Cat. It's not like you to get upset by one of our little adventures."

She nipped her lip. Gazed at the sections of black iron bars, now flat on the ground. Harmless. What *was* her problem, anyway? That collapsed cage symbolized her breaking away from the Wongs, didn't it? No sense in feeling stupid because she'd never guessed it was such a *flimsy* prison.

"They used it as a . . . playpen of sorts," she hedged. No need to reveal all the sordid details or bring back the Wongs' lies, was there? "'Cat in a Cage,' they called their game. Seeing it brought back a jolt I hadn't expected." She kept an arm around Bruce and welcomed the other two into her embrace. "Sorry I overreacted, guys. Actually . . . some very hot, wanton things happened while I was in it, so if you want to have your fun, well, carry on! No harm done. Honest."

Grant looked at the other two and then bussed her cheek. "We can play later. Why don't we explore your gorgeous island while you reacquaint yourself with those folks on your porch?"

Cat watched them dash lithely toward the beach. Three shirts and vests fluttered off behind them to land on the sand with belts and swords. Such exuberance—such a sense of fun!—reminded her she needed to devote more time to *play*. It was the stuff stories were made of, after all.

Like with Jack, right? Did I choose you a fine playmate or what?

"Yes, you did, Spike," she murmured as she gazed out toward the *Captive Fantasy*. On the chance the captain would see her, she waved both arms above her head at him. Just thinking of him restored her sense of rightness—

Yeah, there's a message there. You listenin', doll?

She chuckled and quickly walked the rock pathway up to the porch, where familiar voices chattered—some that warmed her heart, but one that gave her pause. Cat stepped under the porch's roof to take in the little celebration already in progress: plates of grilled shrimp and tropical fruits were arranged on the colorful table, and the spice of freshly baked breads made her stomach rumble.

The Contessa was helping herself to a skewer of shrimp—gesturing prettily with it—when the conversation stopped. The owner of that distinctive mannish voice turned around to look at her.

"Ebonique," Cat said, hoping she sounded like the mistress in this situation rather than the slave. "Welcome to my home! I hear the Contessa has freed those poor hostages—"

"Every last one of them, we did. Yes, ma'am," the ebony-skinned woman assured her. Draped in a sari of bright lime and turquoise, with a coronet of fresh flowers on her head, Ebonique looked more like a Caribbean queen than the dominatrix Cat had met in the slave compound.

Valenzia came over then, from the table where Ramon and Leilani cuddled over their brunch.

"*Such* a pleasure to meet you where we can speak freely, sweetheart!" she gushed, still the fashionista in her candy-pink sheath and upswept hair. "When Leilani came out of those drugs Arthur slipped her—told me you'd bought Porto Di Angelo—I knew it was time to set the wheels of justice in motion."

Here it came—the explanation that would make sense of her whole absurd situation with those Wongs.

"You see, Arthur wasn't always in such a filthy business," she began in an indignant tone. "When we first met, at a software conference in the Silicon Valley, he dreamed of setting up shop on his own turf—so he could play by his own rules. I sensed he'd make a huge success of whatever he undertook—"

"Software conference?" Ramon challenged from the table behind them. "Now, Valenzia, this is *me* you're talking to, and you don't know up from down about computers."

"No, but I know where to meet powerful men, don't I? And

computer geeks are so damn grateful when a beautiful woman—
that would be *me*—takes an interest in them."

Cat choked on a chuckle: the Contessa had just stated her
secret for success. And as the flamboyant Italian slid two grilled
shrimp from her skewer between her teeth, grinning girlishly at
her caretakers, Cat sensed Valenzia Borgia was living the ultimate rags-to-riches story. She could take a few lessons in that
herself.

She'd just confirmed Cat's original hunch, too, that Wong
had been a technology executive. Interesting affirmation of her
intuition, wasn't it?

"Please—go on with your story!" she urged. "All I could
piece together was that Arthur was an American who'd escaped
the States' taxes—"

"And when he bought that wonderful island from a floundering monastery," Valenzia continued, "he wasn't smuggling
dolphins or slaves. But the Internet has brought many an enter-
prising man into many a new global arena . . . opportunities
abounding at the click of a mouse," she added with a shake of
her pretty head.

"When Arthur invited me to visit—and I decided to make
the most of *that* opportunity," Valenzia continued with a sly
chuckle, "he kept his under-the-table dealings a secret. Kept me
too . . . *busy* to wander into that low-slung building that housed
so many lost and stolen souls."

"And when I caught her poking around," Ebonique chimed
in, "I realized this was no ordinary girlfriend Arthur was entertaining. We girls kept our secrets, waiting for the right time—
the right hostage to come along—"

"To spin Arthur's greed out of control," the Contessa added.

"And that would be me." Cat considered all these details,
putting the rest of this puzzle together. "As the new owner of
Porto Di Angelo, unfamiliar with the Caribbean—no family to
trace me, and offshore accounts bulging with a Powerball jack-

pot—I was a prime candidate for bringing him a big, fat ransom."

"Which Captain Jack wisely refused to pay," Ramon stated. "And while Arthur was a genius with computers, his son Charlie got too excited about playing with your cute little Mac. Didn't have a clue about security software that could pinpoint its location."

"So it worked! Just like Trevor said!"

"Took some luck for all the connections to get made, but, yes," the big black man said with a grin. "By the time Jack and the IMB boys figured out what you were spelling with your fingers, your attorney and his buddies were already on their way to find you. Happened pretty fast, all things considered. Thank goodness for that!"

An incredible story . . . and again, one that hung on the right details falling into the right hands at the right time. Syncronicity at its finest.

Or angelic intervention, a smoky voice nudged her. *I made Jack click on a Web site URL he'd never heard of, and there you were under the heading of "RUhot4it."*

"Escape Artist dot com," she murmured.

"Yes, you're certainly that!" Valenzia slipped a slender arm around Cat's shoulders to hug her proudly. "When I saw you sending signals to Arthur's video cam, I sensed I should do something to distract him. So I lifted my dress to play with myself, pretending the sight of Thomas taking you from behind was more than I could sanely watch—"

"But he saw me during his replay," Cat recalled. She smiled at the alluring woman, who confessed such secrets like an old friend, and who'd taken her in as a new friend. "I have to say you look better with your natural hair and your own chic clothing, Contessa."

"Why, thank you, dear!" she said with a giggle. "Arthur insisted that all of us in the film disguise ourselves, so—"

"I recognized you right off!" Ramon crowed. Then he gave his wife a big, grateful kiss. "And when I saw you were there, Contessa, I knew everything would be all right for Leilani and Cat."

Valenzia smiled fondly at the cuddling couple. "Well, I'd had my fun. What's not to love about reducing a domineering hard-ass like Arthur Wong to a sniveling, fawning little prick who can't get it up without a whacking? But I'd tired of him. Cat and Leilani's arrival was my signal from the universe to move on."

"And so you did," Ebonique chimed in. "And I'm damn glad you brought me along for the ride, honey! Girls just wanna have fun, and it's time for a whole new gig."

Cat laughed. This Ebonique on her porch was a total turn-around from the dominatrix of that subterranean slave compound. More like a high-energy pop singer than a mistress of discipline.

"And what *is* your next gig? *Not* that I want you to rush off." Cat closed her eyes over the delicious grilled shrimp Valenzia coaxed between her lips. It felt good to be talking to these two strong women as an equal. Gave her a real appreciation for how deceiving appearances could be.

The Contessa's body tightened slightly. "I hope this will be all right with you, Ms. Gamble," she began—although it was no secret she'd do as she damn pleased. "I've made Ebonique my partner in a new holistic spa venture on Arthur's island—which is *my* island now. Wong lost the property to me in a game of strip poker after I screwed his brains out. Never admitted it to his sons, of course, but I have the deed to prove it."

Cat's jaw dropped. "I can't imagine an arrogant, controlling man like Wong ever playing—"

"Oh, Arthur was a player, all right," the Contessa purred. "I just made sure we always played my games, by my rules, in case he ever did anything unchivalrous. Like getting rid of me before I could ditch *him*."

While Cat was trying to assimilate all this, she felt how erect and rigid Valenzia was holding herself. A sure sign something else was at stake.

"A spa sounds like the perfect business for that island." She smiled at the two women, fishing. "With that pagoda, and the pretty little grotto with the waterfall—"

"I'll see that Thomas and Charles are proven innocent of their father's evil schemes, too, so they can become our shaman of spiritual enlightenment and chef."

Once again Cat's mouth fell open. Ms. Borgia sounded utterly convinced she could accomplish this feat, even though Wong's two sons were integral parts of his slave trading, the way she saw it.

"And I hope you won't be too upset that Leilani and Ramon have agreed to work for me, as well," the Contessa went on. "The three of us shared a very special relationship when Porto Di Angelo was mine, you know. Now that this fine home belongs to you, dear, I want you to feel free to change it—and to hire help you choose yourself—"

And we know who that's gonna be, don't we, doll?

"—to manage your new estate," she finished with a smile. Her dark eyes sparkled with warmth as she glanced at her two intimate friends and then back at Cat. "I sense you'll be spending a lot of time aboard the *Captive Fantasy*, but you'll still bring a whole new energy and spirit to this home. I loved every minute I spent as mistress of this little piece of paradise, but it's time to move on. Bigger fish to fry and all that."

"And I wish you well at your new endeavor—*all* of you!" Cat replied with a sweeping gesture of her arm. Enthusiastic shrieks came from the beach then, and she saw her three friends dashing along the edge of the waves, brandishing their pirate swords. "Those first two fellows, Bruce and Grant, will soon be my new groundskeeper and estate manager—with a little friendly persuasion, of course."

"What's to persuade?" Ramon chortled. "Looks to me like they already feel quite at home here. Took them all of five minutes to toss their shirts."

It was true, wasn't it? They had a knack for being happy wherever they went together. "I wouldn't be surprised if the third one, Trevor Teague, will hire out for architectural jobs all around these islands, making Porto Di Angelo his home base," Cat remarked. Fishing again, but sincere about it.

"He's an architect?" Ebonique's appreciative gaze lingered on each of the men in turn ... on their fine, tight asses in those pirate pants, mostly. "We could certainly use his expertise as we renovate the pagoda and that slave compound, couldn't we, Val?"

"Damn straight." She released Cat's shoulders to stand at the deck railing beside her dark-skinned partner. The two of them radiated a very potent, colorful energy as they watched the three men frolic on the white sand.

"Would you mind terribly, Catalina dear, if I kept your beach boys employed when you don't need them? When you're sailing with Jack, perhaps?" Valenzia ventured in a voice that vibrated with power. "I see endless potential there for the wealthy female clientele who'll frequent my spa. And expert guidance for my landscaping, legal matters, and renovations, of course."

Cat grinned. Not here an hour, and already Bruce, Grant, and Trevor were in demand—and in a position to negotiate more money than they'd ever dreamed of while working in St. Louis. "You'll have to ask *them*, Valenzia. They don't know they've already assumed these positions in our minds."

"They can assume any positions they want," Ebonique murmured, "and I'll be watching every move. Even if it's not me they're pleasuring."

"They'll come running at the sight of your studded leather

outfit and whip!" Cat assured her. "They greatly respect women who control their own destinies. And their love slaves."

Still chuckling, Cat went to the brunch table. She picked a pastry redolent with cinnamon—an apple pie center that filled her mouth with its soft sweetness. Amazing how many things fell into place during a single conversation, when it was the right people with the right ideas making it all happen. Of course, most of the Contessa's high-flying plans hinged on having things go her way, didn't they?

"So how will you spring Thomas and Charlie?" she asked quietly. "It seemed to me they were a vital part—did the dirty work—of their father's smuggling enterprises."

The Contessa clasped her hands before her, looking regally serene as she turned to face Cat. "As you will learn very soon, when you've settled into your new station in life," she replied in an erudite voice, "the combination of wealth, brains, and beauty serves us well in this male-dominated island culture. I've cultivated good friends in high places, Catalina. They'll see it as a great favor if I not only pad their pockets but relieve them of two court cases involving American citizens. And besides, the records of Arthur's transactions are in my possession now. They all bear his signature. Not his sons'."

Was this woman really as powerful as she claimed? Was Valenzia Borgia even a contessa, really?

Does it matter? She has the presence to make people believe—the pluck to pull off her schemes and dreams. There's a lesson there.

Yes, there was. Cat grinned, feeling she'd just been made privy to a delicious secret: the secret of how to arrange *her* life, now that she was truly in control of her finances. Her *future*.

She caught a whiff of sweet, druggy smoke—or was it the scent of those angel's trumpets on the breeze? Swore Spike's breath tickled her ear—and sensed he was very, very pleased with himself for the way things were falling into place for her.

"If you're looking for help with the legalities concerning Thomas and Charles, you might consult Grant Carey." She pointed out the older man, whose well-cut hair and thicker body set him apart him from Bruce, the golden beach boy, and Trevor, the athletic artiste. The three of them were headed around the hillside, taking in the lay of the island and the sparkling Caribbean Sea, all of them talking and gesturing at once.

"Grant appreciates clients who pay attention to the details and give him all the information he needs to win their cases. An absolute *shark* in court," she added emphatically. "Without his extraordinary efforts, I'd still be floundering in the quicksand surrounding my husband's suicide and . . . financial misman-agement."

Silence shrouded the covered porch then. The Contessa, Ebonique, Leilani, and Ramon studied her with faces so sym-pathetic she could feel their compassion wrapping around her like invisible arms. Maybe she should've kept her mouth shut. Now she'd gone and ruined the fine, feisty mood these enter-prising women had—

"Cat, I am so sorry," Valenzia whispered. She and her dark partner came to take each of her hands. "Now I'm even happier that *you* have purchased Porto Di Angelo—"

"And that you've hooked up with Captain Jack," Ramon chimed in from behind her. "You're a class act, Miss Gamble. Anything you need to know about how things work here on the island, we'll be happy to show you and your new manager man."

"You *go*, girlfriend," Ebonique said with a hard squeeze to her hand. "No doubt in my mind you'll make this new life work out *your* way!"

Leilani left the table then. She wrapped her slender arms around Cat's waist . . . rested her head against the center of her back. "I thank you again for getting us out of Arthur Wong's clutches, dear friend. I see fine things in your future here."

"Like . . . ?" That fortune teller's mystique piqued her again, and Cat knew she'd miss having Leilani around to tell her about such stuff.

"I see healing solitude here by the sea," the housekeeper began softly. "A fresh new outlook on your life—not to mention your writing career ascending to new heights. . . . Fame and fortune for you there!"

Leilani's voice rose, taking Cat's excitement level with it. "And love!" she proclaimed. "Sweltering hot sex with Captain Jack, who will cherish you as his queen and share his adventurous life with you. Joy is yours for the taking now, Cat!"

Were these three goddesses surrounding her, blessing her with their benedictions? Cat closed her eyes, daring to envision all those fine, fun things Leilani had just predicted: hot sex, a devoted man. A skyrocketing career, and healing . . . and joy.

Joy!

How long since she'd used that word, much less felt it? She let out a shuddery breath. Her smile wavered in a rush of emotion. "Thank you," she murmured. "Thank you all for being a part of my . . . transformation. I feel like a butterfly breaking free from its cocoon. I really, really owe you for this."

"Owe us for what?" a familiar voice teased.

Cat turned to see her three friends, who watched this little scene from the edge of the porch. They were shirtless but wearing their pirate pants and bright smiles. She grinned at them. Didn't they look absolutely *gorgeous* with sand on their legs and their hair combed by the tropical breeze?

"Well, I owe you big-time for that winning lottery ticket, of course," she replied playfully, "but it might be you owing *me* very soon. If you're brave enough to say *yes*."

Grant's eyebrow quirked. "Do I smell a trap?"

Cat shrugged, feigning innocence. "Do you call my island life a trap, dear man? Would any of you turn down the chance to live out your career fantasies on Porto Di Angelo? Because if you say *yes* fast enough, these ladies and I have work lined up for you."

"What sort of work?" Bruce slicked his damp blond hair back from his temples and looked warily each of them.

"Well, I for one need a groundskeeper," Cat replied, opening her arms to the lush tropical trees shading this second-story porch.

"And I need architectural expertise to renovate the Wong compound for our new spa," the Contessa chirped. When she batted her lashes she *did* resemble Sophia Loren, just as Grant had suggested.

"I need an estate manager, too, since Leilani and Ramon will be working for Valenzia now—"

"And, Grant," the Contessa spoke above her, "I have more legal work than you can shake your ... *sword* at, now that Arthur Wong's property is mine."

Cat laughed. The three men just gawked at each other, at a total loss for words—the first time she'd ever seen that! Then Trevor broke away to take her by the shoulders, looking at Ebonique and Valenzia, as well.

"But the real question is, does anybody need three *pirates*?" he asked quietly. "If I can't occasionally sail the sea, looking for adventure, I see no point in leaving my home and business to come here and *slave* for three women! Three relentless, driven women who—"

"Yessss! Count me in!" Bruce crowed. His grin rivaled the Caribbean sun as it finally hit him: he could *live* this island life! He could leave traffic and smog and urban sprawl behind!

"And—and we could share this extraordinary house with you, Cat?" Grant asked happily.

"Absolutely, gentlemen." She flashed them her finest feline smile. "And Captain Jack assures me he has plans for you three swashbucklers, anytime you care to come aboard and indulge those fantasies."

"Hot damn!" Grant grabbed her face to give her an exuberant kiss. "Hot damn! I vote we pack it in stateside and then pack our bags, guys! Not that we haven't loved living in your wonderful home, Trev—"

"But Cat's made us an offer we can't refuse! We can all cash in on her ticket!" Bruce proclaimed. Then he whipped his sword from its sheath. "YO HO HO—"

"—and a bottle of rum!"

"—it's a poi-rate's loife fer me!" they sang out.

The Contessa and Ebonique giggled so hard tears streamed down their cheeks. And when Ramon and Leilani completed the circle, it felt like one of those electrifying huddles at a pep rally—

—or like you're surrounded by more love than you ever dreamed possible.

She grinned gratefully. "Ramon, if you'd be so kind as to escort these pirates back to the airport when they're ready—"

"Consider it done, Cat."

"—we can all look forward to bright, shiny new lives, starting at this moment of *yes*," she breathed. "And I can't tell you how that excites me!"

"A toast!" Ramon fetched the pitcher of sangria from the table while Leilani got the goblets. Moments later, as they raised their glasses, there wasn't a dry eye on the deck.

"To life, liberty, and the pursuit of happiness!" Grant offered.

The ringing of their crystal rims hadn't died away before Cat raised her glass again. "To love and bold adventure—in every area of our lives!"

"Hear, hear!"

"And to pirates!" Trevor Teague exclaimed. "Long live Captain Jack and Cat as they sail through life aboard the *Captive Fantasy*!"

"Aye, aye! To Captain Jack and Cat!"

To Captain Jack, indeed, Cat toasted silently, looking out to sea. She had so much to tell him now! She could already see the sparkle in those blue eyes and hear the British innuendo in that velvet voice . . . felt the wind whipping her hair as Jack held her at the ship's railing to survey his domain—his paradise.

And hers now, too.

30

Very quickly, it seemed, she was alone. Cat waved one last time to Rodrigo's ferry boat, which carried Ramon and her three new partners, bound for the airport. The Contessa had already left with Ebonique and Leilani, who'd packed up their clothes and personal effects in short order. Cat was amazed at how fast this had happened—how few earthly possessions Ramon and his wife counted as their own or important enough to take along.

They live light, they travel light. Something to be said for taking yourself lightly.

"You got that right, Spike." She leaned on the railing of the porch to gaze out at the shimmering turquoise sea, alight with thousands of dancing diamonds. As she watched, spellbound, the afternoon mellowed into sunset and dusk.

Would she ever tire of that sight? The only thing better would be to see the *Captive Fantasy* approaching.

For the first time in months, she was totally alone. And even though every nerve ending in her body craved Jack Spankevopoulos, right now, at this moment, she'd never felt more alive. Never felt *happier*.

She sighed with this profound realization. The sweet, druggy scent of the angel's trumpets wafted around her and Cat inhaled deeply, already high on the miraculous things that had transpired today.

She'd lost her caretakers but gained three hot, handsome companions.

She'd come home.

She'd learned of bold new plans that only Valenzia and Ebonique could put into play—and she'd chipped in on their success by insisting on her own.

She'd come so far! It took only a few moments of inhaling that sea breeze and gazing at that red ball of sun as it dipped into the ocean, to realize how quickly and completely her life had turned around.

Smiling placidly, Cat went inside. Leilani had cleaned up from their porch party and left the house spotless. She gazed up at those brightly colored Caribbean angels who hung from the chandeliers and the ceiling . . . breathed in the deep satisfaction of belonging here, in this exotic yet peaceful home that so surpassed anything she'd ever known before.

Never thought I could pull this off, did you, Laird? she mused. *Some things I'll miss about you, but I feel pretty damn fine knowing you can't spoil any of this, or lose it at the tables. I've found a better way!*

Swiping at brief tears, she walked slowly upstairs, loving the way the evening light settled into the large, open living room below . . . the way those angels drifted serenely on the breeze. After all that had happened this past week, entering her pristine white bedroom felt like a cleansing ritual.

Cat stood in the room's center, taking in the high bed with its white comforter, and the walls so bright they vibrated, and the desk near the French doors, where she planned to write a new—

"It's back! Yessss!"

Cat nipped her lip against another wave of emotion: the Contessa had reclaimed her Mac, and Ramon had reconnected her. . . . A few clicks on familiar icons proved that her files—even her pirate romance!—were still intact. Her pink phone was plugged in and recharging. The six sundresses from her duffel hung in the closet as if she'd never left.

So, except for a week of being on constant display, and some inner dignity, she'd lost nothing to the Wongs.

Deep down, she thought it was cool that the Contessa wanted Thomas and his brother to work for her. They'd done her no real harm, after all—and they'd shown her sides of herself she would never have known, had they not held her as their lover . . . their captive . . . a woman who'd fascinated them enough to compete for her body and the pleasure of tending her.

She tightened inside. Sure, the cage and the leash had enraged her at the time, and those Web casts had exposed her in a big way. But it had all worked out, hadn't it? And Arthur got caught. Poetic justice would lead to happily-ever-after now, right? Just like in one of her books.

Cat picked up the cell phone. Turned it on with her thumbnail, a huge grin playing with her face. She scrolled down her directory list and nailed his number.

Ringggg . . . ringggg . . .

"Hello? This is your captain speaking."

Cat closed her eyes to swim in the rich timbre of that British voice. While he probably answered his phone that way out of habit—maybe his enslaved passengers had this number, under the circumstances—it wasn't lost on her that he'd called her *his* captain.

She cleared her throat. "I'm home, Jack. Alone. What're you going to do about it?"

Jack sucked air. He'd been gazing at that fabulous sunset, at the way the Caribbean seemed to bleed with the intensity of its rich red rays. His arms suddenly ached for Cat Gamble, so they could savor this splendor together.

"Cat, darling?" His whole body vibrated. "Is everything all right, that you're alone? I thought Ramon and Leilani would be—"

"They've signed on with the Contessa! She and Ebonique are opening a holistic spa!" Cat closed her eyes to imagine him in his crow's-nest office or by the picture window in his suite. Probably shifting to allow his cock room in those snug pirate pants. "It's too complicated to cover on the phone. Happened so damn fast, my head's still spinning, but—"

"And that leaves you without help on the island?"

He checked the *Fantasy's* position on his lighted route map, calculating the time and distance to Porto Di Angelo—to *her*, and that house where they could revel in each other, uninterrupted. He was rock hard already.

"Only for a while," she replied. She sounded breathless and excited—about talking to him, or about her plans? Not that it mattered: Cat's exuberance fueled his own. "You see, our three pirates are headed to the airport to—"

"Just a moment, my love. Duty calls." Jack pressed the phone against his chest and picked up the two-way radio. "Stavros? Pick up!"

Static crackled. "What's up, Cuz?"

"I'll leave that to your vivid imagination. We're changing course. Set sail for Porto Di Angelo, as fast as you can safely get us there."

There was a pause. A snide chuckle. "Got it bad, dontcha?"

"That's envy I hear. Cat's on the phone, and she's on that island all by her lonesome. I hear paradise calling, loud and clear."

"You don't think the passengers will squawk? We've dropped anchor there twice this week—just this morning to take her home, so—"

"Am I the captain of the *Fantasy*, First Mate Spankevopoulos?"

His cousin paused. "Yessir, of course you are. I just thought—"

"Well, think no more!" Jack felt bravado bubbling in his veins, fueled by his passion for Cat. "This is a cruise where we take passengers as love slaves, so now they'll bow to *my* needs for a bit. Chances are they'll be too engrossed in gaming or drinking or each other to even notice my absence. Anyone who complains can be assured of a partial refund."

"Aye, aye, sir. We can have you there in a couple of hours."

"Thank you, Stavros. I foresee a raise in your pay. Over and out."

He chuckled and rejoined the woman awaiting him on the phone . . . home alone, perhaps naked on her balcony, watching for the *Fantasy*.

"Now," he continued in a low voice, "you were telling me about your three St. Louis friends going back to the airport? I had the distinct impression they loved it here enough to stay at least another—"

"Oh, they're staying! As in, permanently!" she exclaimed. "Going home to tie up loose ends with their businesses, and Trevor has a house to sell, and—"

"And they'll be living *where*?"

Her pause suggested he could've said that without sounding so damned territorial. Or . . . threatened?

"The house is large, so I've invited them here to live in the other suite," she stated. "And really, with helping the Contessa—perhaps pulling a few gigs aboard the *Fantasy*—they'll only be here to tend to business for me. Grant's my estate man-ager, and Bruce is my groundskeeper. I guess we'll call Trevor my cabana boy, since that's the only position left open!" she teased.

He exhaled slowly. She sounded happy. Carefree and open to living life to the hilt. "Forgive me for sounding like a jealous lover," he crooned. "It *is* your house, darling. Considering how you got abducted last week, I really do feel safer knowing you have . . . male staff arriving."

"Yes, each of them has a '*staff*,' dear man," she quipped, tickling his ear with her giggle. "We had an agreement while I was living at Trevor's, that we wouldn't intrude on each others' privacy or sensibilities. It sounds like a fair way to live while they're under my roof, don't you think? After all, they have the entire island for their playground."

"And so do we, my love," he breathed. What a wonderful thing, the way their thoughts wove into such provocative con-versation. "Matter of fact, I'll be there in, say, a couple of hours?"

When her breath caught, the sound filled him with joy. And lust.

"Really, Jack? I—I was calling to tease you, mostly, and to say—"

"I love you, Cat," he breathed into the phone, "and I can't wait until next week's cruise to see you again. If that's all right with you."

"Oh, Jack . . . Jack . . ."

Would he ever get enough of hearing her say his name that way? He closed his eyes, feeling the shift in the evening breeze as the ship turned in a wide circle.

"Will you wait for me on the shore? No clothes?" he chal-lenged. "I can imagine you in the marvelous moonlight this perfect evening promises—your skin glows in the moonlight, did you know that? The waves are ruffling around your ankles, and the breeze is playing in your golden hair."

"I can do that," she whispered, and then she let out a throaty little laugh. "I was looking forward to some time alone to sort things out, but, well, *your* thing has a way of sorting out the essentials, doesn't it?"

"I hope you're ready, darling," he murmured hoarsely. "Here I come."

31

Cat clicked off her phone. She gazed beyond her balcony for the first glimmer of the *Captive Fantasy*'s lights on the deep velvet horizon. Captain Spank was midcruise, yet he'd turned his ship around to come to *her*! How romantic was that?

How horny must he be? came Spike's reply.

But wasn't it awesome, to know a handsome man like Jack—a pirate, no less!—had changed the course of his voyage—and his life—to be with her? When had she ever felt this needed? This cherished?

This hot for it?

"Spike, really! You go overboard sometimes."

She fumbled with the knot at the shoulder of her simple sundress—too damn many clothes, that was her problem! As the fuchsia silk slithered to the white tile floor, Cat vibrated with a wild, crazy excitement. The kind that only happened in her romance novels. She fingered her black lace panties—the ones Jack gave her when they had played a slave game in his suite—and left them on.

She was going to the shore to wait for her lover. And he was coming to claim her for the happily-ever-after he wanted as badly as she did.

He's leavin' no part of you untouched, missy. He's wanted this from the get-go, Spike murmured. *You've made love to him dozens of times, but after tonight there's no goin' back. This is your heart and soul we're talkin' about. You ready for that, kid?*

"Heart and soul." Cat walked languidly across her moonlit room. "Great title for a song, eh, Spike?"

Don't mock me, doll. I'll be gone when he gets here.

She stopped at the top of the stairway to catch some glimmer—some physical sign—of his presence. "Why not? Jealous of a pirate?"

You got no further need for me, Cat.

"And who decided that?" Her voice echoed in the large living room as she descended into it. Anyone listening would think she was crazy for talking to this unseen being.

Maybe she *was* crazy.

Yeah, crazy in love! came Spike's reply. *I'll maybe drop in on you now and again, but Jack's the guy you'll be leanin' on now. My mission's accomplished. A total success, I might add! You can thank me any way you care to, baby-cakes.*

Cat's lips quirked. Such an attitude this angel had! She swore that was beer she smelled, and cigarettes—in a home where no one had smoked! She reached the center of the main room and bowed deeply to the north . . . to the south . . . to the east . . . to the west. Those fabric angels flying above her cheered her on.

"I honestly can't thank you enough, Spike," she admitted. She was suddenly near tears: she'd come to depend on that gravelly voice for advice—had taken his presence for granted. But there was no need to get weepy and red-eyed on this night filled with promise, was there? Hadn't her angel taught her better than that during his brief stay?

"Look where I was when you came to me and where I am now!" she mused aloud. "Rags to riches. The Cinderella in my own sparkling fairy tale."

Hunka-hunka burnin' love's more like it. But, yeah—Cupid's got nothin' on me!

"Walk with me to the beach, Spike. And . . . may I ask you one last favor?"

You wanna see what I look like. All the girls ask me that.

Cat's lips twitched as she started for the door. "Why do I even bother with these little chats, since you can hear what I'm going to say before I—"

She halted on the dark porch. Was it her imagination—the play of moonlight in the shadows and trees? Or was that a very large male face on the other side of the railing?

Dark, doelike eyes gazed at her. His hair swayed in a breeze created by the fluttering of huge, luminous wings. He had no color: Cat saw the blooms of the angel's trumpet trees clearly when she looked through him. His gossamer body floated farther back so she could see all of him at once; so she could define his burly shoulders, his tapered waist and sensational abs—

"Spike, you—behave yourself!"

He wiggled his bare ass at her, and in the whisper of the waves she heard his snicker. He blew a kiss over his shoulder and winked—or was that the twinkling of a star? Then he disintegrated—evaporated—whatever angels did when they became invisible again.

Cat rushed to the rail, searching the starry sky, the angel's trumpet trees, and a beach that glowed in the moonlight, but he'd gone.

She started slowly down the stone path, saddened yet giddy. She'd had an *angel*! She knew his name—and had truly heard his voice!

And he says you're ready to fly solo now. Or with Captain Jack. Either way, you can't lose! How wonderful is that?

The night breeze made her nipples prickle—or was it the excitement of meeting her lover as she'd always dreamed? Cat stepped onto the moonlit beach to await Jack. As the warm sand rose between her toes, she felt an indescribable sense of freedom. It was a soul-deep certainty that she was on the right path now—and that the sleek pirate ship in the distance would carry her to her destiny.

She stopped at the shoreline, to watch the waves ebb and flow around her ankles with lacy foam that hypnotized her for minutes on end. As the breeze lifted her hair like a lover craving her kiss, Cat focused on those billowing ivory sails and the stately masts silhouetted against the azure sky.

Had there ever been a more breathtaking sight?

The *Captive Fantasy* cut smoothly through the water, now close enough that she could distinguish the rumble of its engines. The *swoosh* of its wake made the waves rush around her knees now.

Cat stepped back, peering toward the ship for the first sign of Jack. The *Fantasy*, more magnificent than anything Disney could create with movie magic, stopped out where the sea was deep enough to accommodate her. A silver boat was being lowered from its stern.

Its engine whined. It turned away from the ship to cut rapidly across the water toward her dock, its beacons aglow on either side.

Cat hooked her thumbs in the black bikini's narrow band. Her pulse thundered in counterpoint to the waves that teased her feet. Knowing how Jack loved the flex of her legs and the full moon of her ass when she bared it, she waited until he'd cut the engines and tied his boat into a slip of her dock.

And there he was! He'd left his ship to be here with her! She swallowed hard to keep from squealing as he ogled her outright and shed his vest. His flowing white shirt fluttered to the sand, and he reached for his fly buttons.

She pushed her thumbs downward, making his grin sizzle in the moonlight.

"Leave that on, love." He'd stopped a few feet in front of her, his breathing hot and audible. "I want to rip it off you myself."

"Are you man enough to do that?" she challenged. "Looks to me like you're just some guy playing pirate—or stuck in a time warp. What would *you* know about seducing—"

Two quick, sloshing steps, and he grabbed her. Crushed her against his half-clad body for a kiss that shut her up—except for that low moan that began inside her, like a siren in the distance. He slipped his hand into her panties and then shoved a very purposeful finger up her slit.

Her need skyrocketed.

"Are you implying I'm one of your pretty-boy pirates, wench?" Jack rasped against her ear. "Do you think I'd let the three of them live anywhere near you, if I couldn't control you with *one finger*?"

Cat's cry rang out again as that finger found the spot deep within her that nailed her to the wall. She clutched him to keep from falling backward. Needy for release, she writhed hard against the palm that cupped her mound.

"Answer me, wench! Or do I continue this torment until you climax?" he badgered her. "You know how neglected I feel when you rush ahead of me."

"You! You—" Gasping, Cat pulled away from his hot hand. "Are you calling me greedy? So out for my own pleasure that I'm ignoring yours?"

"Aye, it would seem that way to—"

"Well, you're *right*! So now you'll have to chase it down to get any." Cat pivoted to dash along the beach, laughing with the sheer joy of such naughtiness. Behind her, Jack's breathing was punctuated by his much bigger feet splashing in the shallow waves.

"Damn it, Cat—I've got to—"

She glanced over her shoulder: the poor captain had stopped to finish dropping his drawers. His cock was riding high and hard, jutting from muscled thighs ... thighs that had pinned her plenty of times. It was a wonder he could run at all in his aroused condition. ...

But this was no time for sentimentality. Laughing, Cat sprinted ahead. Her whole body glowed with this game of Chase Me, Fuck Me, and even though she'd lose it, she felt like a little girl about to win a big race.

And the prize was Captain Jack!

He advanced on her with strides that splashed much farther apart now, because his long legs were made for chasing wanton women this way. "You're going to pay and pay for this!"

"*Right*! The last thing you're getting is my money, Spank!"

"You're about to take flight, Cat. When I grab you to—"

"Not anytime soon!" She ran harder to stay ahead of him. Moments like this made her glad her smallish breasts bobbed on her chest like—

Two large hands closed firmly around them. Cat shrieked with laughter when Jack again crushed her in his hug.

"Open up. I'm coming in," he muttered. He folded her forward—parted her legs by moving her wet, sandy feet with his. Lance was already rubbing her crotch, reminding her who would give and who would take it now.

"You're wet for me, wench," he growled. "Bend over and—"

"Can't make me!"

With a single yank, he sent her panties to her ankles. Then the captain slipped his hands beneath her hips and lifted her off the ground. "Come again, wench? What was that part about *making* you?"

Cat squawked and squirmed, loving the strength in his body. His hands had slipped beneath her knees, so she hung suspended with her back against his chest. She gaped open ... so hot and ready for him, even as she pretended she wasn't.

"This is just your version of 'might makes right,'" she protested tightly. "What ever happened to Lancelot's knightly chivalry for a damsel in distress?"

"You call this *distress*, wench?" he rasped against her ear. "Lance does live up to his noble name—he lances a *lot*! Like so!"

Cat cried out with surprise that quickly turned to need when Captain Jack impaled her on his high, hot cock. He braced himself . . . burrowed his feet into the sand, shoulder-width apart, and arched back slightly to balance her weight on his pelvis.

Her eyes widened with the depth of him—the way his tip pressed against her innermost parts as she remained spread wide. She felt helpless in his grasp.

"You wanted to be plundered by a pirate? Well, here it is, love!" His chest rumbled with a rough chuckle as he raised and lowered her, stroking himself with her as though she were his sex toy.

This man felt so hot, so perfectly fitted to her, Cat couldn't recall how anyone else had ever been. The whole world revolved around their coupling: this moment, this night. This yearning to climax and commit.

"I'm gonna come, Jack," she rasped. "Don't say I didn't warn—"

"You're milking me dry, woman! I—I—"

His words became a wanton mating call that carried out over the sea. Cat's body became a tempestuous place where pressure and heat and release came together quite suddenly.

They stiffened, offering themselves to the moon. Their eyes stayed closed and their mouths open, until their cries subsided. Jack let out his breath and gently let her legs find the beach.

Cat flashed him a dazzling smile. "I've never—"

"Neither have I, but I loved it."

"—made love naked on the beach." Jack opened his arms,

and she walked into them. "How did you know—again—what I was thinking?"

He shrugged. She was so lovely, with the moonlight shimmering in her hair and those impassioned eyes fixed on his. So he kissed her, rather than messing up a tender moment with mere words.

"We have an inexplicable connection," he agreed. "It scares me a little, but we'll become accustomed to it as time goes by."

"I'm not sure I want to predict everything you'll do and say. Or have you finish all my sentences, either."

"I'll do my damnedest not to be predictable, love." Jack's adoration shone from every line and angle of his face. "After all, did you think I'd leave my ship on a moment's notice? Did you believe we'd have sex on the beach without getting sand in our cracks?"

Cat's laughter rang like the call of an exotic night bird. "You always seem to be a step or two ahead of me on such things."

"Ah, but you started it all by running ahead of *me*." He brought her hand to his lips. "Far more enjoyable exercise than that elliptical machine in the *Fantasy*'s gym. You'll always keep me younger than my age."

"Which is?"

His grin quirked. "Young enough to want you, *now*, in that upstairs room. Old enough to fear I'll nod off the moment we hit the sheets."

"That's no answer. And there's no shame in that." Cat's eyebrow angled coyly. "I pride myself in giving you such a fine ride you have to rest before the next one. Thirty-six," she added in a whisper.

Jack focused playfully on her breasts, which rested against his chest. "You underrate yourself, my dear. I would guess at least forty or forty-two inches of lush, enticing flesh—"

"You're changing the subject, Jack."

"Ah, but is there a lovelier subject on this earth than your attributes, Cat?" He waggled his eyebrows at her. "You wear them—and your age—very well, by the way. Forty here, but who's counting? Life as I want to know it began the moment I met you."

Her mouth dropped open. She felt dangerously near tears. Had any man ever expressed himself so eloquently—not to mention in that enthralling accent that made her insides quiver? She couldn't recall Laird ever saying—

Laird? Who's Laird?

She smiled up into Jack's swarthy face. "Thank you," she breathed. "I—I hope you don't think my lack of response meant—"

"Lack of response, love? Is that what you call the way you squeezed it out of me just now?" His hands smoothed the hair back from her face. "I sense your husband—may he rest in peace—wasn't much of a romancer, so you aren't accustomed to a man who sings your praises. And meanwhile, I'm hearing exactly what I want to know every time I look into your eyes."

Her lips twitched. "All right, Mr. Sees All And Knows All, what am I thinking right now?"

"That you've never met such a wonderful man, and you never intend to let him go."

He said that with a straight face! Not even a blink to interrupt the gaze he entranced her with right now . . . a gaze so deep and loving, Cat wanted to get lost in it forever.

"You are so right, Captain Jack," she murmured. "You're all my fantasies rolled into one. More happiness than I ever dreamed I could find. It's probably way too soon—"

"Who says so?"

"—but I *love* you, Jack!" she rushed on. "And I hope you'll want to share my island and my home—"

"We could start with your bed."

"—and I can't wait to spend endless days aboard the *Captive Fantasy*—"

"You can count on that, love."

Cat clapped her mouth shut. She'd been babbling, hadn't she? So lost in the moment and in this man's hot, hungry gaze she had no clue what she'd just said—except that he'd agreed to every word. Unconditional love and acceptance were written all over his handsome face.

Stunned. Awestruck. Spellbound. That's how Jack looked, and it's how she felt, as well. She licked her lips, speechless. In the back of her mind, she hoped she'd recall this moment—put words to these feelings—when she wrote that big book Leilani had assured her would happen soon.

"Are you hot for it, Cat?"

She swallowed hard at the raw emotion—the lust, mostly—residing in those words. "Damn straight I am. Are *you*?"

"Always. You make me that way."

Something long and hard prodded her bare thigh. She took Jack's hand between both of her own; kissed it as she held his rakish gaze. "Let's go upstairs," she whispered. "You can be the pirate who makes me your slave. Then we'll play it the other way around, all right?"

"Too late. You already have total control, darling."

They walked slowly up the stepping stones to the house, their bodies rubbing up a light, delicious friction. As they reached the porch, Cat paused to gaze out over the moonlit sea, framed by the gently swaying palm trees and her white sand beach. A dream come true in so many ways.

Thank you, Spike. I owe you big-time. She sent the thought out into the diamond-speckled sky, and Jack watched it with her.

Was it her imagination, or did those stars above them flicker? One of them winked—seemed to sizzle!—and then it shot out with a burst of star fire! Just like she'd seen from Trevor's balcony the night she felt so lost and alone, before this whole adventure began.

"That's what happened right before I won the lottery!" she wheezed. "I made my wish, and it's—it's—"

"It's a *sign*, my love." Jack chuckled and slung his arm around her. "In all my years of sailing, I'd never seen a shooting star until a couple weeks ago—the night I swore off Mad Maria and wondered if I was doomed to navigate this life alone. So I made a wish, too. On the same star you did."

Cat's pounding pulse steadied into a thrum. A very suggestive thrum. . . .

"And here we are, love—you and I, together." Jack lowered his lips to hers to seal this sacred moment. "We're very highly connected right now."

"Connected," Cat echoed with a sly grin. She took his hand to lead him into her room. "Maybe you and Lance should show me how that works again."